A
Proof Reader's
Adventures
of
Sherlock Holmes

A
Proof Reader's Adventures
of
Sherlock Holmes

by
Nick Dunn-Meynell

edited by
David Marcum

First Edition published in 2020
© Copyright 2020 by Nick Dunn-Meynell

ISBN Hardback 978-1-78705-699-2
ISBN Paperback 978-1-78705-700-5
AUK ePub ISBN 978-1-78705-701-2
AUK PDF ISBN 978-1-78705-702-9

Published in the UK by
MX Publishing
335 Princess Park Manor, Royal Drive,
London, N11 3GX
www.mxpublishing.co.uk

Editor Foreword ©2020 by David Marcum
David Marcum can be reached at:
thepapersofsherlockholmes@gmail.com

Cover design by Brian Belanger
www.belangerbooks.com and *www.redbubble.com/people/zhahadun*

Illustration by Sidney Paget

Referenced Artwork can be found
at the London National Gallery

CONTENTS

Forewords

Adventures

Forewarned
by Nick Dunn-Meynell

In "The Blanched Soldier", Godfrey Emsworth is diagnosed as suffering from psychosomatically induced ichthyosis, also known as pseudo-leprosy.

That is, he had pseudo-pseudo-leprosy.

I have written the literary equivalent of that imaginary complaint.

These are not pastiches in the style of Dr Watson's accounts. Nor are they records of fictitious cases investigated by Mr Sherlock Holmes. They are not even intended to be creative re-workings of Watson's published stories. Instead I have sifted through his fables in search of the very few absolute and undeniable facts. Then I have let them lead me where they would.

At first I tried to express my conclusions in conventional essay form. The results were dry and uninteresting. I realised I was in the position as Sherlock Holmes when he came to write "The Blanched Soldier", having complained for years his hagiographer had reduced impersonal scientific investigations to a collection of fairy tales. Had Holmes written as he wished to, he would never have found a publisher.

And yet he had a point. The good doctor had been like the manufacturer who had the brilliant idea of making children's toothpaste more palatable by adding sugar: It rather undermined the stated purpose of the enterprise. One ought not to sweeten a pill marketed as a cure for diabetes. Nor should one promise to teach readers how to think critically conditional upon their first suspending all disbelief.

How could Holmes ever have been so foolish as to attempt to compromise as he did between fact and fiction? Perhaps his brother Mycroft urged him to it. Mycroft was like the British Empire: He could soothe his conscience and justify his imperial authority by arguing that one day he would hand power over to the people – but not just yet. They were still children and had to be educated first, lest in modern democracies they be hoodwinked by tricksters peddling pleasing lies.

Plato's Socrates condemned democracies because most men are seduced by the shadows of shadows. That best and wisest of men would surely have approved of Mycroft. By contrast, he would have been appalled by the silhouette of a man in a deerstalker with a magnifying glass in his hand as the public's picture of the quintessential philosopher.

1

An amateur hypnotist realised that a certain television celebrity would win a political election – not in spite of the fact he talked nonsense, but because he did. The shyster mesmerised his followers by supplying simple mantras to be repeated over and over again. He gave them stories in single sentences with a beginning, middle, and end that promised to take them back to the future. He assured them that since only those things the heart believes are true, they could choose whichever alternative facts and realities they wished.

Watson was like that. He was a pickpocket who embraced the reader and whispered into their ear that they ought to be on their guard against pickpockets. He promised them the truth if only they would trust him, for he was a doctor.

In fact, he was a writer as doctor gone wrong. Instead of drawing upon his medical experience to ensure the accuracy of his accounts, at least from a medical point of view, he drew upon his appreciation of the credulity of patients. He knew he could get away with murdering the truth. He could say that a face was still twisted with hatred and fear and rage hours after death and his readers would accept it.

How could Holmes have countered such deceptions? I eventually concluded he could only have done so by supplementing Watson's mythologized versions of his investigations with dialogues of his own. In these, he might reveal the truth he had deemed best to conceal from his friend, lest he pass it on to readers, many of whom belonged to the criminal underworld. Worse, some were investigative journalists.

"Try it yourself," I heard the ghost of Holmes reply. So I did so.

I have found that it's never a problem to find holes in the plots that can be turned into clues. Watson's plots are nets consisting of practically nothing but holes, rather as matter seems solid but in reality is mostly empty space. I eventually realised the real trick would have to be to keep the holes together.

Bulletproof glass was discovered by chance when a flask fell and shattered into a hundred pieces yet retained its shape. It had contained liquid plastic and had not been properly cleaned, so that an invisible layer of the substance still coated it. The man who made the discovery was a painter and a composer who also happened to be a chemist. Perhaps only such a kindred spirit to Sherlock Holmes could have made such a discovery and seen how it could be put to use. One has to apply the methods of a Holmes to expose the difficulties with Watson's accounts, and yet keep the spider webs from unravelling.

One of my chief aims has been to discredit the myth propagated by Watson that Holmes was a thinking machine without a drop of art in his veins. Holmes chose to live at 221b Baker Street, around the corner from the Wallace Collection. This boasts choice examples of the art of Greuze, Delaroche, and the Vernets. He could also pop down to the National Gallery any time he wanted. Mycroft lived in Pall Mall, an even easier walk away from it, though in his case he probably took a cab.

Like Holmes, I was brought up as a Catholic. My first teachers were nuns and priests. They taught me how the events of Christ's early life had been deduced by hagiographers obeying to the letter Jesus' instruction to "search the scriptures". Those first Christian interpreters turned to the most sacred texts of their societies, including the myths of ancient Egypt, Greece, Rome, as well as those of the Jewish people. These were analysed, and previously inexplicable passages identified as prophecies that had now been fulfilled by such events as the deduced journey of the Magi to Bethlehem. The surmise that Sherlock Holmes as the last Magus who must have been born on the feast of the Adoration of the Magi is in that same logical tradition.

Let me end by repeating that I have presented my trains of thought as continuations of Watson's tales for one reason and one reason only: To make them slightly less indigestible. But please do not imagine that, because these records have been presented like fiction, they are no better than the good doctor's own "novelised" biographical sketches.

Nick Dunn-Meynell
May 2020

"... but the sequel was rather unusual." *
by David Marcum

First of all, you should know that these are curiously different Sherlockian tales – every one is a unique continuation and analysis of the original twelve stories in *The Adventure of Sherlock Holmes*, which first appeared in *The Strand* from 1891 to 1892. Within them, you'll find a series of conversations between Holmes and Watson, each immediately taking place at the conclusion of one of the *Adventures*.

Next, it should be known that these are not typical Holmes narratives where you'll find Holmes and Watson solving a new mystery – A visitor to Baker Street tells a strange story. Holmes jumps up and does things, maybe in disguise, maybe stopping to receive a report from an Irregular. Maybe there's the smoking of three pipes, or a visit to the Diogenes Club, or the lair of some informant. Then an exciting twist, followed by the explanatory *denouement* for a puzzled Dr. Watson.

No, you won't find that here, and these stories are not like that. You should know that up front. Rather, they take the inconsistencies and contradictions to be found in those original twelve *Adventures* and pull them apart, twist them, double back on them, and construct them into something that's sly and new and thoroughly thought-provoking.

Since I'm known as a long-time and adamant defender of the pure traditional Holmes story – Canon and pastiche – some might wonder that I'm associated with these stories, which are *not* pure or traditional or Canonical. As a pretty firm rule, I only promote and support tales that can stand alongside those original sixty Canon adventures.

But . . . .

Several years ago, I first heard of Mr. Nick Dunn-Meynell when he wrote a letter to *The Baker Street Journal*, commenting on an essay of mine that had run in a previous issue, "Basil Rathbone's Solar Pons Films" [Vol. 63, No. 4, Winter 2013]. Nick disagreed with my premise, writing a response that was possibly longer than my original offering. *BSJ* editor, Steve Rothman, included Nick's letter in the Autumn 2014 issue [Vol. 64, No. 3] and emailed me that he thought I'd find it amusing. I told Steve that I was mostly flattered – whether I agreed with Nick or not – that someone had taken the time and trouble to write a rebuttal to my own ideas

Not long after, Nick and I began exchanging occasional emails, and at some point a couple of years later, he sent me a piece of a pastiche that he'd written, something of a sequel to the events of "The Crooked Man", which laid out in detail everything that Watson had missed in the published version, and how the description of the case as narrated in the original story wasn't the actual truth at all. Holmes had observed layers beyond layers deeper than what was initially seen by Watson – leaving the latter with the choice to publish the version that we know now as something that could be better understood by the general public. And not long after Nick sent that first piece of the story, he sent another, and then another, until finally it was a pretty substantial whole.

Around that time, I was deeply involved in accumulated stories for and editing *Sherlock Holmes: Adventures Beyond the Canon* for Belanger Books (3 volumes, 2018). Seeing that Nick was sending me a sequel of sorts to one of the Canonical stories, I asked if he'd be willing to let me include it in the upcoming collection – and he was. The story he sent, eventually titled "The Adventure of the Upright Man", appeared in Volume I of the set. I realized at the time that it was something quite a bit different from the traditional pastiches that people expect, but if one paid attention to where Nick's arguments led, one could see that there was much more to "The Crooked Man" than was initially obvious. It's true that some people preferred the straight pastiche formula – and that's what I espouse as well – but as a collector and chronologicizer of literally thousands of traditional Canonical pastiches for over forty-five years, I also appreciate those between-cases types of stories where Holmes and Watson simply have a conversation about something – such as this instance, where they dissect the hidden layers of a previous case, much like the old Golden Age mystery solutions of Ellery Queen or Agatha Christie where, after the public solution has been explained, the deeper and more private one is revealed.

Time passed after that collection's publication, and in due course Nick sent another similar story for inclusion in one of the volumes of the ongoing series that I created and edit, *The MX Book of New Sherlock Holmes Stories*. In this case, it was a story serving as a sequel to one of *The Adventures*, and it was simply too convoluted and a little too off-trail from traditional pastiches to be included for the casual reader. But it was well written and showed an amazing ability to pick out the contradictions within the original narrative and weave them into most unexpected new directions, and it needed to be seen. Realizing that, I encouraged Nick to write others, possibly for inclusion in a book of his own. He did, eventually surprising me by coming up with twelve such narratives, one for each of the original *Adventures*.

These efforts are dense with material and are filled with Easter Eggs for the perceptive Sherlockian. Nick's subtle sense of humor and affection for Holmes and Watson peeks through at every turn. There are references in each of the individual stories that refer to the others within this collection, giving hints of a bigger narrative at play. Reading these cannot and should not be hurried. They must be pondered.

Chronology here is thrown out the window. Holmes and Watson here are not quite the Holmes and Watson of the Canon – and neither are Mrs. Watson nor certain Scotland Yard inspectors, nor other beloved characters. These stories must be taken as a whole on their own terms, and those who do so will find a great deal to enjoy.

In addition to the Sherlockian aspects, Nick has managed to weave a work of art from London's National Gallery into each story, pointing out hidden or ignored aspects, symbols, and meanings. Due to the nature of publishing a book, each painting is presented, but in black and white and reduced to fit on a relatively small page. I urge every reader to go online and look at these paintings in full-color to fully appreciate the subtle clues that Nick highlights within his stories.

There's much to enjoy and ponder about these stories. Some of these stories caught me by surprise and made me laugh out loud, while others left me painfully aware of contradictions and mistakes that I'd previously ignored in The Canon – something like what Martin Dakin did in his volume of Sherlockian analysis, *A Sherlock Holmes Commentary* (1972), but to a much deeper degree. (I can only imagine how deeply Nick studied each original *Adventure* looking for the smallest of clues that just didn't make sense.) As I read, I constantly wondered if Nick shouldn't explore certain aspects of these versions as actual traditional pastiches – he has the skill for it, and I encourage him to also write one that could have come directly from Watson's Tin Dispatch Box.

As I wrote at the beginning, these aren't typical Holmes adventures, but they are worth the time to savour and explore. Enjoy.

David Marcum
November 2020

NOTE

* ". . . *but the sequel was rather unusual*." – Sherlock Holmes, "A Scandal in Bohemia"

"Few are the pains the vulgar take to find the truth, being ready to give credence instead to the first story to hand."

Thucydides – *History of the Peloponnesian War*

"In almost every instance where we have found it necessary to disagree withThucydides and to offer a different interpretation, the evidence that raised the doubt and furnished the material for a divergent readingcomes from his own account."

Donald Kagan –
Thucydides: The Reinvention of History
(p. 228), Viking (2009)

The Following Paintings Accompany Each Story:

"The Adventure of the Game of Thrones"
Hans Holbein – *Christina of Denmark*

"The Adventure of the William Morris Settee"
Paul Delaroche – *The Execution of Lady Jane Grey*

"The Adventure of the Mistaken Identity"
Hans Holbein – *The Ambassadors*

"The Adventure of the Remarkable Worms"
Lucas Cranach – *Cupid Complaining to Venus*

"The Adventure of the Writing on the Wall"
Rembrandt – *Belshazzar's Feast*

"The Adventure of the Amateur Mendicant Society"
Bartolome Bermejo – *St. Michael*

"The Adventure of the Gaslit Detective"
Anglo-French School – *The Wilton Diptych*

"The Adventure of the Worm that Turned"
Agnolo Bronzino – *Allegory with Venus and Cupid*

"The Adventure of the Rule of Thumb"
Joseph Wright of Derby – *An Experiment with the Air Pump*

"The Reappearance of Lady Diana Spencer"
William Hogarth – *Marriage a la Mode: 1 The Marriage Settlement*

"The Adventure of the First Clue"
Titian – *Bacchus and Ariadne*

"The Adventure of the Peachy Copper"
Carlo Crivelli – *The Annunciation with St. Emidius*

A
Proof Reader's
Adventures
of
Sherlock Holmes

Hans Holbein – *"Christina of Denmark"*

The Adventure of the
Game of Thrones
Continuing "A Scandal in Bohemia"

Part I: The Eagle, the Serpent, and the Hare

"*To Sherlock Holmes she is always the woman . . . And when he speaks of Irene Adler, or when he refers to her photograph, it is always under the honourable title of the woman.*"

I paused, though not in any serious hope of applause. Holmes did not stir in his chair opposite mine before the fire in 221b, nor had he stirred during all that reading of "A Scandal in Bohemia". So I sighed and resigned myself to playing the game.

I tried to slam my flimsy issue of the hand-printed *Baker Street Journal* as best I could to supply the excuse and cue he was awaiting. It did the trick. He half-opened his eyes as if after long sleep. We both knew he had actually paid the keenest attention to every word. A split infinitive and I would not have heard the end of it.

"But why, Watson?" said he, almost closing his eyes again and sinking deeper into the chair. "Have you once thought to ask yourself the simple question 'Why?'?"

It was Thursday the 22nd of March, 1890, the first anniversary of what I had supposed was the conclusion to the affair of the King of Bohemia and the incriminating photographs. One was presumably at bottom of the waters near the Island of Elba with the bodies of Mr. and Mrs. Godfrey Norton. The other, a framed portrait of Irene Adler as she then was in evening dress and oddly resembling sixteenth century mourning weeds, had survived. It occupied pride of place on Holmes's mantelpiece behind his gold-plated hypodermic, a gift from a grateful King Hamlet III of Denmark. The hypodermic was inscribed with the words: "*Adieu, adieu, remember me.*"

Holmes made no comment when a telegram arrived from King Wilhelm II of Bohemia's agent informing him that she and her husband Godfrey Norton had been lost overboard in gale off the Island of Elba while fleeing from England. On behalf of His Majesty the agent had expressed his sadness at the unforeseen tragedy: "*Dear me, Mr. Holmes. Dear me!*"

To my disappointment, Holmes himself showed neither surprise nor grief. On the contrary, he at once covered over her photograph with black as if to blot out the memory of her, in accordance with his principle that the brain should not be cluttered up with irrelevant facts and distracting passions. After that he had lain upon his sofa, where I found him on returning to 221b two days later. Whether he had moved in the meantime it was impossible to say. The only difference I could perceive was that he had turned his head and was gazing at the photograph still draped in black as if straining to pierce the veil. What problem he was concerning himself with I could not say.

"Why should I publish? I thought it would be a nice tribute to her. My number of subscribers has risen to a hundred-and-twenty-three, you know," I added with some pride. "I am thinking of reprinting some of my accounts elsewhere once those two years of silence we committed ourselves to have expired. Of course even then some facts will have to be amended for the general public."

"A hundred-and-twenty-two," Holmes corrected me cruelly. "I think we may safely assume that Jack Stapleton's arm will not rise up, pen in hand out of the Grimpen Mire to renew his subscription. But you misunderstand me. I meant why '*the* woman'? Do you suppose I am ashamed to name a lady of dubious and questionable memory? Or are you thinking of Haggard's *She*?"

I was, but I was not about to admit that to Holmes. "I should have thought that was obvious. It was because, well, she was *the* woman. You know, just as Birdy Edwards was '*the* man'. It just means we shall not look upon their like again." This was perhaps to state the obvious but sometimes that is the simplest way. I hoped for once it would suffice.

"No, that is not it at all," he snapped, and as his eyes transfixed me I felt like a mouse who in nibbling cheese has grazed a cat's cobweb-fine feline whiskers and been confronted by its analytical gaze. "The problem is not that you are being obvious, but that you are being obvious in the wrong way. Try again. Why am I so scrupulously wary of speaking her name? But remind me, what is her name?"

"Why you know that," said I, a little bemused. "It was Irene Adler – or rather Irene Norton, I should say. Or Adler, whichever you prefer."

"Well, which is it?"

"Norton. The late Irene Norton." I made a mental note to correct the text of "A Scandal in Bohemia" should it ever be reprinted. I had referred to her there as "the *late* Irene Adler". "At least that was the name we chose to call her by."

"You are a careless writer. That is not a criticism. It is useful that you pepper your accounts with erroneous dates and spurious names. It muddies the waters very nicely and should make it well nigh impossible for the new breed of investigative journalists to unearth the truth. But with me it is different. If I were to speak of Irene Adler as you do then someone would put two and two together and ask themselves if Irene Norton ever existed. She cannot afford that."

I thought it best not question Holmes on his interest in spiritual telegraphy. It seemed that just as my wife would sometimes communicate with her deceased mother via a medium so my friend was still in contact with the spirit of Mrs. Norton, intrigued as he was by all the latest technological developments. He had a fine collection of photographs of spirits, which he far preferred to eyewitness accounts. I believe he envied the camera its infallible eye. "You wish to protect the Norton name."

"That's not it at all. You were quite wrong to speak of the late Irene Adler, though not because you ought to have said 'Norton'. The woman never was swept off the *Uhlan* in a gale. She did not suffer the fate of Birdy Edwards. For that matter neither did Birdy Edwards. You see the problem? To suspect the reported death of the one would at once be to cast doubts upon the death of the other. You cannot reveal that she lives, until quite another death has brought about the absolute separation of King Wilhelm from Irene Adler he so earnestly desired."

It saddened me to see Holmes still in a state of what for want of a better word I would call denial. He had never forgiven himself for luring Birdy Edwards, or John Douglas as we then thought of him, out of his hiding place only to urge him to fly England, thus making his murder at sea a foregone conclusion. Holmes's revenge had been to have his Baker Street Irregulars spread dark rumours concerning the predilections of the mastermind behind the plot. His reputation ruined, Professor Moriarty had become mere Mr. Moriarty and retired from his university town to London, that monstrous quagmire into which all the broken men and women of our empire are so irretrievably drained. The last we heard he had been reduced to the horrible life of an army examinations coach. He is a webless spider now. Yet by insisting that Moriarty or one of his many imitators had thought to murder Mrs. Norton and had failed thanks to him, Holmes could tell himself he had made amends for that earlier blunder. I thought it best not to disenchant him.

Now, had I betrayed the slightest curiosity he would have teased me and told me nothing. It was quite another matter when he sensed I had concluded he was deceiving himself. That was perfectly unendurable to his proud spirit. "You disbelieve me?" said he sternly. The "dare to" in the accusation was unspoken but implicit. "I assure you this is no mere wishful thinking on my part. I say they live. I shall prove it. We will concern ourselves with Irene Adler alone for the present. I tell you I understood Wilhelm's intentions towards her from the instant I saw the photograph she left me. I understood it was as dangerous as the one he had

19

so desired I recover. The game of kings is a ruthless one. It requires sacrifices, and she who is made queen one day will be shoved off the board the next instant. That, of course, is the secret message of her photograph. No, do not trouble searching for it. You would not know how to look."

Holmes imagines me incapable of appreciating art. "Well, what of the facts of the case? They seemed perfectly straightforward to me."

"We shall reconsider them. You recall the details of the affair?"

"I have an exceptionally good memory for stories," said I proudly. "You may notice I almost never take notes. I never need to. It is my medical training, you see. Just as I never make mistakes with my prescriptions, so I never supply an incorrect date or quotation."

"If one accepts my axiom that one should never make exceptions then that must be so, for the logical conclusion has then to be that all the times you have appeared to blunder must prove the rule that you never do," said he with tightened lips that quivered as if desperate to prevent laughter from ever being born. "I can still recall your prescribing strychnine in large doses as a sedative to Thaddeus Sholto, which should indeed have done the trick. Tell me then how the case of the King of Bohemia commenced for you?"

"I was returning from seeing a patient when I happened to find myself by chance under the windows of 221b."

"Rather as Romeo happened to find himself beneath the balcony of Juliet," said Holmes unnecessarily, for he was far too fond of drawing inappropriate Shakespearean parallels. "And what did you observe? More precisely, what did you see?"

"You had lit your room brilliantly and I saw you were alone, for your figure was perfectly silhouetted against the blinds. You were pacing back and forth like a caged panther in a state of feverish excitement, so I deduced you had shaken off the narcotic effects of your cocaine and were hot on the trail of your prey."

"Cocaine is a stimulant, not a narcotic," said my pedantic friend. "The only reason it is so described by disapproving doctors such as yourself is in the hope that when the use of narcotics is legally restricted a ban on cocaine may be sneaked in with them. So as I understand it what you saw was behaviour associated with a disturbed state of mind and a sense of urgency, but what you observed was a man alone arguing some matter out with himself. That is the so, is it not?"

"Precisely," said I, not sure I quite understood what this distinction between seeing and observing really meant. "You were waving your arms about and talking to yourself – or rather you seemed to be addressing an imaginary audience. You might have been addressing the gentlemen of the jury. It was clear you were in the middle of an exceptionally challenging case. Of course, afterwards I realised it was the one you were about to take."

"And about which I knew nothing."

"Exactly. I was right, was I not? You were weighing up the facts of your latest case?"

Holmes nodded. "You were absolutely correct, though it is clear you failed to deduce what that case must be."

"Why, there can be no doubt about that," said in some confusion. "It was how to recover the incriminating photograph showing King Wilhelm II of Bohemia and his former mistress Irene Adler in an, um, false position."

"Indeed? I had gathered from your accounts I was the inept lover putting myself in false positions. However, photography is still in its infancy. The false positions you are at this moment picturing would be too blurred for accurate identification. Now tell me, do you recall my reply when you inspected that note from Wilhelm and asked me what I made of it?"

"I do have ears," said I with wary resentment, for I suspected a trap. "I can hear, you know. You declined to speculate on the grounds that you had no data."

"Oh, you heard, I have no doubt about that, but do you ever listen? The distinction is clear. Given that I hold to the principle that nothing is so dangerous as to theorise before one knows what it is one is theorising about, how likely is it that my agitated state was due to an attempt to solve a case before I had one?"

"You knew you were about to be visited by an illustrious client, Holmes. At least you would have done if you deduced as I did that the costly paper on which the note was written suggested a man of great wealth. Since he would come masked, I further deduced he must be famous. He clearly wanted to keep a low profile."

Holmes laughed. "A low profile? Like my silhouette I took care would be exceedingly sharp when seen from the street? But we will come to that. The man came dressed like the reincarnation of his hero Henry VIII. King Wilhelm II of Bohemia is very like his cousin Kaiser Wilhelm II of Germany, you know. He is forever dressing up as a mighty warrior to compensate for the fact that he is nothing of the kind. There are in the world certain narcissistic souls, my dear self-effacing doctor, who feel a constant need to steal the limelight by playing part after part. Like a lady's attire, that mask was intended to draw attention to what it concealed. As for his being an illustrious client, my dear fellow, that meant nothing to me. In my experience, the more exalted the client, the more mundane the matter to be considered. No, I promise you I was not giving our pedestrian mystery man a second thought save to note in passing that he was rather like Jack the Ripper, who was a vast shadow cast by an insignificant little chap who happened to hear voices. But it is invariably the shadow men attend to. Mine will be remembered long after I am forgotten."

"Then what was the case you were investigating?"

"That of the gentleman who was with me at the time."

"But you were alone!" I persisted. "At least I could see no one with you, which amounts to the same thing."

Holmes bestowed upon me a pitying look. "Really? Well, sometimes it does, as we shall see. But I have enemies. Did it not occur to you that by supplying my silhouetted form against those blinds, I was tempting providence? Of course it was for that very reason I was moving back and forth so speedily, yet a man like Colonel Moran, were he still pursuing his true vocation instead of wasting his talents assisting Mr. Moriarty in coaching dullards for military exams, might still have put a bullet through my brains. Why do you think I thought it safe to take such a chance?"

"I have no idea."

"But really, my dear fellow, the reason ought to be obvious. I knew I was safe because at that moment I was not the target. Do you not see that there had to be someone with me? It was his life that had been entrusted to me. I lit the room brilliantly and let all below see my figure alone so none would suspect he was there. And can you not deduce who that other man must have been? Consider the date. It was 20 March, 1889, was it not? You surely read the morning papers. What were they reporting from the previous day?"

This seemed like an unreasonable question. How could Holmes expect me to recall what I happened to read over breakfast that day? Then I remembered how puzzled I was that Holmes had never been asked to give evidence regarding letters published by *The Times* ostensibly written by the politician Charles Parnell – letters that appeared to prove his complicity in the brutal Phoenix Park murders of Lord Cavendish and Thomas Henry Burke. The correspondence had been vouched for by leading graphologists. None of them, though, paid the least attention to the character the handwriting betrayed, and that was Holmes's speciality. He would have detected atavistic tendencies and the most sinister weaknesses of character. I was naturally astonished and indignant he was never asked to supply his expert opinion.

When I had seen Holmes so excited I supposed he was being consulted at last, particularly since my morning paper had reproduced part of Sir William Harcourt's thoroughly inflammatory speech of the previous day. In it he had painted the master spy Thomas Miller Beach, alias the Irish American Major Henri Le Caron of the Fenian Brotherhood, as no hero of the Birdy Edwards breed, but rather as a treacherous cad. His testimony given against Parnell was therefore to be dismissed out of hand. "Ah!"

"Yes, as you so eruditely put it, 'Ah'. You will recall that by flushing out John Douglas, alias Birdy Edwards, in that trifling affair you have already serialised in your little *Baker Street Journal* under the title *The Valley of Fear*, I may inadvertently have played into the then Professor Moriarty's hands, for in a sense I did his work for him. Had I not become involved and had I not felt the need to best America's greatest living detective, there would have been need for him to fake his death a second time. To make amends for having inconvenienced Birdy somewhat, I was determined to assist Beach in his own sudden and tragic death at the hands of Fenian avengers. He was to be blown overboard like Edwards before him in a gale off a fittingly symbolic isle, preferably one with Napoleonic associations. It was all planned. It would have succeeded. Then along came Wilhelm II and the deception had to be shelved. I have rescheduled it for 1 April of 1891, barring unforeseen events. My little April Fool joke, you see."

I was horrified. "You were keeping Le Caron at 221b? What of Mrs. Hudson? Did you never consider the danger you were placing her in?"

"Watson," said he in mild chastisement, "I can forgive you for failing to count the number of steps to 221b, which I know you have failed to do ever since I told you there were seventeen, but you might at least have observed that the woman you assumed was my landlady and who confiscated your doctor's black bag in her care before belatedly taking you up to your old rooms was not a disguised Mrs. Hudson but someone calling herself Mrs. Turner."

"Preposterous," I muttered. "Did she think I was smuggling you up more of your transcendental drugs? But I suppose you had instructed her to regard with suspicion all doctors as potential Grimesby Roylotts intent upon poisoning you. A pointless precaution I should say, since the man most likely to poison you is yourself. Did she really think me so very suspicious a character that she would not allow me to ascend to my own old rooms without her accompanying me? And if she meant to lead the way, why did she insist I go first? Do you know, I had to wait ten minutes while she checked the contents of the bag to see if I was what I claimed to be. Then she became suspicious because there was no stethoscope. She particularly questioned me about the contents of one bottle whose label had fallen off. To prove it was not poison, I had to dab myself with it. Only iodoform, I assure you."

"Ah, yes, you had removed your stethoscope and put it in your hat just before knocking at the front door. I trust your more astute patients

23

were able to deduce its earlier secretion there from its subsequently smelling of the lime cream to which dirt and hairs had adhered. You also stained the tip of one forefinger black with nitrate of silver. You see, you had nobody to blame but yourself. She naturally suspected you of merely masquerading as a doctor, since a genuine surgeon would never fail to wash his hands after examining a patient. It will console you to know I put her mind to rest later. I explained you were nervous about seeing me after so long a breach and were working in accordance with your revolutionary theory that the way to a detective's heart is through his brain. You meant to break the ice at our reunion with a little party game."

I blushed even redder than when imagining His Majesty and Irene Adler in anatomically interesting positions. I had hoped my ruse would not be so obvious. Doubtless it would not have been had not Mrs. Turner insisted I employ iodoform as an unreliable alternative to *Eau de Cologne*. "So she was one of your agents?"

"A remarkable woman, almost as remarkable as *the* woman. She instantly identified you as a doctor likely to go wrong. Had you not seemed to know the way to what you said were your old rooms the pistol she had secreted in her hat would have been repositioned between your ribs and you would have found yourself handcuffed an instant later. I assure you I later defended you to the hilt. I stressed that whenever you do quite innocently prescribe deadly poisons, it is merely carelessness, and there is no evil intent. Except in the case of Thaddeus Sholto, of course."

I have developed an immunity to Holmes's perverted sense of humour. "And Mrs. Hudson?"

"Was never at risk. She was taken by Detective-Sergeant Patrick Macintyre of Scotland Yard's political department to secure rooms round the corner in Marylebone Street. Unfortunately, with a feared assassination of Queen Victoria in the offing, he had more pressing duties to attend to."

"And you were not asked to assist in foiling a murder attempt on Her Majesty?" I asked in surprise.

"Oh, she was never the real target. The aim was to divert the police away from Beach. Besides, a lackey from Buckingham Palace did drop by at 221b meaning to propose I assist. He changed his mind the moment he saw my '*V.R.*' done in bullet-pocks on a wall. As if that were the same as a portrait of Her Majesty with bullet-pocks *through* it! Incredible imbecility! I ask you, did Her Majesty take it amiss when Hiram Maxim demonstrated his automatic machine gun to her by creating a '*VR*' out of bullet holes a few years back? She read it as a proof of loyalty and not the contrary."

24

"So you lost your chance to add '*By Royal Appointment*' to your business card?" I commiserated sadly. "How unfair!"

"I would not have accepted the commission had it been offered me," said he with the twisted lips of one suffering from what I diagnosed as a severe after-taste of sour grapes. "Beach was a higher priority. I have long admired him for his infiltration of the Fenian Brotherhood, an achievement against which Birdy Edwards's membership of the Scowrers was as masterly an achievement as boarding an underground train without a ticket."

With relief I understood at last why Holmes's response to my sudden appearance that night had been so ambivalent. I pride myself on being able to read his every emotion as no other man or woman can, yet was confused by his lukewarm greeting. I could not be certain he was glad to see me at all. Now I realised it was because Beach must have been concealed nearby, which would also explain his somewhat curt dismissal of me as soon as King Wilhelm had departed.

A thought struck me and I hazarded a guess. Imitating my master's methods, I presented it as a deduction. "Was that why you dismissed the love letters from Wilhelm to Irene Adler as of no importance? The leading graphologists who authenticated the Parnell papers were subsequently proven to have been not entirely correct. If ever there was a time when such letters might have been shrugged off, it was just then."

Holmes snorted his contempt. "Leading graphologists! They were the fakes. Why did they not at once take note of spelling mistakes and insist the suspected forger write out the words? Behold the dangers of too narrow a specialisation! They could not see the words for the lines they were composed of. Nobody would have thought of it had not brother Mycroft drawn their attention to the oversight. I said *oversight*, but I was tempted to say *blindness*, save that it would be a gross insult to the blind, who are generally very perceptive. There is more sense in a bat-blind Carrados than in an all-seeing Carlyle, and more knowledge of the world. You are right, though. For a brief moment I did lose faith in graphology, hence my failure to analyse the handwriting of that note written by the King of Bohemia. I have done so since. There is murder in the viciously sharpened points of his dagger-like '*t*'s and an insinuating serpentine treachery in his slitheringly sensual '*s*'s. Had I only scrutinised them earlier, I would never have consented to take the dragon's side against the damsel. However, the aftermath of that matter rather complicated things as regards Beach."

"How so?"

"Why, to have faked a second death so soon after that of Birdy Edwards was dangerous enough, but to have faked two more would certainly have aroused fatal suspicions. I could let Irene Adler have herself blown off a deck by a sudden gust of wind in the same manner as Birdy ostensibly was. The criminal fraternity would rejoice that Sherlock Holmes had been tricked into unwittingly working for Moriarty a second time, and that in spite of the fact his criminal career has been terminated. No, once again the professor's favourite puppet was tricked into encouraging the target to panic and fly. But to have had her and Beach both die at the hands of assassins and in the same month was out of the question. Beach very chivalrously agreed to delay his death for a further year or two."

I must have looked confused. Holmes says he can always tell when I am startled or at a loss from an expression akin to that of a startled sheep. Actually he says he can tell when a sheep is startled from its displaying an expression reminiscent of mine when at a loss, but I think that is his idea of a jest. At any rate I must have borne such a look at that moment.

"You are doubtful. You cannot see how I could have known that her life was in danger. It is simple. She told me."

"She communicated with you in secret after the case concluded?"

"Not afterwards. You forget the letter she left for the king to collect when we called to steal that incriminating photograph. Reading between the lines of it, I learnt that the accompanying photograph contained a coded message alerting me to the King's dishonourable intentions. It also revealed precisely what the nature of that other photograph was that Wilhelm was so desperate to recover. This will come as a shock to you, but His Majesty was not entirely honest with us. There *was* a secret wedding. The photograph was a double portrait of the happy couple and included witnesses such as the priest. It follows that what his Highness actually desired was a separation of the most absolute kind, one that would not require any public revelation that they had ever been married. It seems that the small print of the wedding contract stipulated that it would be rendered null and avoid should either of them die. I gather it is a standard legal loophole."

"Holmes!" I cried. "You cannot mean His Majesty meant to dispose of the woman he had married!"

"It is not entirely insignificant that His Majesty modelled himself chiefly on Holbein's portraits of Henry VIII. I have studied the life and times of that evil gentleman well and concluded that the rash of very convenient deaths of Anne Boleyn's adversaries about the time of her coronation were not wholly coincidental. Wilhelm would have delighted in emulating his hero. You recall how he insisted to us that the future history of Europe depended on silencing Irene Adler? It is the old argument that the end justifies the means. As a matter of fact, the future of Europe was at stake as Irene Adler herself sought to warn me, but we will come to that in due course. For the present, note only her pointed promise that the King could '*rest in peace*'. Do you not see what she meant?"

"Why, that since she loved another and better man and was loved by him, he had nothing more to fear. She had no desire to be avenged upon him."

"She never had. However, the King had no guarantee that the man she appeared to claim she loved really was any better than himself. Godfrey Norton was a lawyer, it is true, but exactly what kind of a lawyer? He had out of the blue in a state of panic to demand Irene Adler wed him instantly and without witnesses who might testify later. A few hours later they were fleeing the country together. Now, what honest lawyer would behave so? Even if he were to keep his old name, he could hardly set up in practise on the Continent. His knowledge and qualifications would be useless there. If we suppose they meant to change their names and disappear, then the attempt would be doubly futile. In all likelihood, then, he was desperate to escape the law before he himself stood in the dock. Such a man might well convince a doting new wife she should blackmail the King purely for financial gain. The wedding had not ended Wilhelm's troubles. It threatened to double them."

"But then why should she say that the King could rest in peace?"

"Is it not obvious? It was a hint to me. He could do so only be ensuring that *she* rested in peace – if not several feet underground then full fathoms five below the sea. Why do you think he was so ecstatic when that servant supplied him with precise details regarding her flight? It made pursuit a simple matter. Do you recall how profusely he thanked me for my failure? He ought to have demanded a full refund. Instead he offered me his hand and the ring in the palm of it, which sadly I had to decline. By then I was otherwise engaged."

"But he explained his delight," I reminded him. "She said she would only use the photograph to protect herself. He swore he accepted her word for it."

"Then he swore to accept a foreswearing. Did he not assert that she had sworn to send the photograph on the day the betrothal was announced? And would she not then be swearing to break that vow? He insisted he could not conceive she would ever break her vow to break her vow. Why should she not do so? Ah, Watson, the sighed oaths of lovers are mere breath and gone with the wind."

Holmes lacks sentimentality. His condition is probably incurable and I have come to accept it with a shrug. But the solution to this conundrum was a simple one. "Well, the King was lying about the threat."

"Precisely!" cried he. "Of course she had never vowed to do so pointless, spiteful, and self-destructive a thing. If as she said the photograph was the only protection she had, then to have released it or would have been to not only lose that protection but guarantee the subsequent vengeance of His Majesty. The reason Wilhelm wished me to steal it was to remove that sole security so Death might presently part them asunder. In my heart I knew this. I allowed myself to be deceived because the end was so excellent. I am sorry to have to admit it, but to play the criminal has always been a dream of mine, as it has been yours too. Oh, do not deny it. You consented to accompany me on that burglary with undisguised delight. Moreover, to have stolen from the daughter of my greatest precursor would have been a dream come true. To dupe the daughter with her father's own devices made the challenge irresistible."

"But she escaped!"

"Oh, Wilhelm's minions were watching her house. They saw her slip out before five that morning. Just in case she caught them napping, that servant was left behind to provide details concerning which train she had taken, where to and under what name. Very obliging of her, was it not? Oh, what a chase that would have been! It would have bettered our pursuit of the *Aurora* out to sea. To have set off after the granddaughter of *Aurore Dupin*!"

"This is incredible!" I gasped. "You cannot be saying she was playing on you all the time you thought you were playing on her? I cannot believe it. The facts are all against it."

"Not at all. The facts are all for it once you understand what the facts are. So let us review the case from the beginning, or better still a little before that. You recall she said in that letter she left that she had been told the King would contact me?

"Very well."

"And that she had my address, which by chance happened to be a short walk from where she had chosen to stay?"

"Certainly."

"Now do not imagine a world citizen like the adventuress Irene Adler had determined to settle down permanently in St John's Wood. She had only rented that house temporarily, knowing that whatever the outcome of impending events, she would soon be on her travels again. She was ready to leave at a moment's notice. But that raises an interesting question. Why did she choose to live there at all? What was the one great advantage to that particular humble abode to outweigh the immense disadvantage that it was just a short walk away from the home of the greatest detective the world has ever known, the very detective she was sure His Majesty would turn to very soon?"

Holmes considered me quizzically and warning bells began to ring. This was a trick question. I knew it. What the trick would be I could not tell. I would find out soon enough. "Security," said I. "She anticipated there would be repeated break-ins and so security had to be her highest priority."

The sleuthhound barked. "Ha!" If dogs could laugh that is what it would sound like. "Ha! No less secure building exists in London. Picture in your mind's eye those sitting-room windows reaching down almost to the ground and with those preposterous English fasteners that a child could open. Were they not an open invitation to any passing burglars? And might one not expect her to introduce rudimentary locks after they had accepted that kind invitation twice? You must surely see she meant the King's men to enter that way and search that room most thoroughly of all. That way when they returned they would focus their attentions on the other rooms in the house and not even trouble to recheck that very obvious recess where she would leave a letter for me later. Of course they must have located the recess in an instant simply by tapping on the walls."

"They need not have entered that way," I pointed out. "I remember you said the one remarkable feature of the house was that the passage window could be reached from the top of the coach-house."

There was a twinkle in his eyes. "Ah, yes, that very peculiar alternative means of egress. I must confess, I entirely failed to realise the crucial meaning of that very curious optional extra. How easy it would have been to put bars on the window after the first, or at least the second, burglary. That, though, would never do. But we are halfway there now. If the house had any advantage, it was not that it was difficult to burgle but exceptionally easy, as she had intended it would be. So ask yourself again what advantage the place had that made it worth staying in, despite the certainty a detective living a short distance away would one day come calling."

I knew that once Holmes had answered his question I would kick myself for not seeing the obvious, yet that did not help. "I give it up. I cannot see it."

"Oh, you see it. The problem is it is staring you in the face, and that is why you strain your neck to overlook it. Is it not obvious? Of course it is. Since nothing could have justified the risk of living practically next door to the one great genius capable of undoing all her plans, the conclusion has to be that it was precisely for that reason she chose to do so. After all, since it was inevitable that I would become involved, what was the point in living at the North Pole knowing the very inaccessibility would be treated by me as a challenge? Do you not see? It works both ways. If I was only a short walk from her, then she was only a short walk from me. She did her homework. She studied my methods. She observed me. She knew when you called and the King too, for so charming a woman would still have had friends at his court."

"So that was the reason for those two-hour journeys in her landau every evening!" I cried. "I thought that was strange. It hardly constituted exercise, and why go out as darkness was falling when she might once again be accosted as she had been twice before?"

Holmes chuckled. "Oh, she never did make those trips, save on that one occasion when she saw I had organised a little scene outside her home for her personal entertainment. You see, while the King's men were tailing the mysterious veiled lady in that landau, an exceptionally beautiful young man in what Irene Adler liked to call her "walking clothes" was out watching 221b from the street below. Of course she slipped out via that passage window I mentioned earlier. As for those "walking clothes", they really were just that. She must have inherited her love of practical male attire from her remarkable grandmother Aurore, who renounced flimsy woman's shoes for masculine metal-heeled boots and found to her delight she could fly from one end of Paris to the other. You understand why feminine feet are crippled in China? It is the most aesthetic of castrations. Our contralto had her husky masculine tones from Aurore too. The latter's own mother once mistook her voice for that of her son."

"She saw me enter 221b?" I squirmed inwardly, for she must have witnessed my uncertain oscillation on the pavement, to say nothing of my smearing nitrate of silver onto a finger. And then there was that stuffing my stethoscope into my hat.

"She did. She also witnessed my indoor perambulations and those of the King that succeeded them. So did the actor who accompanied her. She also saw me leave as a drunken groom and again as an eccentric nonconformist in the company of a gentleman carrying a plumber's rocket in place of the Penang lawyer of his previous visit. What a woman, Watson. Oh, what a woman! I have never loved and I swear on my grandmother Anais's grave I never will, but as an approximation she wrote truly in that letter when she said she loved and was loved by a better man than His Majesty." He bowed low to Irene Adler in homage to his dearest foe. "There has never been a woman like her. There never will be again. Like me, she is unique. No, no, do not smile, and do not I beg you convert my statement of strict scientific fact into mere sentimentality. When you consider her ancestry, you must see that what I say is true."

By now I was thoroughly intrigued if hopelessly at sea. "And yet your entry on her said nothing more than that she was born in New Jersey in 1858. It was silent on her antecedents. Who was she?"

"You of all people ought to know that," said he with a curious twinkle to that hawkish eye. "Do not forget my initial attraction for you was that you imagined you saw in me a creature of fiction made flesh. But to begin with her New Jersey birth in 1858 – both the place and the year were false. The former was little more than a joke to portray her as the New Jersey Lily and so cast the King of Bohemia as to her what our Prince Pagan, as the Prince of Wales has been dubbed, was to Lily Langtry. Others have countered that the briony should be her plant since it is a climber with heart-shaped leaves."

"And her age?"

"A gentleman never gives a lady's true age. The lady is herself still more discreet. Yet to say that the stated year of her birth was false is perhaps a little unfair. It was her correct 'stage' age, which traditionally is ten years less than the biological one. It is perfectly fitting that King Wilhelm has adopted the same practice, for if ever there was a player king it is he. He is besides a young head on old shoulders and shall be to his dying day. With her the situation is reversed. But come now. Apply your special knowledge of crime to the problem. See if you can deduce who her father must have been."

"I have no special knowledge," said I reasonably enough. "You are the only detective whose methods I have ever studied. Of criminals I knowing nothing, save for the ones you have introduced me to."

"Not true, not true! Think back to the moment I revealed my profession. What was the first thing you did?"

It had been on the fourth of March in 1881 that Holmes declared himself to be the world's only consulting detective. The boast was a justifiable one save that he implied he was also the first. "I pointed out you might have been modelled on Lecoq and Dupin. I praised you for achieving in the world what they had only done in stories. If you will forgive me, Holmes, you took offence where you should not have done. Had I compared you to real life detectives, I might have understood it."

"But you did," said he calmly. "I did not wish to disillusion you at the time, but you are old enough now to take it. Lecoq, it is true, is a fictional character, but he is based on the very real if somewhat self-mythologising Eugene Vidocq. Why do you suppose that I said that Lecoq *was* a bungler? If he never lived then he could never die. I spoke of him in the past tense because I knew him to be nothing more than an idealised portrait of the late Eugene Vidocq, of dubious and questionable memory."

"And you are saying he was Irene Adler's father?"

"Watson," said he severely, "will you ever learn to listen? Have I not just said that you ought to be able to deduce the identity of Irene Adler's father from your present knowledge of crime? Who else did you compare me to?"

I thought for a moment. "Why, to Poe's Auguste Dupin."

Holmes opened his mouth to correct me and then thought better of it. "You are right. He is Poe's Dupin, for the real man bore about as much resemblance to Poe's portrayal of him as I do to your fairy-tale thinking machine. Now draw upon your knowledge of Poe's accounts and see if you cannot think of some affair his Dupin was involved in that might invite comparisons with the business of the Irene Adler papers and photographs."

Once Holmes had told me where to look I suddenly realised how obvious it was. "Why, of course. There was that business of the blackmailer and the purloined letter Dupin was able to recover from his home. That is curious. Now that I come to think of it, the resemblances are striking. Why, he even staged a distraction in the street so that he might switch the stolen letter for his counterfeit of it while the blackmailer was gazing out into the street. Of course, your distraction was far more spectacular."

Holmes gave a self-critical humph. "We will come to that. How would you explain those similarities? I forbid you to put them down to coincidence."

That was unreasonable. "How could they be anything other than coincidence? It is not as if you were competing with him. Were you? Good God. You were."

Holmes bowed his head in acknowledgement and perhaps in mock shame. "Guilty as charged, Doctor. That is precisely what I was doing. And why do you suppose I was doing so? Why on that particular occasion would I have wished to?"

"I have no idea."

"Consider that it took Lecoq six months to identify an unknown prisoner. I told you I could have done it in twenty-four hours. You thought I was boasting but I spoke the truth. The trick, as I have since explained, is to look for the singular while others are concentrating on the typical. So apply my method to the problem of Irene Adler's true identity. What is typical about her and what is entirely atypical? Recall King Willy's characterisation of her."

I could not see what this had to do with his attempting to outdo Dupin, but bitter experience had taught me it would be a waste of time pointing this out. So I did as I was told. "The King said that she had the face of the most beautiful of women with the mind of the most resolute of men."

"Very good. So your average investigator would seize upon what?"

"Obviously that she was a great beauty." I recalled how when I had lain in bed beside my wife that night I had been haunted by the face of *the* woman. Yes, she was a dangerous creature.

"And having done so he would choose from a smorgasbord of famously desirable *femme fatales* before concluding she had to be Sarah Bernhardt or Lola Montes or any one of a hundred other of the usual suspects. But that is not what you are going to do. I have too much respect for you to suppose that is what you are going to do. You are going to concentrate on the *second* part of that statement. The King might have said she had the resolution that only a woman scorned is capable of. He did not. He said her resolution was masculine. She did not simply dress as a man from time to time, you see. She *became* a man, or at least she ceased to be a woman. Now, who can you think of for whom that was true?"

"You have already told me. You said her grandmother Aurore Dupin liked to dress in men's clothes."

"More than that, she was able to move freely both physically and mentally and go undetected. The trick, you see, is first to exorcise one's own self so that another may take its place. Aurore Dupin expressed it nicely: "Not to be observed as a *man*, one has first to grow accustomed to not being observed as a *woman*." It is all a matter of self-effacement. You may notice I invariably choose to play characters as different from myself as possible. I once played the gravedigger in *Hamlet*. I would never choose to play the Dane. The part would be too close to the player. That was the melancholy Prince's own blunder when he chose to put an antic disposition on."

"But I have never heard of Aurore Dupin," I complained. "How was I supposed to deduce she was Irene Adler's grandmother when I knew nothing about her?"

"Then name me some other woman of this century renowned for her beauty and hailed as an unparalleled genius who was also notorious for dressing as a man."

I could think of only one. "George Sand the novelist."

"Very good. As it happens that was Aurore Dupin's *nom de plume*. And as a clue to the identity of Miss Adler's father, I should just say that one of Sand's recurring themes was incest. Now, can you not think why I was so determined to beat Irene Adler employing the same trick used by Auguste Dupin to recover the purloined letter? Why do so not merely to defeat Irene Adler, but to have her dance to my tune as if she were my puppet?"

I understood. "You believed you would be defeating Auguste Dupin in the person of his daughter."

"Or his granddaughter or both. Aurore's daughter Solange, a noted *grande horizontale* of her day, was convinced her true father had been one of her mother's lovers, and out of spite she lured one or two of them away."

"And you believe that Auguste Dupin was Solange's lover and perhaps Aurore's too? But you have no proof. There is nothing in Poe's accounts to suggest any such thing. Besides, I am still not wholly convinced Auguste Dupin ever existed."

"That is the intentional result of those accounts. Dupin wished to vanish – and not without reason. What does Poe tell us about his friend's background?"

I strained to think of anything. It occurred to me Poe had been particularly coy. "He does not seem to have been especially interested in supplying us with details concerning Dupin's past. He does not even give us any dates. As I recall he said no more than that Dupin came from an illustrious family but owing to a variety of untoward events, he declines to say what they were, the energy of his character succumbed and he determined to conceal himself away from the world. Accordingly, he lived in a dilapidated house closing all the shutters at first light to avoid prying eyes. He reminds me of Poe's character Roderick Usher. He clearly suffered from the eccentricities of genius."

"Oh, that is your idea, is it? He was an eccentric? It does not occur to you to ask why he behaved so? Is it not obvious there was a scandal? Now consider that the Dupin family, while illustrious, was nothing if not bohemian. A scandal in such a family was one to scandalise the scandalous. No, Dupin concealed himself from his family and friends and from the world itself not just because *he* had renounced *them*, but because *they* had renounced *him*. Only a man as eccentric, as you would say, as Poe could be a companion to him. And now, tell me that other outstanding event in Irene Adler's life we should pay particular attention to in determining her ancestry."

"But I know nothing about her," I protested feebly. "She was a closed book to me before our brief encounter with her."

"That is all you need."

"Then I can only say that she defeated the world's greatest detective. That is quite noteworthy."

"Precisely!" cried Holmes. "She defeated *me*! So the next question we have to ask is whether it was nothing but a fluke, as it may well have been, or whether she did so because I had at last met an antagonist who was my intellectual equal. If the former, then your expressed belief that I was defeated by a woman's wit may be correct. If the latter, than *the* woman was more than witty. She would have needed to possess a genius of the same kind as my own. You know my theories concerning nature and nurture. If I am correct, then that would be consistent with my conclusion that Irene Adler was Jeanne-Gabrielle, the illegitimate daughter of Auguste Dupin and Aurore Dupin's daughter Solange, who vanished soon after her birth in 1848. I once praised your wife Mary as possessing a genius for investigative work, but you must understand I meant 'genius' as nothing more than a taking of pains that might be developed given the right training. But if Irene Adler was defeating me at every turn, then hers was genius in the one true sense. She taught me a thing or two. You may thank the stars, that I and that violinist's great-granddaughter did not make sweet music together. The world is not yet ready for the monstrosity that might easily have resulted from such an experiment. Elizabeth Barrett-Browning, you know, called Aurore Dupin the most brilliant woman of any age, and I must confess Auguste Dupin had a good intellect too. Think what the awful result would have been had the brains of three such geniuses been combined in one being!"

Here Holmes's hand strayed absent-mindedly to a sovereign strung like a ring upon his watch-chain. Irene Adler had given it to her drunken groom after her second secret wedding. Holmes liked to refer to it as the queen's shilling.

"But can you be certain of this?"

"Not entirely. It is, as I say, a question of *nature* versus *nurture*. But when you consider that Mycroft and I are both exceptionally brilliant, it does seem likely. I was quite tempted to engender such a creature purely out of a spirit of enquiry and to study the result, assuming she consented to the experiment."

"No, no, I mean her ancestry! You say the proof is she was playing you, but what evidence is there that this was so?"

Sherlock Holmes placed his artistic Aubrey Beardsley hands together as if in mock prayer as he gazed at the photograph of the adventuress with his cold, grey eyes. What he was thinking I could not tell. He was doubtless arranging facts in his mind and stripping away any sentimentality that might bias his judgement.

"You will recall, I commenced my campaign against her by visiting her home disguised as an inebriated groom. Having established that her home was a burglar's dream come true, I then dropped by at the mews, where a pair of overpaid and underworked ostlers happily paid me to do their chores for them. Though they could see that the last thing I needed was further liquid refreshment, they insisted on pouring what they claimed was half-and-half down my throat. Subsequent events would suggest that this was imprecise. It was almost half porter, almost half ale, and about seven percent something more potent. They also supplied me with my favourite shag tobacco, which was very thoughtful of her."

"Of *her*?" said I in surprise.

"Obviously of her," said he impatiently. "Do you honestly suppose that after her home had been burgled twice, the servants in the neighbourhood were not all paranoid about strangers who turned up eager to pump them for information? She knew I would make an appearance. She had warned them that should any exceptionally tall, lean fellow appear, they were to tell him exactly what she wished me to hear. They kept me there as long as they could while she was busy elsewhere arranging matters. That I had come as a drunken groom suggested a delicious trick. I vaguely noticed a stable lad leave the coach-house soon after I made my appearance. It may have been her.

"After parting from those ostlers, I took to trudging back and forth before her house on the opposite side of the road. Her lawyer made his appearance and thrust his way past her maid straight into her sitting-room, where he proceeded to put on a dumbshow as if addressing the gentlemen of the jury rather than proposing marriage. He had certainly attended the Parnell hearings and been mightily impressed by the performance of Sir Charles Russell, Q.C., M.P., whose broken voice and whole manner suiting with forms to his conceit rightly earned the applause of his adoring public. Additionally, as I say, our actor drew upon my own little performance the night you saw me pacing back and forth as if debating an abstruse point with myself. The difference is that whereas I was not alone and you assumed I was, he was alone and I assumed he was not. I supposed our *grande horizontale* had assumed the position and was decorously prostrate on a bearskin rug. I further surmised that after he had left she slithered out like a Washo hunter impersonating a serpent. Of course she was not there at all. It was only once she had signalled to him she had returned and all was prepared that he abruptly terminated the dumbshow and hurried out. She returned to the house by her usual route from the top of the coach house to that passage window. She clearly has a peculiar taste in these matters."

"But Holmes," I objected, "what was the point of it all?"

"Well, I have said that they must have drugged my half-and-half. The best way to play a part is to be it, and since I had unknowingly volunteered for the role of drunken groom, she had thought I might as well be properly immersed in the part. I have myself found a cocktail of transcendental medicines works best. In this case adrenalin was to be added to the mix. You know how I enjoy an intoxicating chase. It is as good as a chaser to me. All that was required was an excuse for one and then I would be fully prepared to play a variation on that drunken groom. By the way, you see the joke to that mad rush to get me to the church on time?

"Not quite."

"Recall how soon after we first met, you thought to play the detective and deduce my profession. With that aim in mind you listed my limits. You were good enough to grant me a good practical knowledge of British law, but I fear that weddings are my blind spot, as indeed they were for the lawyer she was supposedly about to marry. You know why until recently it was illegal to be pronounced man and wife after high noon?"

"I have no idea."

"Because in the past the likelihood was that the groom would be drunk after twelve. Marriage is a somewhat distasteful affair and one I try to avoid thinking about. Understanding this, Irene Adler thought it worth the risk to stage that frantic race against the clock to the church. She gambled that the rush of adrenalin would work with whatever was added to my half-and-half to leave me thoroughly disoriented. It never occurred to me how very unlikely that wedding was. There was the surpliced gentleman, I shall not call him a priest, arguing with the lawyer at the altar that a witness was absolutely essential. It was three minutes before the hour struck and Cinderella found herself in rags once more. If they really had needed witnesses why did they not summon her coachman John and the cabbie? Why settle for a drunk who had wandered into the church by chance and would most likely never be seen again?"

"There was no time. If there were only three minutes in which to perform the ceremony then every second counted," I pointed out. "It is incredible that it was still performed before twelve struck."

"Oh very remarkable," said he, refilling his clay pipe with that foul shag of his. "Particularly since having prudently cut corners to strip down the ceremony, cutting all that poetry about till death do us part and such balderdash, our surpliced friend proceeded to invent perfectly superfluous new material for the witness to repeat. By the time it was over just as the church clock was tolling twelve I could no longer swear which groom had been married to the woman. It was one of the most unnerving experiences of my life."

"Unnerving?" I was thinking of how on returning to 221b he had proceeded to laugh as I have not seen any man laugh outside my surgery. He laughed heartily, with a high ringing note, leaning back in his chair, and shaking his sides. On and on it went. He simply could not stop. "Surely you thought it quite droll."

"Droll?" Holmes let forth one of those laughs like the last breath of a dying man that were so much more typical of him. He has mastered the technique, along with the silent munching of toast, as absolutely necessary at the Diogenes for when he and his brother Mycroft breakfast together there. They semaphore news and pieces of wit to each other beneath a sign on which is written the single club imperative: "*Silence*". "Hysterical would be a better word. Really, Doctor, all your medical instincts ought to have risen up against that laugh. In another man it might have been dismissed as hilarity. In me it should have been diagnosed instantly as the possible onset of brain fever. I must confess, I was troubled by very curious dreams that night."

I thought it best not to enquire. "I still don't understand the point of it all. Why so ridiculous a charade?"

"To leave me with the vague suspicion that I had been the hare to the Adler eagle. I would want my revenge in kind. If she had played on me then I would play on her. I would stage my own scene and she would be my puppet to perform just as I scripted her to do. Of course you can see why she was so confident she could manipulate me into staging the scene I did."

"I'm sorry, I don't think I do."

Holmes looked surprised. "But did you not note earlier the striking similarities between Auguste Dupin's plot to recover the eponymous purloined letter and my own to steal the photograph? I confessed I was competing with Dupin. I was determined to defeat him in the person of his daughter using his very methods. She knew I would wish to do that. She also understood I would try to upstage her father with something infinitely more showy and superficial. He had had one man discharge a musket without a ball outside the blackmailer's house as a distraction. Since the King of Bohemia was supplying me with unlimited funds, how could I resist the temptation to hire a whole theatre of extras for that scene?"

Holmes made a wry face and I knew he was picturing his spectacular show. "At that moment, I entirely lacked the supreme gift of the artist, the knowledge of when to stop. I was working on the principle that nothing exceeds like excess. Did I pause for an instant to consider that she was an actress of sorts and accustomed to crowd scenes in the opera house and the theatre? The more extras I used the more likely she would recognise a face or two and even know them personally. Incredible imbecility!"

"I must confess," said I, a little bemused, "it was not like you to be so careless."

"Precisely!" he cried. "It was not like me. I was not myself. Have I not told you again and again that all emotion is antithetical to rational thought? And do we not have here the proof of it? I was jealous, I was angry, I was confused. I was bent upon revenge. Strong emotions were working within me. Your thinking machine would never have behaved so.

38

She did that to me. I admit it. Treat that as a cautionary tale, my friend. Never trust a woman, and above all never trust yourself."

"But you did gain entry into her house," I objected, for I felt I should play devil's advocate since my friend was intent upon being his own worst critic. I thought he was being far too hard upon himself. "Personally I believe it was beautifully done. She stepped out of her landau straight into the fist fight you had orchestrated. Your rushed to her defence in the role of a clergyman was perfectly timed. Once you had fallen to the ground, clapping that red paint to your forehead, she had no choice but to take you into her home and to the very room where you had deduced the photograph must be concealed. Surely it all went according to plan. It was *your* plan, not hers. Then I threw that plumber's rocket in through the window when you signalled me to do so and your troupe of extras cried out "Fire!" in unison. It was just like being in the theatre! She rushed to the recess to recover the photograph, realised that the fire had been faked and at once replaced it before leaving you alone in the room. Your only mistake, if you will forgive me for saying so, is that you should have performed your wonderful imitation of the action of the tiger. In one bound you could have removed the photograph and in another you would have been out of that long open window with your extras creating a barrier between you and any pursuers. I am only surprised you did not do so."

"Oh, that would never have done," said he in a tone of self-recrimination. "Deny myself my coming big scene and the applause I so richly deserved? For of course I had to have an audience. On that occasion there were only actors. Do you not see how much better it would be to return the next morning with you and the King of Bohemia? And of course we would at once be ushered into her home with no questions asked and left alone in the room where the photograph had been concealed. Does that not make perfect sense to you, my friend?"

It is curious but until Holmes had pointed out the absurdity of the thing it had never occurred to me how ridiculous it all was. The King of Bohemia was the last person to be invited into her home. Why would she have concealed her most precious possession in the very room where visitors were left alone? Why place it in the most obvious of recesses and one with no lock upon it! I gave Holmes a reproachful look. My hero had disappointed me.

"I was mad – insane," he pleaded in his defence.

"But did you not deceive her for an instant?" I asked hopefully.

"Not for a second. Think of the iodoform."

"The iodoform?"

"You wished to break the ice by having me deduce your new profession, so when Mrs. Turner insisted you prove the iodoform was not poison you dabbed it behind your ears. If we grant that the blood of Auguste Dupin ran in her veins, what easy Adler Test might she have applied to that wet red paint on my broken head once she had so very thoughtfully wiped it away?"

I thought about that. "Oh. I see. She could have sniffed you."

Holmes sighed. "Many a bride has shown more wit than I did then. A little pig's blood would have done the trick. Pride, Watson. Pride had addled my brains."

"You think that was your mistake?"

"The entire plot was my mistake! Have I not said that I have used that cry of 'Fire!' several times? It did me good service in the case of the Darlington Subsitution Scandal and was praised by the press when I repeated the ruse on the occasion of the Arnsworth Castle business. Knowing I would be her adversary' do you suppose she failed to follow my career in the press every bit as diligently as you did? She realised I was copying her father's ploy with variations. With a little encouragement, she could guarantee I would repeat it once more. Never again! Should I ever be tempted to reuse once more it promise me you will whisper 'Norwood' in my ear."

"Er, 'Norbury', Holmes," I corrected him. The name of his other shame was Norbury.

"Yes, of course. Norbury," said he irritably, for he hates to be corrected. "Forgive me, my mind was on where Beach is to be buried once his death has been announced. But to finish our review of that farcical scene, you see what she did next?"

"She detailed her actions in the letter she left for you in that recess. First she thought about what had just happened. Then she went upstairs, undressed and redressed in her male attire. Having done so, she went back downstairs just in time to see you leaving by the front door."

Holmes looked at me expectantly.

"Oh, I see. You said that you at once made your excuses and left as quickly as you could. You doubt she could have done all that in the few seconds it took you to make your exit."

"So what did she actually do?" Holmes again paused kindly to give me time to think, should I choose to do so. I seized the opportunity to try. I flatter myself I succeeded quite well.

"Her landau was still parked outside her home, ready to rush your clergyman to hospital. She could not have undressed and stepped into her gentleman's shoes so quickly. I see that. It took you a full five minutes to change back from your drunken groom disguise. Since she knew your address she must have taken her landau and changed while in it. All that makes sense. But cheer up," I added, sensing he was feeling bad about his crass errors of judgement, "She was not infallible herself. She should never have passed you by as a man and wished you a goodnight. It is incredible you did not recognise her voice."

"But I did," said he with a frown. "She knew I would. I see that now."

"You knew it was her?"

Holmes was thoughtful. "I don't think it was quite as bad as that. Or should I say it was worse? I would appear to have chosen to tell myself I could not identify her. That act of self-deception was easy enough. All I had to do was search my mental files for a man whose voice her contralto matched. Naturally I failed, as I secretly meant to do."

"But why?"

"Oh, it is obvious enough now," said he wearily. "Just as it would not have done to permit that affair you serialised in your journal as *The Sign of the Four* to have concluded without an exciting chase so one was called for in this later affair. We would arrive at eight and discover that the eagle had flown. We would set off in hot pursuit. The mad drive to the church had whetted my appetite, you see, and I was determined that the pursuit of Aurore's granddaughter would be as exciting as our coursing of the Aurora down the Thames. I was particularly annoyed with the King for foiling my plans. He was meant to fling his arms into the air with a cry of despair, I would assure him all was not lost and that the game was afoot. With luck she would leap from her train at a station stop and we would discover it too late. Then we would follow her luggage to France. She might have led us a merry dance right across Europe. The race would conclude at some dead end overlooking a bottomless abyss. We might have fallen to our deaths locked in each other's arms. What a finish! Well, perhaps another time." Holmes had fallen silent reminiscing, on what might have been and plotting what was to come.

"And all because of the note she left for you and the photograph for him. If it had not been for them, he would have continued to hound her to the ends of the earth."

"Ah, but he still intended to. You see, the truth is that it was the note that was meant for him and the photograph was for me."

I thought Holmes must have made a mistake. "Surely not. Why should she leave you a photograph? It must have been for him, just as the note said."

"Oh, Watson, do use that head of yours," said he with his customary impatience. "His Majesty was desperately hunting down every image of her to destroy them all. Is it likely he desired another? What did he dread more than that his fiancée should discover the woman's picture down the very divan they had once shared? No, she addressed the letter to me so I would pick up the photograph first. Had it gone straight to the King, he would have cast it into the fire in a second. She claimed it was a gift for him, knowing I would at once realise how absurd that was, and so see it must contain some cryptic message making it as dangerous as that wedding portrait. More so, in fact. It was the photograph and not the note that worked on me like the flash of lightning that blinded Saul and opened his eyes on the Damascus road. After that, there was no question of my accepting the King's marriage proposal."

I stared at Holmes in astonishment.

"Well, not quite that," said he with a chuckle. "You remember how he offered me his hand with a snake ring in its palm? It was the second secret wedding I found myself being drawn into. But I had this charm to protect me." He touched the pierced sovereign on his watch-chain. "I had taken the queen's shilling, you see, and become one of her irregular knights. 'Adler', you know, means 'eagle' in German, and the eagle is the antithesis of the serpent."

He looked up from that sovereign to the photograph of the woman in black on the mantelpiece and I did so too, each of us lost in his own thoughts.

Part II: The Adventure of the Last Trump

I was just turning away from it when suddenly I understood. It had been so obvious that I had missed it before. "Holmes," I exclaimed in amazement, dazzled by the simplicity of simplicity. "Someone had died!"

He put a hand on my shoulder. "Good, Watson. You do begin to pierce the veil. And many more must die too. A little late, perhaps, but you have perceived, I see, that hers is no evening dress. That black skull cap is perhaps a trifle suggestive."

"I had supposed she was dressed for some costume ball," said I defensively. "That robe does look as if it might belong to some sixteenth century character. She could be Ophelia at the funeral of Hamlet's father and greeting the Prince with a sweet smile." Had I been Hamlet and received such a smile Shakespeare's tragedy would never have been written.

"Certainly she is the daintiest thing under a black widow's cap. But do you not recognise the pose? No? Perhaps I forgot to mention I am at present once again playing the knight to protect a damsel in distress plus a couple of curious gentlemen besides. There are fears of abductions. Did you perhaps wonder why the curtains were drawn over the windows? Draw back the one on the right."

I did so and was astounded at the sight. There was Irene Adler herself dressed just as in the photograph. At least it might have been her, so similar was the smile and the perfect asymmetry of her beautiful face, which permitted two contrasting aspects of her personality to be exhibited. This might indeed have been a portrait of *the* woman. I recognised it as Holbein's Christina of Denmark, Duchess of Milan, on loan to the National Gallery in Trafalgar Square. Yet it was just how I imagined Irene Adler must have been in her teens. As I drew aside that curtain it was to the moment in Rider Haggard's great novel when the eponymous "She who must be obeyed" unveils her enslaving beauty. Was this one of her many incarnations?

My thoughts were interrupted by the realisation that Holmes's human voice was in evidence drawing me reluctantly back to the mundane world. I forced myself to listen.

". . . When Holbein painted this, Christina's husband had just died, his condition doubtless exacerbated by an earlier poisoning attempt. He was Francesco Sforza, Duke of Milan. It is not his death, though, that concerns me. As a student of crime I find the murder in accordance with Sforza's instructions of Merveilles, the French envoy to Milan, much more to my taste. But you could not be more wrong. This is no incarnation of '*She who must be obeyed*'. This is her innocent twin sister '*She who obeys unquestioningly*'. Is it possible that you did not see that?"

Holmes must have noticed my bookmarked copy of *She* and deduced I was rereading it for the fourth time. "You must at least confess she is queenly," said I, determined to champion so lovely a lady.

"'Queenly'? Yes and no." He was smiling as at some private joke. "One has first to receive the royal jelly to be transformed into the queen of the hive. If not, then one remains a pawn. She never became a queen, though I have no doubt Wilhelm's hero Henry VIII must have sighed that she would have made a fine one. This is a portrait of what might have been. You can see that from her headpiece."

I could not, though I did not doubt Holmes would proceed to deduce her whole tragic history from it as he had recently done that of one Henry Baker at the start of our adventure of the Blue Carbuncle. "It seems like a very ordinary black cap," I confessed. "It is merely part of her widow's weeds, I can say no more than that. I cannot guess what you are about to surmise from it."

"Good. Don't. Guessing is a filthy habit. But surely you can tell me something more than that."

"Nothing, save that Holbein seems to have twisted it about to one side."

"And you don't know why? Well, well, it is better than nothing, though I have to say since I have already slipped in its significance, you ought to see it. I say again that this is a portrait of a pawn who might have become a queen. Do you not see that? Holbein has turned her cap about to increase her resemblance to that chesspiece standing upon the penultimate square of the board. Her husband has died. Henry VIII's third wife, Jane Seymour, has died. He desires a fourth wife. As a good Protestant, Holbein wishes to see him wed this good Protestant, so he creates a vision of *the* woman of the King's dreams. She is waiting obediently for His Majesty to instruct her to take one step forward into his waiting arms. Then she will instantly cast off these weeds to be redressed as his queen. Both shall cease to mourn and be reborn. It is as if Hamlet had not succumbed to melancholy and had wedded Ophelia as he ought to have done."

Holmes can see deeply into the manifold wickedness in the hearts of men and women, but love is a closed book to him. Accordingly, I had to doubt his assertion that this was really a portrait of *the* woman of Henry's dreams. "How can you possibly tell that this would be the King's ideal woman? You only say that because she happens to resemble Irene Adler," I added teasingly.

"Nothing of the kind. You have read *Frankenstein*? The laudable aim of that eminent doctor was to manufacture a perfect being by amalgamating the best parts of various dead men. Holbein has adopted the same approach by combining what Henry would have considered the best bits of his first three wives.

"Not first that Christina is passive. She patiently awaits the command to step forwards out of the picture. If she does so, she will be transformed and will never forget she owes everything to her creator. Henry shall be her Pygmalion, which is to say her creator and god. So the pious and obedient Jane Seymour is in evidence here. That is easily combined with the fidelity of the good wife Catherine of Aragon, since Christina dutifully remains in widow's weeds. But mark the asymmetry of the face and note the mouth in particular. This is a girl with a pretty twisted lip. It is the infamous Habsburg lip, to be precise, which doubtless gave her a little pleasing lisp. Holbein has cleverly used this mouth to make one side of her face seem all innocence while on our left the lips are larger and more sensuous. She is made to combine the innocence of Jane Seymour with the erotic charge of an Anne Boleyn."

"She had a lucky escape," I muttered.

"Undoubtedly. It was doubtless with the benefit of hindsight she is said to have commented how gladly she would have given Henry a hand in marriage if she could as easily have afforded to lose a head. The truth is, she did as she was told, just as the King of Bohemia's bride Clotilde did. Such women are educated to place duty far above whatever meagre rights they might seem to have. They understand that such matches are nothing but moves in the game of kings. Christina would never have

44

refused Henry if ordered to accept him, any more than Clotilde would have refused King Wilhelm."

"She was a pawn indeed," I murmured.

"Sir Thomas More, you know, spoke of the game of kings as mostly played out on scaffolds. He pointedly observed that the King would not hesitate to sacrifice an English knight to gain a French castle. I mentioned that one Merveilles had to die to ensure the marriage of Christina to the Duke of Milan. It was a political killing to guarantee a political wedding. Sforza needed the permission of the Holy Roman Emperor Charles V, you see, and Charles would only grant it if Sforza first broke the Treaty of Milan signed to create an alliance against the Empire. So you see that from the age of eleven, when she was first betrothed to Sforza, poor Christina understood rulers control by force not love."

I turned back from that painting to reconsider Irene Adler posing as the Duchess of Milan. In throwing light upon the photograph, Holmes had revealed the dense darkness which surrounded her. "So she harboured similar fears?"

"Undoubtedly," said he grimly. "As in the case of Henry's wives, such pawns could easily find that the final square once achieved turned into a scaffold and beyond it the abyss. Wilhelm envied Henry the ease with which he disposed of unwanted wives. He required a like separation from Irene Adler following that secret marriage, but could not achieve it by means of divorce. He had to keep the union a secret. But as I say, the small print of the marriage contract states death can annul it, so that is the separation he had in mind. She left full details of her flight so that his men might find her easily. Her photograph communicated to me what she expected. If I wished to assist her then she might live on, while the King would imagine he had succeeded. Needless to say I helped in the subterfuge. I hope she will outlive Wilhelm."

"But if she was content to continue to conceal their secret marriage, why was he so determined to dispose of her?"

"Because that was the least of the revelations he feared. You see, there had been a good deal of pillow talk and mutterings in his asleep. He had revealed things to her he ought not to have done, and these included the plans of his cousin Wilhelm of Germany. Should she communicate such data to me, I might pass them on to my brother Mycroft, who might in turn transmit them to others. By coming to me first and convincing me she was a blackmailer, he recruited me to his side before ever she could contact me. It was only be means of that photograph she could finally open my eyes. You see now that the pose recalled the portrait of Christina. That in turn was intended to make me think of another work. In doing so I would come to understand her greater fears for the future of our world."

Night had fallen and the gas lamps in Baker Street had been lit. Holmes rose from his chair by the fire and strode over to draw back a curtain and reveal a second painting. I recognised it as Holbein's great double portrait of two unknown men also on display in the National Gallery.

"This, too, has been targeted, and the forgery of it that was to have been substituted for it is at present on display there until the would-be thieves can be taken. A scarlet thread of murder links these two Holbeins. It was by means of this thread that I at last penetrated the labyrinth to its dark heart. What we have here is nothing less than a prophecy of the end of a world. It is a prophecy that is not without significance for us in our own age."

I did not understand how Holmes could suppose this picture of two supremely confident Renaissance men standing on either side of a table piled high with all the instruments of reason and imagination might be read as Apocalyptic. "Surely you are mistaken. Theirs was a golden age of optimism much like our own. The sun was rising on a better world than had ever been before."

"The lute, Watson, the lute. That is the key. Kindly attend to it."

There was indeed a lute upon the lower shelf of the table. Considering it more carefully I noticed that one of the strings was snapped. "It is broken. That happens. You break the strings of your Stradivarius from time to time. What of that?"

"Oh, nothing. Except that the Latin word '*fides*' means both '*lute*' and '*faith*', so you see a broken lute can mean a broken word. Now, the emblem created to signify the Treaty of Milan had been a lute, meaning that if but one string was snapped all harmony would be lost. The breaking of the thread of life of the French envoy Merveilles was such a tragic loss of harmony."

I thought to myself how often I had been tempted to break a string or two of my friend's Stradivarius to end his improvised scrapings. "It need not mean anything. It could be nothing more than a broken string."

"Granted. But if it does refer to the French envoy's murder, then it probably tells us something about these two anonymous men. Why should they take any interest in the death of a French ambassador? Only if they themselves are French ambassadors and particularly so if they are in a like situation. They might, say, find themselves at the court of a man ready to disregard international conventions and laws on the grounds that what he has the right to do he will do, and in so doing he may extend his rights further. The painting is dated 1533. Who would be our most likely candidate at that time?"

46

The image of the Herculean King Wilhelm of Bohemia in all his barbaric and theatrical opulence flashed across my mind. In an instant I saw him changed into Holbein's Henry VIII. "Why, the fellow on the left is posed just like this painter's most famous depiction of Henry."

"Just so. Let us then work on the assumption that these are French ambassadors at the court of Henry VIII in the year he separated from Catherine of Aragon his wife and secretly married his mistress Anne Boleyn."

"Whatever happened to avoiding speculation until one had all the data?" said I cheekily.

"I told you I learnt a thing or two from Irene Adler. In particular she taught me to apply such principles more flexibly. Let us first theorise and then see if the facts confirm or contradict our theory."

I had thought better of my thinking machine. "You are in danger of producing a circular argument to prove your assumptions by your assumptions."

Holmes sniffed. "No doubt you imagine you praised me when you likened me to a thinking machine, just as those who supposed Newton's brain a piece of clockwork meant to praise the man they imagined had reduced the universe to nothing more than that. You would make of me a living version of Wolfgang von Kempelen's chess-playing automaton. I am not an uncritical admirer of Irene Adler's father, as you know, yet she has forced me to reassess some of his ideas. He spoke truly when he said chess playing need not be the mark of a creative intellect. In theory, one might indeed create a chess-playing machine capable of winning every game, though the games played between pairs of such automatons would be entirely devoid of aesthetic interest. Success would be dependent not upon the presence of thought but its entire absence. How would you define faith?"

I was startled into attentiveness by that unexpected question. "Why, it is to believe something without evidence."

"That is imprecise. It is to apprehend truths that cannot be arrived at through proof. Now, you must see that this can either mean to believe what no evidence supports because one has closed one's eyes or to see directly what is true but that cannot be proven through other facts. The one kind of faith is the worst sort of dogmatism. The other is the clearest of perceptions. The problem is that the one can easily masquerade as the other. If I see the colour blue, I cannot prove it to a blind man. I see it and there is an end to the matter. Reason is useless here. But it is easy to tell oneself one has seen a colour unknown to science when one has done nothing of the kind. That is the false kind of faith. You must see that one faith is diametrically opposed to the other. When Christ accused his followers of lacking faith, he meant they were so lost in the dogma they called faith that they had ceased to be able to see. And if one cannot see then all observation, being preconditioned, is worthless. Irene Adler has taught me that."

"A woman?" said I in amazement.

"*The* woman," corrected Holmes. "The Ophelia to my Hamlet. That was part of the point of her playing Christina of Denmark in deep mourning, yet so full of life. But your condemnation of circularity is not entirely unjust. We have made a leap of faith. Now let us retrace our route step by painstaking step. What and where is the first step? Clearly it is to be found beneath the right shoe of the gentleman on our left."

Here I recalled how at the start of "A Scandal in Bohemia", Holmes had deduced from my clean shoes that I had been out walking in the country some time before and that I had a very careless servant girl. Such deductions would be impossible here. "You are most assuredly joking. How can you possibly learn anything from those painted shoes?"

"Watson, you hear but you do not listen. I never claimed I could. I said the clue lay beneath it. That tells us who this gentleman is, what he is, where he is and why he is there. Of course that is only to scratch the surface. It also relates to man's significance or lack of it in the universe, but we will not go into that."

Holmes seemed quite serious, so based on my knowledge of the man I assumed I was right and he must be joking. "I don't believe it. There is nothing beneath his shoes but the floor."

"Most astute. Dupin, you know, describes a game in which the aim is to discover a name upon a map. The novice chooses the tiniest word. The adept selects the largest characters and the novice misses them entirely. But you, my friend, have missed the map itself! Look at this floor again."

I did so and frowned. "All I can see is a pattern consisting of nine circles. Is this a palimpsest? Do you detect a secret map concealed beneath this pattern?"

"Not at all. Have you not heard of the music of the spheres? Ah, but I was forgetting. You have been seduced by that Copernican nonsense about the earth falling up instead of the sun going down. There are eight celestial spheres and there is God. That is what these nine circles represent."

I laughed. "Well, I know you like to boast you can see an ocean in a drop of water, but really, it is going a bit too far to turn this patterned floor into a map of all of creation."

Holmes likes a challenge. "Really? Then consider the pavement on which kings and queens are enthroned before the high altar in Westminster

Abbey. It is patterned thus. Moreover, there was an inlaid inscription, probably torn up during the English reformation, instructing the reader – mark that, Watson – to read it as a map of the cosmos and to give a value of three to each and every sphere, multiplying three by itself as one proceeds from circle to circle until one arrives at a final figure for the lifespan of the universe. So you see that the gentleman on our left has his right foot at the centre of a circle representing a sphere with a value of three." Holmes paused to permit me to appreciate his triumph.

"Well?" said I. "What of it?"

"But is it possible you do not see?" he cried incredulously. "Is it not obvious? It is a very simple pun."

"'Three'?"

"Yes, yes. One, two, three. His sphere of influence is three!"

I struggled to think of anywhere called *Three*. The best I could come up with was the Firth of Forth. I could think of no other place named after a number. "I am at a loss," I sighed.

"Watson," said he solemnly, "did we not agree that these gentlemen were French?" He paused while the communication travelled from his mouth to my ear and thence to my brain. He clearly assumed it would take some time.

Suddenly I understood. "Troyes!"

"Troyes," confirmed Holmes. "This gentleman's sphere of influence was Troyes in France, which is of course pronounced like '*trois*'."

That was certainly ingenious, but was it not a trifle too much so? "I don't think that can be right. Why would a Frenchman identify himself by means of the floor in Westminster Abbey? What had that to do with him?"

"Ah, but you have committed the error of framing a question rhetorically the better to justify never addressing it at all," said he smugly. "Now, had you asked that question seriously, then it would cease to be a problem and would at once become its own solution. Why would a Frenchman identify himself by means of the floor of Westminster Abbey, unless it had some special meaning for him? The date 1533 is inscribed into the floor here. This Frenchman must have been in the Abbey in that year. Now, Watson, think back to you school days studying English history. What happened in Westminster Abbey in 1533?

I thought it wise to guess without confessing I was doing so. "The coronation of Anne Boleyn."

"Just so. And the French ambassador Jean de Dinteville, the Bailly of Troyes, was the chief guest at that singular event. But who is the other man? Any ideas?"

"They cannot both be French ambassadors," said I helpfully. "There would only have been one in England at a time."

"No? Not even of one of them was here to represent the French state and the other the French Church? Both would be necessary if in separating from Catherine of Aragon, Henry was risking excommunication at the hands of the papacy. The support of the church in France would have been most welcome. The man on our right is obviously a French bishop."

I smiled and shook my head. "It may be obvious to you. I do not see it at all."

"Oh, you see it. Now let me teach you to observe it too." He stretched out his hand for one of his reference tomes and opened it at a picture of the inner sanctuary of Westminster Abbey as it was prior to the English reformation. "You see those statues of Edward the Confessor and Thomas Becket to the sides of the altar? They represent the Church and state. Now, in your mind's eye superimpose its key features onto those in this painting. The effect is akin to a palimpsest. You see that this table takes the place of the altar. These two gentlemen representing the Church and state stand in for the statues. That is clear, is it not?"

"Not quite," said I contritely. "How can you tell that one of these men represents the Church and the other the state?"

"Why, from their crowns," answered Holmes. "They are quite different."

I toyed with the idea of pointing out that there were no crowns but prudently thought better of it. My magician would be perfectly capable of producing a hat out of a rabbit. "Well, where are they?"

"I shall not insult your intelligence by drawing your attention to the pair of crowns to the sides of the gentleman on the left's head in the patterned curtain. That tells us this is the French ambassador Jean de Dinteville, who as such is the image of King Francis I of France."

I nodded. "That is obvious enough. What then of the gentleman on the right?"

"The curtain supplies Georges de Selve with a crown too, though his is of a different nature. You shall see it clearly enough with your mind's eye if I tell you de Dinteville's costume features lynx fur. That is a clue. It was thought the rays from the eyes of the lynx could penetrate solid matter, so that it could see through every veil. Just imagine you have the eyes of a lynx and then it will appear."

I attempted to decode my friend's unnecessarily cryptic clue. He had to mean this de Selve fellow was standing in front of where the crown would be. I followed the repeated pattern and suddenly I understood.

"Yes, well might you gasp. Were it a bullet it would go plumb through the middle of the back of the head and smack into the brain."

"Wonderful!" I cried. "Why, it is directly behind his brows. Yet it could be coincidence."

"It cannot be coincidence," said he dogmatically as is his fashion. "Do you not see this patterned curtain proclaims he is a bishop elected by God? He has received the charismatic gift of a tongue of fire like the first Christians at Pentecost. He is not even consecrated yet. He could not be until the completion of his twenty-fifth year. You see his age is supplied on the edge of that locked book he is leaning upon so heavily. He cannot open it until after his consecration."

I saw that there was indeed an inscription: "*aetatis suae 25*". "You are wrong," I pointed out with a quick pang of precipitate pleasure. "He *was* twenty-five."

"You are misled by the Arabic numerals. The inscription is a Latin one and is short for '*anno aetatis suae*', which you should know means '*in the year of his age*'. Since the Romans had no zero, one's first birthday was one's day of birth. De Selve was in his twenty-fifth year. He was not yet twenty-five."

I would say it is unwise to correct Holmes. That is not quite true. It is only unwise if he is wrong. "Well, perhaps. But where is this tongue of fire you claim to see?"

"Oh, you see it too. Once again you simply do not observe it. Look directly above his head and you will perceive there is a shape in the curtain as if such a huge tongue of fire had descended upon him. It is the celestial fire invoked in the hymn you can read in the open book before the broken lute. It is a Lutheran hymnal and the hymn on that page is employed to call upon the Holy Ghost. It is sung to invoke unity at times of division in the Church. It is in German. The Church no longer speaks with one tongue and from the same hymn sheet. But bishops like de Selve would work to recover such unity."

"Why," said I, "that ghostly flame is like a mitre too. But why the need for such cryptic symbolism?"

"For the same reason that Irene Adler needed to communicate with me in code. Dark times demand dark speakings. This bishop is travelling incognito in England as Catholic priests would one day do again after the English reformation. But his aim is to prevent further rifts. As for that secret mark upon his brows, you will understand its meaning better if you contrast it with its antithesis. This is a man of peace. Who was the first man of violence, the one who made my profession possible?"

That was easy. "It was the first murderer, the man who bore the mark of Cain. He slew his brother Abel because the latter's sacrifice was more acceptable to God."

"And so he offered up the old human sacrifice. Traditionally he did so at the holy ground of a place of sacrifice, which is to say in the equivalent of the sanctuary of a temple. And would not such sacrifices

51

soon occur with the dissolution of the monasteries? And did not the murderers bear the mark of Cain? That is what is being foretold here."

Although Holmes is a lapsed Catholic, it is still in his blood. "What makes you think so?"

"My dear Watson, I have already told you this floor recalls the sanctuary floor in Westminster Abbey where kings and queens are crowned and enthroned. Now consider that dirty cloud in the foreground eclipsing the star at the centre of the floor's design. It screams murder in the sanctuary. That is obvious, is it not? Hmm. Would it not be good practice if before removing corpses from crime scenes such as this chalk outlines were always made on the ground? No, it would not. Better to photograph the scene."

There was a clear danger that Holmes would veer off at a wild tangent. I stepped in to prevent it. "But what makes you think this cloud, as you call it, marks the spot of a murder? It looks to me as if some iconoclast has hurled whitewash at the painting. Perhaps your profession causes you to see all scenes as scenes of crimes. You really should learn to see things from a different point of view."

He seemed amused at the suggestion. "Very well. Let us put your theory to the test. Let us consider this painting from a different angle. Just step over to the right hand side of it and gaze down at that shape. Tell me what you see."

I did so. It took me a moment to discover the optimum viewpoint. At first it seemed as if I was gazing into a semi-transparent serpent's egg to perceive the creature growing within it. And then I saw what the creature was. "Why, it is a distorted skull!"

"Just so. Rather fine, is it not?" said he, like one sipping a fine vintage. "It streaks across this map of the cosmos like a jarring note amidst the music of the spheres. It constitutes a somewhat ironic answer to the invocation of the Holy Spirit in that Lutheran hymnal. What it signifies, of course, is a murder committed in the sanctuary of the Abbey."

"And you have identified what that murder was?"

"Naturally. The year before this picture was painted, Sir William Pennington of the Catherine of Aragon party was struck down while fleeing from Richard Southwell of the Anne Boleyn faction. Officially it was a private quarrel. This painting communicates the opinion of these ambassadors. Sir William said he would see Henry's mistress crowned queen over his dead body. Southwell was happy to arrange it. So you see, this skull recalls that murder at the same time as it marks a spot corresponding to the one before the high altar where Anne Boleyn was consecrated and enthroned. She was six months pregnant at the time.

Discovering this skull is like looking into her womb to see what is growing there."

I found this hard to swallow. "Surely you are being needlessly apocalyptic. You don't seriously imagine these French ambassadors could have been so fearful about the future? They seem to live in an age as wonderfully optimistic as our own. All those objects on that table undoubtedly represent the achievements of Renaissance man."

"Well, they were religious men as well as men of reason. The murderer Richard Southwell, who subsequently played a key role in the dissolution of the monasteries and grew rich in the process, had one ominous distinguishing mark that would feature in any police description of such a criminal today. You see, he bore the mark of Cain."

"Holmes, you are joking!"

"Oh, I am quite serious. As you know, my cousin Rivington is Royal Librarian at Windsor Castle. This is a copy of the Library's Holbein's sketch for his portrait of Southwell."

He handed me what I took to be a photographic reproduction of a surprisingly harmless looking man. It was not a brutal countenance, but it was prim, hard and stern, with a firm-set, thin-lipped mouth, and a coldly intolerant eye. It seemed to remind me of someone but I could not think who. Then I had it.

"Good heavens!" I cried in amazement. The face of a classic Baskerville had sprung out of the page.

"Ha, you see it now. The Southwells and the Baskervilles were related. But you perceive the mark upon his brows?"

I did, though it was probably just damage to the original, which must after all have been centuries old. I said so. "Some religious fanatic has tampered with the picture for purposes of propaganda. They have given him the mark of the Beast."

"No, no, that same mark appears in the finished portrait and in a copy of it. He really did bear the mark of Cain. From the point of view of many living at the time, he was predetermined to be a villain. Of course today we would dismiss such nonsense as the merest superstition. They lacked our modern techniques to read the face. Any phrenologist could tell you he bears all the stigmata of a born murderer. Lombroso is good on the subject."

As I reconsidered that bland visage and then turned back to the distorted skull I seemed to sense the shape of some monstrous and growing villainy, half-seen, half-guessed, looming through the darkness, the shape of awful things to come in the brave new world that was about to dawn. I saw that the skull eclipsed a Star of Bethlehem at the centre of the patterned floor. It seemed to prophesy the birth of an Antichrist.

"You understand now," said my own man of the future gravely. "In that clinical murder all the unspoken instincts of these Renaissance men, their vague suspicions, suddenly took shape. In that impassive, colourless man they glimpsed something terrible. A time was coming when cruel and immoral men would seize power and declare that the only right is might. The checks and balances would fail. That screeching comet of a skull over the sacred geometry of the spheres was to their ears like the last trump."

"But then why all these instruments on the table? Why all this evidence of the achievements of man's reason?"

"You have forgotten that this composition looks to the view of the high altar in Westminster Abbey. The message is clear. Man shall replace the sacred table with this secular one and trust to worldly wisdom alone. That is what this skull signifies. Divine wisdom is to make way for knowledge of worldly things alone. The warning is as relevant today as it ever was."

"Well, they were wrong, were they not?" I pleaded. "Look at that world globe there. Does it not proclaim the great achievements of that age of discovery? Had not men reached the Americas?"

"If you look more closely, you will notice that there is an extra line on this globe. It is the line of division drawn by the Pope to divide the New World between Spain and Portugal. This was done in the name of Jesus Christ. But the text you see before that globe is a book of mathematics for businessmen and the page that is it open at begins with the instruction "*Dividirt*", which means "*Let there be division.*" They are dividing the dirt in the name of the Good Shepherd, you understand. That is why there is also what appears to be the sign of the cross but is actually a mathematical device seen at an angle. Yet apply the mathematical operation described there to one of the dates supplied by the shepherd's sundial to the right of the celestial globe on the table's top shelf and that pious claim is given the lie."

I saw that there was something that looked like a golden tower to the right of the heavenly globe. "What date would that be?"

"Why, it is 11 April, which in 1533 was a Good Friday. Not just any Good Friday, for since Christ was said to have died aged thirty-three, or in his thirty-third year by their calculations, it was arguably the fifteen hundredth anniversary of that event. They could interpret that as the apocalyptic time-and-half-a-time when the Antichrist would begin to work in the world."

I could not help smiling. "And what magical mathematical operation revealed the number of the Beast?"

"A very simple one," said he with what was surely mock solemnity. "The first step of the operation called the casting out of nines described

54

here in that mathematics book was to add together the figures of a number. Now, take January as the first month in accordance with the ancient Roman practice, and 11 April gives us the number six. The year 1533 supplies two more sixes. So you see that Good Friday 1533 gave them the three sixes of the number of the Beast."

"Well, what of that? One can always find such chance numbers if one wishes to."

"No doubt. But Good Friday 1533 had been set by Henry VIII as the deadline for the papacy to agree to the annulment of his marriage to his wife Catherine of Aragon. From the point of view of good Catholics like these two gentlemen that must have seemed ominous. Both sides were exploiting such symbolism to declare that they were working for Jesus and preparing for the final great war to end all wars. That is why there is a battle in the heavens glimpsed upon that celestial globe. That bird at the centre of it seeming to assault an eagle is a chicken, the symbol of France. The eagle stands for the Holy Roman Emperor, just as it can represent Germany today."

"Well, it is very ingenious," said I, laughing, "but since this is ancient history it all seems to be rather a waste of energy. I can understand why Irene Adler would pose as Christina of Denmark to alert you to her fears for her safety, but if she meant you to consider this painting too then I can only suppose she had grown paranoid. I know King Wilhelm said his marriage would change the course of history, but that was bombastic. She surely had no reason to think we are to face any such disaster in the future. Modern man is simply too civilised to engage in such madness. With all our modern weaponry it would be suicidal. It would mean the end of our civilisation."

"You do not consider that King Wilhelm is a close cousin of Kaiser Wilhelm," said he gravely. "Oh, I know that they both like to dress up as great warriors because they are nothing of the kind, but such toy soldiers can be the most dangerous of all. It is precisely such little boys full of hot air and desperate to play at being men who are most likely to sound the last trump."

I was reluctant to listen. "Even if Kaiser Wilhelm had told King Wilhelm his future plans, I cannot believe the King would have confided them to his mistress in turn."

"Perhaps. Perhaps not. But what dreams may he have come as they lay together? What did he murmur in his sleep? No, I believe this skull of worldly knowledge without any accompanying spiritual wisdom is indeed the shape of things to come. There is a wind coming, Watson. After it has passed we shall need complete men and women like Irene Adler. Without them we shall never succeed in creating a cleaner, better and truly globalised world."

Paul Delaroche – "*The Execution of Lady Jane Grey*"

The Adventure of the
William Morris Settee

Continuing "The Red-Headed League"

"You reasoned it out beautifully," I exclaimed in unfeigned admiration. "It is so long a chain, and yet every link rings true."

"It saved me from *ennui*," he answered yawning. "Alas, I already feel it closing in upon me! My life is spent in one long effort to escape from the commonplaces of existence. These little problems help me to do so."

"And you are a benefactor to the race," said I.

He shrugged his shoulders. "Well, perhaps, after all, it is of some little use," he remarked. "'*L'homme c'est rien, l'oeuvre c'est tout*,' as Gustave Flaubert wrote to George Sand."

I thought it prudent not to correct Holmes's execrable French grammar, though it did lead me to wonder afresh at his assertions of French descent. To avoid his eye I allowed mine to wander to where his fingers were absent-mindedly playing with the sovereign on his Albert watch chain. It was a gift from George Sand's granddaughter and one of his most treasured possessions. He could never love, yet I sometimes wonder whether he did not regret that he could not have made her the exception to the rule. I deduced he was recalling *the* woman's grandmother's contemptuous response to Flaubert's '*small coin of empty words*'. My friend had once mentioned with amused disapproval Sand's smart rebuff to the author's declaration of faith in art for art's sake.

I left my former resident patient with some misgivings and returned home to write up my account and post it to my agent, which I did as the dawn was breaking. After that I joined my sleeping wife to try and snatch an hour of rest before surgery began, but all in vain. I found myself tossing and turning as my thoughts kept returning to Holmes. Once his whisky was gone, he would stretch his long white hand out to the mantelpiece for a different kind of bottle. I pictured him putting the final touch to that tattoo of pock marks on his thin, sinewy left forearm, dotting the "*R*" in the "*V.R.*" with the point of his syringe.

Well, it was not my affair. I was no longer his doctor. I could wash my hands of him. Why, then, did I feel so guilty?

Fortunately, there were few patients for me to see that day, though there were a number of house calls to make that evening. Walking home from these I happened to pause to consult my late brother's gold watch. As I ran my fingers over its scratched surfaces, I recalled how Holmes had decoded a history of alcoholism from them, rather as a cardsharp's shaven fingertips can detect the minute pinpricks on the hidden faces of trick cards.

As I looked up from it I was surprised to find that by chance I had stopped directly before 221b. There above me were the panes that had replaced the old bow window demolished by Jefferson Hope at the climax to the affair I had chronicled in my contribution to Conan Doyle's *A Study in Scarlet*. And there – yes, there was the shadow of my friend pacing back and forth and in an evident state of delirious excitement!

So he had not taken the cocaine. I exhaled a great sigh of relief, for it meant he must be at work once more. Yet the next moment that exhalation turned into a sharp intake. He had suddenly disappeared! He had not moved to one side but had vanished vertically. He had either collapsed or ducked down out of sight. I waited. A long minute passed. Still he failed to reappear.

Had he heard the whistle of a bullet? Had he over-dosed on some new cocktail of transcendental drugs? A cold sweat broke out upon me at the thought. Without realising how it had happened I found myself flying up the old stairs three steps at a time. Quite forgetting the staircase had an odd number of steps I stumbled and fell at the top. Then I was up and had burst into our rooms, dreading what I would find. Would my friend be stretched out on the bearskin rug with his hypodermic sticking into the final dot of that "*V.R.*" just completed on his arm? Having lost my brother through inaction I could not have borne to lose him too.

To my astonishment he was nowhere to be seen. Here was a locked room mystery indeed! I tried to figure it out. Perhaps he had unintentionally trapped himself inside his safe? The combination was *431881*, as I had good reason to remember. No, it was empty save for a few papers and one or two precious gems. Then he must have installed a trap door beneath the bearskin rug. He was even then peering out at me from the gaping mouth of the beast! I thought of sticking my head into it but imagined Holmes snapping the jaws shut to give me a fright. Instead I gingerly raised the rug. There was no trap door. What did that leave? Holmes was quite the chameleon of concealment yet surely not even he could masquerade as a lampshade or a potted plant! Nevertheless, I lifted and examined those too, feeling I was being ridiculous even as I did so.

Having searched every nook and cranny I slumped down upon the new settee, though not before looking behind and beneath that too. I knew his methods. Could I not apply them? I had eliminated the impossible. What remained? Ah, I remembered how in that affair of the four, an assassin had penetrated a locked room by means of a hole in the ceiling. I looked up at ours somewhat apprehensively, for I half expected to see the cannibal Tonga with his blow pipe to his mouth. But again, there was nothing.

"I said he was the fourth smartest man in London. Was I right?"

Looking down I saw Holmes's severed head on the couch beside me. I sprang to my feet in horror. So Tonga had indeed survived his ducking into the Thames and had returned to take his revenge at last! Was he even now sinking those strong yellow teeth into my poor friend's roasted heart? No, of course not, he preferred his meat raw. But was Holmes's family accursed? I remembered how his ancestor Marguerite-Emelie Vernet had suffered a like fate during the reign of Madame Guillotine.

Clutching at my own heart I groped frantically in my hat for my stethoscope. It was not so much for myself as for my friend. What, did I think to take his pulse? I had heard tales of guillotined heads continuing to grimace and distort for hours afterwards. But did I really imagine if I found the rest of Holmes, I might sew the head back on? And could I seriously have considered searching for a pulse at the neck? But there was no neck. At the thought I began to giggle. Stop it!" I cried. "Pull yourself together!" With a supreme effort I managed to do so.

And then I laughed for joy. Suddenly I had realised how foolish I was being. Tussaud's was a stone's throw away. That was it! They were about to add a waxwork of Holmes and had posted the head for his approval. Reconsidering it more critically I could plainly see it was indeed nothing but a bust. Ah, yes, but what a bust! I remembered how Holmes had spoken with admiration of the work of the great sculptor Oscar Meunier. It had to be his work. Only he could have captured Holmes's Red Indian stoicism so perfectly, though even he had overdone the masklike calm.

"Holmes!" I cried. "It is wonderful! But come now, show yourself. Where are you hiding?"

"What a question, doctor. I am here. The head is the only vital part of the body, you know. Everything else exists simply to support it."

Once again, I leaped up from the settee as if I had just received an electric shock. The lips had moved! I had always suspected Holmes must once have been an entertainer upon the stage. Evidently, he had been a ventriloquist in earlier years and had just thrown his voice into this most ingenious mechanical head. Slyly I craned over the side of the settee, realising he had secreted himself there after I had collapsed back onto it. But no, there was no sign of him.

Turning back to the disembodied head I gaped as widely as that silently roaring bearskin rug, for the head had been reattached to the body! Mr. Sherlock Holmes was wriggling his way out of that settee as a fat white rabbit might from a magician's hat when almost defeated by its unsatisfactory cubic capacity. I think I almost passed out. Certainly, I

61

found myself in the land of mist for an instant or two. Then Holmes's face slowly materialised above me as out of a pea souper. I noted with relief that, yes, it was fully and firmly attached to its appendix.

"My dear fellow," said he with what was almost certainly sincere concern, "I owe you a heartfelt apology. I would never have played such a prank had I known what its effect would be. I had been exploring the interior of this admirable device, you see, when I heard your inimitable little trip at the top of the seventeen steps – not eighteen, do try to remember it – and I thought I would entertain you with a magic trick. It was very wicked of me and I swear on my dear grandmother Anais's grave I shall never play any such joke on you again. Unless it is absolutely necessary, of course."

"Well," said I, "I forgive you as always. But what do you mean by calling this settee a *device*? And do you mean to say you yourself did not know of it before?"

"Not exactly. I am as you know accustomed to receiving occasional trifling gifts from grateful clients. Have I shown you this snuffbox the King of Bohemia sent me? Here it is. Take a pinch of the white powder in it and I guarantee it will revive your spirits. No? Well, it is an acquired taste. Snuffboxes are one thing, though, and anonymously delivered settees quite another. You will note its green slipcover bears a William Morris design borrowed from the patterned curtains in the Holbein painting the National Gallery is set to acquire. To be precise, they shall shortly come into possession of an exceptionally fine copy of it, for the original has recently been exchanged for a forgery and the masterpiece itself is presently on display in the study of a certain professor. But note the pattern of pomegranates, crowns, and rings. Ironically, that was what first put me on my guard."

"Why ironically?"

"Because it was meant to be and was so thoroughly diverting as to cause my critical faculties to momentarily lapse. That Holbein I mentioned alludes to a blasphemous murder committed in Westminster Abbey in 1532. A settee recalling such a painting was guaranteed to delight me. Only those of the professor's inner circle would have known that."

"You mean Professor Moriarty?" I ventured. "But you told me he was a spent force. Surely he slouched off from his university in disgrace to lead the horrible life of a disgraced academic in London. Is he not now an army coach? I supposed him to be *persona non grata*."

Holmes nodded. "Someone spread the most grotesque tales about his predilections. All those pretty little Greuze-faced urchins coming and going at all hours! His university decided he could not be trusted with young scholarly *protégés*. But his banishment left a vacuum in the underworld too. Doubtless this ruse is the work of one of his less-official students ambitious to fill it."

A Mona Lisa-smile flickered momentarily across my friend's face and I thought I knew who was responsible for all those dark rumours. "Then who do you suppose did send it?"

"A bright little fish from his cesspool of corrupted talents. This sofa scam could only have been devised by one of his most Machiavellian *protégés*. I think it was the gentleman I praised yesterday as the fourth smartest in London."

"You mean John Clay?"

Holmes laughed. "Clay? No, no, not Clay. By no means Clay. We met the man I have in mind briefly at Wilson's so-called pawnshop. We will come to him presently via this settee. Before I forget, Doctor, here is your stethoscope returned with many thanks." Holmes dropped it back into my hat. "And here is your hypodermic." He added it to the headpiece. "I was tempted to use both but settled on the stethoscope alone."

"To do what?"

"To determine this sofa's contents. I applied the stethoscope to the couch and confirmed it was breathing just a mite too rapidly for a traditionally sedentary item of decor. Its occupant had to be either an assassin or a spy."

"An assassin!" I cried, springing up for the third time at the thought of what in my imagination still lurked within it. "Holmes, you told me to 'try the settee'! I might have been stabbed in the back. "

"Not at all," said Holmes smoothly. "You really do need to brush up on your anatomy, Doctor. Besides, I have devised an antidote to those envenomed darts that played so significant a role in the affair I believe you have just published as 'The Sign of Seven'. And such darts would have been meant for me. But have no fear, Tonga the cannibal is at the bottom of the Thames with one of your bullets through his black heart. So much for the Hippocratic oath. As for this settee, I assure you it contained nothing more than an undersized eavesdropper installed for a very specific purpose. Someone was exceedingly anxious to overhear our little discussion concerning Mr. Jabez Wilson's tale of the Red-Headed League once he had left."

"But who?"

"I have already said who it was," said he impatiently. "Do you never listen, Watson? It was the fourth smartest and the third most daring man in London, who was most assuredly not that numbskull Clay. It was the Jack-in-the-Box of Wilson's pawnshop who leaped to the door before we could open it and so prevented us from catching a glimpse of its interior, which I fancy must have resembled the excavated gardens of Pondicherry

Lodge. Think of all the earth from that tunnel! As for the gentleman who gave us directions to the Strand, I am surprised you did not remember him from Lord's."

"But it was Clay, was it not?"

"Watson," said Holmes gravely, "the longer I know you, the more certain I am that you and infinity are far more alike than first appearances might lead one to suppose. I can never get the limits of either of you. Did I not observe that the knees of the gentleman's trousers were slightly discoloured as if from kneeling upon a dirty floor?"

"I remember you deduced he must have been engaged in digging a tunnel from the pawnshop's cellar to that of the abutting bank."

"And do you also recall why it was that you entirely failed to notice the disgraceful state of those trouser knees?"

I hung my head at the just rebuke. "I know, Holmes. I am appallingly unobservant."

Holmes shook his. "No, no, that will not do. That is not nearly good enough. Proper dress is your department, Watson. Nobody has a more critical eye than you when it comes to sartorial rectitude. But imperceptiveness starts with oneself. Know yourself, Watson, and do not commit the sin of modesty by dishonestly selling yourself short. Are you not a stickler when it comes to dress codes, as one might expect of a former army surgeon? Did you not inspect Wilson the pawnbroker as if he were on parade and ought to be reported? Were you not thoroughly offended by his not-over-clean black frock-coat, unbuttoned at the front, to say nothing of his drab waistcoat? Did you not bite your stiff upper lip at the sight of his frayed top hat and his faded brown overcoat with its wrinkled velvet collar? Did you not screw your discerning nose up at the sight of his dirty and crumpled *Morning Chronicle*? When we lodged together at 221b you insisted your morning *Times* be freshly ironed. A spot of marmalade on page one was practically a capital offence. Now ask yourself how you of all people could possibly have failed to perceive that the smart young gentleman's trousers needed more than mere pressing. You were distracted, were you not? Ask yourself by what."

I considered. "I was busy scrutinising his face."

"Do be precise. Which features especially?" As he spoke Holmes involuntarily raised one hand to his forehead though too late to brush away a fly that must just then have flown away. With his other he pinched an itching right ear lobe. I think he was trying to distract me.

Then I remembered. "Why, I perused his brows in search of that white acid mark Clay told Wilson bore witness to some past chemistry experiment. I could not find it, though. Oh, yes, and I examined his ears hoping to spot where they were pierced for earrings."

64

"And were they?"

"We know they were."

"Forget what we know. What did you see?"

"Well, they were pierced. I did see where they were pierced. But they must have been pierced. He had used makeup to conceal the holes. He had to avoid being identified. That was why he had hidden the acid mark too."

"No, he had not. Have you forgotten how Wilson said Clay turned conversations to those features? Did he not tell anecdotal tales concerning their acquisition? He claimed the forehead mark was a consequence of acid splashed on his face and that his ears had been pierced by a gypsy. Why did he go out of his way to draw attention to identifying characteristics? He could have concealed them had he wished to. He had dyed the red hair that marked him out as a member of the Holdernesse family – albeit an illegitimate one. Conclusion?"

"That Wilson was lying?"

"Excellent, Watson!" I sighed, for Holmes seemed particularly pleased at this. I surmised it meant he had previously considered that explanation and discarded it. "Ah, but wait a moment." He paused for thought. "I do remember now that when Clay broke into that dark cellar where the gold had been stored the light was too poor for you to make out those distinguishing attributes. You have not trained your eyes as I have to see in the dark. He had them both on that occasion. Inference?"

I understood. "When Clay met us at the door to Wilson's pawnshop he was in disguise. Of course, he had to be, for I did not recognise him as the gentleman who emerged out of that cellar floor."

"Watson," said Holmes, honouring me so far as to make a half-hearted attempt at concealing his impatience, "please do apply my principles with more care. When one has eliminated all other possibilities then the single remaining one, no matter how improbable, must be the truth, but only – I repeat only – if one has indeed eliminated all other possibilities. Now, is there any alternative explanation you may have overlooked? Do not fail to consider the blindingly obvious."

"I can think of none, Holmes." And then, as an afterthought, I added, "Except that they were two different men."

"At last!" Holmes raised his eyes as I presume, he offered up a prayer to Huxley's God of Systematised Commonsense. "Yes, as you so astutely if belatedly observe, my very dear Watson, they could have been two different men. Ah. Please excuse me for one moment. A purely routine precaution."

In an instant Holmes had sprung like a tiger across the room to plunge the hypodermic that had appeared as if by magic in his hand through the dot after the "*V*" of the patriotic "*V.R.*" tattooed with bullet pocks into the wall. It matched that on his forearm. The wall squeaked pitifully. "That's all right," said he, calmly returning to his seat. "Have no fear, doctor. It was an exceedingly weak solution of cocaine. Not more than two-and-three-quarter percent. Our neighbour's rat will be the terror of the local cats until the effect wears off. Walls have ears as well as eyes, you know, and I had to be sure. Where was I?"

"You were suggesting that the man at the door of Wilson's was not John Clay."

"I suggest nothing. I state undeniable facts. The man we encountered first was Clay's nominal apprentice, though only in the same sense as I was guided by that mediocrity Auguste Dupin and learnt acting from the equally over-rated Vidocq. That habit of his of dressing up as a nun and old women was quite needlessly showy. I would never stoop to it. The student oft surpasses his mentor. Did you perceive how swiftly Clay's own apprentice spotted my little trip? Smart, very smart! Oh, I was forgetting, you were engrossed in your inspection of his smooth brows and un-pierced ear lobes to note it. I refer with shame to my crass error in travelling to Saxe-Coburg Square by the Underground."

"I pleaded with you to allow me to me hail a cab, Holmes," I grumbled, for being a doctor I had deeply resented that thoroughly unhealthy and entirely unnecessary choice. "Did I not warn you of the damage it would do to our lungs? Clay's could not have suffered half so much while he was digging that tunnel from Wilson's to the bank's vault. He had no need to fear sulphurous fumes. Think of the filthy state of our clothes when we at last emerged coughing and spluttering back into the light! Does that not help us to picture what our insides must have looked like?"

"*Mea culpa*," said Holmes solemnly. "Rather as the state of my lungs is doubtless mirrored by the state of my clay pipe's bowl. The choice of transportation was an unpardonable blunder on my part, and for the reason you have stated, though not in the manner you imagine. Personally, I found the concentrated atmosphere of the subterranean train service singularly invigorating, particularly when aided and abetted by a briar liberally stocked with shag. But that was the difficulty. Two can play at the same game, you see Watson, and if I could deduce our gentleman's intentions from the state of his clothes, he could most assuredly read mine in like manner. More than that, he could read *my* mind."

I laughed. "From your clothes? You are joking of course."

"Not at all. Have you forgotten that I smoked three pipes before ever we set forth on our little expedition? I smoked two more during the journey. My clothes were covered in ash. They reeked of the weed. If I deduced Wilson partook of snuff, could not our fourth smartest man tell that I was a heavy smoker? And shag has a most distinctive bouquet, as did our fragrant gentleman's Sullivan cigarettes. Word has got about in the London nether world that I love a good shag almost as much as our bank director Merryweather does his Saturday night rubber, and who better for Wilson to visit for advice than Mr. Sherlock Holmes?"

"But you asserted more than that. You said the state of your clothes permitted him to read your mind."

"Of course it did. Here were two well-dressed men, and yet the dirty state of their dress advertised they had quite unnecessarily resorted to the Underground. Now, why should such gentlemen stupidly elect to travel by so deplorable a means of transportation?"

"Why indeed?" I muttered. "You never did explain that."

"Only because I did not know myself. The brain is a queer thing, Watson. I sometimes think of writing a little monograph on the mental underworld and its relation to crime. It was only when startled by the electric flash of revelation in our adversary's clear blue eyes that I suddenly realised what could have possessed me to do such a thing. Do you not see that with what I shall dub the subterranean portion of my brain I had embarked upon a particular train of thought? Without knowing it, I was thinking along the lines of secret tunnels. The overground portion of my mind was perfectly oblivious until that moment to what the underground brain was processing."

I wondered afresh at this amazing man. I had always supposed Holmes could not possess anything other than a computing brain, yet here he was confessing there was a second box of tricks operating in an entirely different manner, and one he seemed to suggest was common to all men. What a specialist in nervous disorders the world lost when Holmes chose to confine himself to the practical study of the criminal mind!

"Yes, a most abnormally perceptive young man," mused Holmes. "I speak in all seriousness, Watson, when I say that I should be proud to join forces with such a rogue. Of course, we would both have to die first. Well, well, one day perhaps. In the meantime, remind me to warn the City and Suburban Bank to employ no complimentary settees until after they have been comprehensively needled. For you see, where the Holdernesse illegitimate has failed, our amateur cracksman will think it good sport to succeed. Ah, Watson, I am delighted he was the one that got away! I can look forward to the return match. And yet to give myself due credit, he was not altogether successful, was he? Witness how I quite saw through that sofa trick and misled him with my cunning talk on the uniqueness of that affair."

"Why, do you mean to say you have investigated a case like that of the Red-Headed League before?" said I with some surprise. "I had understood it to be unprecedented."

"Far from it. Surely you have not forgotten last year's trifling matter of the Stockbroker's Clerk? One needs no more than a moderately astute eye to see past a spot of repainting and then the old spokes of the wheel are recognisable as they come up once more. But to give the devil his due, the old plot has been much improved upon. Make no mistake, Watson, we are dealing with a proper artist, which is to say one not so lazy as to endlessly repeat his own work. Once one starts along that road one becomes one's own imposter."

I cast my mind back to the business of the clerk Hall Pycroft and the attempted burglary of Mawson's, but could not for the life of me see any similarities between it and the matter under consideration. "Surely you are mistaken, Holmes. Hall Pycroft was recruited for a bogus post to ensure he could not take up a genuine one with Mawson's. An impersonator took his place and burgled that institution. Fortunately, Pycroft saw something was amiss a few hours before the robbery was due to take place and came to you. But there was no tunnel, there were no red-headed men, there was no French gold in a cellar deep underground, and no copying out of the *Encyclopaedia Britannica*. Where are the similarities?"

Holmes rationed me out but one meagre nod of that finely chiselled head per point as I ticked them off. "You have summarised the superficial differences well," he conceded. "And yet are you not missing the key point? Forget the fact that Pycroft was set to work copying out lists of hardware addresses while Wilson transcribed the *Encyclopaedia Britannica*. Forget that the earlier job took a week and was for more than a million while this present one required three months of degrading and dangerous work for a comparatively paltry twelve-thousand pounds in thirty thousand napoleon coins. Forget all the other crucial differences you have just itemised. Do you not see the one shared point to those two tales, as told us by two very different men?"

I cudgelled my brains but they would not mend their pace with beating. "I'm sorry, Holmes, I cannot."

"And do you know why you cannot?" he enquired earnestly. "It is because the solution is concealed within your question. You ask what points of similarity can there be between these two tales told by two men who came to me mere hours before the crimes were due to occur. Do you not see that it is not what they said, but that they said it which matters? In both cases, we have men who claimed they had been duped and discovered the fact just before the scheduled burglaries. In both cases they happened to come to me to tell their tales. I frankly admit I have not as yet achieved the recognition due to me from an ill-informed public, in part owing to that unfortunate co-authored effort of yours and Doyle's entitled *A Study in Scarlet*. Since then my name has figured in no newspaper. Yet both those men assured me I was the obvious man to assist them, as if mine were already the household name it will one day become. How did they know of me? They appeared not to have heard of you or your works. What do you make of that, Watson?"

"It was a coincidence, Holmes. It had to be or their stories would not have been so different."

"I have already stressed the most pertinent difference," insisted Holmes, "which is that the later tale is an improvement upon the earlier affair. Our phantom crime writer did not repeat himself out of laziness but on the contrary because, being a perfectionist, he was dissatisfied with his first attempt and was determined to get it right. The later refinements were so marked that I feel I am doing him a disservice to say he repeated himself at all."

I could not approve of Holmes's tendency to regard crimes as works of art. "And you call that an improvement, Holmes? Why, this recent business is far less plausible than the earlier affair. Had I been in Pycroft's shoes, I might have been taken in as he was, but I honestly do not believe I would have been deceived for a moment by that plan to repopulate the earth with redheads. I might have agreed to copy out lists of hardware suppliers, but I would have drawn the line at the *Encyclopaedia Britannica*."

Holmes chuckled. "Delightful! The sheer absurdity of it! Do you not see that our ghostly crime writer has learnt to play the game for its own sake? The earlier affair was merely workmanlike. This revised version of it displays the touch of a master."

"But Holmes," I reminded my friend, "you have said many times the true artist always knows when to stop. Pycroft would never have suspected anything had it not been for the accident of a single gold filling. Only one in a million could have been deceived by the Red-Headed League hoax. Surely all those baroque flourishes were failings and ought not to be praised."

"And yet it seems Wilson was deceived. So trusting was he that he had to be given a hearty nudge in our direction, for of course there was no reason to inform him that the League had been dissolved before the burglary and every reason not to do so. That was the one flaw to an otherwise perfect work of art. The deliberate mistake was too obviously intended to ensure Wilson's visit to 221b. I was to be intrigued. I was to work to thwart the plot."

"To thwart the plot?" I echoed stupidly.

"Why, of course. And that is my point. A work of art is overdone when it fails in its intent. Now, had the aim here been to succeed then it would have failed. Since the aim was to fail it succeeded brilliantly." Holmes eyed me mischievously to see if I had followed. I suspected he hoped I had not. If so, he had succeeded brilliantly.

"Holmes," said I slowly, "what you seem to be saying is that the man who plotted this crime meant you to foil it. But you cannot mean that. The idea is fantastic. Are you really suggesting this crime writer of yours had some kind of a death wish?"

"Quite the contrary. In the case of the Stockbroker's Clerk, he or she may have been working to eliminate dangerous potential rivals by supplying a plot I was meant to see through. That may originally have been true of this present affair too, but not by the eleventh hour. The stakes had changed. He was no longer playing to win a game. Something much bigger was at stake and he was playing to save it."

"And by 'he' you mean the otherwise smart man in the disreputable trousers we met at the pawnshop?"

Holmes shook his head. "Hardly. I'll wager he was no Jonathan Wild to run a crooked Scotland Yard and so acquire mastery of the city's underworld. No, he was in the tradition of Wild's adversary the eighteenth-century loner Jack Sheppard, a truly great thief when it came to stealing himself out of every prison cell. If our man was labouring for Clay or his ghost writer, it was only to learn the ropes prior to cutting the painter. He may have been the one who contrived that pillow talk sofa and secreted a street Arab inside it. Had I suspected as much earlier I would never have stressed quite so obviously the uniqueness of this case."

"Why not?"

"So smart a man must soon have understood my aim was to lull our crime plotter behind the scenes into a false sense of security. Now that our loner knows I have picked up the scent, he will lie low until I and that crime plotter to crooks have met and one or other of us has perished. Then he will treat himself to a stealing spree. Yes, I will most certainly instruct the City and Suburban to accept with caution any chest of fool's gold or silver big enough to hold a man."

"Well, then, who is your mastermind? And why are you so sure it could not be Moriarty?"

"Oh, really, Watson, how could it be?" said Holmes petulantly. "Even if his reputation were not in tatters thanks to me he would never think to become the ruler of the London's gangland. He is a kind of underworld version of what brother Mycroft is in the overworld of our rulers. Both men are utterly devoid of ambition. Like Mycroft, the Professor will always be an academic at heart, happy enough in the past to plot crimes for others but never willing to become actively engaged in his own little dramas. No, let us not be distracted by yesterday's man. Let us leave him and Colonel Moran in their cramming school to lecture on the campaigns of Napoleon and the other iconic criminals of history."

"But you must suspect someone," I persisted. "Can you not apply your own principle of eliminating the impossible until you are finally left with one highly improbable solution that nevertheless has to be the truth?"

Holmes shook his head. "My unknown adversary is a genius. He knows how I think and will act accordingly. He must be someone I have overlooked. My only hope is that he makes one little trip, and to that end I must ensure that he never realises I so much as suspect his or her existence. You recall I said we could not speak freely outside Wilson's pawnshop because the walls had ears? Ever since I uncovered the Amateur Mendicant Society I have grown wary of beggars and vagabonds. They go everywhere, see everything, and are overlooked by everyone."

"You have a remarkable power of detaching your brains, Holmes," said I in a spontaneous burst of unfeigned admiration. "If you harbour such fears, it is all the more impressive you could relax so entirely at the concert we attended immediately after our visit to Wilson's. I will never forget the sight of you dreamily waving a hand about as if you yourself were conducting the music. Of course I cannot forget the looks of annoyance on the faces of music lovers in the audience either."

Holmes chuckled. "Oh, that. I was sorry to irritate my fellow concert-goers but it was absolutely necessary. My dancing fingers constituted a code, you see. I was semaphoring my message to a certain little bird. It was tweeted in turn to brother Mycroft and so on to the powers that be. You should have realised that, Watson. The concert programme was German. You know I only use German music to introspect. I turn to French music when I wish to dream."

"In that case, I suppose your sudden attack of *ennui* after the case was closed was feigned too," said I with a touch of irritation. "You have no idea how anxious I was for you, Holmes."

Holmes seemed perversely pleased. "I did deceive you rather well, didn't I? I am thinking of writing a little monograph on the art of putting antic dispositions on. The enemy could not be tipped off that I knew the game was afoot and the stakes never higher."

But I was not convinced by this idea of a vast conspiracy. "It seems to me, Holmes," said I cautiously, "that even if we suppose one mastermind was behind both the Stockbroker's Clerk and the Red-Headed League affairs, he would have to be in decline, for in the earlier robbery the prize was more than a million pounds, whereas in this latest one it was only twelve thousand or so in gold, always supposing it could have been removed up a steeply inclined tunnel from that deep cellar to Wilson's pawnshop. Surely the fact that three months were devoted to such a task with no guarantee that the gold would still be there at the end of it smacks of desperation."

Holmes bestowed upon me a rare look of approval. "You have hit upon it, Watson," said he warmly. "And to confirm the truth of what you say, consider two of the inspirations behind this latest job. I initially toyed with the idea that the great Napoleon of Crime Adam Worth had masterminded it, the resemblances between this and two of his finest works were so striking. In 1870, while passing through Liverpool, and chiefly to keep his thieving hand in, Worth abstracted £25,000 in jewels from the safe of the city's largest pawnshop. Tut, tut. How embarrassing to think that Worth had bagged twice as much by burgling a pawnshop as Clay had thought to do by tunnelling from a pawnshop into a bank! And those thousands were a mere bagatelle to Worth, who had bagged a million in money and securities from the Boylston National Bank the previous year by tunnelling into the bank vault from an adjacent building.

"But why are you so sure Worth was not involved?"

"For the reason you have just stated. The pawnshop burglary took little time and effort and was for twice the sum of the City and Suburban. The Boylston stunt took a week for a haul that the Pinks have estimated is in excess of a million. Worth would never have wasted three months for pocket money when he might have committed a dozen crimes in the same period and each worth much more."

I had to concur.

"And besides, Watson, why would he have troubled to dig a tunnel when he might have gone in through the door? That cellar was not connected to the bank. The entrance was unguarded and in a side alley. Why squander those three months when it would not have taken three hours to pick the locks on the gates of the cellar or blow them off?"

"Those gates were very solid, Holmes," said I doubtfully. "Are you sure that would have been possible?"

"A chain is only as strong as its weakest link. It is irrelevant how massive those gates were. Do you not see that the very fact there were so many of them was an involuntary admission not one of them was burglar proof? Why have more than one if that one had been good enough? No, they could only have slowed down professional burglars armed with explosives to answer any lock. If silence had been essential, then a sword of Toledo steel and honed to cutthroat razor sharpness would have sliced through those locks like butter. A Samurai sword would have been even quicker. But that cellar was so very deep underground explosions would have gone unheard. And that raises an intriguing question. Why was the gold there at all when it would have been so much more secure in the chief vault of the headquarters of the City and Suburban? There was no reason for it to be located near to any particular one of its local branches, even should its need be exceptional. As long as the City and Suburban was in possession of the gold, that would have been enough."

I was a little bewildered. "Not connected to the bank? What do you mean, Holmes? I assumed the cellar *was* the vault. You told me the pawnshop abutted onto the bank and that was the reason why it was chosen for the digging of the tunnel."

Holmes chuckled. "If all that had been true, then the pawnshop would have been the worst place of all to dig such a tunnel. Remember all those stairs we had to descend to reach that cellar? It must have been at least a hundred feet below the ground. Now, Wilson's basement was only just below street level, so the tunnel would have been an almost sheer drop. That would have been a problem had they meant to remove those more than four-hundred pounds of gold that way, which of course they never did. But think how hard it would have been to climb back up again! The gentleman at the shop would have been filthy from head to foot after all that mountaineering. Yet his slightly soiled trousers gave the false impression he had been able to move along the tunnel on his knees."

"What did you mean when you said they never meant to remove the gold via the tunnel?"

"And then sneak those fifteen crates out of the pawnshop and into a square in plain sight! Could they really have forgotten the fate of that Beddington brother who had stepped out of Mawson's with his swag and walked straight into the long arms of a passing officer of the law? Now please consider that the cellar lacked a vault lining and its floor was paved with flagstones so large they had only to raise one of them to climb through into the cellar. Is it not obvious what they meant to do? The gold was to be placed in the tunnel and the flagstone replaced. They would then pick or blow the locks of the gates leading back to the door and so exited that way. No doubt there was a concealed but sleepy old watchman in the vicinity whom they could have proceeded to very easily outpace. Afterwards it would be supposed they must have left with the gold by that route. Nobody would think to check for the possibility of a tunnel. The gold would be safe there until the search for it had fizzled out."

"But how could they have removed it later?"

"Quite simply. As I have said, that crypt could have been connected to no bank. It was cavernous, far bigger than any mere bank branch would have required. It was doubtless used for housing many things. The robbers had only to store boxes of their own in it. Then it would have been a matter of returning to that cellar via their tunnel to deposit the gold coins in their own purported chest of silver prior to making a withdrawal."

I could see a flaw to this ingenious theory. "If that had been their plan, then why did they discontinue the deceit of the Red-Headed League? Surely it would have been wiser to ensure that Wilson still stayed away from his shop for several hours every day for another week or two in case they needed to return to the cellar via the tunnel so as to pack the gold into boxes during daylight hours."

"Precisely, Watson. That ridiculous red-head ruse could only have been terminated when it was so as to ensure the robbery would fail. The abrupt dissolution of the League justified Wilson's visit to 221b and guaranteed my involvement in a case I would not have missed for the world. But we have yet to explain *why* the gold was so far from the bank branch. Think of it, Watson. Suppose that your tin despatch box crammed with records of cases had been deposited in that bank and removed from thence to such a cellar. Every time you wished to consult it, a clerk would have had to leave his post in the bank to go with you out into the street. You would have gone together down that side alley and then through that door and gate after gate with descent after descent. What a waste of time! And let us suppose you were a burglar. You could have hit that clerk over the head and helped yourself to whatever you wished. It makes no sense."

"I have a theory," said I hesitantly, "if you would care to hear it."

"I should be grateful for any assistance," said he gravely.

"Well, Holmes, the chairman of directors Merryweather said his bank had received several warnings that a robbery was imminent. With that in mind, might they not have thought to secretly relocate the gold? Nobody would have thought of searching for it in so obscure a cellar."

Holmes considered that. "Well, Watson, there is this to be said for your theory. It would have been the best argument Merryweather could have made to persuade his fellow directors to allow him to keep those crates in that cellar. But you do see the inherent danger to such a scheme?"

I nodded. "Should it ever get out that the gold was there, then the chief advantage to the ruse would be lost and it might easily be stolen."

"And that is precisely what happened. Someone inside the bank passed on the information. The question is who that insider could have been and why he did it. Of course, that is clear, is it not?"

My eyes were round. "Holmes, you are surely not suggesting Merryweather was the informant? That is ridiculous! Why would he betray his own bank?"

"Oh, he could have told himself he was doing it for the bank's own good. And besides, when Clay came to open the chests, he would have found that they contained nothing but lead. The gold was long gone and spent."

Sherlock Holmes is unsurpassed within his limits, but he has his blind spots as even he occasionally recognises, and it is here that I am of some use. I may not have mastered the science of deduction, but I do have a good understanding of human nature. "You are overlooking one thing, Holmes," I pointed out. "Merryweather was a devoted whist player, and that is the infallible sign of a plain-dealing man. You have often told me that chess is the game of scheming minds. Whist, you know, is different. It is a harmless entertainment. Can you really believe that a lover of whist could be a master criminal?"

Holmes was forced to acknowledge the truth of this though with his usual *caveats*. "It is certainly the case that the chess player is capable of plotting his game several moves in advance," he conceded, "but there is a difference between chess and whist that you have failed to take into account. In chess, all one's cards are on the table and face upwards. In whist one must look elsewhere to determine what all those poker-faced cards are. One must be adept at concealing one's own situation and intentions while reading one's opponents to determine theirs. Now, you supposed Merryweather an amusing and harmless old man because he kept grumbling about having been dragged away from whist for the first time in thirty-seven years on a wild goose chase with no blue carbuncle or golden egg at the end of it. You took seriously his constant complaints about being coerced into catching his death of pneumonia – or an excessive lead intake should guns be involved – while sitting in a dark and dank cellar deep underground for several hours on the off-chance that someone might choose that night to break into it."

"Well, he did have a point, Holmes. I cannot understand why the police bullied that poor old man into putting his life at risk without even deigning to explain to him that they believed a tunnel had been dug into the cellar. Usually they dislike having members of the public present on such occasions. Imagine if Merryweather had ended up riddled with bullets! The press would have had a field day."

"Oh, I assure you, Watson, that though I asked him if he wished to come, the police were absolutely adamant they could not permit him to do so. For all they knew a gang of armed and dangerous men might have poured forth from that tunnel and with a single shot, the light of our lamp would have been put out. In the ensuing darkness, the director could have been killed in the crossfire. But Merryweather's whist companions include men of considerable influence, to say nothing of that most imperious of ladies the Countess of Balmoral, and so he was able to pull strings as I suspected he would. That was why I invited him, to see if he would accept, and indeed stubbornly insist upon being present. He was clearly determined to be there. And of course the police had told him of the tunnel. Had they not outlined the anticipated robbery, we would never have been taken seriously, nor would the bank have given us permission to enter the cellar."

I was confused. "Holmes, I don't understand," I was forced to admit. "You say that he wanted to be present to greet the burglars? But he spoke like a man who had had his card-dealing arm twisted half off to be there. And you say he was told about the tunnel? How could he have been? Why, he thumped vigorously upon its flagstones with his stick two or three times. He would hardly have done that had he known the robbers might be working below."

"Ah, Watson, Watson," said Holmes with a sad smile, "it always depresses me that what ordinary folk regard as genius is often nothing more than an ability to see the obvious. Astronomers such as the mole-like Moriarty demonstrate in darkened rooms and with the assistance of their reflector lanterns and globes that the earth simply must go around the sun, when if they would only stare up at the heavens it would be blindingly obvious that the converse must be the case. Come, come, can you not accept it? Merryweather tapped on the floor to warn the thieves off. It was the prearranged danger signal to let Clay know that the plot had been discovered. That was why he insisted on being in the cellar. The real question is why the thieves ignored the warning and proceeded with the robbery."

"Well, if you speak of the obvious, Holmes, I have the answer to that. They were not in the tunnel and so they could not. Surely that shows your suspicions of Merryweather are unfounded. If he was the gang's insider, then he would have known when they would be there. He would not have tapped on the floor until he was confident, they would hear the signal. That could only have been after Wilson had gone to bed and they were free to enter the building and set to work."

"Not at all. Consider that the gentleman who answered my knocking on the pawnshop door was not Clay. Where was Clay? He was already in the tunnel. The lookout had been placed upstairs to warn of the return of Wilson, always supposing that Wilson was what he appeared to be. But that meant other members of the gang were in the house and at work deep underground. Once Wilson returned, they had to remain in the tunnel."

"But if they heard the warning signal, why did they proceed with the robbery?"

"Because only Clay knew it was the warning signal. Doubtless he argued that the utter silence following those couple of sharp taps proved that the sound meant nothing. Of course, the opposite was the case. If that tapping had been part of some routine activity in the cellar, then it would have been accompanied by others. But crooks do not often possess even the middle-of-the-road imbecility of the man in the street. Clay was persuasive and the work proceeded."

"At the risk of swinging for it?"

"No, to avoid that end. But we will come to that. First let us consider why our devout whist player was assisting Clay to steal that gold. You have supplied the answer, Watson, though you did not know it."

"I have?"

"Think, Doctor. You thought it inconceivable that so dedicated a card player could turn to crime. Can you not see that his passion supplied him with a motive?"

I scratched my head thoughtfully. "I am afraid I don't quite follow."

"Why, he was a born gambler and addicted to the adrenalin surge that always comes with defying the odds. It is a not uncommon complaint in the City. Speaking confidentially, I am reliably informed that Lord Revelstoke's father won his fine Berkeley Square home at cards. I would not be surprised if the son loses it on another such turn of fortune's wheel. In fact, Barings may presently prove to be a house of cards and built on quicksand. Did I say quicksand? Perhaps cesspool would be nearer the mark. There is undoubtedly an east wind approaching the City, you see, Watson, and Merryweather knows it."

I was stunned. "But you cannot mean that," I gasped. "Not Barings!"

"Oh, do not be amazed, my dear fellow," said my companion with some amusement. "Did not Coxon's fail last year over its Venezuelan loan? I can tell you in confidence Barings is soon to be in similar difficulties over Revelstoke's rash investments in Argentina. Rumour has it Merryweather, having missed that particular leaky boat, has boarded another and speculated no less foolishly in San Pedro with equally unfortunate consequences. You have heard of the uprising there?"

I recalled the headlines. Following a revolution, the lecherous tyrant "Don Juan" Murillo, the Tiger of San Pedro, had fled that tin pot country in a ship top heavy with treasure. There had been much speculation concerning who might have invested so heavily there and incredulity that the monster had managed to vanish with all those massive loans. Holmes had surmised some unknown criminal consultant had to have assisted him. He stubbornly declined to consider it could have been Moriarty.

"Yes, Don Juan," said Holmes, who had read my mind as was his habit. "And that explains Merryweather's part in the attempted gold theft. The gentleman who plotted Murillo's escape knew his treasure came from the City and Suburban, a fact that the bank itself would have been intrigued to learn. Merryweather borrowed rather more than the spare change sum of twelve-thousand pounds worth of French gold, intending to win back his losses on the San Pedro bet. 'Twelve' may have been the number agreed upon by the directors. At Barings, it was the custom to refer to eight-thousands of pounds, say, simply as 'eight'. When Merryweather suggested 'twelve' the directors would have agreed. He could then have added a nought or two to what they imagined he meant in his request to the Bank of France. Predictably he quickly succeeded in losing that gold too. It came to the attention of the same crime writer who plotted Don Juan's disappearing trick. I have no doubt our mastermind has cardsharps on his payroll. Think of Moriarty, whose right-hand man was the devoted card player Colonel Moran. Someone like the Colonel probably relieved Merryweather of much of that gold in the first place. That same cardsharp could then have contacted the chairman with an offer he could hardly refuse."

But I was more confused than ever. "Holmes, if what you say is true then that gold was no longer in those crates. Clay and his gang would have been stealing empty boxes."

"Not entirely empty. Merryweather had doubtless filled them up with lead bars packed between layers of lead foil. And of course he neglected to let the crooks know the gold was gone."

"But what was the point?"

"Oh, he would have insured the gold and for its true value, which is more likely to have been twelve-hundred-thousand-pounds than twelve-thousand."

I was doubtful. "I fear, Holmes, that matters could hardly be arranged so easily. Did he not consider what would be his fate when Clay knew he had been double crossed?"

"But the loss would not have been discovered immediately. The crates would have been left in the tunnel to be collected weeks after the theft and only once the police had concluded the robbers had escaped with the gold via that side door. Long before that an anonymous tipoff would have led the police to Clay. He was wanted for murder. He would have died on the scaffold indignantly protesting to the end that his handcuffs had not been not gold plated, there was no red carpet, and they had forgotten the silken rope."

"What was Merryweather's role in the robbery?"

"Think, Watson. Do try it. Like caviar, you may even acquire a taste for it. The refined Clay, born with a golden spoon in his mouth and a blue chip on his shoulder, outraged when a policemen common as muck dared to lay dirty hands upon him, nevertheless happily debased himself for a month slaving as a lowly pawnbroker's apprentice. The subsequent tunnelling took a further two months working in conditions of danger and discomfort that a Welsh miner might have rebelled against. Moreover, there ought to have been no guarantee that at the end of the three months those crates would still be in that cellar, particularly since it was known they were being targeted. He would have been caught red-faced rather than red-handed had he broken into the cellar only to discover the gold had been removed long before. Someone had to have told Clay an immense quantity of the gold was there and guaranteed it would remain unmoved when common sense dictated it ought to be relocated. Only an insider in a position of great influence could have managed all that. Who else could it have been?"

Holmes can be very convincing even when making questionable claims, but on this occasion, I felt I had to keep my feet firmly rooted in the ground. In a whirlwind of ideas, being a stick-in-the-mud becomes a virtue. "You cannot seriously be suggesting Clay allowed himself to be captured, Holmes. Where is your proof?"

"Why, consider his behaviour at the time. You recall how he levered up that flagstone?"

"But that is my point," I persisted. "He did it in absolute silence. He would not have been so cautious had he wished to be taken."

"Then why did he allow the light from his dark lantern to show through? And why did he not peer into the cellar?"

"There would have been no point, Holmes. The cellar was lost in darkness and his eyes must have adjusted to the light in the tunnel. Besides, he did put his hand through to grope about."

"For what? Was he feeling for our shoes? It was a melodramatic gesture intended to make our skins crawl. Think how those fingers writhed like a Medusan hairful of Indian swamp adders! Do you recall what happened next?"

"He emerged through the flagstone."

"He did not!" cried Holmes triumphantly. "What did you hear? Be precise."

I thought hard. There had been a curious rending, tearing sound and then one of the flagstones had been turned over on its side. "That is curious," said I in some confusion. "I don't understand, Holmes. He had been able to raise the first flagstone silently. I don't see why he did not climb through that opening. Why did he raise another? And why did he make such a racket the second time?"

"Ah," sighed Holmes. "Once again you see the truth and yet you fail to accept it. Is it not clear that it was for theatrical effect? He was putting on a show in accordance with his instructions. Think of how he enquired of his companion Archie whether he had possessed the foresight to bring a chisel and some bags. What burglar would ask such a question at such a

79

time? Why did he not think to ask him if he had remembered to turn off the gas as well? And what did they need a chisel for anyway? To cut away at the first flagstone to raise it soundlessly? But that had been achieved. No, Watson, everything was just a touch overdone. None of it rang true. "

"Holmes," said I impatiently, "you have still not given me any idea *why* he might have wished to be taken. Don't think you can palm me off with your usual talk of relegating motives to realms of conjecture. If as you say he was wanted for murder, what could he possibly have gained?

"A clean slate. It was part of the deal he had been offered by our crime writer. Clay would never stand in the dock or on the scaffold. He would be released scot-free."

"You mean there was a second tunnel? His friends were planning to rescue him out of prison?"

Holmes chuckled. "How very exciting! But remember the rules. I have rationed you to no more than one secret room or passage or tunnel per fairy-tale. If you read the papers on Monday morning, you will find the explanation there."

"You think that when the press covers the robbery they will explain it?"

"I mean that when you search for coverage of a robbery brilliantly foiled by the incomparable Inspector Peter Athelney Jones, you will find no mention of it, to the dismay of that imbecilic lobster. Nor, for that matter, will you read that a certain Brunton of Brunton, Bourke, and Company, stockbrokers, has been despatched to Bertram Currie of Glyns on an urgent mission to save Barings and in the process the reputation of the City of London."

I stared at my friend. "How could you possibly know that, Holmes?"

"Because of my brother Mycroft."

I had met Holmes's brother and knew something of that lazy and unambitious if troublingly brilliant man. "Mycroft? But you led me to understand he is a mere nonentity in Whitehall. How could he have been privy to such confidential information?"

Holmes was strangely taken aback at my query. He appeared to be perplexed for an instant and then to understand. "Ah, but of course. Yes, Watson, you have once again unwittingly supplied the solution in raising the question. That must be it. Because he is thought of as the lowest of the low, he is free to overhear conversations that in the presence of any other would be held in whispers. Think of my street urchin spies, who are free to go everywhere, see everything and are themselves overlooked by all averted eyes. In the American Civil War, you know, black slaves served Southern generals at their dinner tables and eavesdropped on discussions concerning campaign strategies as freely as did their masters' dogs. It was a necessary article of faith that the blacks did not possess the brains to understand what was being said. Now, Mycroft has a mind superior to that of any of his betters, yet he is so silent and sluggish they think him an *idiot savant* good for mere computing and nothing more. He does not mean to listen in, you understand – it is simply that he has a perfect memory and is incapable of forgetting anything he hears. Copernicus, Carlyle, and all manner of rubbish can never be erased from that great brain. He is genuinely indifferent to all political questions, but to make conversation when we meet in the Stranger's Room of the Diogenes, he throws me amusing titbits of political and financial gossip."

"Such as?" I asked eagerly.

"Why, such as that the Bank of England shall shortly be called upon to request a loan of three-million pounds in French gold to signal to a jittery City its determination to support Barings. But will she get it, Watson? That is the question. Will she get it?"

Here Holmes looked at me enquiringly as if there could be any doubt about it. "I should have thought so. Why should the French hesitate?"

"Well, that is the question, is it not? Any hesitation would be fatal. Now, what would the French think if the papers were full of news of an attempt to steal that first loan of Gallic gold from the City and Suburban? What if they learnt it had been stored so carelessly in an unguarded cellar and all warnings that a robbery was imminent had been disregarded? They might ask themselves whether it would not be wise to keep their remaining gold for themselves in case the City of London failed, and a global panic ensued. And besides, if the City went under, than Paris might replace her one day as the financial centre of the world."

"Oh, come now," I laughed. "You complain that I am sometimes too melodramatic, but really, I cannot hold a candle to you. The City fail? That is rather far-fetched. Barings is not the City and the City is not Barings. The fall of a house is not the fall of an entire city."

"But if that city consists of dozens of houses of cards standing cheek by jowl?" enquired Holmes earnestly. "Let me draw a parallel. Let us suppose some nihilist were to detonate a bomb beneath Pulitzer's *New York World* building a few decades hence when dozens of such towers of Babel have been erected. Picture the *New York World* falling to left or right like a flaming domino. It strikes an adjacent monument to Mammon and that falls upon nearby buildings in turn. Soon the New York world is burning."

"But the City is not like that, Holmes," I reminded him. "We have no sky scrapers, as I think *Punch* calls them, threatening the heavens."

"No, but the City has its head in the clouds. It is driven by the dreams and nightmares of gamblers. The individual investor is an insoluble

81

puzzle, but in the aggregate they can be reduced to a mathematical certainty. They would go over the falls like a stampeding herd of lemmings. Every house of playing cards would fold. It would lead to the greatest depression the world has ever seen." Holmes suddenly seemed to understand what he was saying and became very serious and silent.

It disturbed me too. "I see now why your brother Mycroft has no ambitions to rise in the political sphere," said I with a grimace. "What you have called the overworld of the criminally rich might almost be the mirror image of the underworld of the criminally poor. I perceive you believe news of the City and Suburban will be suppressed lest it make the French jittery. You think Clay was arrested for form's sake and shall be released at once. That would certainly explain why he allowed himself to be taken. The charge of murder will have to be dropped too. But you have yet to explain why our mastermind thought it best to sabotage his own plot."

Holmes seemed uncertain. "I have a general idea of his or her intentions, you understand. No more than that. He or she may have thought of Clay as a maverick and a rival and so set him up. Our mastermind might mean to take control of crime in London. Had all gone according to his original plan, then a second gang would have removed the gold via that tunnel after Clay had been arrested. And yet that never happened."

"It would have been a masterstroke to have seized the gold that Clay had been forced to abandon," said I. "Except, of course, that if you are correct the gold was already gone."

Holmes nodded. "True enough, but that is a minor detail. The question is why our great brain threw away the chance to win the game so spectacularly. I can think of only one possible reason. He realised that the stakes had suddenly changed and were now too high. It was no longer a question of merely winning the game."

"So what was at stake?"

"Only the game, Watson. The game was for the game itself."

"How do you mean?"

"Think of it this way. No one has a higher respect for private property than a thief. It is just that he also happens to regard all property as theft and present possession as nine-tenths of the law. Or possibly ten. After all, that is why the meek have been disinherited of the earth. Now, I suspect our mastermind is quite a cultured fellow. He has read the final part of William Morris's serialised *News from Nowhere, or An Epoch of Rest*, which as it happens appeared only last Saturday. It supplies a dystopian vision of the future as a return to the past, only with no crime since there will be no property." Holmes shuddered at the thought. "Can you imagine with what horror our mastermind would have regarded such a ghastly prospect?"

"I certainly can," said I with a smile.

"Consider, too, that last year was the centenary of the French Revolution. It can be no coincidence that there was such severe rioting in the London streets. Why, the protesters even exchanged rude semaphore messages with members of the Diogenes. Let us suppose the City were to fall as the result of the simultaneous failures of both Barings and the City and Suburban, leading to an uncontrollable panic. Might not Morris's prophesied social revolution sweep away the industrial one? Our mastermind concluded, and I would concur, it was simply not worth the risk. Better to lose one game than imperil the game itself."

"But if Merryweather really has gambled away that loan of French gold, won't his bank go under once the loss is discovered? Will that not be the last straw you fear?"

"Our crime writer will show him a way out. If the director makes one of this mastermind's cardsharps his partner in crime, then together they will fleece wealthy aristocrats and make up the director's lost gold. In return, our spider will have acquired a thread into the City, and a bank through which to funnel his ill-gotten gains, as well as those of such illustrious clients as 'Don Juan' Murillo. Plus, he will have access to details of all the bank's accounts. Useful information if one is intent upon blackmailing and bribing others. Such are the fringe benefits that come with saving the world."

I could not help laughing. "So you would make Moriarty – or his successor since you refuse to believe it could be him – a benefactor of the race! You have to admit, Holmes, there is perhaps something just a little funny about so outlandish an idea."

Holmes smiled with his mouth but not his eyes. "Mankind's benefactor, you say? Well, perhaps he is at that, though quite unintentionally. His motives for acting so have been entirely selfish. Nevertheless, I acknowledge your genius, sir." Here Holmes bowed low to an invisible adversary. "You reasoned it out beautifully and your logic was impeccable."

"Logic, Holmes?" said I, somewhat put out by Holmes's amoral admiration for Machiavellian villainy. "He can only be a criminal and intent upon short term gain. It may cost him his immortal soul."

"Perhaps. But at least he understood that the long-term need to save capitalism easily trumped short-term greed. More than that, he has grasped a profound truth. *Le joueur c'est rien, le jeu c'est tout.*"

It is a matter of history – that secret history which when publicised is disbelieved in favour of myths that conceal even the known facts – that

83

Barings did survive and the City of London remained the financial centre of the world. The City and Suburban Bank was not so fortunate.

I flatter myself "The Red-Headed League" assisted in the suppression of the truth concerning that scandal. This was at the express wish of the Prime Minister, the late Lord Holdhurst, as communicated to Sherlock Holmes via his brother Mycroft, whom it later transpired was somewhat more ambitious than Holmes had imagined. It seems doubtful at the present time that the true version of events supplied here will ever be authorised for public consumption.

The final blow fell for the City and Suburban with the second and more successful burglary of one of its branches in the April of 1893. This was perpetrated by the now infamous amateur cracksman Arthur J. Raffles, who was undoubtedly the gentleman who scrutinised Holmes and myself so astutely when we paid a call on Wilson's sham pawnbroker's on Saturday, 11 October, 1890. In my published account, I attempted to muddy the waters as regards the precise dating lest a connection be discerned with the visit of Sidney Brunton to Curry and Glyns the following Monday on behalf of Barings. That was the same day as the burglary of the City and Suburban would have been discovered. Had that theft succeeded, it is doubtful that either Barings or the City and Suburban would have survived for more than a few months or even weeks.

As it is, the City and Suburban limped on until the 1893 Raffles burglary. That thief later disappeared, presumed drowned in July 1895. Holmes has hinted that he had a hand in the gentleman's apparent demise off Napoleon's island of Elba. Raffles's fiancée at that time, recorded as one "Werner", may have been the "Verner" who purchased my failing practice following Holmes's resurrection in 1894. I am no longer certain that she was either a doctor or related to Holmes, but she may have been one of his agents.

Those who wish to read a fuller account of the 1893 City and Suburban burglary may care to consult Harry "The Rabbit" Manders's "The Chest of Silver", one of his confessions in the volume A Thief in the Night, *which recounts crimes he aided and abetted Raffles in committing. Readers should approach these with caution. The Rabbit is not a reliable witness.*

In "The Knees of the Gods" in the volume The Black Mask, *Manders again records the presumed death of Raffles, this time in 1900 while fighting the Boers in South Africa.*

At the close of "His Last Bow" Holmes is made to hint that neither he nor I would survive the Great War. The decision was taken to have my occasional collaborator Conan Doyle write this story in the third person, the better to encourage the reader to deduce as much. In reality, Holmes,

84

Raffles, and I are still alive at the time of writing. So is another who has asked that she not be named.

Holmes got his wish to work with Raffles for a cause in which he insists the end justifies somewhat unorthodox means.

For The Game never ends.

Hans Holbein – *"The Ambassadors"*

The Adventure of the Mistaken Identity

Continuing "A Case of Identity"

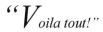 *"Voila tout!"*

"And Miss Sutherland?"

"If I tell her she will not believe me. You remember the old Persian saying, *"There is danger for him who taketh the tiger cub, and danger also for whoso snatches a delusion from a woman."* There is as much sense in Hafiz as in Horace, and as much knowledge of the world."

We both sat in silence for a while, though the qualities of our silences differed. His was the one hand clapping silence that always preceded the onset of one of his black dog moods. Mine was like the silence between the lightning flash and the thunder. I had experienced it once as an army surgeon before going over the top.

At the end of that pregnant pause I took a deep breath. It had to be said. "Actually, Holmes, the point is an academic one. I am afraid the lady is dead."

My friend had often amazed me with his revelations, and I had long looked forward to the day I would astonish him in turn, yet now that the day had come I could take no pleasure in his look of bewilderment. He opened his mouth to speak and found no words. Finally, he managed two: "Dead? How?"

"She died three hours after I delivered her daughter. I did all I could for them. I managed to save the girl, but the mother . . . ."

Holmes looked incredulous. "Watson, if this is a joke . . . ."

"No, no, I am quite serious. She confessed that on the night when she met her stepfather disguised as Hosmer Angel, they both of them were swept away. You remember I said a case of great gravity had engaged me for most of today. I would have told you before, but you see Windibank arrived just as I was about to do so. Then I thought it best not to until the stepfather had left."

Holmes nodded. "Very wise, very wise. A case of gravity and the grave, it seems." I might have taken offence at his attempt at levity, save that I suspected it masked how secretly shaken he was. "But I cannot quite understand this. How could I have failed to perceive her condition? I, the most observant of men! Halloa! Halloa! Halloa! What, in the name of the devil!"

With the speed of a tiger's paw Holmes's right hand had shot up to put his long, thin, white forefinger to the edge of the offending eye. The next moment he was scrutinising his finger's glistening tip with a look of distaste such as I had only seen once before. That had been when he discovered a crack in his favourite high-powered lens. "I confess this is beyond me. It cannot be for that woman. Why, what's she to me, or me to her that I should weep for her?" But if not for her then for whom? Curious, Watson, very curious!"

I recalled how Holmes's had claimed in his extravagant article "The Book of Life" that the ideal reasoner could infer the possibility of a Reichenbach Falls from a single drop of water or deduce heaven from a wild flower. Now he seemed to think that in a single tear drop he might glimpse all the sorrows of the world as a wizard might while peering into his crystal ball. Yet I noted with wonder that despite being shaken, he remained as admirably dispassionate and as clinically objective in his consideration of that tear as if it had been nothing more than a drop of dew.

"Any ideas? What could have caused it? And more to the point, how do you explain my failure to perceive that the gross Miss Sutherland was not simply a female Mycroft? A spectacular oversight, was it not? To have failed to perceive I had not one client but two? Worth more than a pregnant pause, I think."

He spoke breezily enough, yet I could tell he was deeply disturbed by that unprecedented blunder on the part of the greatest detective the world has ever known. "You must be my eyes and ears, Doctor, as I evidently cannot trust my own any more. Come, come, Watson, you know my methods. Read my mind for me. Retrace my thoughts. I must get to the bottom of this, else how may I trust myself again!"

All the time he had been speaking he had avoided my eyes. His gaze had been fixed upon the latest picture to be displayed above his mantelpiece. In view of its crucial importance later I had best explain at the start that I say "the latest" because Holmes insisted no picture be displayed for longer than it remained a mystery. What appeared to be an unfinished copy of Paul Delaroche's *The Execution of Lady Jane Grey* had been hanging there for the past six days, which had to be a record. He pretended to be intrigued by it now.

I remembered that he had feigned interest in it earlier too, staring up at it with his feet propped up on the mantelpiece as he recited the chain of events of the Miss Sutherland affair to her treacherous stepfather Windibank. It was only when he had glanced back and perceived the sneer on that scoundrel's face that he had quite forgotten himself and assaulted the seducer in a blind rage. I was relieved that the villain escaped with his life. I truly feared Holmes was ready to beat him as ruthlessly and as efficiently as he were one of the corpses, he liked to lash black and blue to determine the effects of bruising after death. Had Windibank not fled, I think Holmes might have been able to make a comparative study of bruises before *and* after death as displayed on one and the same corpse.

"You want me to read your mind?" I asked doubtfully. "You read mine while I was studying my portraits of Beecher and Gordon, but that was when I was attending to nothing else. I can hardly say what was going on in yours when you stared at that painting. You were not attending to the Delaroche execution scene at all. Surely your thoughts were wholly devoted to the mystery of the disappearance of the bridegroom Hosmer Angel from the cab on his way to his wedding."

I was uncertain whether Holmes had heard me, for he had not moved a muscle. He might have been turned to marble as he kept those eyes as steel grey as Athena's riveted to what begged to become a Tussaud's Chamber of Horrors tableau. Was it coincidence that Tussaud's took the step of permanently establishing itself in the Baker Street Bazaar the year after the success of that painting? Perhaps it was a memory of it that led Holmes to create a living *tableau* with dummy borrowed from there to take the wicked Colonel Moran. But that adventure lay in the future.

At last he spoke. "Watson," said he quietly, "that may be the most revelatory thing you have ever said. Sometimes to be entirely wrong can be far less dangerous than to be very nearly right. To mistake magnetic for true north is be lulled into a false sense of security. Sooner or later one will hit a rock. I assure you I had not been thinking about the bridegroom. No, not for a moment. My thoughts were all directed towards that painting and my words were those of a man talking in his sleep. It follows that my tear must have been for Lady Jane Grey, except – no, that would be absurd. And yet it must have been so. I suppose Miss Sutherland waited to pounce on you in the fog outside 221b?"

"Yes, she was there," said I, accustomed as I was to his sudden changes of subject as one thought vanished and another loomed out. "She asked me if I would perform a termination. Naturally I refused. I told her that the child's life was not her own. She should keep her hands off it. That did no good."

"And yet you managed to change her mind?"

"I asked her if she had considered any names. She had. Once the unborn baby ceased to be nameless, she found it impossible to consider killing her."

"The girl's name she chose was Georgiana."

I gaped. "Holmes, you followed us! How else could you possibly have known that? Admit it. You were our cabbie."

89

He smiled, but it was not his usual tip-of-the-iceberg smile as worn whenever struggling to conceal from himself and me how much he savoured my amazement. This smile verged on becoming a grimace. "An ideal reasoner. One who like my brother Mycroft has never shed a tear in his life, might deduce her entire story from that one word. No, no, I did not follow you. Ah, but they are very impressive, are they not? All those parlour tricks of mine. I see that there are different kinds of intelligence and a man may be a congenital idiot in one way and a genius in another."

I wondered whether to be flattered or insulted. "I suppose you are referring to my role as a lightning conductor for your own flashes of genius."

"No, no, I was thinking of myself as much as you, my dear fellow. What a man we would have made had we only been born one instead of two! Neither of us is really complete without the other."

"I am not sure what my wife would say to that," said I in some embarrassment. "But what do you mean? How can a man be wise and foolish at the same time?"

"Ask Hamlet, my good Horatio. And do not ask me how I knew the name for the unborn daughter had to be Georgiana. That will become evident enough in due course.

"As for our contemplation of Miss Mary Sutherland, all the time I thought you so very unobservant you were doing your job as a doctor while I was distracting myself with trifling observations upon the toecaps of Miss Sutherland's shoes, the hole in a glove, and the wrinkles to her sleeves. Amazing. I understand now how Newton felt while studying pebbles on a beach as a boy only to look up and see the neglected ocean beyond. I did not fail to perceive her pregnancy. I see that. I succeeded brilliantly in overlooking what I had no intention of acknowledging. Now that I am close to accepting the truth, I am sorely tempted to forget it. I confess it is as distasteful to me as the notion that man may not find himself located at the centre of the solar system."

Holmes was alluding to his eccentric desire to believe we live in an egocentric universe.

"You will never guess what intrigued me most about Miss Sutherland. It was the angle at which she wore that preposterous hat of hers. You have seen my latest addition to the décor?"

Holmes waved me towards a "wanted" poster that featured Gainsborough's abducted portrait of Georgiana Spencer, Duchess of Devonshire, and promised a reward of a thousand pounds for her recovery. The painting had been stolen from Agnew's back in 1876, the very year Holmes had set up shop as a consulting detective. It was only twelve years later that he finally solved the crime during a visit to a certain corrupt professor's study. That gentleman was an admiring student of the great Adam Worth and meant the detective to know it. The Professor had hung Greuze's painting "*La Jeune Fille a l'agneau*" behind his desk without drawing its protective curtain to be sure Holmes would see it. The pun on '*agneau*' and '*Agnew's*' was unmissable. The Professor was imitating Worth, hence Worth had to have the Agnew's Gainsborough.

"The only mystery remaining was why Worth never sold the painting. I have found the answer to that. Gainsborough's Duchess bears a strong resemblance to the remarkable Kitty Flynn, the wife of Worth's partner Piano Charley. Something of a *ménage a trois*, you understand, and not unlike that in the Duke of Devonshire's household, where Georgiana's most intimate friend was also her husband's mistress. That must have intrigued Miss Sutherland, given the curious situation in which she found herself. And you see, Watson? Precisely the same tilt to the hat, as indeed were the outrageous dimensions of both their headpieces. Our Mary Sutherland was clearly modelling herself upon Georgiana."

"You read a great deal into a painting. How can you be so sure that Worth and Miss Sutherland viewed it in such terms?" If as my friend boasted he had paint in his veins I sometimes wondered whether he was not suffering from lead poisoning. I later thought to hold him up as a cautionary tale to my late friend the illustrator Sidney Paget, who had the dangerous habit of sucking his paintbrush.

"Oh, they were not the first to use it as a mirror held up to nature. It disappeared, you know, about the time the Duke discovered his wife was pregnant by her lover, Lord Charles Grey, who incidentally steered through the Reform Act in the self-same year Paul Delaroche began work on that painting of Bloody Mary's counter-reformation execution of Lady Jane Grey. Mycroft is of the opinion that had Lord Grey failed, there would have been a guillotine erected in Trafalgar Square and Grey's head under it. So you see that the past is a glass held up to the present to show it possible futures. Mycroft believes we escaped the tyranny of the people by the skin of our teeth."

The cynicism of so prominent a member of the Diogenes Club did not surprise me. Mycroft Holmes is not a wholehearted believer in democracy. He regards politics as a game and elections as a circus entertainment to trick the masses into believing they *are* the British government. According to Mycroft the government suffers from a similar delusion.

"But we were speaking of the gorgeous Georgiana. You know that at the time of one of her pregnancies she invented a false front to conceal her condition? Of course, it was quickly adopted by high society as a fashion statement and worn whether the ladies were expecting or not. Ah. Miss Sutherland was wearing one. Women are such inexplicable creatures."

I thought that was the pot calling the kettle black but knew better than to say so. I joined into the digression instead. "I see the effect was like that achieved in Jan van Eyck's Arnolfini double portrait, in which the wife appears to be pregnant though in reality it is an illusion due to her heavy dress."

Holmes shook his head. "No, no, it is a posthumous portrait and she died in childbirth. That is why there is a little statue of St. Margaret in the background. She is bursting out of the belly of a dragon as if about to rise up to heaven. Margaret was the patron saint of childbirth. Thus, is signifies the promise that if the mother dies while giving birth then her soul will burst free of her body to fly up to paradise and be received by her heavenly Father. But I see you are growing impatient, Doctor," said he with what must have been a touch of asperity. Surely it was not wariness. What had he to be wary about? "You are about to make some objection to my theory concerning Miss Sutherland."

I had indeed been bursting to speak and raise an obvious objection to my friend's extravagant deductions, for he seemed to me to be talking out of his own hat. He had once condemned my friend Conan Doyle's exciting account of mad Mormons in *A Study in Scarlet* as producing an effect akin to working a love triangle into the fifth proposition of Euclid. Was he not doing something worse? "Surely the shared angle of their hats is a coincidence! Someone as respectable as Miss Sutherland would hardly take a woman as bohemian as the scandalous Georgiana Spencer as a role model. Why, the Duchess practically ruined her husband with her gambling! It was in her blood, I am told. Her mother suffered from the same addiction. I gather Georgiana showed symptoms of having inherited the complaint even in her childhood. I do believe I read somewhere she spent an entire day playing cards when only nine."

Holmes tilted his head upwards, closed his eyes and swore. "Fool! Fool! Fool!" Wth every "Fool!" he struck his splendid brows most forcibly with his clay pipe. It broke. He picked up another. It was his third of the day.

I sighed, for I was used to such insults.

"No, no, not you, Doctor. Me! Of course, she had to be a gambler. Ah, I see it now. Except unlike Georgiana, she was a highly successful one. Why on earth did I not observe it before? I ought to have detected it before she was halfway across the Baker Street road on her way to our front door!"

I laughed. "Come now. How could you possibly have done so?"

"How? By using my eyes. From the fact that she failed to use hers, feeble though they were. Surely you saw how she looked neither to the right nor to the left before plunging suicidally into that traffic. That in spite of being purblind! It took nerves of steel. I would rather have gone over Niagara in a barrel. Of course, she had nothing to lose, for had she been killed it would have ended all her difficulties. But it was a game. She lived for the adrenalin rush, even as Georgiana Spencer did. Oh, I know the type. For them life is commonplace, and anything is to be embraced that will relieve their boredom for a second. She had to play the game."

I was still sceptical, for she had made a poor impression on me. "Come, now, a more vacuous face I never saw." ɂ

"Vacuous, you say? Like this?" Holmes passed his hand down over his own face and in an instant became a Red Indian to reveal nothing. "Say rather it was the face of a gambler that tells you no more than she means it to."

"Well, the mind matters more than the face."

"Precisely! Oxycephalic, Watson, Oxycephalic! Think of dear old Pericles of ancient Athens. Why do you suppose he was invariably depicted wearing a helmet? It concealed a grotesque skull that served as an ironic receptacle for a beautiful mind. Miss Sutherland's hat did much the same. It is a question of cubic capacity, my dear doctor. The cap not only fitted but *permitted* her to hide the light under it. The same was certainly true of her hero, Georgiana Spencer, who at times *was* the government of her day. But that, of course, is part of the secret history of our country that we will never know. By the way, remind me to return Sarah Cushing her skull. I borrowed it the other day to show friend Lombroso at the Congress of Criminal Anthropology in Paris, you know. We concurred it displayed precisely the same degenerate features as that of Charlotte Corday."

I presumed Holmes had "borrowed" it in much the same sense that his ancestor John Didrik Holm "borrowed" Swedenborg's, which was dolicephalic like Holmes's own. I have often suspected a criminal strain runs in the Holmes family, though fortunately it has always been confined to scientific enterprises. "And you think the shape of Miss Sutherland's skull marked her out as a gambler?"

"Oh, not only that. By no means only that. I see now that the creases to her sleeves above her wrists could never have come from typing. How could they have done, when no professional typewriter would think to rest her wrists upon the edge of her work surface but would always keep them overhead her machine? They came from pressing against a gambling table at the crisis prior to her predetermined triumph. I blame you for my crass error, Watson, for had you learned how to type I would have witnessed you at work and could never have committed such a blunder. You really must learn to do so, Doctor. Think of all the inaccuracies that will vanish from your accounts, to say nothing of the lives saved, once your prescriptions for your patients cease to be illegible."

I chose not to acknowledge Holmes's notion of wit. "How can you know she invariably won?"

"From the hole in the forefinger of her right glove and the fact that the fingertip showing through it was stained violet."

"But you explained all that," I reminded Holmes. "She left home in a distressed state of mind, which is why she never noticed the rent to her glove. As for the stain, that was because she wrote a note just before she left and did not have time to wash her hands."

"Ah, but the glove was not torn."

"Not torn?"

"No, Watson."

"But I distinctly saw it was torn."

"Not torn. Unstitched."

I was thoroughly confused. "Unstitched? Who would do that? And why?"

Holmes directed my eye towards a reproduction of a card game by the debauched Italian painter Caravaggio. "Observe the gentleman in the background and in particular the hand he is waving about like an aesthete at a concert. Do you observe any similarities between it and that of Miss Sutherland?"

I considered it critically. "The gloves are the same particular shade of grey as hers were. Why, that is curious. He has a hole near the tip of one finger of his right glove just like hers. What a remarkable coincidence!"

Holmes chuckled. "No coincidence. I noticed as soon as she registered the painting's presence there she gave a start and bent her finger to hide the hole. She knew that work and so fully comprehended its meaning. Our friend Caravaggio was not unfamiliar with the practices of the underworld. Most of what we know of him comes from police reports, for he was no angel. Unless, of course, you count the Hosmer Angels of this world. I daresay he encountered such a gentleman during one of his numerous tavern brawls. That rogue there is a cardsharp and has unstitched his glove to permit the tip of his finger to touch the cards. It is a very useful dodge that I have employed myself. One shaves the skin away from the finger to increase sensitivity. It enables one to detect tiny pricks."

"And you think Miss Sutherland was employing such a trick?"

"Why else would she have taken such care over her appearance and yet have stained her finger violet? It was to prevent me seeing that she, too, had a shaven fingertip."

"But Holmes," I protested, "why should she have let you see it at all? Why not conceal it?"

Holmes gazed dreamily into the distance as he raised his right hand and with a thumb as thin as a hoodlum's forefinger proceeded to touch each of the other four fingers in turn. Then he repeated the operation with the first three. Finally he tapped the middle finger again twice and I knew he had selected one out of seven possible solutions.

"Because she was a gambler. You saw how she never ceased to fidget with her gloves all the time she was staring up at us while standing before the empty yellow house opposite, though she ceased her fidgeting once she was with us. During the journey here she would have been playing with them incessantly. She must have discovered that hole almost as soon as she left her home. When she did so her first thought was one of horror, for she knew even the most mediocre of Scotland Yard detectives would deduce its significance. Ah, but then it occurred to her if I believed her too poor to be able to afford a new pair of gloves and too proud to admit it I would take pity on her. She could not resist doing me on a wager – even on a wager against herself! It was playing the game for its own sake. Admirable, admirable!"

I shook my head in wondering disbelief. "None of this makes any sense. If she was such a schemer, how was her stepfather able to tyrannise over her so? How could he ever have kept her incarcerated in her home for so many years and absolutely forbidden her to wed?"

"He never did. She was still unmarried at the age of twenty-five because she had no wish to be bound to a husband. No, no, believe me, such women exist. When a woman weds a man, she ceases to exist as a separate legal entity. She has no rights and no property, being herself the property of her husband. For a few women born with an abnormal desire for complete independence, such a state of affairs would be intolerable. Miss Sutherland was just such a creature. Professor Lombroso is good on the subject."

"But how did he make her stay at home for so long?"

"He did not. It was her mother and for years before Windibank appeared. The mother was also the one who put her husband up to masquerading as Hosmer Angel. She had seen how he had eyed her daughter, for do not suppose Windibank loved a wife a full fifteen years older than himself whom he had only married for her money. Not that it did him any good, for you will recall Miss Sutherland told us no sooner had she handed over the interest from her New Zealand stock than the mother snatched it out of his hand. Did you catch the resentment in his voice when he whined to us that "I am not quite my own master, you know"? He is one of passion's slaves and a pipe for that strumpet Fortune's finger to sound what stop she please. And it was the daughter he desired. That desire may have been reciprocated, though Miss Sutherland would have died before she admitted it. I do not know whether she really failed to recognise him in his disguise. I do know that neither of them could restrain themselves."

I was incredulous. "But Holmes, if the mother was jealous, why on earth would she have wished to bring them together?"

"Because revenge is a dish best served cold. Did I not demonstrate that last year when I invited your noble bachelor St Simon to sit down to a cold supper with his bigamous bride? The wife's diabolical revenge was to bring them as far as the church door and then part them forever. Our travelling wine salesman was thereafter to suffer torments worse than those of Tantalus, for unlike Tantalus he had tasted the forbidden fruit. What Mrs. Windibank did not count on was the pregnancy of her daughter. But all that is really rather trite and need not concern us, particularly since Sutherland is dead. The case is closed. The real mystery is the singular behaviour of the detective."

I saw the truth of this. I had always considered Holmes to be nothing but an automaton – a calculating machine. I had supposed him a brain without a heart and incapable of any human feelings. His inexplicable shifts of mood and his irrational rationalisations on this occasion had proved me entirely wrong. And then there were other difficulties.

Why had he invited the stepfather but not the wife and daughter to 221b? It was the mother whose conscience might more readily have been pricked, and surely the daughter would have accepted the truth if he had confessed in her hearing. As for inviting Windibank, Holmes's only aim in speaking to him seemed to be to wholeheartedly concur with the blaggard's boast that he had committed the perfect crime since technically no crime at all – or so he said. And Holmes had remained inhumanly detached for a time, staring up at the ceiling, as I had supposed, while he rehearsed the events as if he had been there to witness them. By contrast, he hardly seemed to be present with us save in body.

But I doubt now that he really had been staring at the ceiling either when with Windibank or with Miss Sutherland. He had certainly not been doing so while with Miss Sutherland. He must have been considering that Delaroche execution scene. I could not see him doing so because I had stationed apart from and behind Holmes as he sat opposite her before the fire. So short-sighted was Miss Sutherland she had been unaware of my presence. Finally Holmes had waved her in my direction, but it was clear she could not see me. Thus I was able to take verbatim notes of her conversation with a mind to future publication.

In the case of Windibank, my friend had finally ceased to study the painting as he turned back towards the monster in time to catch his twisted lip. Holmes's consequent eruption had been frightening to behold. I had glimpsed the fires in the boiler of the racing engine. I knew it then to be a machine fully capable of murder. There, but for the grace of God . . . .

But after that Holmes had apathetically washed his beryl-of-nitrate-stained hands of his duty to his client and excused himself by protesting that to speak the truth would be both dangerous and superfluous. Windibank was predestined for the gallows without any assistance from him. I found myself wondering whether it was Miss Sutherland or he who was really determined to avoid the truth. What that truth was I could no longer say.

"You see the point, Watson," said he, and I realised he had been reading my thoughts better than I could ever have done myself. "Your highly questionable collaborator Conan something or other has rightly chided you for the foolish inconsistency of your characters, save of course for portrayal of yourself, but none of them is more contradictory than your wonderfully implausible hero, Mr. Sherlock Holmes. He is your Hamlet, my dear Horatio, for at one moment he thinks too much and does not act and the next he acts without any thought at all."

"I am flattered you liken my Holmes to Hamlet," said I with the smile. "But the credit must go to you."

"But there is a crucial difference between your Holmes and Shakespeare's *Hamlet*. Intelligently considered, the Dane is seen to be perfectly and plausibly consistent in his very inconsistency. Think how trigger-happy he is after finding Claudius at prayer. He wishes to dispatch him but after the most cold-blooded weighing of the pros-and-cons decides he cannot. He fears lest dying praying, the sinner's soul might escape by a legal loophole into heaven. So he vows to kill the King when he is caught about some dirty business and so swiftly he shall have no time to cry out to God to receive his soul.

"Then what happens? In the very next scene the Prince runs through a spy concealed behind an arras on the off chance it is Claudius. The Prince does not trouble to confirm first that it is the King for in doing so he would give the man time to confess his sins and so escape damnation. The Dane of the Elsinores has done exactly what he promised he would do. Thus you see the one scene explains the other and so reveals the method in his madness. There's genius in that. Now, Doctor, if you wish to appease your questionable friend Conman Doyle, you must work as Shakespeare did to render rational the most mysterious of mood changes and so justify the ways of Holmes to men. If you do not, then you are no biographer at all. You are nothing better than a second rate hagiographer."

I averted my mind's eye from the ingratitude of my friend, who did not appreciate how hard his Horatio had worked to tell his Hamlet's story. I determined to redouble my efforts until the day I succeeded. "But if you yourself do not understand why you behaved thus, how can you expect me to? You cannot ask me to find a safe passage into that Grimpen Mire of a soul of yours if even your great mind is not up to the task."

"No, no. Sometimes the average man may see what the exceptional one overlooks. On one or two occasions your mundane eye has noted tracks I have missed, and precisely because I was studying the ground with such minute care. It all comes down to that painting and its effect upon me." He had put his feet back up on the edge of the mantelpiece and was reconsidering the image of Lady Jane Grey kneeling blindfolded before the block. "I care not a whit for her fate. Why should I weep a tear for Hecuba? And why, for that matter, did my ancestors the Vernets shed buckets and buckets of salt water when first they saw this picture back in 1834?"

"I believe you mentioned a Vernet went to the guillotine at the time of the Terror that followed hard on the heels of the French Revolution. Marguerite-Emelie Vernet, was it not?" I had researched the family in a vain attempt to determine Holmes's parentage, with a mind to publishing a proper biography on my friend. "And what if Louise Vernet posed as Lady Jane? She was the painter's wife, you know."

"Excellent, Watson!" cried Holmes, and he mockingly applauded me in that silent way of his with those Aubrey Beardsley thin and painterly hands. "I do believe you are on to something. But as is also so often the case in your accounts, there is a trifling difficulty with chronology. My ancestor Louise Vernet did indeed marry Delaroche, but in 1835, not long after he met her and some time after this picture was first exhibited. He had commenced painting it in 1832 and then abandoned it temporarily that same year, obviously in order to nurse some family member who had contracted cholera."

"Why do you say that?"

Holmes waved me towards Delaroche's semi-delirious woman in the background who had collapsed onto the scaffold. "Artists are like detectives and surgeons. They cannot help seeing the world with a clinical eye. I have always found it to be a most useful defence mechanism. Now, that Lady's expression is one of the best things in this painting and is surely based on the close observation of a sufferer near to death. I surmise that while Delaroche was nursing a family member – either that or a lover, since only for his nearest and dearest would he have risked contracting the sickness himself – he sketched their feverish resignation and then used it for this distressed female."

I thought of how I had cared for my alcoholic brother for a time, though as it transpired not for long enough. With an inward shudder and sense of shame, I understood I had noted his symptoms as a concerned sibling but also with professional satisfaction. He had been a textbook case. One of Holmes's more outlandish speculations, that every man has not one brain but two, seemed for a moment just a little less far-fetched. I hastily shook the thought off. That way madness lay. "But why cholera?"

"Well, you recall the words of the sleepwalking Lady Macbeth as she broods upon the corpse of the murdered king? "Yet who would have thought the old man to have had so much blood in him?" Shakespeare borrowed that from an eyewitness account of Lady Jane's death. Those who witnessed it were amazed at how profusely the blood spurted forth from her little neck, like crimson champagne from a well-shaken bottle."

"I still don't follow."

Holmes waved a chastising finger at me. "Why, Doctor, Doctor, you know extreme dehydration is a symptom of cholera. The sluggish blood turns black, tarry, and flows as sluggishly as Lethe's stream. Blood-letting was the one generally accepted treatment to free up the arteries of the victim, but was often impossible.

"Now, Bishop Stephen Gardiner had played the good gardener to preach to the sickly Queen Mary Tudor on the need for good husbandry. A little pruning was called for in her demi-Eden. In his words, *"the rotten and hurtful members of the Commonweal"* were to be cut away. I believe your friend Doyle has written a poem to justify the ways of God as tree surgeon in like manner. Let me see, let me see . . . .

> *"And still he trains the branch of good*
> *Where the high blossoms be,*
> *And wieldeth still the shears of ill*
> *To prune and prune the tree.*

"One can combine that with the idea of blood-letting as necessary for the good of the patient, which in this case is the body politic. Except that Jane Grey's was not the corrupted blood. That showed our surgeon had cut off the wrong branch. The symbolism is, if you will forgive me saying so, bleeding obvious. Bloody Mary's was the bad blood."

I felt a little annoyed that Holmes should attempt to better me in my own field of expertise. I shall not be surprised if one day I come across his end-of-term report card on me overpitched into the dog-grate: *"Knowledge of Medicine. – Nil"*.

99

"That is very clever," said I grumpily, "but how does it prove Louise Vernet could not have posed for this lady? He might have met her in secret years before they wed."

"Hmm." Holmes was thoughtful. "It is just possible. I believe there was some vague talk of their having been lovers in 1833. Delaroche was seen in a carriage with a woman who was seated on his left-hand side. Note that, Watson. It was to tell friends not to acknowledge him. Had she been of unimpeachable reputation she would have sat to the right. Some said the lady in question was the notable *Comedie Franca*ise actress Anais Aubert, who specialised in playing innocent young girls and boys on account of her diminutive stature. Delaroche argued a case of mistaken identity, insisting the lady had been his future fiancée. Yet stories persisted Anais had borne him a daughter sent to England to be brought up and educated. She may already have sent a son here."

I nodded. "General Edward Stopford Claremont, the lover of Yolande Duvernay, considered by some to have been the most beautiful and the richest widow in England. With one possible exception." I nodded towards where what I supposed was a portrait of *the* woman, concealed behind the patriotic "*V.R.*" Holmes had bullet-pocked into the wall with my souvenir Maiwand jezail. I rubbed my leg. One of those bullets had ricocheted.

Holmes raised his eyebrows.

"Oh, just gossip I picked up at the club."

"It was not that," said he with a chuckle. "I had not realised that Her Majesty was your type. But we were speaking of Anais Aubert. Her professional career portraying virginal innocents required her to play the part of the naïve little girl offstage as well as on it. Had the child's birth been confirmed, Anais' career would have been over. What became of her daughter, if there ever was a daughter, is entirely unknown. I asked about her when I was still a child but was told not to be so inquisitive. I was forever being told not to be inquisitive. You see that Delaroche portrait you have impelled me to conceal my musket work behind?"

"The one of Irene Adler?"

Holmes paused for thought. "Hmm. Now that you come to mention it, the resemblance is striking. Quite a coincidence. No, that charming lady is Anais herself. It was a gift to me from a grateful client."

She was indeed a very beautiful and sweet looking woman. I could not help noticing yet another resemblance. "Holmes . . . ."

My friend shook his head. "No, no, that is quite out of the question. If rumour is right and she was pregnant by Delaroche at just the time he painted his masterpiece, then she could hardly have posed for hours in so uncomfortable a position. Put that possibility out of your mind."

"But surely she might have posed for the face of Lady Jane while another model supplied the body."

Holmes stared at me. He turned back to the painting. "Why did I not consider that?" he muttered. "I ought to have done. I did not. Therefore, I chose not to. Quite intriguing. Singular, in fact."

I could see that this blind spot bothered Holmes. I thought it best to distract my friend by returning to the subject supposedly in hand. "As for why the painting might have affected you, perhaps you saw some parallel between the situation of Miss Sutherland and Lady Jane. I take it they were both victims forced into marriages with unsuitable partners in accordance with the wishes of their fathers. That is how I read it."

Holmes seemed relieved at my cunning redirection of the conversation away from the mystery of how he could have slipped so badly. "I confess you may be onto something there, Watson. Yes, indeed. Consider that paternal old gentleman helping to guide the blindfolded Jane so very considerately towards the block. Note that her wedding ring is prominently on display on her left hand. I think that the message is clear: Her father had directed her towards the wedding altar as in a game of blind man's buff and she went as a sacrificial lamb to the slaughter. Now another kindly gentleman helps her towards the place of her ultimate martyrdom. All her life she had been led astray by well-meaning guides. As you say, the parallel with Miss Sutherland misdirected by her parents is obvious."

"Then we have our answer. You were considering the fate of Jane when you happened to look back at Windibank and caught sight of his sneer. It must have seemed to you that the wheel had turned and history was repeating itself. Thinking on that just now caused you to shed that singular tear."

"Yes, that could explain it," said Holmes doubtfully. "Yet it seems somehow inadequate. The fates of Lady Jane and Miss Sutherland are of no concern to me. Had the woman who posed for Jane indeed been my grandmother, it might have been a different matter."

"You mean Delaroche's later wife Louise?" said I in some surprise. "But Louise was Vernet's *daughter*. You told me your grandmother was his sister."

Holmes squirmed uncomfortably in his seat, for he had been sitting in the same position for some time. "To tell you the truth, I am not entirely sure who my grandmother was. My parents were somewhat reticent on the subject. Doubtless some scandal in the family. It could have been Louise. But as I say, the point is purely academic since this is *not* Louise. You are right that it must be Delaroche's lover Anais, whom he abandoned shortly before his marriage. And there is no reason why I should weep for an actress."

I pictured Holmes as a boy with his older brother Mycroft by his side gazing up at this painting as if they really were witnesses to a public execution. Knowing how ready my friend is to fight the good fight and wrong injustices, I could imagine his indignation and his desire to step into the picture, mount that scaffold, and demand so blatant a travesty of justice be halted. For this tragedy could not be cathartic. On the contrary, it was sickening.

I found myself asking questions I did not dare speak aloud. Had it all begun then? Had my friend's entire career as a detective been an attempt to step into that painting and put an end to the injustice it depicted? But how could that be?

Then in a flash I saw the truth. I doubt I will ever experience anything like that Eureka moment again, for lightning does not often strike twice in the same place. It was another case of mistaken identity. Of course! Suddenly it all seemed absurdly simple.

Delaroche's lover Anais was indeed the woman in the painting, but it was not for her that Holmes had shed his single tear. It was for the daughter she had borne him and had had sent away to England. In due course that girl wed a widowed English squire and bore him a son, though probably at the cost her own life. I saw as clear as day who that son was.

I had the words in my mouth and was on the verge of blurting them out: "I have found out who this lady is. Why, Holmes, it is your – ?" Thank God I stopped myself in time. The romance was there, certainly. Yet if I had told him could he have believed me? More to the point would he have forgiven me? As if in answer to my questions, my friend's own wise words came back to me from an earlier affair: "Some facts should be suppressed – or, at least, a just sense of proportion should be observed in treating them."

There is as much sense in Holmes as in Homer, and as much knowledge of the world.

Lucas Cranach – *"Cupid Complaining to Venus"*

The Adventure of the
Remarkable Worms

Continuing "The Boscombe Valley Mystery"

"God help us!" said Holmes, after a long silence. "Why does Fate play such tricks with poor helpless worms? I never hear of such cases as this that I do not think of Baxter's words, and say: '*There, but for the grace of God, goes Sherlock Holmes.*'"

I opened my mouth to correct my friend's mistake but thought better of it. The words could not be Bradford's. If Holmes said it was Baxter, then Baxter it had to be. So I closed my mouth again, feeling vaguely uncomfortable and confused.

An hour later we three were alone in a first-class train compartment, meaning myself, Holmes, and the lady he had acquired from the manager of the Hereford Arms. The train pulled out of Ross and soon we were hurtling back to our beloved cesspool at a rapid rate, able to take for granted that on arrival our watches would require no adjustment. Such is the miracle of train time, though it is a greater wonder that already we take it for granted. It is hard to believe our fathers lived in a world in which time was still relative as varying from place to place. Science has rationalised both time and space. It was my privilege to have been befriended by the man who above all others personifies the spirit of our scientific age as we work to force unruly nature to conform to our logic.

For this reason, it was embarrassing to see the man of the future sprawled along one side of our compartment and unashamedly scrutinising our painted lady through his magnifying glass. I assume that was what he was doing. Surely he could have been interested in the bees defending their hive from the winged child to her right. I took him to be Cupid. That meant the naked lady in a hat set at a coquettish Duchess of Devonshire tilt must be Venus. She was not my idea of Venus, though. The forest to the left could then have stood for notorious St. John's Wood, and she one of the adventuresses kept there.

A wide-ranging experience of women in many countries had long since inoculated me against such *belle dames sans merci* and I flatter myself I am now immune to Cupid's honey-coated arrows. Besides, I have been an army surgeon. "The Trojans say you should never look a gift whore in the mouth, sir," a syphilitic private had advised me once. I knew better. Behind this lady's smirk, which declared that she might not know much about art but knew what her audience liked, I was sure there lay concealed a mouth full of rotted teeth. She had raised her left arm to waft the scent from her armpit my way, but I stopped my nose against it. That armpit was where the venereal spots would first appear.

I must confess I was to blame for her unwanted presence. What had caused my fit of temper? And yet I had only bruised her slightly. Nevertheless, Holmes had felt obliged to purchase her from the Hereford Arms and for the princely sum of no less than fifty-five shillings!

It happened this way.

Mr. Holmes had gone with Detective Inspector Lestrade, the rat-faced gentleman with the bulldog chin that I had previously met at the time of the Lauriston Gardens Mystery, to interrogate James McCarthy in his cell concerning the murder of his father Charles McCarthy. I had stayed behind at the Hereford Arms, where I overcame my distaste and forced myself to study the latest *Holywell Street Journal*. I had to determine what sorts of story the editor currently favoured.

Readers who have acquaintances who have heard tales of Holywell Street will raise their eyebrows at this, but they should put themselves in my shoes. At the time when I had been forced to contribute reminiscences to the *Journal*, they were distinctly down at heel. It will be recalled how, after being wounded at Maiwand, I had been shipped to England with my health irretrievably ruined owing to the medical treatment I had received. My war wound pension was quite inadequate. My Strand hotel was an easy walk from the offices of the *Holywell Street Journal*. They welcomed my tales of experiences in two separate continents, since expanded to three following a comprehensive investigation of the Australian bush. Of course, I was aware of that street of shame's reputation, but a young writer is obliged to share sheets with strange bedfellows.

The Boscombe Valley investigation was one of the earliest in which I was privileged to accompany Holmes, but for reasons that shall become apparent when writing the above account of it, I had to conceal the true date. To do this I therefore pasted in an introductory scene with my wife and I breakfasting. In truth, that lay years in the future. So did the days when I would at last be free to write of nothing but Sherlock Holmes, first in my own ill-fated privately printed *Baker Street Journal*, and then in *The Strand Magazine*.

So there I was in the Hereford Arms with a yellow-backed volume of the *Holywell Street Journal* on my lap reconsidering "The Adventure of the Mahratta Minister's Daughter (and Her Pig)", from my own series "Confessions of a Wayward Stethoscope". Suffice it to say that to my surgeon's eye the accompanying illustration was anatomically preposterous, and yet somehow managed to leave nothing to the imagination. Glancing away from it in disgust, my ordinary eyes happened to fall upon another piece of erotica, though this was masqueraded as art. It was on the wall opposite and I realised with a shock that the lady depicted might have modelled for the illustrator's rendering of my heroine.

That was the last straw. With a cry of, "That's done it!" I hurled my hated literary rag across the room. Unfortunately, owing to my shoulder wound I aimed badly, and it missed the duck's-egg wallpaper to inadvertently strike the offending artwork, denting it indiscernibly.

I say the damage was imperceptible. I ought to have said it was imperceptible to the human eye. I had reckoned without Holmes and his beloved magnifying glass. How he could have deduced what had happened is quite beyond me. Of course, even then I had begun to suspect he was a mind reader. For that very reason when he returned, I took the greatest care to look at the ceiling, the floor, the walls, the furniture, and indeed everywhere save for the painting, for I was certain that if I did so much as glance guiltily towards it the game would be up. Nevertheless, he made a bee line for it and a moment later was poring over its surface with his glass just as he would have done were it the scene of a crime, which in a sense it was.

Detecting the tiny dent, he proceeded to reconstruct the entire chain of events leading up to my temper tantrum. Having done so, he quite unnecessarily insisted on purchasing the thing from our hotel manager, who was an honest man and confessed his wife had acquired the atrocity from a Jew broker's in Tottenham Court Road for only ten shillings. Despite his protestations, Holmes was adamant he would not pay a penny less than the princely sum of fifty-five shillings. Being a methodical man, he had the manager sign a paper witnessed by myself and Lestrade, transferring every possible right in the painting to him.

Did he imagine Venus would come to life and be flown by a flock of doves back to Ross, there to be welcomed with open arms by the manager? Despite all her charms, the good man was clearly glad to see the back of her. Holmes's determination to have it was all the more puzzling since he fancied himself something of an art connoisseur, and who with any understanding of art could wish to have something like that hanging in his bedroom?"

"No, I am sure of it. It was Bradford."

That started me out of my meditations. "Why, I am glad to hear you say so, Holmes," said I in some surprise. "I knew you had made a mistake, yet I could not quite bring myself to say so."

"I? A mistake?" He was not in the least bit indignant and seemed merely puzzled. "What are you talking about, Watson? It was you who made the mistake. I said it was Bradford and you opened your mouth to object it was Baxter. You wisely thought better of it."

107

"But you said – " I broke off in confusion. Had I misheard him? No, he had said Baxter. I swallowed my words once again rather than contradict Holmes, contenting myself with a non-committal shrug of the shoulders. The matter was too trifling to be worthy of further consideration. It was best to forget it.

Still Holmes frowned. "I can't understand it," he muttered, as if his very little trip were the most serious matter in the world. "You are right, Watson. But this is unthinkable. It is unprecedented. It has to be explained. Why, consider what this means. If you were right and I was wrong . . . How could that be? I remember now. I said Baxter. Ah, Doctor, Doctor, to read the minds of lesser beings is child's play, but to read one's own – why, that is the real challenge! Especially when you are Sherlock Holmes."

"That is a little arrogant, don't you think?" said I in mild rebuke, for happy though I am to blow Holmes's trumpet, I have always disapproved of his readiness to blow it himself.

"No, no. When one strives to transform oneself into a thinking machine, then one necessarily loses touch with one's more instinctual side. When I introspect, it is only to look outwards. I do not trust myself, you see, and so try to have as little to do with myself as possible. We are barely on speaking terms. Now, though, it is necessary. What could account for that ridiculous slip? Wait a moment, though. Ha, I have it! By God, Doctor, this opens up startling possibilities. Heavens, here is an entire new continent of crime! That one word . . . The ideal reasoner . . . ."

"You mean like the word 'rat' spoken by the dying McCarthy?" I suggested helpfully. "That solved the Boscombe Valley Mystery."

"It did indeed," said Holmes thoughtfully, still probing Venus with his eyes, "though not perhaps in the way you imagine. I could not tell you the truth of course until you had finished scribbling your official account of the so-called mystery, for I would not have you knowingly mislead your future public. And obviously I needed you to sign Turner's confession with a clear conscience just in case it was needed in court. I would not have you perjure yourself. But you did seriously suppose I would have saved the remorseless John Turner from the scaffold after he had widowed and orphaned so many? Did you really fall for that rich man's 'life of martyrdom' act? No, no, the one I spared was worthier of pity, I hope, and that may help to explain what I think I shall call my *Freudian Slip*."

"Your what, Holmes?"

"A joke, Watson, nothing more. Freud was a gentleman I happened to encounter during one of my investigations abroad last year. We exchanged ideas and I recommended he experiment with one or two mind-enhancing drugs to aid him in his researches. I also teased him about his tendency to grow a trifle confused when excited and dubbed his unintentionally amusing linguistic blunders 'Freudian Slips'. We made quite a game of it. Let that pass."

"But if Turner did not murder McCarthy, then who did?"

"The footprints at the scene of the crime were helpful though not conclusive. Still, I thought it best to obliterate them just in case the police had second thoughts."

I confess I was shocked at this and withdrew into incredulity. "Not you, Holmes. You were appalled at the way the police had contaminated the crime scene. You did not do it."

"Actually, I was impressed by how well they had managed to preserve the scene intact a full four days after the murder. Of course, it was important that Lestrade in particular should not object, as I proceeded to desecrate the ground, so I kept up a running commentary while I dashed this way and that, accusing the police of having ruined the crime scene even as I did so myself. Hypocrisy is an undervalued skill, Watson – officially that is – and one I recommend you cultivate."

"But why do so?" I asked, ignoring Holmes's transparent attempts to shock me.

"It was vital that I obliterate the most remarkable tracks of all. Fortunately, the police had discounted those before ever they began to study the site, but it was always possible they might gird their loins to think the unthinkable, even as I was forced to do."

"You are speaking of the footprints that John Turner left?"

Holmes smiled. "Oh, those would indeed have been unique in the annals of crime had they resembled the ones I described to you. What was it I said? Huge strides of a lame man walking on tiptoes? Let me suggest an experiment. The next time you find yourself haunted by ancient memories of your cruelty towards some schoolboy struck about the shins with a wicket, inflicting wounds of the mind that shall never heal, and your phantom limp returns, try walking on tiptoes while taking seven-league boot strides. See how long you can manage that before you fall over. No, I made all that up. The footprints I discovered were of a very different nature. They staggered me for a moment. Then I recalled a precedent and understood who had done that horrid thing. But, of course, I knew the answer in my heart before ever I arrived at the crime scene. I invented evidence to protect the true culprit."

I could not understand why my friend was striving to deceive me so. "But you know that is not true, Holmes. At the very least you could not have been lying about the murder weapon. It had to be that stone you picked up in the wood."

"Nothing of the sort. I had already spotted the stone Turner actually used. Do you recall how I laid down my waterproof and stretched out upon it? That was to conceal the true stone beneath it. By way of misdirection I picked up a perfectly innocent stone that I only showed you once we were safely away from the crime scene. My one aim was to increase Lestrade's exasperation, the better to ensure he would refuse to consider engaging in any further investigations."

How could Holmes be so hypocritical? He was engaging in transparent sophistries. "But your proofs!"

"Which were?"

"The grass growing under the rock."

"There was none. Did you not see me pick it up out of moss? Before you can observe, Watson, first learn to see."

"There was no sign of where it was taken from."

"Proving it had not been taken from elsewhere."

"It corresponded to the injuries."

"So I claimed, but neither you nor I had examined those injuries. And the erroneous conclusions of the examiners were that the skull had been struck repeatedly by a heavy, blunt object. The stone I showed Lestrade was small, light, and jagged."

"There was no sign of any other weapon."

"Have you forgotten the gun with the blunt butt end James McCarthy had left at the crime scene? What was to prevent the murderer from removing any other weapon when they left? And why do you suppose I ridiculed Lestrade for wading out into the pool in search of the murder weapon? I had to justify refusing to do so myself in case it was there."

"But the context!"

"Precisely. The three most important factors to take into account when assessing any finds are location, location, and location. The archaeologist records in minute detail where his discovery is made. The tomb robber works to conceal it. By removing that stone, I instantly destroyed almost all the significance it might have had, which is why I did so." Holmes pointed to a rock below Venus's foot in the painting beside me. "You see that stone? There is a tiny dragon etched upon it holding an apple, or more likely a ring in its mouth. I cannot go into details. Suffice it to say its deeper meaning would be lost forever were that stone to be plucked out of the painting and tossed away. Only be cross-referencing it with other elements in the painting, and by considering what such a depiction of Cupid stung by bees and complaining to Venus would have meant to its original audience, can such a philosopher's stone be made to reveal its secrets? But one criminal investigation at a time, and the Trial of Worms need not concern us here."

I was beginning to suspect Holmes was regretting having permitted me to accompany him on a further adventure. He was afraid I would tell all. It hurt that he imagined I would ever publish an account that would reveal to Turner's daughter Alice her father's darkest secrets as a cold-blooded multiple murderer and a thief. I knew what that would mean. Far less serious revelations in the case of the *Gloria Scott*, Holmes's first ever criminal affair, had left the son of Justice Trevor a broken man forced to flee England to escape the sympathy and scorn of friends. And did Holmes suppose I would be so unchivalrous as to destroy that ravishing beauty's prospects for the sake of good copy? How little he could have known me then!

Still I was determined to make him admit the truth. "That was not the only clue, Holmes. I watched you closely. I saw you gather up tobacco ash from Turner's cigar on the forest floor."

"And did you also see me pick up the cigar stub I later claimed to have found but never produced?"

"Well, no, but you did put that tobacco ash into an envelope. I thought it was dust."

"Did that not strike you as strange?"

"Strange? Why? The last time we worked with Lestrade we found Drebber's corpse in one of the dustiest rooms I have ever encountered. You gathered up tobacco ash I took for dust then too."

"Precisely! Ask yourself how it is that when you saw me perform the exact same procedure you did not at once conclude I was again collecting tobacco ash."

"I'm sorry, Holmes," said I humbly, and as always my features were treacherous servants. I blushed. "I am very stupid."

"No! And then again, yes!" Holmes seemed quite angry at my contrition. "You are stupid indeed to suppose that you could have been so stupid. You are not a fool, Watson. Are you too obtuse to see it? You had every reason to assume it was tobacco ash, and yet once again you concluded it had to be dust. Why did you do that? But do not cudgel your brains about it, for your dull ass will not mend his pace with beating. What colour was it?"

The question surprised me. "Why, it was the colour of tobacco."

"Do try to be precise. What does that mean? 'The colour of tobacco'! "It conveys nothing. It was the dusty shade of brown of your own beloved Arcadian mixture. We were not in Arcadia, though, despite the presence of death that made it a paradise for me. Did it not occur to you to consider that tobacco ash is never the colour of tobacco? Had it been the colour of dust, then it would have been a different matter. If you had troubled to study my monograph on tobacco ashes of the world and the accompanying

111

fifty hand-coloured illustrations, you would have realised that tobacco ash always comes in shades of grey. Light grey ash means high quality tobacco from good, nutrient-rich earth with plentiful deposits of calcium. Priest's black ash means fewer minerals but more potassium. But the dust I picked up was the colour of your tobacco. Therefore, it was not tobacco. It was dust. I don't know why I need to explain this. Had it rained, then perhaps some ash would not have blown away. Since the ground had remained bone dry for four days, it is inconceivable any ash could have remained. It would all have been vanished."

"I trusted you."

"Unforgivable! In that case the fault was entirely yours. Never take anything on trust, Watson. It betrays a lack of faith in the scientific method. Besides, you were most remiss in failing to ask me why I examined the bark of that beech so minutely with my glass."

Holmes had paused and was reconsidering his painting. He seemed particularly intrigued by the hollow apple tree one branch of which Venus was clutching in a suggestive manner. I wondered whether he was examining it for signs that Cupid had been using it for target practice. "I supposed you were looking for scratches where Turner had struck a match upon it. Or wait a minute – Turner was diabetic. That meant he would have urinated freely and frequently."

"Ah, so that was the scent the old sleuthhound was following! And would Turner have lit a match on bark a foot above even my reach? But you are warm. I did not discover just one graze but many. That beech resembled an epileptic drunkard's timepiece. Someone had been coming to that spot day after day to master a very special piece of weaponry. Of course, the conclusion I had been fighting against was becoming ever harder to avoid, to my sorrow. Ah, Watson, I was so sure the rain would come and ruin the scene!"

I thought I had him. "Holmes, you know that is untrue. You rightly predicted there would be no rain! You told me the barometer stood at twenty-nine so there was no need to visit Boscombe Pool until the day after we arrived."

"You really are a repeat offender, Doctor," said he with a solemn shake of the head as he passed this dreadful judgement upon me. "Ah, Petrarch, you were right! '*Who naught suspects is easily deceived.*' Must you persist in believing everything I say? When will you finally realise that everybody lies? Please recall how I excused my refusal to visit the site as soon as we arrived from London."

"Why, your explanation was a good one. You were exhausted after the long train journey from London."

"Most of which I spent reading Petrarch in accordance with my principle that the best rest a man may take from labours is to change from one kind of work to another. And to quote again from the master, '*Continued work and application form my soul's nourishment. So soon as I commenced to rest and relax, I should cease to live.*' Then diagnose and prescribe, Doctor. If sitting quietly and reading had tired me so, what would be the worst remedy once I was out of that train and what the best kind of the rest?"

"Why, Holmes," said I in some surprise, "how could you have been so foolish? The worst thing you could have done was the very thing you did! You insisted on going with Lestrade on yet another tedious train journey to interrogate James McCarthy, who had absolutely declined to reveal his secrets to the police. That must have been uphill work for you. Why did you not think to stretch your legs at the crime scene as you followed the scent?"

"Always the rhetorical questions!" He wagged a cautionary forefinger. "How much better if they were real ones. Were you to ask, then you should receive. I have as good as told you why. I was still hoping against hope that it would rain clowders of cats and cries of hounds to ruin the crime scene before ever we got there."

"But the barometer!"

"Oh, bother the barometer!" swore my friend, or intemperate words to that effect. "You will never make a detective, my friend, so long as you continue to accept statements as authoritative purely on the basis of their authors. Did it not occur to you to check the barometer in the hotel for yourself?"

"You mean it did not stand at twenty-nine?"

"I mean that next to the '*29*', you would have read the word '*Rain*'. Ah, but I am too generous. While I am chiding you, I am neglecting to censure myself. It was cowardice, Watson. I had intuited the truth and I did not wish to confront any evidence that would confirm my apprehension. That was why I still strove so desperately to delay our visit to the crime scene even at the eleventh hour. Why else do you suppose I insisted on visiting McCarthy's home first?"

"But that was essential, Holmes. You had to take the measurements of the shoes he had been wearing on the day he was murdered so you could compare them with the footprints."

"Oh, let us keep flat-footed on the ground! Do you seriously imagine the police sent back the dead man's shoes to his home in case his soul arose to go in search of them? They preserved them as evidence. Moreover, as a matter of routine they took ink impressions of the soles. I daresay you were impressed by how painstakingly I took eight different

113

measurements of each shoe as if for a change I was playing at being Bertillon instead of Bertillon playing at being me. But really, Watson, you must see I was engaging in brazen delaying tactics. Even if the shoes had been the ones McCarthy had been wearing at the time of his death, to record a hundred or a thousand measurements and yet never to think of taking ink impressions of their soles would be like measuring the dimensions of a finger down to the last millimetre without troubling to take a finger mark. No, I was still praying for the rains to come before I had finished there. Have I not said I had already intuited who the killer was? The evidence that the lodge-keeper's daughter, Patience Moran, supplied me with during our visit to the lodge was but further confirmation of their identity."

"She was nowhere to be seen when we visited the lodge."

"That was the further confirmation. And besides, you are incorrect. I saw her hiding in the bushes when we left."

"But how could you have identified the murderer already? You cannot you mean you had solved the case before ever we arrived at Boscombe Valley!"

"Well, that would be an exaggeration. But think of the newspaper reports, which included Patience Moran's testimony to the police. She insisted that on seeing the son James leaning on his gun while shaking his fist at his father in a fury she had at once raced away from Boscombe Pool back to the lodge to summon help. Consider, then, that hardly had the terrified girl begun to babble forth her incoherent account of the altercation than in walked James himself with blood on his right hand and sleeve. You know how I like to rummage about in my mental lumber room for precedents. This time I dug deep. I had been seven at the time. You could say the affair represented my very first case. Not that I was alone. It turned the whole country into armchair detectives. More of that anon. You see the present difficulty? If Patience Moran had rushed straight home as she claimed, then how is it he could have followed her so quickly, given that he claimed he left his father soon after the latter had responded in kind to his raised fist. Had then gone some distance from him only to hear the scream of a man in terrible agony; had returned to find his father dying and struggling to gasp out something about a rat; had waited until certain his father dead. Had remained holding him in his arms for several minutes; and only then had gone to the lodge for a doctor and the police? And yet he arrived there at the same time as the girl! And besides, why on earth head for the lodge-keeper's home at all?"

"Because the lodge was nearer than his home," I suggested sensibly, for every Don Quixote needs his Sancho Panza to point out the obvious from time to time. "The McCarthy's residence was almost a quarter-of-a-mile away. The lodge was not half that. It could not have been much more than a hundred yards away. Surely time was of the essence."

"But the lodge-keeper had no horse and cart as the McCarthys did. The first thing to do was to send for the doctor and police. Why then did he not think to post his groom to Ross to get both? But leave that for the present. James McCarthy claimed he first left his father when the latter responded in kind to his threats and only returned when he heard a scream as of someone being mercilessly beaten to death. Of course, as a doctor you must realise that this could not have been McCarthy, for if he had indeed been struck so savagely on the back of the head he would have been rendered instantly unconscious. Have you ever heard an unconscious man scream? No, Turner himself uttered that shriek after striking McCarthy on the back of his head. He did so to lure the son back. It ensured he would be accused of the murder."

"Perhaps," said I doubtfully. "But Holmes, are you not overlooking an obvious point?" The reader will think it presumptuous of me to have dared to speak thus, yet in concerning himself chiefly with trifles Holmes did occasionally miss the wood for the individual leaf. That proved to be the case when on a later occasion he followed the hoof prints of Silver Blaze out on Dartmoor using his magnifying glass while I relied solely upon the naked eye. I saw as he did not that they doubled back, an observation that saved us a long walk. And so I dared to speak now. "Patience Moran was only fourteen years old. James McCarthy ran faster."

Holmes would have none of it. "We are talking about a near hysterical girl running that hundred yards for dear life and as if from the devil himself. No, no, Doctor. Either James or the girl was lying or they both were. And since everyone lies, the third option is by far the most probable."

Holmes is distressingly cynical but there is nothing to be done about that. It is part of his profession. His is the detective's equivalent of the callousness that enables surgeons to eat ham and eggs in the presence of bloody corpses. I have done so on the battlefield. "Even supposing James lied because of the danger he felt he was in, why suppose that the little girl was lying too?"

"Because she had seen things that she thought it prudent to conceal. Patience had a ringside seat when Turner cracked open Humpty Dumpty's skull, rather as we might do one of Mrs. Hudson's hard-boiled eggs on a morning when she has been engrossed in the latest complimentary issue of your *Holywell Street Journal*. Then the girl saw James McCarthy return. She witnessed his very suspicious behaviour. And it goes without saying she knew who the murderer was."

"But it was Turner! You just said it was."

"I said nothing of the kind."

Was this another of my friend's curious "Freudian Slips"? "Holmes, you know you did. Or are you now saying Turner administered a rock to McCarthy's skull in an attempt at emergency trepanning and to save his life?"

My friend roared with silent laughter. "Ah, Watson, that is splendid. Really imaginative. Not quite. But you are doing so well I hardly think there is any need for me to name the real murderer. You must have deduced it."

"I know who you think it is," said I uncertainly. "Why you imagine it was McCarthy's son James is quite beyond me. John Turner confessed. Circumstantial evidence is one thing, but a full and free confession made by a dying man is quite another."

Holmes snorted. "Dying? Oh, Turner will be dead within a year. I grant you that. But dying? Hardly. He is a dead man walking. The distinction is hardly trivial."

"Speaking as a retired army surgeon I have to say I cannot see the difference. Have you forgotten, Holmes, that even before our arrival he was so sick the police were not even permitted to interview him for a few minutes? And by the time of our encounter his condition had worsened to the point where he was clearly on his deathbed."

Holmes gave me his plate-glass penetrating look. "Watson, would you say that I am a cruel man?"

I felt a little embarrassed. "Not cruel, Holmes, not actually cruel. Perhaps a little lacking in humanity from time to time."

"Hmm. Humanity. Humanity is overrated. Nor was that my question. Do you seriously suppose that if I believed he might die at any time I would have sent him a note peremptorily instructing him to pick up his bed and walk? Why did I not go to his home to speak to him there?"

"But you explained that. It would have led to gossip."

Holmes assessed me with keen interest. He seemed to be deciding how best to explain something so obvious to him that he found my incomprehension quite incomprehensible. "Hmm. Let me put it in terms you should understand. A man lies dying on a battlefield. As an army surgeon, you can either go to him or send him a message ordering him to crawl to you, though he might die before he reaches you. The reason you need to speak with him is because there have been several cases of venereal disease and you believe he is responsible for them. Do you then demand he comes to you so as to ensure there is no gossip?"

"Of course not. But that is hardly the same thing, Holmes. You had no excuse for visiting Turner."

"The police wished to interview him and were unable to. I was associated with the investigation. I had promised his daughter Alice Turner I would keep her informed of developments, so I should have visited her anyway. What more natural than that I should also ask to speak with him while there? But to have commanded a dying man to leave his room at the risk of his life to attend a private meeting with a detective investigating the murder of his neighbour? That would indeed have caused precisely the talk I claimed to be so anxious to avoid. Do you not see? It was not he I needed to speak with. It was Patience Moran."

"But you never did speak to her."

"Oh, yes I did. Do you not recall that I left you for ten minutes while I popped back into the lodge a second time? You remember why I did so?"

"You said it was to have a word with Moran and to leave a note."

"Which Moran?" asked Holmes innocently.

"Why, that is obvious," said I in some irritation. "Since you had a note for Moran the lodge keeper to take up to Turner, it had to be he you spoke to."

"That was what I had intended you to deduce. Never tell a straight lie when you can equivocate, Watson. Plausible deniability is always worth the extra effort. I sent the father away with that note instructing Turner concerning the scene we were to play in your presence, unless of course he wished to stand trial for several murders committed in the Australian bush and one or two minor jobs in England's green and pleasant land. Efficient assassins are always in demand. Once the father was off on his errand, I summoned forth Patience out of the bushes and persuaded her to reveal what she had actually witnessed at the time of the murder. She saw everything."

"Well, I can see why you needed to send Moran off, so as to speak with the daughter alone. You thought she might be shielding him. But you still have not explained what you meant when you said Turner was no dying man and yet would be dead within a year. It is a very peculiar diagnosis."

"It is a question of atmospheric pressure. An east wind is coming."

"And you think it will bring rain?"

Holmes sighed. "Don't be obtuse, Watson. Turner boasted his slaughter sprees are still spoken of in Australia. He treated killing as a game and the more crosses he notched on his rifle the higher rose his prestige in the Australian underworld. Think of all those grieving widows and orphans he left with a burning dream of revenge. The death of McCarthy has made the front page in that continent, which I may require you to visit soon on a little errand.

117

"Naturally a description of McCarthy's colossal Australian neighbour and benefactor Turner was included, and those with good reason to hate the murderer Black Jack will have apprehended this is he. The shadow of death shall fall upon Boscombe Valley. One avenger may fail, but another will come, and yet another, until someday justice will be done – that is as certain as tomorrow's red dawn. One does not need to consult the barometer to predict a storm long overdue."

"And his confession?" I was still not convinced Turner was acting.

"Oh, that," said he with a dismissive wave of the hand such I once saw him make at a concert to the annoyance of the conductor. "Never take account of confessions when made outside of the confessional. I have devised a portable one that has done me good service. As for any other pieces of circumstantial evidence, including those we spoke of earlier, the Australians have a word for the manner in which such so-called evidence can rebound. Surely you have not forgotten so soon that when James arrived at the lodge, he had blood on his right sleeve and hand?"

"But Holmes," I protested feebly, "Turner was struck on the left side of his skull! The posterior third of the left parietal bone and the left half of the occipital bone," I added more confidently, feeling I was in my professional element. "Surely that means the blow had to have been delivered by a left-handed man."

"It means nothing of the sort, doctor," said he sternly. "To begin with, you have ignored the possibility McCarthy was turning away when the blow was delivered."

"Was he?"

"No. He was on the ground. That made it much easier for the old and enfeebled Turner to bring the stone down upon the wound with all the strength he could muster and using both hands. He could never have smashed the skull otherwise. But the fact that there was blood on McCarthy's right sleeve and hand is of the greatest import. I might almost say it is final."

"To prove his innocence!"

Holmes blew a beautiful blue smoke ring from his Viennese cigar straight into the face of the painted Venus, who seemed determined to persist in her futile attempts to woo a stone-hearted Pygmalion. "Well, to begin with, it means James McCarthy's claim that he held his dead dad in his arms for some minutes before he thought to seek a second opinion was a straight lie. You have to see that. The skull had been completely smashed in and blood was gushing forth. How was it, then, that there was no blood on the son save for his right sleeve and hand? Obviously, he had used his other hand to smear blood there precisely because the wound to the skull was on the left. It was a clumsy attempt to guarantee he would not be

118

suspected of the murder. He knew he had been seen following his father earlier with a gun in his hand. His exasperation with his father must have been well known locally. He had to be the prime suspect."

My friend reads too much sensational literature and it sometimes results in wild flights of fancy. "Oh, come now, Holmes, this is too much! Surely you must see that if he had acted as you described then there would have been blood on both hands."

"You are forgetting that nondescript grey cloth he observed lying twelve paces to his left as he knelt beside his dying father."

"What, you mean he used it to wipe away the blood on his left hand?"

Holmes groaned as if in pain. "Of course not. When next he glanced over, it was gone. Someone had removed it. Well, that is not quite correct, but let it pass as a working approximation to the truth for the present. Now, if it was a little to the left of the son, you may readily perceive it would have taken a Washo hunter or myself to remove it without his being aware of the theft. Let us assume neither was available. In that case, it could not have been where he said it was at the time of its removal. It was no longer on his left, but *behind* him."

Holmes waited. I tried looking lost but on this occasion that did not satisfy him. "Oh, come, Watson. Have you forgotten your shaving mirror?"

"My what, Holmes?"

"Ah. He has. Do you not recall how soon after we first met I deduced the window in your hotel bedroom had been on the right?"

I felt my chin in some embarrassment, for Holmes had guessed at its location from the fact that one side was less well-shaven than the other, though I could not now recall which.

"Oh, do stop stroking your chin, Watson," said he impatiently. "Surely you must realise now that 'on the right' was a meaningless observation since I did not say on the right of what. Do you see? McCarthy said the body was on his left, and so it was at first. But then he moved. He had his back to it when it vanished."

"But what makes you think he moved?"

"Is it possible? You really don't know? Have I not said just this second why? Perhaps not in so many words, but we were speaking of the blood on his right hand applied using his left. He had to go to the pool to splash the left hand about in the water to wash it clean of blood. Obviously, he could not use his right hand to help him do this since that had to remain bloody. While he was absorbed in his task, the long grey travelling-cloak, or whatever it may have been, got up and left. He could not hear the sound of the running feet over that of running water."

"And you think Turner removed his cloak to ensure there would be no evidence McCarthy was not the killer."

"No, though he certainly grasped with both hands that heaven sent opportunity to kill two birds with one stone, the better to save a third from a fate worse than death. He would slip a hangman's noose around James McCarthy's neck as the only way to prevent the knot eternal binding Alice to James. Forget the cloak for the present. You see now why Turner administered that superfluous blow to the skull of the dying McCarthy? His highest priority was to ensure his daughter was not suspected of the murder by concealing the true nature of the first and fatal wound."

All the time he was speaking, Holmes was contemplating his teenaged Venus, who had evidently conceived the infant Cupid by her side at the earliest possible opportunity. While she was stroking a branch beneath her left foot, her left hand was still clutching an overhead bough, tipped with a pair of golden apples. She might be about to break it off, and I thought for once I could follow Holmes's own unspoken thoughts. "Do you really think Alice Turner would have had the strength to kill McCarthy, and in so brutal a manner? You imagine, perhaps, she broke off a branch from that beech you examined so carefully and struck him with it?

"Why Watson, that is very good. You have perceived my methods, though you do not yet know how to apply them. I was indeed contemplating Venus as the *belle dame sans merci par excellence*. You know she was born out of the foam released into the waters off Cyprus when Uranus was castrated and his testicles cast into the sea. That golden bough she could so easily break away is meant to remind us of her origins and her true nature. What is it Petrarch says? '*Rarely do great beauty and great virtue dwell together.*' But I take your point and your objection is a pertinent one. How could a young girl have slain McCarthy when she could hardly have reached up to where the wound was made? That argues for a very curious piece of weaponry. You recall the findings of the inquest? The wound had been the result of repeated and savage blows delivered by some heavy and blunt object. Then they changed their minds and decided it had been a single clout. Why were they so confused? Because they never considered the possibility that the obvious damage done was incidental and intended to cover up the immediate cause of his death. They failed to see the truth because they had never seen anything like his wound before. Mark that, Watson. It is why Turner was convinced only his daughter could have been responsible for it."

"Then how did he die?"

"Need you ask? Did not McCarthy tell us? Do you not remember? He did so with his last gasp."

"All he said was '*a rat*'."

"That is what his well-educated son thought he said. You are forgetting that James was raised in this country, while the father hailed from Australia. He spoke with a strong Australian accent, and the son automatically translated what he seemed to be saying accordingly. Australians tend to change '*a*' into '*eh*'. McCarthy actually said '*e rit*', so the son supposed he meant '*a rat*'. It did not occur to him that he really had said '*e rit*'. But what could he have meant by that? Any ideas, doctor?"

I thought of an article I had been reading on Clousseau's Syndrome, a rare condition resulting from damage to the linguistic centre of the brain. "If it was a crime of passion, he might have been trying to say so. If the blow to the head had impaired his speech, then the words he was trying to speak could have come out garbled. He said that he had been killed in *a rit of fealous jage*. Of course he meant *a fit of jealous rage*."

Holmes looked very serious as a dignified man might do who feels it his duty not to laugh.

"Well," said I irritably, "You have not convinced me he was not trying to name Turner as the murderer."

"Then why did he not do so? Why try to say 'Black Jack of Ballarat', which would have meant nothing to anyone in England? But he could not name the killer. He did not know who it was. All he knew for sure was the weapon used to kill him and that was what he was trying to name."

"I am cudgelling my brains, Holmes, but I can think of none."

"You do not have my specialist knowledge. And besides, we must also take into account McCarthy's ancestry on his mother's side. That you can deduce from Turner's account of how he had intended to blow McCarthy's brains out when he and his gang of murderers ambushed a gold convoy and killed all save for him. Does that not strike you as curious?"

"Hardly, Holmes. Turner explained to us he was a good man at heart who had had the misfortune to fall into bad company."

"Ah, the old, old story," sighed my modern Diogenes through twisted lips. "The boy with a heart of gold misled by others. I believe the same was said of Jonathan Wild. I'll wager there was not a mother's son in that bloody gang who did not blame all the others as the bad company that corrupted him alone. Are you not overlooking one crucial fact? How was it that McCarthy was later able to identify a man he had seen only briefly many years before?"

The face of the dead Enoch J. Drebber came to me as if I had seen it only yesterday. Never shall I forget those features twisted into a demonic mask of hatred and fear. "There are some things that remain with you for the whole of your life, Holmes." Now the face of Drebber was replaced by

121

that of the Afghan Joan of Arc Malalai that I had glimpsed for a second at Maiwand, waving the veil she had torn from her face as a banner. A strange enigma is woman! It was her bullet that shattered the bone in my shoulder.

"Stop reminiscing, Watson," said he sternly. I realised I had been hugging the area where the bullet had struck. "Again you are wildly off target. He knew Turner's face because that murderer did not bother to wear a mask. Why not? Because he never took prisoners. And yet he claimed he saw McCarthy, who must have feared he would receive a bullet through his brains in the next second, only intent upon memorising the features of the last face he might ever see, presumably with the intention of giving evidence when his assassin was tried at a higher court than the Assizes. How absurd. McCarthy was searching that cruel face for a sign of humanity and finding none. Turner did not hold his hand. It was held back by another, most likely one who felt a special kinship with McCarthy and understood the murderous hatred Turner felt towards their race. You recall Turner's description of McCarthy?"

"It was rather vague. He only told us he had the face of a devil."

"That is enough. Trying seeing McCarthy through the eyes of John Turner, whom I may tell you was descended from transported convicts and was desperate to play the gentleman. Why do you think he was so very determined his daughter should never marry the man she loved? It was because of James McCarthy's bad blood. Is it not obvious? James's grandmother was an Aboriginal Australian, and in this cold-blooded killer's view, that meant James was barely human."

I was appalled at such prejudice, for I have always regarded the primary aim and justification of our great Empire is to spread civilisation about the globe. We should not hate savages, but treat them kindly and help them as one would children to become men. All they need is organisation. "But how does that help us to identify the weapon?"

"You almost hit upon that when you supposed the killer broke off a branch from that beech tree I studied so narrowly through my glass. You forget, though, that it was not the *branches* I scrutinised, but the *bark*. I told you, I found ample evidence of damage caused by some weapon. You disbelieved me because still convinced the fatal wound was inflicted using a stone. I say again McCarthy's cry of '*e rit*' was his attempt to name the true weapon. Have you never –" And here he bent forwards and lowered his voice. " – have you never heard of the *boomerit*?"

"I never have."

"Not even under its other name? McCarthy was using an Aboriginal Australian's term for a quite unique weapon. For years I have been aware of its existence, though I have never before had an opportunity of handling one. It is fast, silent, invisible in motion, and of tremendous power. They

122

use it to take down kangaroos. There are two types, the hunting and the returning boomerits. In this case the hunting variety was used, which means it had to be retrieved, and that was why the murderer was forced to venture forth out of the wood. Unfortunately, first Turner, and then James McCarthy returned there, and the murderer was forced to take cover."

"Take cover? But how could they? They could not have hidden amidst the reeds unless . . . Why, I think I see. They were underwater and using a reed to breathe through!"

Holmes clapped his hands with delight. "Splendid! You should patent that. Ah, but you are too late. That was how Scyllis was said to have cut loose the ships of Xerxes" fleet. Besides, it is quite impossible. I have tried it. But do remember to introduce it into one of your fairy tales before anyone else does. As for their concealment, you are forgetting that grey clothing."

It was my turn to laugh. "But you are joking! Alice Turner was not that tall, I grant you, for all that she was a veritable Aphrodite. I have rarely seen so perfect a figure. Yet not even she could have concealed herself beneath that travelling cloak or whatever it was without McCarthy realising someone had to be under it."

"Perfectly correct. However, it was not she who was concealed there. And besides, you have made certain assumptions that prevent you from seeing the truth."

"What assumptions, Holmes? I have made none."

"Oh, yes you have. You suppose the clothing was owned by the murderer and recovered lest it lead to their identification. But that could not have been the case."

"Why not?"

"I would not insult your intelligence by explaining. You must see that the murderer expected James McCarthy to leap up at any moment to race off and fetch both a doctor and the police. The son would hardly have wasted time searching for clues, nor would he have burdened himself with them as he ran for assistance, since his beloved father's life hung by a thread. Having reasoned thus the murderer would have waited until the son had left, and only then would they have collected the clothing. The idea that they would have risked being seen by James for the sake of that piece of cloth is patently ridiculous. I hardly need to explain all that to you, Watson."

I was flattered that Holmes had allowed me to work this all out for myself. However, whilst I have always revered Holmes as my master when it comes to pure logic, in the realm of common sense I am his. "What is the use in arguing they could not have recovered it when we know they did? It is like proving God does not exist after one has died and is standing before him."

Holmes did not answer at once and I supposed he was struggling to accept the truth of what I said. He diverted himself with scanning the painting yet again, as if it might supply some counter argument. It occurred to me quite irrelevantly that if he had been Job on his dunghill and God had spoken out of a whirlwind, then Holmes would have replied "I accuse *you!*" and God himself would have been stunned into silence. Indeed, in accordance with the principle that the least likely suspect is often the guilty party, Holmes would be quite capable of deducing that God was responsible for the snake in the garden that introduced death into Eden. When he finally spoke, it confirmed he had entirely missed my point.

"You are wrong, Watson. I have proved that the clothing was not recovered. It is equally certain it did not belong to the murderer but to the murdered man. That is beyond all doubt."

I proved Holmes wrong. I dared to doubt it. "It could not have done! The son would certainly have recognised it as his father's."

"Not if McCarthy had purchased it during the three days while James was away seeing his secret wife in Bristol."

"But you have no proof that McCarthy did so."

"You forget, Watson, that the son was seen following his father within sight of him, yet he claimed he had no idea it was he. He may of course have been deceiving himself, but such a deception would not have been plausible had the father been dressed in clothes well known to the son."

"But James saw his father setting off for his rendezvous at Boscombe Pool! He must at least have noticed that he was dressed in grey."

"Not if only the lining was that colour. The lining was all he saw at Boscombe Pool."

Holmes can be truly infuriating. Sometimes I see him as a modern Socrates, but at others he seems to me to be like those sophists Socrates condemned whose one aim is to win every argument. "If the clothing did not belong to the murderer then why would he run the risk of removing it?"

"They did not. They were only intent upon removing themselves. When McCarthy first returned to the scene, the only thing that concerned him was the figure of his dying father. He hardly registered the presence of that clothing, though it is true that if even a small-sized woman had been hiding beneath it, he would have sensed it. But this person was even smaller than that. Nevertheless, the chances were still high that the son would think to investigate it eventually. Therefore, when he went to the pool's edge to wash his left hand, they seized their chance to escape."

"But why take the clothing with them?"

"I have already said they were not recovering the clothing. It follows that the clothing was recovering them. They concealed themselves beneath it as they fled in case he should look up." Holmes pointed towards Venus in her Duchess of Devonshire hat. "You see those twelve balled ostrich feathers like the constellations orbiting about Draco the Dragon? Think of the proverbial ostrich with her head in the sand. If she cannot see you, then you cannot see her. It was the same principle."

"That seems a little childish."

"Out of the mouths of babes! Childish is exactly what it was. But then what can you expect from children?"

"But Alice Turner was eighteen. I would hardly call her a child."

"Quite right. But then I never said she was the murderer. I only said Turner *assumed* it had to be her, as he imagined nobody else in Boscombe Valley knew how to use a boomerang, as it is now called. He was mistaken. I confirmed that was the case when I revisited the home of the Morans. An Australian household, Watson. My instinct felt the presence of those weapons upon the wall before my eyes ever saw them. I applied the Sung T'zu Test by unbottling some flies, which instantly settled on one of three boomerangs displayed there. The blood sang out, if you will excuse an Anglo-French pun."

I did excuse it. I had no idea what it could be. "You mean Moran was the killer? And the daughter was shielding him?"

Holmes has the maddening habit of changing the subject just when he seems about to get to the point. One moment he might be discussing the true identity of a corpse and the next he has passed on to a consideration of Wallis's *The Death of Chatterton.* Then the only question to be asked is why the writer George Meredith modelled for the face of a dead forger. My heart sank as I saw him once again pointedly perusing the painting of Venus and Cupid. Sure enough, when he spoke, I had to resign myself to yet another pointless digression.

"Observe that tree, Watson. It bears twenty-four apples, and yet consider it more carefully. There is a hive there in the hollow heart of it. Fruitful and yet rotten, you see, like a honey-sweet but diseased courtesan with a heart of stone. Venus is that tree. As you have no doubt noted, Doctor, she must have grown pregnant at the first conceivable opportunity and discarded her child the instant he was discharged. He has been bawling his head off in moral outrage that the bees dare to sting him. It never occurs to him to let go of the stolen honeycomb. A fallen Adam, you see, who continues to clutch the forbidden fruit. But his father was the sheep thief Mercury, so like father like son. First viewers of this work would have understood it related to the Diet of Worms of 1521."

I saw that although Holmes had changed the subject it was only to pass from one trial to another. It was better to let him run his course. "You mean the trial of Luther for heresy."

"No, that was not the trial I had in mind. Some bees had stung a child to death in Worms. They were condemned as heretics to be burnt in the town square. If Luther witnessed the sentence being carried out, he might have paused to consider that there, but for the grace of God, went he. It would also have occurred to him that man plays the martyr like Cupid here as one more sinned against than sinning, just like our friend Turner declaring he has led a life of martyrdom as one compassed about by diabolical buzzers. And why? In Turner's case, it was because instead of confessing his sins, he preferred to be blackmailed in perpetuity. Contrast that with the case of Constance Kent. Well, perhaps that was before your time. Ah, Watson, what tricks fate plays on such worms as these! I call them worms, for the medieval bestiaries classified wasps and bees as such. Bees are so much better than men. Their struggle is the nobler. I have a theory I am still evolving, Watson, that mankind is a tree whose roots are thoroughly diseased. No matter how good any of the branches may be, they can turn rotten at any time. Think of how syphilis, which was once called Job's Disease, can be inherited by the most pious of men and communicated from them in turn to their children. The Morans may well be damned in that matter. Patience Moran's father was with Turner in Australia, of course. It could not have been otherwise, for he is Turner's first line of defence against the day avengers come knocking."

I saw a way out of the labyrinth and back into the wood by Boscombe Pool. "Mr. Moran had been playing with Turner's daughter, teaching her how to use the boomerang!"

"Near, Watson. You have almost apprehended Turner's mistake. With his strong prejudices, he was determined his daughter would only move in the best circles, and so he forbade her to wed James McCarthy. He would not permit her to have anything to do with their inferiors as he saw them. She had to meet any friends unworthy of her in his eyes in absolute secrecy. They did so in the wood, and there they achieved a complete mastery of the art of the boomerang. They love each other and hated McCarthy for his treatment of the Turners. It was a Biblical hatred. They hated him with a perfect hate."

"Holmes," I said, "I see at last the direction of all your indirect ways. You are as devious as a boomerang! The Moran who murdered McCarthy was not the father. The true culprit is – "

"Patience! Have patience, my friend." He raised a long and solemn finger to thin pursed lips. I could not comprehend why he was so intent upon protecting the killer.

126

"Surely, Holmes, if as you say those who lack the grace of God are predestined for villainy, is it not criminal to permit them to remain at large? Surely this person will rise from crime to crime until they end up on the gallows. How can you take such a risk?"

"Baxter."

"Beg pardon?"

"As should we all. Baxter. That one word tells us a whole story."

"I am sorry, Holmes, but theology is a closed book to me," said I meekly. "My understanding of sin is as imperfect as it is of crime. I know Baxter believed there are some who are beyond redemption and destined from birth for the pit. So I understand your 'Freudian Slip' in misattributing words of Bradford to Baxter, if that idea was what you were preoccupied with. But would that not argue against allowing the girl to remain at large? Is she not predestined for a life of sin?"

"You misunderstand. That was not the reason for my Freudian Slip. My mind went back to the first criminal investigation I ever attempted and at the tender age of seven. You recall the Road Hill House murder of 1861?"

"I glanced at Stapleton's account of it. The girl Constance Kent brutally slew her infant stepbrother. It could not be proven. A few years later she unexpectedly and voluntarily confessed. I believe she is still serving her sentence."

"She is due to be released next month. As part of my investigation into this present affair, I visited her in prison, and we had a little chat. She confided in me concerning her childhood and said something that stuck in my mind. Can you guess what it was?"

"I would not try, Holmes. Guessing is a filthy habit."

"Bravo! She said she tried to be religious in her youth, but on reading Baxter became convinced she was damned as one without the grace of God. Like Shakespeare's *Richard III*, she was '*determined to be a villain*'. Richard, you know, squared life's endless circle of misery and violence and fear. He reconciled free will and predestination by means of a splendid pun. It was predetermined by the great Author of us all he would be without the grace of God, and so the villain of the play. He cheerfully embraced his fate – not out of resignation but as an act of self-assertion. Thinking a comedy what seemed to others to be a tragedy he became its all-licensed fool. Constance made a like choice, read up on cases of famous murderers, even as I was doing the same. Like Richard she was determined to become the best villain she could be."

"And you believe Baxter was right?"

"Oh, he poisoned her with his books just as some suppose De Quincey did me with his."

127

"What, his *Confessions of an Opium Eater*?"

"That, and *On Murder Considered as One of the Fine Arts*, But to answer your question: Thanks to Constance Kent, I now know that he was wrong. Having spoken with her, I am convinced anyone may turn back to the good, including the present unnamed party. By the way, I have prescribed Constance a long sea voyage to Australia, there to start a new life. It is a scientific experiment, actually, to determine whether nature and nurture can indeed be countered even at the eleventh hour. Will you go with her, Doctor, to make sure she settles in and also to observe her initial progress? The air and scenery are perfect. You have been looking a little pale lately. I think the change would do you good."

He had laid his hand on my shoulder. How could I refuse? "Willingly, Holmes. I confess, Turner's tales of Ballarat have quite whetted my appetite. I would quite like to be a gold digger."

"When you return, you can reminiscence on experiences in yet another separate continent," said he with a wink and a knowing smile that probably concealed his secret annoyance. It was not my fault that my present editors preferred my adventures to his. I gently ventured to point that out to him. "And besides, Holmes, I could hardly put a tale like this one into print. Alice Turner would recognise herself in the story, and you rightly wish her never to know the truth about her father."

Holmes swatted the difficulty away. "That is not a problem. Simply muddy the waters a little with a few misleading claims. Include an opening passage that would seem to date it to several years hence, and finish with a few lines implying the case closed less than a year before publication. Let me see. Yes, this will do . . . ."

> *Turner lived for seven months after our interview, but he is now dead; and there is every prospect that the son and daughter may come to live happily together, in ignorance of the black cloud which rests upon their past.*

Rembrandt – *"Belshazzar's Feast"*

The Adventure of the
Writing on the Wall

Continuing "The Five Orange Pips"

"**W**hat will you do, then?'"

"Oh, I have my hand upon him. He and the two mates are, as I learn, the only native-born Americans in the ship. I know also that they were all three away from the ship last night. I had it from the stevedore, who has been loading their cargo. By the time their sailing ship reaches Savannah, the mail-boat will have carried this letter, and the cable will have informed the police of Savannah that these three gentlemen are badly wanted here upon a charge of murder."

"But if he receives the pips from you upon his arrival at Savannah, will he not set sail at once? And besides, Holmes, do you have anything more than the most circumstantial evidence they had anything whatsoever to do with John Openshaw's murder? They could hardly be arrested on the grounds that they were all Americans and in London on the night of the murder."

Holmes did not appear to be listening to me, but rather to some sound undetectable to my ears, like a hound that has heard its prey and is deaf to all else. He held up a hand that might have modelled for a medieval saint's, so long and white were the fingers, to signal silence. Then with the bound of a tiger to a monkey as it starts to scramble up a tree, he was at the chimney and had his head up the fireplace. He emerged with soot on his face. Sensing my amusement, he gave me a black look.

"Thank you, Watson, but I am aware of that. Are you aware of the significance of it? The sweep dislodged the soot as he scrambled up and out."

"Sweep? What sweep?"

"The one you only thought you imagined you heard sobbing."

"Holmes!" I cried. "You are a mind reader!"

"It was perfectly simple. You were reading Clark Russell's new novel *The Dead Ship*. You had earlier praised his likening of a tempest to tortured children shrieking. In that pleasant state in which fact and fiction become indistinguishable, you could no longer separate the howling of the wind in Baker Street from Russell's description of a storm at sea. Naturally you assumed that the sobbing of the child in the chimney was nothing but the wind. But I am not the only one to employ street Arabs. They make splendid eavesdroppers."

This was the cocaine speaking. My best bedside manner was called for. "Doubtless you think the Ku Klux Klan mean to know your plans. But surely if that was their intention, there would be less outlandish means to learn them. Could they not have bribed that new maid of yours to listen at the door?"

At that instant I heard a curious scurrying off from outside our door as of a Giant Rat from Sumatra.

"She leaves tonight," said Holmes indifferently. "Of course, she was only installed so that I might discover her and thenceforth think myself safe. No, no, it was the sweep who was the real spy. We may speak freely now. I can tell you the truth."

"The truth?" I echoed stupidly. "But Holmes, you have already told me the truth. John Openshaw was murdered by the Klan like his father and uncle before him because they were desperate to recover incriminating material. What could be clearer than that?"

"You know, Watson," said he, considering me through one of his smoke rings as if it were his magnifying glass, "that I have been likened by Lestrade to Don Quixote. That makes you my Sancho Panza, striving to keep my feet upon the ground. The truth is in keeping hold of my feet you are sometimes swept away yourself. You swallow my fairy tales whole, my good fellow. You must see that the tale I told you is hardly credible."

"I think I am reasonably sceptical, Holmes," said I defensively. "Have I not just pointed out to you that by sending this Captain James Caldwell Calhoun of the *Lone Star* the five orange pips, you were sportingly giving him fair warning that the police will come calling to ask him questions? And have I not said they could do no more than that? All you have against him and two of his crew is that they were not on board the vessel on the night of the murder, but then how many of the crew would not have been on shore leave? You say that one dock worker you questioned thought that those three crew members were not on the ship. He could only have been so sure because it was practically deserted, for he could not have known them personally. I think that shows quite a critical turn of mind."

Holmes shrugged his shoulders. "Well, it hardly matters now. By now the *Lone Star* has in all likelihood been blown at the moon."

I felt a cold shudder go down my spine. "You speak as if your hand were God's, Holmes," said I reprovingly. "You cannot prophecy such an act of God."

"Oh, God shall have nothing to do with it," said he with a grim smile. "No, Watson, you need not fear. It is not I who have arranged it. Really, it ought to be perfectly obvious who has planted an infernal device on board

132

the vessel. You practically deduced as much for yourself the moment John Openshaw walked into our sitting-room."

"I cannot recall making any such deductions," said I with a smile that had nothing to do with the compliment he had paid me and that I had no doubt he would presently withdraw. I was pleased that Holmes should refer to it as *our* sitting-room, despite the fact I was only there for a few days while my wife was away on her spiritualist course refining her mediumistic skills.

"Why, my dear Watson, you do yourself an injustice. Did you not very shrewdly observe on seeing our visitor enter in a shining waterproof and with his umbrella dripping that it was raining outside? Admittedly the sound of the rain beating against our window and the howling of the equinoctial winds were additional clues that you might have picked up on earlier, but it is better to learn wisdom late than not at all. You doubtless noted too that he had no hat upon his head, for of course it must have blown away during his walk from the station, must it not?"

"As a matter of fact, I did," said I diffidently, for I was beginning to suspect Holmes was being sarcastic.

"And very astute too. One thing puzzles me, though. Given his terror of sudden assassination, why did he not take a cab rather than risk a sudden stab in the back?"

"He could have read in the papers of the Jefferson Hope affair. For that matter he may have read my serialised account of it in my *Baker Street Journal*, or the reprint in *Beeton's Christmas Annual*. For all he knew, the assassins might have done too and thought to copy Jefferson Hope's trick of turning cabbie. Holmes, I know that my deductions cannot compete with yours. I was filled with admiration when you perceived he had come from the south-west based on the chalk and clay upon his shoes. I did not do so very badly, though, and I would appreciate it if you could be a little less sarcastic about my thinking, what was doubtless all too obvious to you."

Holmes nodded his head seriously enough, which was about as close to an apology as he was capable of getting. "I accept your rebuke, Watson, for the fact that your elementary deductions happened to be wrong cannot excuse me. My own were as wide of the mark."

"How do you mean?"

"Why, he had to have smeared his shoes with that chalk and clay mixture just before he stepped out of his cab. He could not have walked here, for then the rain would have washed it off and it would quickly have been replaced by what we delicately identify as London mud. I have written a trifling monograph on the subject complete with a hundred-and-forty hand-coloured illustrations and accompanying cards of my own invention. Scratch the card and sniff facsimile scents of the cesspool's various precincts. I am particularly proud of the one for the House of Lords."

"You mean of the tweed soaked in urine during the dyeing process?"

"That may be the cause. Or that could be the excuse to conceal the incontinence of their Lordships. A reminder of mortality, Watson. Luther stressed his inspiration that the righteous are justified by faith alone came to him while he was on the toilet, thus making of himself a Job on his dunghill complaining to God that he had done nothing to deserve this. This is Luther's point. We complain about dunghills of our own making."

Holmes can be a fascinating conversationalist when he chooses, but he does tend to flit from subject to subject with the bewildering rapidity of an electric butterfly. Normally I edit out his digressions, but have thought it best just this once to give my more discerning readers a taste of what it was actually like to pantingly follow his labyrinthine speech. I seriously doubted, though, that the context of Luther's revelation concerning predestination and the nature of God's grace were entirely relevant to the subject under discussion. I steered him back to it. "But what of the streaming umbrella and the state of his waterproof?"

"Why, obviously the fact that it was dripping proves he came by taxi. You must see that."

"But it could only have been so wet because he had been walking for some time in the downpour."

"In an equinoctial gale? He could not possibly have unfurled it. There is a drainpipe outside our window, and I could hear its stream discharging down to the gutter. The sound transformed itself into a pattering for some seconds after Openshaw rang our bell. The reason was clear. He had unfurled his umbrella and was it directly beneath the end of the drainpipe. It was obtuse of me not to have understood that at once. It was only when he claimed to have come from Horsham that I realised he had gone to some pains to convince me that this was so. Horsham has no chalk and clay soil. He was anxious to conceal his less recent arrival in London, for he needed to perform a task of the utmost significance. I have already said what that task was. No? Ah, you heard but did not heed. Later. For the present it is enough to note he would not permit the maid to take his waterproof or his umbrella. He was anxious to enter 221b playing the part of a man who has just swum heroically against the current of the gale foot by painful foot down Baker Street's sheer pavement."

I was deeply troubled. "Good gracious, Holmes. If what you say is true, then how can we trust anything he said?"

"Oh, I never did trust him," said he indifferently. Then he frowned. "That is not the problem. I chide myself for failing to distrust myself. You observed of course that I turned my lamp towards where Openshaw would sit, the better to half-blind him when he did so?"

"So that you might observe him, no doubt," said I shrewdly. "Or so that he could not observe you."

Holmes flashed me a rare look of approval. "There you have it!" he cried. "But what light did it cast upon myself that I should resort to such underhand tactics? You know my methods, Watson. When I wish to enter into the mind of a character, I attempt to become him. You recall what I had been doing when the bell rang?"

"You were moodily cross-indexing your records of crime."

"Not exactly. Say rather that I was attempting to determine the nature and extent of a spider's web that may or may not exist. There are plenty of threads, you understand, but though they brush against my face I cannot get any of them into my hand. Now, you may recall my mentioning that the lately disgraced ex-Professor Moriarty happened to be irresistibly drained into my beloved cesspool just at the moment we were absent investigating that trifling business of the engineer's thumb last month. The man is a spent force and is unworthy of further consideration. Nature abhors a vacuum, though, and some successor is bound to arise to take his place. I begin to feel such a presence. Since I have no idea yet who it could be I was striving instead to enter into the character of the man most likely to have mentored a new mastermind. I gather Moriarty has opened an establishment pretentiously named the Army Medical School with his former right-hand man, Colonel Moran, nominally to cram those taking examinations. In reality, it is training the next generation of criminals."

"But what has that to do with your turning the lamp to shine into Openshaw's eyes?"

"Goodness, but you are so dull today! Have you already forgotten the Birlstone business? By a curious chance I was considering the disputed drowning of Birdy Edwards off St. Helena when the bell rang. I believe you have serialised his tragedy in *Dr. Watson's Baker Street Journal* as 'The Adventure of the Walk through the Valley of the Shadow of Death'?"

I nodded, making a mental note that should I ever managed to reprint it I would shorten the title.

"At that moment I was in character as Moriarty. I had absorbed his habits. That was why I turned the lamp away from myself and towards the visitor, and so made myself the inquisitor and he the one to be quizzed. You see why I cannot trust myself? Since my thoughts were running on the Professor, as I shall continue to call him in deference to his standing among those who cannot forget his former greatness in the criminal underworld, it was inevitable that I would engage in a piece of wishful thinking. I rang an alarm bell in my brain and cried wolf in my sleep. I told

135

myself here he was at work once again. But I must accept that he belongs to the past and that the great age of crime is over." He gazed gloomily into the flames he claimed had been overheating the behind of some unhappy little sweep.

I shook my head back and forth violently to dispel the idea that the wind in the chimney really was a sad urchin roasting over an open fire. "Then you must confess that your scepticism concerning Openshaw could be wishful thinking too."

Holmes shook his own head as if to rid himself of so dangerous a thought as Openshaw might have shaken his umbrella before entering 221b but didn't. "Not in view of his opening statement. The first thing he said was that his persecution could have nothing to do with himself. When a man tells you that he is being hounded by invisible forces for no reason at all, you can wager he is concealing some shameful secret. It had everything to do with him. So did the deaths of his uncle and father. I shall go further. Take John Openshaw out of the equation, and neither Elias nor Joseph Openshaw would ever have died."

"Oh, come now, Holmes," I scoffed. "I think I am a good judge of character. If ever a man was innocent it was John Openshaw. The fellow was refined and delicate almost to the point of effeminacy. I would not have wanted someone like that beside me at Maiwand. Either he would have been petrified with fear, or he have turned tail and run the moment the guns got to blazing. How such a shrimp could be related to a man so heroic as Colonel Elias Openshaw is perfectly beyond me."

Holmes seemed amused by my contempt. "There speaks the former army surgeon! In your heart of hearts, you would prefer to serve under the Colonel, for all that he was a former slave owner, and heaven knows what else to boot. Think about that. Use it. You, as a military man of sorts, feel an instinctive distaste for a fellow who frankly confesses himself to be like a rabbit frozen with terror at the sight of a snake. Would you not expect the Colonel to have despised his spineless nephew just as much? And yet that solitary, drunken, coarse-tongued brutal exploiter of other human beings took a fancy to that refined twelve-year old. According to John Openshaw he begged the boy's father to give him his son to be his solitary companion. What was the nature of this curious attraction? And why was the father so ready to part with his own flesh and blood? Is it normal to surrender one's heir into the hands of a brother one is estranged from, and who evidently has no intention of ever inviting one into his home? Bear in mind, too, that Colonel Elias Openshaw was the kind of man to take liberties with his property. Would you, Watson, trust a son of yours in the hands of such a former slave owner?

136

"I gather that he needed someone to play backgammon and draughts with," said I with growing unease. The Cleveland Street scandal was still front-page news. I could hardly fail to apprehend the dangerous drift of Holmes's insinuations.

"Aye, but what other games did he engage in? I understand your reluctance to accept the possibility, Doctor, for what father would abandon a son into the bloody hands and lecherous lips of a beast such as brother Elijah may have been? But a doctor must observe sickness as unblinkingly as the detective does the crime."

"But there need not have been any crime in this case," said I, for I was dutifully and desperately determined play the devil's advocate. "Opposites attract, you know, Holmes. I have seen it again and again, for as you know I have had experiences of men and women in three separate continents. It was doubtless the feminine nature of the boy that the Colonel found so appealing."

"No doubt," said Holmes grimly. "This Ganymede would be his cup bearer. But you wilfully persist in missing the point, Watson. John Openshaw characterised his father as a man of exceptional obstinacy with whom it was vain to argue. As for the Colonel, he was accustomed to issuing orders to cannon fodder and to slaves. Are we then to believe he went cap in hand as a beggar to a brother he cared nothing for and who cared nothing for him to plead for the surrender of his son *gratis*? And would Joseph have done so without a fight, knowing in his heart he might never see his son again? It does not ring true, Watson. It does not ring true." He raised a hand and rubbed two fingers and thumb together.

"That is monstrous, Holmes!" I cried. "I cannot and I will not believe it. You are suggesting the father as good as sold his son? Why should he? You forget Joseph Openshaw had been a successful businessman. His unbreakable bicycle tyre made him a fortune. He retired early to live a life of luxury. Why should he sell an heir when he had no need for more money?"

"Indeed?" said he with eyebrows raised like crows of ill omen looming over a cornfield. "Then why did Joseph move straight into Elias's home after his death, if not because he was uncomfortable in his own? All that boasting of an unbreakable tyre was pure hot air, Watson. Once punctured it was utterly deflated. He did not retire a wealthy man. Such businessmen build dynasties to bequeath to their children. They do not sell both the businesses and their children to the highest bidder. No, no, the Wheel of Fortune turned, and it crushed him under it. If anyone went cap in hand to anyone it was brother Joseph to Elias, to plead for assistance and promise anything and anyone in return. Come, come, do not look so shocked. If he was negotiating the unsuitable marriage of his daughter into

137

a titled family, you would not think it odd at all. Because it was his son, you think it infinitely worse."

"I will not credit it," said I aghast. "Why assume the unbreakable tyre was a myth? I read just the other day that the chief difficulty with those new pneumatic tyres is they puncture so easily."

Holmes chuckled. "But I know rather more about the subject than you do. It falls into my specialism, you see."

I laughed. "Into crime? You believe that future bank robbers will attempt to escape on bicycles?"

"That is not what I meant. I freely confess these thoughts are not my own. Brother Mycroft sees beyond the particular to the general and past present difficulties to those of the next century. He sees the way the wheel turns and extrapolates where it will be a hundred years hence. He has deduced that the bicycle will soon result in female terrorism such as the world has never dreamed of."

I laughed again. "Surely he is joking, Holmes!"

"Mycroft never jokes. He is forever grave. His reasoning runs as follows: Because politicians are incapable of real foresight, they will fail to legislate to prohibit female cyclists. But female cyclists are impractical things due to their bulky attire. Therefore, multiple petticoats and corsets shall be discarded and rationally dressed women riders shall don trousers. Young ladies on bicycles shall shed their chaperones. Tasting a new freedom of motion in the bicycle saddle and out of it, they shall proceed to dream of a more dramatic liberation. With increased liberty shall come the freedom to cry they want some more. The day shall come when they shall demand the vote, and when that is denied they shall turn violent. When laws are perceived to be intolerably unjust, it becomes a badge of pride to break them. It will come, Watson. The Furies shall descend from the skies, riding on bicycles."

I had long ago diagnosed Holmes as an incurable misogynist who entirely fails to appreciate the sweet nature of the fairer sex. "You are wrong, Holmes," said I with a confident chuckle. "It would be quite contrary to a woman's character to behave thus. Has not Lombroso demonstrated scientifically that masculinity in a woman is an indication of degeneration and typically found only in criminals? You smile, and I see this is something you will not understand. Well, let us drop that. What is this special knowledge that convinces you the Openshaw unbreakable bicycle tyre is a myth?

"The knowledge that until recently bicycle wheels were made of iron and possessed no tyres at all. As you say, pneumatic tyres are viewed with suspicion because they do puncture so easily, which is one reason why they were banned from the race at the Oval earlier this month. I gather

Arthur de Cros, the son of the chairman of the Pneumatic Tyre Company, is planning to ride through the streets of London instead. Were Openshaw to have developed an unbreakable tyre, he might indeed have made a fortune, but the dates are all wrong. I am told John Dunlop only applied for a patent for his pneumatic tyre last year and it has yet to be decided. No, Watson. Joseph Openshaw lost everything, and his brother had to bail him out, in return for which he acquired the use of the son as cupbearer."

Holmes often overlooks human nature. "The boy would have objected," I reminded him. "Surely if what you say was true, then John Openshaw would have grown to hate both his uncle and his father."

"And wished them dead," said he, seeing the common sense, of this though too proud to admit it. "One would then have to rethink the case entirely and wonder whether Openshaw was quite correct to assume their deaths had nothing to do with him or his own personal history. Why, had he not given us that assurance, one might even wonder whether John Openshaw could have had a hand in their deaths!"

Holmes was again stooping to sarcasm. "Really, Holmes, you cannot doubt they were murdered by the Klan, just as John Openshaw himself was. How else can you explain the five orange pips that all three received? And were not all their envelopes marked 'K.K.K.'? Surely that proves they were from the Klan?"

Holmes paused as he perceived my objections were unanswerable. Finally he spoke.

"Forgive me, Watson, I must confess I found myself briefly at a loss for words. For the sake of argument let us accept your points and move on. Why do you suppose the Klan was so anxious to recover those papers from Elias?"

"I would have thought that was obvious, Holmes," said I reprovingly. "The papers incriminated them, and they wished to destroy them."

"I see. And in order to do so they sent Elias an envelope marked with their initials, so giving in evidence against themselves the better to find and burn all papers that might be used against them. Rather inconsistent, was it not? And how did Elias intend to thwart their plans?"

"He burnt the papers."

"Really. So to prevent them from destroying the papers he destroyed the papers. Think about that, Watson. Let it sink in. They were his one bargaining chip, his sole source of security when threatened by his former colleagues, and so he burnt them to 'checkmate them still'. By sacrificing his king? An odd way to win the game, would you not say? Hardly the mark of a scheming mind. Now, is not the conclusion obvious?"

"That he had gone mad?"

"No, that is not the solution. He burnt the papers to prevent them from falling into the wrong hands. Consider that the letters '*K.K.K.*' were written on the envelope and not on a sheet of paper slipped into it. Elias would have concluded from this that the aim was to incriminate the Klan. He would then have deduced the pips were sent by those he had persecuted and desired revenge. To have incriminated the Klan would be delicious."

"But Holmes," I protested, "if their aim was to recover those papers and use them as evidence against the Klan, they would hardly have written to Elias weeks before their arrival. That would give him plenty of time to destroy the papers and vanish away. Besides, if they had meant to take revenge, they would have attempted it years before."

"You forget, Watson, that the Klan went masked. They would have been known to each other but not to their victims. Elias concluded he had only recently been betrayed to his enemies."

"But how could they have learnt who he was and where he was to be found?"

"A most pertinent question, and one that Elias would certainly have asked himself. Let us leave that for the present. As for why he supposed they were seeking him out at that time, he would have supposed that they saw it as their last chance. Are you up to date with your American history?"

"I believe there has been an election for the American President. I think a Republican won."

"I share your indifference to such questions. Mycroft does not. He tells me that while the Republicans were in power the Klansmen had lived in fear of retribution. Grant became President on March 4th, 1869, and you will recall that according to the paper John Openshaw recovered it was on that day the mysterious Hudson came. Following his or her appearance there was a frantic flurry of activity. Clearly there was an anxiety to intimidate as many potential witnesses against them as possible, lest Grant be about to suppress them with a vengeance. It was on the fourth of March 1881, as you will no doubt remember, that the short-lived presidency of the Republican Garfield began. That was long after we had become lodgers of Mrs. Hudson's. Then with the inauguration of the Democrat Grover Cleveland on March 4th, 1885, the Klan was at last able to breathe a sigh of relief. The papers Elias possessed were instantly rendered harmless."

"But then why should Elias have burnt them? I seem to recall he received the letter on March 10th, 1885, six days later."

"Elias would remain locked in his bedroom for weeks with numerous bottles of brandy and an equal number of chamber pots. He had little to do with the world at the best of times and was usually so drunk he would not

140

have remembered what had happened from one day to the next. His terror at the sight of those orange pips caused him to act intemperately. Only later would he have read the papers and understood that the Klan's enemies could not have been after them. He would then have assumed that in their frustration at having lost any chance of achieving justice by legal means their one aim was then to at least take personal revenge against all those past Klan members they could identify."

Here I feel I must break off this narrative to explain to those who have read "The Five Orange Pips" that the dates supplied there are all two years too early. For that I must take the blame. I had just returned from Switzerland, where with my mind's eye I had seen Holmes fall to his death locked in the arms of Moriarty, a deduction reinforced for me when my account appeared in *The Strand* and Sidney Paget's illustration depicted their end in just such a manner. I think I may have succumbed to a brief bout of brain fever, during which my curious phantom limp recurred. Somehow, I was able to copy out my account of the Openshaw affair and it became the first to be sent on to my copyist after Holmes's apparent demise. However, what with the blinding tears that blotted the papers and the uncontrollable trembling of my hand that copious quantities of medicinal brandy quite failed to cure, what I wrote was illegible in places. My copyist Conan Doyle thought I had dated the case to 1887, and not 1889. Seeing that this would have been inconsistent with the other dates and assuming I could not have been mistaken about that key one, he altered all the others accordingly. Thus the year in which the Klan was suppressed was altered from 1871 to 1869, the year Elias died was changed from 1885 to 1883, Joseph died in 1885 rather than 1887 and so on. I was very upset about this, for I am always scrupulous in ensuring my dates are absolutely accurate, as my readers will know. I trust this digression may be forgiven.

"And besides," Holmes added in a matter of fact manner, "I never said the Klan or its enemies sent the pips."

"But then who posted them."

"That is surely self-evident. Nobody."

"Nobody?"

"Nobody.

I flung my hands into the air in a dramatic gesture of despair.

Holmes laughed. He always finds my confusion amusing. "It is perfectly simple. The Klan received a letter begging their assistance. His enemies were closing in on Elias. They set sail and sent word that help was on its way. The letter was received and destroyed. The pips were placed in the envelope in its place and the letters 'K.K.K.' written in red on the inside. Once Elias was dead the Klan was sent a second letter warning them that the police were investigating and urging them to fly."

141

"But who was responsible?"

"Precisely the question that Elias asked himself, though he did so thinking that he had been betrayed. Of course, his conclusion was that it had to have been his brother Joseph, who had been forced to surrender his son to the tender mercies of a man who had habitually exploited and abused his human possessions. Certainly, Joseph wept precious few crocodile tears for Elias. You will recall that John Openshaw said whenever he suggested to his father the death of Elias had been murder rather than suicide, brother Joseph burst out laughing. The tears he shed were tears of mirth."

I thought of my own brother's death of alcoholism and the sense of guilt I had felt at having let him die. "But Elias could not have suspected Joseph, Holmes. He left him his entire fortune."

"And not a penny to John. Is that not suggestive?"

"I do not see how."

"He advised John that if events proceeded as he expected them to do, then should he inherit the estate upon his father's death he ought to leave it to his worst enemy. You understand? Brother Elias practised what he preached. He left his estate to the man he surmised was his worst enemy. He left it to the brother he believed had betrayed him, meaning to ensure he suffered the same fate as himself. But he was wrong."

"Surely not, Holmes," I corrected him. "Joseph did indeed suffer the same fate."

"No, I mean he was wrong to suppose his brother his worst enemy. Joseph was only the second."

"And the first?"

Holmes puffed smugly on his pipe. "Consider that the Colonel was a drunkard who must have spoken in his cups of his past life and murmured of it in his sleep. Only one person was privy to all those conversations. That was his nephew John. Understanding how much Elias feared the day of reckoning, John borrowed the keys to the lumber room and that box containing the Klan papers while Elias was in one of his drunken stupors. He used the information in the box to address a letter to the Klan urging, them to hasten to Elias's assistance."

"I cannot believe it," I gasped. "How could so nervous a young man as John Openshaw had been so devious?"

"His nervousness was in large part owing to the abuse he had suffered at Elias's hands. Think of your old school chum Percy Phelps, Doctor. Your bullying of him scarred him for life. But you must see the Klan would never have written to Elias so long before they arrived if they meant to seize upon him. They would have wished to take him by surprise and before he could take flight."

I thought of indignantly repudiating Holmes's charge, for I had always taken the greatest care never to leave Phelps so much as obviously bruised, so there could hardly have been any remaining scars. But it was better not to get distracted. "The envelope to Joseph was sent in advance of their arrival too. If you are right, Holmes, then only John would have been targeted by them, for in his case alone the delay was minimal."

"Precisely! The implication of that is clear. The Klan were not involved in the deaths of either Elias or of Joseph. On both occasion,s letters were written to them by John urging them to come to the aid of the Openshaws, and on both occasions he received and removed their replies and put pips in their place. Both times he wrote to them again following the deaths to warn them the police were investigating, and they should escape."

"They would have grown suspicious!"

"Certainly. Slowly but surely the doubt grew that perhaps John Openshaw, the one who had twice written to them urging their aid, was the killer."

"Impossible!" I cried. "Did you not say, Holmes, that only a gang could have killed them and yet left not a trace? No one man could have done so without so much as leaving a single footprint behind at the scenes of the crimes."

"Pshaw!" Holmes would often express his contempt thus. Actually, he sometimes used stronger language. "Why do you persist in swallowing my rationalisations without permitting yourself so much as a grain of salt for seasoning? That was for the benefit of our captive audience in the chimney. Cannot you see that the opposite was the case? A single individual will leave more footprints than a gang. As for no strangers having been seen in the neighbourhood, that was because there were none, though if there had been, then one stranger could have been more easily overlooked than several. No, no. Accept that there was no gang involved and the deaths become much simpler. Let us take that of Elias first. You recall the circumstances?"

"I believe that he had locked himself up in his room to drink, and was later found outside drowned with his head in a pond."

"You see how easily John Openshaw could have managed it? During all those years he would certainly have made copies of the keys. He slipped into Elias's bedroom and found the man dead drunk. He put on his shoes and bore the man out to the pond to give him one last drink. That explains why there were none save for Elias's shoeprints leading to the scene of the crime. Of course, the murderer simply retraced his steps afterwards. It is a very easy trick. I have often employed it myself."

"And Joseph?"

"Ah. There we enter the realm of pleasing speculations where even brother Mycroft can only dream. His suggestion is worthy of mention, though. John Openshaw could have read newspaper accounts of how the escaped convict Selden fell to his death while flying from the luminous Hound of the Baskervilles. That would have made him think of Elias's tales of how in the early days of the Klan they would dress up as the ghosts of soldiers to terrorise their victims. It would have been a matter of recovering the old Klan robes from the lumber room and applying a spot of phosphorous paint. Then John could have appeared as the ghost of Elias the Klansman as Joseph was walking home by the edge of the unfenced chalk-pit to urge him to repent of his sale of his son. Joseph would then have taken a step back in terror and gone over the edge. It is as good a theory as any, and rather better than any of mine."

"And who killed John Openshaw? Who could have lured him down to the river's edge to drown him?"

Holmes chuckled. "That is rather too obvious, is it not? There was only one man who could have done it. Whom did he trust with his life? The very man into whose hands he had put his life."

"Holmes!"

"A good guess, though 'a good guess' is something of a contradiction in terms. No. It was not Holmes. It was the policeman who had appeared at John Openshaw's home claiming he had been sent there for his protection after the police themselves had smiled at his tale of orange pips and treated it as a joke. How likely is it that the police of Horsham would have spared one of their men to remain with Openshaw in his home for an indefinite period when they clearly thought the man deluded? And supposing they had done so, would they have given that policeman strict instructions never to leave the house whether Openshaw was in it or not?"

"You mean that he was the murderer?"

Holmes considered a corner of the ceiling. "You recall that the papers reported one Constable Cook of H Division on duty at Waterloo Bridge heard a cry for help and a splash, as of a body falling into the Thames. The police assumed that this Constable Cook was the creation of the gentleman of the press, whose comprehension of the dividing line between fact and fiction is about as clears as it is to you, my dear Watson. Their motive seemed clear enough. H Division covers Whitechapel and not Westminster, so the motive in claiming that such a constable was on duty there would have been clear. It seemed to imply that this was a Ripper killing, and the constable had shadowed the suspected man there. But Cook shared this in common with Jack the Ripper. He was a myth. There never was any such person."

144

I should just mention that the reason Holmes never took the slightest interest in the murders attributed to Jack the Ripper was that he declined to believe that the legendary murderer was anything other than a creation of the newspapers. And Holmes absolutely refuses to have anything to do with fictional characters.

"Well, that is always possible," said I doubtfully. "It think it unlikely, though. This police impersonator could have followed Openshaw up to London and, on seeing him leave 221b, he might have decided he had to be disposed of before you became actively involved in the case. But why did he not kill him during the train journey?"

Holmes smiled mischievously. "Did I not say that it was rather too obvious who had to have killed John Openshaw? It was intended that I should read of how a Constable Cook of H Division had heard the cry for help from the victim. I would at once assume that Cook was an impostor. So he was. But he was Openshaw's accomplice. Whether it was Openshaw or Cook who gave that cry, always supposing there was a cry, we shall never know. Nor can we ever know who Cook really was. He could have been a servant of Colonel Openshaw's who witnessed his murder, but who felt he deserved to die, given his numerous crimes against humanity and in particular against his nephew. If so, then he would have been the same servant who identified the corpse as John Openshaw's."

I could see the flaw to all this surmise. "You are forgetting the envelope, Holmes!" I cried. "It was found in the pocket of the body they fished out of the Thames and the address was still legible. It proved that the drowned man had to be Openshaw!"

"Holmes clapped solemnly. "Very good, Watson. Had there been a drowned man, then you would have a point. There was none."

"No drowned man?"

"No drowned man, Watson. As you know, Doctor, when a man drowns his lungs fill water and the increase in weight causes the corpse to sink. But that could not have been the case on this occasion since the body was recovered without much difficulty, and fairly quickly, as had it not been then the water would have obliterated the address on the envelope. The man must therefore had been dead before ever he was dumped into the Thames. But there were no signs of physical harm outwardly. Had he still been alive and had he indeed cried out, and since he did not drown, he could not have died. It follows that, in all likelihood, he had been poisoned. To test for poison is a tedious business requiring different tests for different poisons. There was no reason to perform such tests since it was thought to be a simple case of death by drowning."

"Well, that may be true, Holmes," said I grumpily, "but it hardly answers my objection concerning the presence of the envelope."

"Oh, do try to think, Watson," said he impatiently. "If the Klan really were intent upon recovering documents, then they would have searched his pockets and found that remaining paper."

"Why, so they did Holmes. The papers made no mention of it."

"But in the process, they would also have discovered that envelope. Are we to suppose that having done so, they carefully replaced it in his pocket? No, Watson, the envelope was placed on the corpse so that it would be misidentified as that of John Openshaw, who no more drowned near Waterloo Bridge than did Birdy Edwards last year near St Helena."

"But Openshaw is dead!"

"Certainly he is dead. At least, that is what you must tell your subscribers, for I have no doubt that among them are to be found my enemies, and I do not wish them to suspect I know the truth. Besides, I may have need of his services in the near future. In truth, though, it is not Openshaw but those remaining Klansmen who are dead men. I said Openshaw arrived in London some time before he put in an appearance at 221b. The little errand I spoke of was to conceal an infernal device upon the *Lone Star*, set to detonate once the ship was well out to sea. It will blow the *Star* to the moon. Now pack your toothbrush and your pistol, Watson, for there are still one or two loose ends to be dealt with, and that requires we visit the scene of the crime."

"You mean Waterloo Bridge."

"No. Horsham."

I could not imagine there could be anything to help us there, but I obeyed without question. Not a word more would Holmes say on the subject, and instead spoke at length on Turner's *Fighting Temeraire*, arguing in a convoluted manner that it was the first painting to celebrate the dawn of the Victorian age while simultaneously lamenting the passing of a more heroic time. Holmes is forever sighing for an earlier time of great villains and heroes. At length, though, we found ourselves in the dining-room at Horsham where three Openshaws had all received the orange pips in the post. I gazed about the room searching in vain for clues and could see none. Holmes pointed towards the floor, which I confess I had failed to consider.

"You see, Watson? I told you Openshaw was intent upon deceiving us. There is our proof."

I stared stupidly at the carpet. "Turkish?" I enquired feebly.

Holmes sighed at my obtuseness.

"The shoes! He said. "The shoes! Do you see the traces of mud upon them? Where is the chalk? There is none. That proves Openshaw smeared his with clay and chalk shortly before entering 221b, just as I said he did. Next consider the chair in which Elias Openshaw was seated when he

146

gazed up from those five orange pips and perceived that his sins had found him out."

Holmes directed my attention towards one of the identical chairs set about the round table. He denied me the pleasure of pointing out that there was no reason to suppose he had not been sitting on another.

"Your problem, Watson, is that you will insist on considering no more than what is in front of you. Have I not told you again and again that you must put yourself in the shoes of others? And what is the easiest way to do so in this case?"

I frowned and attempted to look thoughtful. Holmes responded by putting his hands on my shoulders to steer me to the chair. He lowered me down onto it. "What do you see?"

I recalled how Holmes had chastised Inspector MacDonald the previous year for failing to pay sufficient attention to the Greuze painting hanging behind Professor Moriarty's desk. I would not make the same mistake. There was a copy of Rembrandt's *Belshazzar's Feast* on the wall directly opposite. The drunken king was shown interrupted in his revelry by the sight of an ectoplasmic hand writing on the wall behind him a cryptic prophecy of doom.

"Only my precursor the detective called Daniel was able to decipher it. To speak more plainly, Belshazzar and his wise men all saw it, but only Daniel observed it. He diagnosed its true meaning. Now, what do you suppose was Elias's reaction when he looked up from those five orange pips and for the first time observed that painting John Openshaw had installed there? But of course we know. He cried out that his sins had found him out. That was why he burnt those papers, believing that in doing so he was signing his own death sentence at the hands of thwarted avengers. It was an attempt to atone for his past acts of cruelty by at least showing loyalty to the Klan. Of course you see why he identified with Belshazzar here?"

I nodded. "Very well. John Openshaw said that Elias's eyes bulged in exactly the same way as Belshazzar's do here, and doubtless they expressed the same kind of terror as the King felt when he received his warning."

"Good. Yet I think we might still squeeze the pips into squeaking just a little more. If you know your Bible, you will recall that Belshazzar, who had been drinking heavily, was so terrified and unmanned by the sight of the ghostly hand that, as the King James delicately puts it, his loins were loosed. As a doctor I think you will know what that means. You can see Rembrandt depicts his accident here."

In spite of years of medical training and some experience of men before a battle I could see no symptoms of such a disturbance here. "If you

147

are asking for a second opinion, Holmes, I am bound to say I think you are mistaken."

"Why, it is easy enough if you read between the lines. Rembrandt painted *The Rape of Ganymede* shortly before this, in which Ganymede as a babe is bring borne away by Jove's eagle. In his terror Ganymede is depicted urinating uncontrollably. Naturally Rembrandt could not be as explicit when he came to paint Belshazzar's distress, but he alludes to his source material very clearly. Do you not see how that cup is spilling it contents? Why do you suppose the wine is yellow? It is to alert us to the king's crisis. Now, you can be sure that the habitually drunk Elias would have suffered a like indignity when he received those orange pips, and so would have seen this painting as a mirror held up to him to show his true nature. I could not have done it, but Mycroft deduced the painting would be here."

It was rare for Holmes to confess when another had got the better of him, but he seemed to take a curious pride in constantly stressing the superiority of his older brother to himself. I was intrigued and longed to know how the smarter Holmes could have deduced what the slower one could not. "But how?"

"It was really quite absurdly simple once it had been explained to me," said Holmes peevishly. "How could I have been so blind to the obvious? Of course, John Openshaw had written to Elias's old colleagues in Florida, and it was they who had set sail for England. They had nothing to do with Texas, and yet the ship was named the *Lone Star* after that state. Why had they renamed it thus?"

"What makes you think they had renamed it?"

"I did not. Mycroft realised they must have done, and that its old name aroused their superstitious fears. Think of that print of Turner's *Fighting Temeraire* you have hanging in your home."

"Holmes! How did you know that?"

"Mycroft knew it. He admires you as the quintessential man in the street. Take that with your love of sea tales, and it was inevitable you would select the best-loved painting of a ship in the country, to say nothing of its being an image of the sun sinking on the old Britain, so as to rise on an empire where it never sets. Remember that it was painted at the time of Victoria's accession."

"As a matter of fact, Mycroft was wrong," said I with some pride. "I grant he was correct that I have a print of the Temeraire in our bedroom, but not for the reasons he imagined. One of my ancestors, Ordinary Seaman David Watson from Aberdeen, was on the ship at the battle of Trafalgar."

"To continue. As you must know, the vessel had been French until captured by the English. They kept the old name in accordance with tradition. But boat the Klan sailed in had to have a change of name. It had been taken from their enemies, and the title they had bestowed upon it was expressive of their hope that the writing would soon be on the wall for the former Klansmen."

"How could Mycroft know that?"

"When I made my enquiries, the docker did not know of any ship called the *Lone Star*, but then he recalled there was a vessel identified only by its initials on its sternpost. Now, what ship would have no more than its initials when it might have its entire name appear there? When I expressed my bewilderment at that to Mycroft, he at once realised what had happened. Having no time for anything else, they had erased all but two of the letters from the old name and made those the initials for the new one. That meant they had to choose some name whose initials would be the same as those two remaining letters. They hit upon *Lone Star* as the only name that sprang immediately to mind."

"And its original name?"

Holmes swelled out his chest in imitation of his brother. "'Elementary, my dear Sherlock. The enemies of the Klan had called it the *Belshazzar*.'"

"But how could Mycroft have deduced from that there would be a copy of Rembrandt's painting here?"

"Oh, even I could have done that. When they answered John Openshaw's urgent request that they sail to the assistance of Elias, they told him they would be travelling on the *Belshazzar*, for they had not yet renamed it. That stuck in the young man's mind. It inspired him to make of the painting the writing on the wall for Elias."

"But why do you not wish me to expose John Openshaw as the murderer of his uncle and father?"

"Because I may be able to make use of him in the future to net a far bigger fish. Remember that spy in the chimney, Watson. The current Napoleon of Crime, Adam Worth, must fall in due course. Someone will take his place and I'll wager that sweep was one of his agents. But a citadel is only as strong as its poorest lock. I mean to make of Openshaw that poor lock. I am assuming, as seems likely, that the sweep was in the chimney to report back on Openshaw's success. Our mastermind may have assisted him but requires his future services by way of payment. But cheer up, Watson, my brother has supplied a splendid conclusion to what shall become your version of events to set before the public.

Holmes fished out of a pocket a paper that he handed to me and on which was written the following:

We did at last hear that somewhere far out in the Atlantic a shattered sternpost of a boat was seen swinging in the trough of a wave, with the letters L.S. *carved upon it, and that is all which we shall ever know of the fate of the* Lone Star.

Bartolome Bermejo – *"St. Michael"*

The Adventure of the Amateur Mendicant Society

Continuing "The Man with the Twisted Lip"

"**I** wish I knew how you reach your results."

"I reached this one," said my friend, "by sitting upon five pillows and consuming an ounce of shag. I think, Watson, that if we drive to Baker Street we shall just be in time for breakfast."

It did not surprise me to find Holmes's prophecy fulfilled. While engaged in any particularly challenging investigation he would do entirely without food and sleep, fending off hunger and fatigue by chewing on coca leaves. Regardless of the time of day or night, for this former Catholic "breakfast" was the first meal taken after a case was "cracked". It was always preceded by his smoking a pipe of tobacco blended to his own secret recipe. The mysterious medley invariably emitted a most curious cracking sound as evaporating water escaped, which is why he spoke of "cracking" a case.

Knowing he had not eaten for two days, Mrs. Hudson had used this as an excuse for marking the occasion with a Scotchwoman's notion of a full English what-you-will. Since it was the fifty-second anniversary of Her Majesty's accession, the patriotic lady had re-hung decorations from the Golden Jubilee of two years before. The bullet-pocks of the patriotic "*V.R.*" Holmes had adorned a wall with on that memorable day had once more been plugged with red, white, and blue-paste carbuncles and beryls. As for the repast itself, it beggared all description, featuring as it did such plenteous delights as Easterhedge pudding, waffles with cinnamon and allspice pear butter, Swiss and Turkish eggs, sausage eggs, egg fritters, bread steaks, pumpkin porridge, finnan haddies, bull's eye, meringued coffee *a la Casparini* sweetened with "*belle dame sans merci*" sugar *a la Klein*, Napoleon dumplings, and hot chocolate with two generous doses of my very own blend of medicinal brandy. For Holmes there was *mate de coca* and toast dipped for twenty seconds, no more or less, in sweet thick milk to the genuine Diogenes Club recipe. He munched silently on the sodden slivers between lassoing a spider in a beer mug with smoke rings from his shaman's pipe. The spider sat Buddha-like at the centre of its web and seemed curiously *blasé*. The web it had spun was *avant-garde* and impractical. The arachnid itself reminded me of someone, but I could not think who.

"What is it, Watson?"

The question started me from my reverie. "Oh, nothing, Holmes, it's just a trifle." I helped myself to some more.

"Then spit it out."

I gave an embarrassed laugh. Trifle sprayed forth.

"Well . . . there is . . . no use . . . denying there *is* . . . something on my mind." I paused to swallow the rest of it. "It really is of no importance. You remember how you startled me awake this morning with your ejaculation? You were so excited I had supposed you had only just then solved the mystery."

"So I had," said he with a slow nod. I felt his eyes studying me from behind that face so like a photographic self-portrait, one meant to cunningly conceal rather than reveal the heart of the sitter's mystery. As his biographer I dreamed of touching it. I decided to spring my trap.

"Then perhaps, Mr. Holmes, you will be good enough to explain how it is that you had already collected a sponge from the bathroom and packed it away in St. Clair's Bellinger bag, ready to wipe the greasepaint off Boone's face? That proves you already knew they were one and the same man."

I had hoped for a reaction as dramatic as when Mrs. St. Clair had pleaded with him to be frank and say if he believed her husband dead and then, having tricked him into committing himself to it, had produced a newly received letter from him previously secreted about her person. As Holmes grudgingly confessed later, she had displayed rather more frontal development of the kind he is partial to than he might have expected in a woman.

"I see. And you think this smacks of the charlatan? Is that it?"

He did not sound resentful. He had anticipated my objection. I began to lose confidence.

"Why, I would not presume so far, Holmes, but you are a dramatist in real life. You apprehended that the murderer and the murdered man were one and the same: You deduced that St. Clair had been playing at being the beggar Boone and preferred to be arrested as the latter, rather than have his guilty secret exposed. You went to the bathroom in the suite Mrs. St. Clair had placed at your disposal and collected the sponge before tiptoeing back to where you had ensconced yourself upon pillows and cushions. Once entrenched there once more, you gave a loud cry as if at some wondrous revelation to awaken me. You have to admit, Holmes, it was a bit childish."

"And if I were to swear to you by the most solemn oaths a man can take that my ejaculation was at a genuine realisation, what would you say then? Pass me down that Bible like a good fellow."

"No, no," said I hastily. "That is hardly necessary. Your affirmation is good enough for me. But I don't understand. What, then, was that sudden revelation if you had already solved the mystery of 'The Man with the Twisted Lip' earlier that night?"

"Watson," said he in his severely schoolmasterly way, "have I not told you seven times seventy-seven times that no solution is anything more than a destination? What is that to the journey taken? It is the method that matters. That being so, did it not strike you as the tiniest bit odd I never so much as hinted as to why it was so vital I return post haste to the home of the St. Clairs? We only arrived there after midnight. Precisely what was the urgent investigation I had been unable to complete on my first visit and that could not wait until the morning? Do not forget that before setting forth I abandoned our driver alone in the most dangerous lane in the entire East End and within throwing distance of an establishment renowned for heaving of bodies out of a trap door into the Thames. What if he had been seen with us just after I had transformed back from that decrepit opium addict into Sherlock Holmes? Revenge might have been taken on me in his person. Do you think I would have taken such a risk without good reason? What, then, was I planning to do at the Cedars in Lee in the county of Kent? Do you suppose I was proposing to creep into the bedrooms of the occupants to eavesdrop on their talk in their sleep? But if that were so, why had Mrs. St. Clair reserved me that bedroom suite?"

It is a curious thing, but it had not occurred to me before just how evasive Holmes had been. When I had asked him what reason he could possibly have for travelling all the way to the Cedars when by his own admission he had nothing to report to Mrs. St. Clair, and that he hated to admit as much to her, he had said no more than that there were enquiries he could only make out there. That had seemed reasonable enough at the time, for he had concealed from me the fact that he had already visited the place. But I had not lived with the world's greatest detective for seven years for nothing. Applying his own methods, I deduced he must have been from the fact that he knew exactly where she would be sit beside a lamp, awaiting the sound of our approaching dog-cart. He also knew where the stable lad slept and was able to awaken him to have him bring us our trap the next morning. I say it was our trap. It may have been the St. Clairs", for they never seemed to use theirs. That would explain how he had managed to locate the lad's bed.

Suddenly your humble lightning conductor had an inspiration. These flashes come upon me at times. I was determined to make the most of it, for not even lightning conductors are struck twice in rapid succession, and it might be long before I shone again. "Holmes, I see it now! You suspected Mrs. St. Clair of murdering her husband! You had plotted a

155

dramatic scene in which she would confess all. You are ever the stage manager. Admit it, though. For once the best plans of Mr. Sherlock Holmes were beaten by a woman's wit."

"You persist in missing the point, sir," said he irritably. I had struck a raw nerve. He had indeed hoped to confront Mrs. St. Clair and she had not proved to be quite the puppet he had meant to make of her. "We are speaking of my methods. Did I reveal all after the case was concluded? I did not. When Inspector Bradstreet asked me how I had solved the case, I evaded the question and said no more than that I had sat on some cushions and smoked. Is it like me to conceal my line of reasoning even after the event? What can you deduce from that?"

I shrugged my shoulders helplessly. The lightning conductor was cold again. "I can deduce nothing."

"Neither could I. Was that not intriguing?"

"I don't understand."

"Neither did I. But I do not mean to speak in riddles. To be plain, then, I knew the solution to the puzzle of St. Clair's disappearance was to be found at the Cedars, but why that was so I could not for the life of me have said. Worse, when the solution came it was out of the blue. That irked me, Watson. It is my methods that must live on after me. Through them I shall achieve immortality. That is why to solve a case means nothing. To understand *how* I have solved it is everything."

"Telepathy!" I cried.

Holmes bestowed upon me an evil eye resembling in its effect Mr. Wells' Martian death ray. "It does not take a mind reader to perceive you have been talking to that indolent doltish dullard, Doyle. There is no such thing as telepathy."

Why, the brazen hypocrisy of it! "Holmes, when Mrs. St. Clair said she sensed her husband had cut his finger far away in their bedroom, you accepted it unquestioningly. How can you have the audacity to say such a thing? Do you doubt there are more things in heaven and earth than are dreamt of in your philosophy, as the Bard puts it?"

He seemed affronted. "Please do not play the Dane, Watson, and kindly do not miscast me as your Horatio. You know I have only ever been the ghost and gravedigger in *Hamlet*. You are right, though, that I had meant her to confess all, for she was not to be trusted for an instant."

That was hardly a revelation! Holmes trusts nobody, not even me. He says I am too honest as the world goes. "But why doubt her in particular?"

"Because there was no trust between the St. Clairs. None whatsoever. Why, he lied to her every day of their lives together, yet we are to imagine that for two years she entirely failed to sense he was living two lives, or rather say two *half*-lives, since he was but the sleepwalking shadow of

156

himself. Now, if theirs was a marriage of true minds and admitted no impediment, she would long since have perceived something was seriously amiss. So I knew she was lying to me, Watson. I could not let her know it, but I had made a window into her soul. Oh, please do not look so sceptical. Have faith. Mind reading is simple enough, but do not pay heed to your friend Doyle's spiritualist nonsense. It is always to be explained by rational means. Do not raise an eyebrow to me, sir. Here, let me demonstrate. You dreamt last night you were back at the Battle of Maiwand and the girl Malalai had just shot you in the shoulder, did you not?"

I attempted to spring from my chair only to sink back into it a second later, for at that instant the inexplicable limp I had suddenly developed shortly before deserting Holmes for a wife had returned with a vengeance. "Holmes, Holmes!" I gasped through my pain. "I am your biographer, yet I would never dream of snooping into your past life. This is how you have repaid my fidelity, by eavesdropping on me as I talked in my sleep!" I stopped. The awful implications of this had just struck me. I talked in my sleep! What awful confessions had I unconsciously made while in bed with my wife? Holmes had ensconced himself in the Bar of Gold opium den to pick up titbits from the incoherent ramblings of the addicts. Had my wife learnt of my experiences in three separate continents from my own mutterings in like manner? Was that why she had called me "James" the previous night? She must have meant me to think of our handsome young neighbour, Dr. James Anstruther, who fills in for me when I am away on adventures with Holmes. Was she trying to make me jealous to get her own back?

"Do not look so worried, Watson," said he with a smile. "You never talk in your sleep, and her calling you James can easily be explained. You did toss and turn, though, and the reason for that was not hard to perceive. You recall that painting after Bermejo of St. Michael vanquishing the devil I sat myself down before in the St. Clairs' bedroom suite? I saw it attracted your attention, not least because Michael is envisaged by the artist as if he were a girl of nineteen or less. That made you think of Malalai, the girl of about that age the Afghans made their Joan of Arc after she died leading them on to victory at Maiwand, having torn off her veil to make of it a banner. When your hand stole up to your old wound while you contemplated the painting I realised it was Malalai who had shot you."

"Holmes," said I gravely, "in another age you would surely have been burnt as a wizard." I was not sure whether I meant it as a compliment.

His grey eyes grew lighter and more watery as they took on that peculiar introspective look and it suddenly struck me I had seen somewhere before. Then I remembered where that had been. While dining at Baskerville Hall, Holmes had frozen in mid-sentence as if turned into that future and too-briefly exhibited Tussaud waxwork of himself. All his attention had become focused upon the opposite wall. I had traced his line of vision and was surprised to find he was staring at what must have been the oldest painting there, a picture of a Goldilocked Franciscan friar depicted holding the paw of a submissive wolf-hound or hound-wolf. Conscious of my curiosity, he had turned hastily away and had begun to speak of the portraits of all the ancient Baskervilles, save for that most ancient one all. It was only later I learnt the picture was of the renowned medieval scholar William of Baskerville, who had been tortured by the Inquisition for his too-daring speculations.

"You are right, Watson, and I almost was," said he as he took note of my expression of dawning comprehension. "I mean I was almost burnt in the person of William of Baskerville. In his person, one surely sees evidence that the doctrine of reincarnation might be reconcilable with Darwin's doctrines. It was from William, you know, that I inherited Occam's Razor."

So that it explained it. "I remember wondering how you managed to remain so clean-shaven while you were living a hermit's life in a Neanderthal hovel out on Dartmoor. The simplest solution is often the best."

As Holmes raised his eyes heavenwards, I seemed to see as in a palimpsest the features of William of Baskerville's face showing faintly through those of my friend. That Franciscan's anonymous portraitist had depicted his subject with eyes upturned in just the same way, and perhaps for the same reason. The painting had evidently been cut, and at one time could have included the heavens opening to receive William's soul, though Holmes has another theory. He believes the work was originally a double portrait of William and his disciple Adso, the latter having made some particularly brilliant Adsonian observation, his master was thanking heaven for having bestowed upon him so exceptional an assistant. Presumably Holmes was offering up a prayer of thanks for his similar good fortune.

What is certain is that the Franciscan had the pious humility to accept he had received much of his inspiration for above. It was a lesson that Sherlock Holmes might have found profitable. It was not too late for him to learn it. Could I teach it? "You should have more faith, Holmes," I ventured. "When I was an army doctor on the battlefield, there was often no time for precise diagnoses. One had to put oneself in the hands of a higher power. Why not admit it was by good luck you solved the difficulty of 'The Man with the Twisted Lip'? Surely there is no shame in that."

Holmes reversed his otter pipe so that the carved figurehead stared me straight in the eyes as if she had just put her head out of water and was as surprised as I at an unforeseen close encounter with a thing from another world. Were I a shaman, I would have taken the little creature as my spirit guide.

"Do you know what I am smoking, Doctor?"

"Only that it is your celebratory blend."

"One of my own devising that includes *nicotiana rustica*, as used by medicine men in South America. Do not chide me. I am well aware of your agenda, Watson, and the little white lies you concoct concerning transcendental medicines and cocaine in particular. It is because you are haunted by the memory of your alcoholic brother. You interpret everything accordingly. For instance, you translated the worn steps of the opium den into evidence of endless drunken feet, whereas if you had read De Quincey *de novo* you would now know opium eaters are rarely drunkards – the experiences are so diametrically opposed. But you were determined to picture inebriates staggering up steps from a gin shop next door only to half-fall down adjacent stairs to the opium den."

I was bemused. "How did you know I read the steps that way?"

"By following you thither with modesty enough and likelihood to lead it. When I visited you at your home last Saturday, I pointed out that the steps to your surgery were worn a good three inches deeper than those of your neighbour sawbones. Moreover they were depressed at all points, which implied visitors who swayed and stumbled as if aboard a ship in a storm. I deduced from your door handle that the previous doctor to occupy your address suffered from St Vitus's Dance, yet such wear and tear to the steps could not have been the work of one man. It was undoubtedly the result of your inheriting a once-successful medical practice that specialised in alcoholics. It is clear you wish to make amends for the neglect of your brother at a time when he needed you. You feel especially guilty since you benefited from the inheritance that ought to have been his, and without which you could not have set yourself up in general practice. You expressed your misgivings to your wife, a pious woman, and unfairly likened yourself to the Biblical Jacob, who cheated his brother Esau out of his birthright. That is why she sometimes calls you James. In that one word the whole story of your imagined relationship with your brother is revealed. I claim no credit for the revelation. It was demonstrated to me by that ideal reasoner in whose footsteps I tread."

Holmes was speaking of his brother Mycroft, who combined my friend's powers of deduction with intuitions akin to those of the controversial Viennese brain fever specialist Sigmund Freud. For example, he construed from my xanthophobia that I must first have

159

serialised my reminiscences in the yellow-backed *Holywell Street Journal*, of dubious and questionable memory.

"But really, Watson, it is very dishonest of you to portray cocaine as a narcotic. I appreciate you cannot concur with your friend Oscar Wilde's view that there are no such things as moral and immoral books. Such a pronouncement seems to you to be self-refuting since those very words propagate the immoral idea that morality is secondary to aesthetics. So you work to depict De Quincey's *Confessions of an Opium Eater* as a poisonous work, and present your writings as an antidote to all such contagious texts. You place morality higher than truth, and think your white lies infinitely better than Wilde's black wit. But when lies are found out, they bring all into question. How could I go without food and sleep during a case if not for my trusty store of coca leaves?"

"I knew it!" I cried. "You were really in that opium den to ingest the vile stuff. You were not there to investigate the case at all."

"An erroneous diagnosis, Doctor. I was quite determined *not* to ingest more opium than was absolutely unavoidable. Fortunately I encountered a certain investigative journalist, one Coulson Kernahan by name, who was in the den hoping to pick up Chinese whispers on the disappearance of St. Clair while gathering material for an article or two on houses of ill repute. A singular waste of time, that. He means to alchemise the Bar of Gold out of all recognition. You recall those stairs descending to it? He plans to convert them into an ironic staircase to heaven!

"Well, Watson, he offered me a cigar out of courtesy and, still in the guise of an aged addict, I amazed him by insisting upon exchanging my opium pipe for his cigars. I assured him it had been smoked by none other than Charles Dickens and suggested he translate our present location to Ratcliff Highway to pique the interest of readers who recall the splendid murders committed there in 1811. And I told him a tale or two about the legendary Adam Worth, whom you may know was last year's winner of the underworld's coveted Napoleon of Crime Award, which he has held ever since his theft of the Agnew Gainsborough portrait of the Duchess of Devonshire in the very year I became a consulting detective. It seemed fitting to speak of a Napoleon the day after the anniversary of Waterloo, for I believe Worth's days are numbered. Expect to see Kernahan publish a tale of a criminal genius masterminding the destruction of the Empire in due course. Hurry into print, Watson. You will certainly be accused of plagiarism should his version appear first."

We both laughed at that. I might just in passing recommend the reader glance at "A Night in an Opium Den," which appeared in the June 1891 issue of *The Strand Magazine*. Though anonymous, I am confident it was written by Holmes's investigative journalist. It preceded my account of the

Irene Adler affair, reprinted in that publication the next month. Had Kernahan published his account after mine, he would not have needed to claim the pipe he smoked was the one that made Dickens sick. It would have been enough to say it had been handled by Sherlock Holmes. Dear me, how did I get writing about that? Where did I leave? Ah, yes. Holmes was speaking of how Kernahan quite inadvertently assisted him towards a solution.

"Once I felt I could trust Kernahan not to expose me and himself," he continued, "I transformed myself in Hyde-to-Jekyll fashion from that aged addict back into Sherlock Holmes. After he had recovered from his amazement, he confessed he had never seen anything so remarkable in his life, though he had read of something of the sort in the series of articles by his fellow investigative journalist St. Clair on his adventures while disguised as a beggar. Then he confided a pretty little theory he had devised that turned on the fact St. Clair's description of himself as a beggar happened to make of him the spit and image of Hugh Boone. His idea was that Boone had inspired St. Clair's disguise. What if they had become lovers? Boone could have tried to blackmail St. Clair and in the ensuing fight the latter was killed. It was an amusing speculation and I mulled it over while distractedly inhaling the equivalent of three pipes of opium. Then the true solution came to me as in a dream. It was a dream that you, my dear Watson, pulled me out of. You see that you were the person from Porlock who quite undermined a poor Sherlock's Quixotic castles in the air. Why do you chuckle?"

I could not help it. "Well, Holmes, I had my own revelation while in that den. The opium fumes must have addled my brains too. Out of the blue words came to me that at the time seemed very profound."

"And they were?"

"'A strong sense of turpentine prevails throughout'." I hoped Holmes would take the hint. His transcendental poisons are sirens masquerading as muses.

Holmes stared. His amazement was most gratifying. Then comprehension dawned.

"Ah. I see. You were remembering the words I once mentioned cousin Wendell had managed to jot down while under the influence of ether. He supposed it would be the secret of the universe. So you think I only imagined I had the answer? That is it, is it not?"

"It makes no sense to suppose you could have stumbled upon the solution in that miasmatic land of mist, Holmes. How could you have done?"

Holmes harrowed his unparalleled brow as he let that germ of an idea take root. "But that is the question. How on earth could I have done? I do not blame you for doubting me, Watson, but you shall see. I did finally manage to deduce how I had intuited that truth, and in doing so drew upon powers of the mind I had never entirely accepted could exist. But I had better retrace my steps. To begin with, do you understand now why you found me in that den?"

"You told me you were there to eavesdrop on the addicts in case they knew who the murderer was," said I hesitantly, for I found now that this was hard to credit. "Holmes, St. Clair had disappeared two days earlier and from three floors above the den. How many who had been in the Bar of Gold on the Monday could still have been haunting it two days later?"

Holmes paused and considered me. I knew he was weighing whether to confide and, for once, I sensed it was out of consideration for my feelings. "Only one resident patient that I knew of, Watson, and in those two days he had never budged from his spot at the steps leading to that infernal soul surgery. Naturally I sat myself down by him. He became my chief suspect. I am referring, of course, to your friend Isa Whitney."

I was incredulous. "Isa Whitney! Why?"

"St. Clair's murderer could not have escaped from the building. The police knew of that trap door leading to the Thames. The killer had to have concealed themselves on the premises, and where better than that opium den? Isa had been there since the day of St. Clair's disappearance and was stationed by the exit. He seemed to be ready for instant flight on receiving the all clear. He was the one obvious candidate."

"Never Isa Whitney!"

Holmes chuckled. "You will be delighted to hear, Doctor, that I soon changed my mind thanks to that investigative journalist Coulson Kernahan. By way of idle conversation, he pointed towards the far end of the den where more stairs led to the upper floors. He only did so to observe that he thought it in exceedingly bad taste that a print of the Crucifixion had been pasted onto a wall there. I perceived as he did not someone kneeling by the brazier there and beating his breast most piteously. Could it be the murderer? Was he praying for forgiveness? I had begun to rise to investigate when he and I were both startled by a sudden cry from Whitney. I confess to my shame I supposed he had named St. Clair's murderer. You will never guess who it was."

I shook my head, unaccountably discomfited. My friend's embarrassed smile told me he was about to give me a shock.

"Yours, Watson."

"Holmes!"

He shrugged apologetically as if to imply that, *Well, it can't be helped.* "I give you my word, my dear fellow, I only entertained the fantastic idea you could be a criminal mastermind for the merest fraction

162

of a second. You must understand it is my method to suspect everyone. After all, you are the least suspicious character I have ever encountered, so I thought it only fair to give you the benefit of the doubt. I therefore asked myself whether yours was not the brilliant act of a previously unsuspected intellectual equal. Was it possible, I mused, that anyone could really be as – let me see, shall we say – as *innocent* as you?"

I was confused. Was Holmes damning me with faint praise, or praising me with faint damnation?

"Rest assured, Watson, that dutiful doubt of mine came and went as swift as a lightning. Had Isa named brother Mycroft, I would have eyed my big brother with suspicion for months afterwards. You must see how amusing it was to imagine I had been living under the same roof as a doctor gone wrong and ready to cut my throat the moment he caught me napping. Who better than my official biographer to report back on my every move to some agent of a higher power? I entertained myself with picturing your so-called literary agent Conan Doyle plotting my demise. One day I would be lured to some lonely spot where the pair of you would seize me as I scrutinised a bee upon a rose. Together you would heave me over the side of a sheer drop into an abyss."

I could at least smile at the idea of the inoffensive Conan Doyle plotting my friend's demise. Then I frowned at the thought that Holmes could ever have doubted my loyalty.

"Besides, we may both have been duped," said he, too lost in pleasing speculations to observe my annoyance. "How was it our mutual friend Stamford was so underworked and overpaid as a dresser at St. Barts that he could think of drinking an hour away at the Criterion Bar during his lunch break? Was it not remarkable he should just happen to meet you there on the very day I was searching for someone to share rooms and you were in need of cheaper accommodation? You see how everything was done to bring us together and to 221b. Providence? Docket that for another day. At least Whitney's crying out your name can be explained easily enough. I instantly remembered how you had held Isa up to me as an awful warning while preaching to me on the dangers of drug use. Apparently you had treated him once or twice while taking the surgeries of your neighbours Anstruther and Jackson. He anticipated that his wife would send you to collect him and take the opportunity to deliver another of your tedious sermons. That was all."

I had done nothing of the sort. I merely observed to Whitney that the heroes of Waterloo had to be turning in their graves while he had turned in his opium berth. I might also have mentioned in passing that in a few hours it would be the anniversary of our great Queen's accession. The degeneration of empires begins with the sad degeneration of the great and the good who ought to be their leading lights.

"But the damage was done, Watson. I had started, the murderer by the brazier had seen my face, and he at once bolted up the back stairs. I hastened after him. The manager blocked my way, eyeing me evilly without ever losing that rictus sardonicus grimace of his, a Hippocratic grin of the kind to be encountered in the reptilian section of the Zoological Gardens. Had the joker recognised me, I would have fared ill. You perceived he lacked his snakelike pigtail?"

"Why, now you mention it his hair did look raggedly cropped."

Holmes almost sniggered but stopped himself in time. "I sometimes sojourn in that den, finding it to be not only a concentrated atmosphere but also a very soothing one. You know my pawky sense of humour. Or should that be porcine? I could not resist raping the locks of that pigtailed gentleman, and he has vowed to return the compliment by severing my own – er – pigtail should he ever get the chance. By the way, should you ever recount this adventure, kindly transform the yellow peril into a rascally Lascar, will you? I particularly like the alliteration of "rascally Lascar" and "St. Clair". More importantly, only the cheapest form of detective fiction features fiendish Chinamen. Nobody would believe it."

Artist he may be and possessed of one of the world's greatest minds, yet Holmes sometimes displays the schoolboy's sense of humour I myself abandoned at about the same time I ceased to hit young Percy Phelps about the shins with a wicket. I made a mental note to trim my moustache more modestly in future, lest he be tempted to shave half of it off one of these days, only to then claim it proved my bedroom window had to be on the right.

"Well, seeing him eyeing me askance without for a second losing his joker smile, I slowed to a saunter and seemed anxious to claim squatter's rights at that newly vacated prime spot by the brazier. It occurred to me that, after all, I might as well. Having deduced you would certainly be dispatched to collect your patient Whitney, I determined to await developments. To avoid the manager's gaze, I became absorbed in the appreciation of that singularly tasteless print of the Crucifixion, my counterfeit connoisseur act being based on the memory of our aesthete friend Thaddeus Sholto sucking on his hookah and lost in religious ecstasy over his precious Bouguereau. The fumes of the opium soon stole into my brain, and I found my thoughts wandering. Idly I wondered why such a work should have been chosen for such a place. That led me to recall the painting of St. Michael triumphing over the devil in the St. Clairs" bedroom. It featured poppies, and that helped me to understand."

"Understand what, Holmes?"

"Why, the Crucifixion picture showed a sponge being thrust into Christ's ruined face. He was offered a pain killer, you know. Some suppose it was gall derived from the poppy. An interesting precedent, that, justifying the use of transcendental drugs to escape this present circle of misery and violence and fear, would you not say, Doctor? No? Well, let it pass. Here was a peculiar connection between those two pictures. Just then you blundered in and broke the spell. How was I to recover that state of mind in which the revelation had occurred? You have read Dr. Elliotson's *Human Physiology*?"

"I have glanced at it," said I with some embarrassment, for the volume had been lent to me by my occasional collaborator Conan Doyle, and I had only had time to consider the cover.

"Hmm. Meaning that as a medical student you were too busy reading *The Moonstone* to attend when his name came up in a lecture on gallstones. I suppose then you know nothing of his theory of state-dependent memory?"

I hung my head as one guilty as charged.

"Well, it is not so very difficult. Let me see if I can put it simply. If one wishes to recover a lost memory, it is sometimes necessary to replicate conditions. For example, Robert Louis Stevenson is said to have had a drug-induced dream that inspired the story *Dr. Jekyll and Mr. Hyde*, one of the very few detective stories worth reading twice – or to speak more plainly worth reading at all. His wife awakened him from that vision. She was his person from Porlock. To recover that dream, he probably took additional drugs. If as is said he scribbled it out in three days without sleep or food, then cocaine kept him going. That would have helped to reproduce the original experience. You see, then, that to recover my vision I needed to reconstruct the conditions of that opium den."

"But then why did you insist we hasten to the Cedars? Why not dismiss me and stay in that abominable hole?"

"Because the bedroom of the St. Clairs and your abominable hole were inscrutably linked. I sensed the picture of St. Michael and that Crucifixion print had been conflated in the mind of the murderer. He or she had to have seen both. Was that because he was Mrs. St. Clair's lover? Or was the murderer Mrs. St. Clair herself? I would sit myself down before the painting just as I had done before that print and drug myself with some substitute for those opium fumes. Then I would await developments. It was quite a four-part problem."

"You mean a four-pipe problem," I corrected my friend.

"It is a curious – though by and large harmless – eccentricity of mine," said he with the driest dignity, "that I invariably mean what I say. It was a four-part problem. I needed to put myself in the shoes or slippers of the four key players in the tragic-comedy. That was best achieved by becoming them.

"First, I would be the cross-legged cripple of Threadneedle Street, playing at being a match seller and preaching to passing bankers on how hard it is for rich men and camels to enter heaven. Unless, of course, they cared to slip through the legal loophole in Christ's palm. By way of payment for the privilege, all they needed to do was drop a coin or two into Hugh Boone's hands as they passed by. You see, Watson? That is why I sat cross-legged with a matchbox placed in front of me: It was the better to become that beggar Boone. I also donned St. Clair's slippers and that electric blue dressing-gown of his you saw hanging so loose about me as I became that honourable gentleman. Of course, I also wished to be the murderer of St. Clair whom I had glimpsed by the brazier. The final role was by far the most challenging of all."

"Isa Whitney?"

"No, Sherlock Holmes. Please restrain from making one of your hurtful remarks about how easy that should be, since I constantly play at being the Great Detective. I had to put myself in the shoes of the Holmes you saw playing at being an old man staring sightlessly at that Crucifixion print. What is it now, Watson?"

He had perceived my dissatisfaction. "Forgive me, Holmes, but why do you keep referring to our suite at the Cedars as the St. Clairs' own bedroom and adjoining bathroom? Then there is Mrs. St. Clair's reputation to think of. Gossips would ask why she reserved you a double bed when you had not indicated you would be bringing anyone with you, or even that you needed somewhere to sleep. By the way, why did she do that?"

I tried to sound no more than idly curious, but the truth is I had begun to wonder. Had Holmes not taken note of an undue eagerness on her part that he should do so? Was that why he had added her to his list of murder suspects? And had he insisted I accompany him on his return visit to the Cedars to act as a chaperon? Or had he meant me to hide under that bed while he tricked her into a pillow talk confession?

As usual he had read my thoughts. "It was I who insisted I spend the night in her bedroom. You know my sense of humour, Watson, and I had anticipated she would look at me in amazement at the seemingly improper suggestion. To my surprise, she seemed quite amenable.. I realise now she understood I had seen something in the suite that required further investigation. But of course it was their bedroom. Do you really imagine they kept so spacious a suite complete with sofa and chairs and an adjoining bathroom for the occasional visiting couple? No, Watson, Mrs. St. Clair had given up using their master bedroom when she and her husband ceased to sleep together at least a week ago. It was she who slept in a guest bedroom on the night we took possession of the suite."

"What makes you think that?" I asked distractedly, less engaged than I would normally have been as I thought of my own wife wondering at what hour I might return if at all. I really ought to send her a note.

"Why, did you not see how I riveted my eyes to a corner of that suite's ceiling? I was considering a spider's web. That was the clue. It had not been swept away. I seize a thread and followed it to a thousand other clues that together proved conclusively their marriage was in serious difficulties. The final confirmation occurred when Mr. St. Clair reacted later to the news his wife had only received the note informing her he was alive yesterday. You recall his cry? Watson?"

"What? Sorry, Holmes. My mind was elsewhere. I think he moaned 'What a week she must have spent'."

"Hmm. Pay attention. Now, today is Thursday, and he was seen at the Bar of Gold last Monday. It follows he was away from her for several days longer that she admitted. By the way, Watson, do try to get the days right this time. As a former army surgeon, even you ought to be able to remember the dates, given that the day before you discovered Isa in the den was the anniversary of Waterloo. Moreover, you may have observed we were obliged to stand every time Mrs. Hudson marched in humming 'God Save the Queen' with yet more of these dishes – from which I deduce that it is the anniversary of Her Majesty's accession."

I did not dignify this carping criticism with a reply. I simply fished out my notebook and displayed the note I had jotted down to ensure no such mistake would be possible: "*June 19, 1889. Found Whitney Bar Gold. Arg with W if Wed. W wrong.*" Since I had collected Isa two days after the day he imagined it to be, that guaranteed I would remember I had collected him on the Wednesday, and not as Whitney imagined a Monday.

"Speaking of Whitney, Holmes, perhaps his confusion over the time he spent in that den was like St. Clair's temporal disorientation in his cell. Both men made mistakes. Whitney thought mere hours had passed when in reality days had gone by. St. Clair's mistake was the opposite of that. He imagined he had lost a week when in fact he had only been detained for two days. Do you remember when we sat in the darkness awaiting the coming of the speckled band? Every quarter-hour seemed like a century."

"Do not exaggerate, Watson," said he disapprovingly. "Ever quarter-hour seemed like a half-hour, no more than that. If, though, you need objective proof that St. Clair's week really was a week, then consider the evidence of the servants at the Cedars. I questioned them on my first visit. They told me he had left so early on the morning of his disappearance he was gone before they had arisen."

But I remembered what Holmes had clearly forgotten. "That was actually quite consistent with what Mrs. St. Clair told you. She said he left unusually early that morning. Does that not confirm he was indeed at the Cedars that morning?"

"And left at the crack of dawn to take the first train from Lee to Cannon Street?"

I nodded uncertainly, for this seemed like a trap and for the world of me I could not see how.

"If he was in such a hurry to get to town early, then why did he not have their groom drive him to the station in their carriage?"

"He was a caring employer. He did not wish to disturb the stable lad and groom unnecessarily."

"The boy did not object when I awakened him at half-past-four. He was accustomed to being treated so."

Then St. Clair was as inconsiderate as you, I thought, though I said nothing of that. I was accustomed to it too. "Well, what of the previous weekend?"

"Mrs. St. Clair had been away and they supposed she had been with him. She returned late on Sunday night after they were all in bed. They supposed he was with her."

Holmes was pursuing his usual vicious circle of cynicism. "Why suppose he was not with her, Holmes? You are forgetting the note he sent her. He called her "Dearest". He would hardly do that if their marriage was failing and he was sleeping elsewhere."

"Ha! St. Clair never wrote that note. Besides, you are overlooking one crucial thing."

"He never wrote it? He must have written it. It was in his hand. What am I overlooking?"

The ring, man, the ring! And as for that note, why, it was written by his *right* hand, I grant you, but I say again it was most certainly not written by him."

I have never met such a pedantic fellow! Of course technically the note had indeed been written by St. Clair's hand and not by him, but it was acting on instructions transmitted to it from his brain and in strict accordance with the impulses of his heart. I really did not wish to waste my time on abstruse philosophical discussions to do with the survival of the personality after the death of the body. Where the philosopher ends, humble physicians like me begin. I decided to put my foot down and like a good foot soldier it obeyed without question. Which surely proved my point.

"Holmes, if his right hand wrote, it he wrote it. I am aware of your eccentric views on such matters, but as a doctor I can assure you that you are not just a brain and the rest of your body is no mere appendix. It is time you accepted it."

His mouth kept tight shut as he trembled with that perfectly silent laughter so essential in his line of work. He had quite stilled the tremor before he spoke again. "Too bad, Watson, too bad! I can never resist dangling some cryptic clue before you. I say again not he but his right hand wrote it, for he was hardly in any position to do so himself. Did you fail to note how insistent Mrs. St. Clair was that the letter was in one of his two hands? Is it possible you missed the immense importance of that? Well, perhaps the answer will come to you. In the meantime let us turn to the signet ring Mrs. St. Clair claimed had been deposited in the envelope with the posted note."

He paused to bestow upon me a meaningful look and I thought I understood. "Why, Holmes, I believe I have it. She told us her husband had cut himself in their bedroom that morning. Boone, which is to say St. Clair, showed the police his cut finger that was bleeding freely at the time of his arrest. It was the same cut finger. Of course St. Clair could not write that note with his usual hand for fear he might stain the page. Had Mrs. St. Clair received a bloody note, she would have fainted in horror, just as he had seen her do at the sight of the blood in Boone's bedroom."

Holmes applauded approvingly. "Bravo, Watson! Most ingenious. You have entirely missed the point, but what of that? You have begun to grasp the method. Just docket those cut fingers for now and be sure to note how St. Clair held up his own bandaged ring finger in the cell when he described how the wound had reopened as he cast his coat out of the window of what we shall call the beggar Boone's bedroom. You are coming along, Watson, you are coming along."

From Holmes this counted as praise. "Well," I grumbled, "I see you are teasing your Watson. But I can cudgel my brains no more. Kindly unravel your riddle. How is it that St. Clair's right hand wrote the letter and he did not?"

Holmes gave a complacent chuckle. "Why, it is so very obvious when you think about it. Only consider this, friend Watson. Under the 1824 Vagrancy Act, the maximum penalty for begging is a month of imprisonment with hard labour. Of course Hugh Boone kept the palms of his bent coppers well greased with oily idealisations of our dear sovereign, but for appearance's sake such constables had to arrest him from time to time. Whenever that happened, he had his right-hand man write to his wife assuring her that all was well. That right hand played Boone in St. Clair's absence. It was simply a matter of accounting for the differences in handwriting by convincing St. Clair her husband had two hands, which in a sense he did."

169

"A pun?" said I in some disappointment. "Is that all?"

"Never disparage the pun, Watson," said he sternly. "Some of the best clues are puns. Think of the great Dane's triumphant cry of '*A rat!*' in *Hamlet*. It was what enabled me to crack the case and so prove the Dane knew he was killing the counsellor Polonius. But one investigation at a time. Let us turn next to the signet ring, for you must see by now why it was so significant. It proves their marriage was in peril."

"I don't see it at all," I protested, still a bit annoyed at Holmes for the linguistic trick he had played on me.

"Dear me. Well, if the marriage was not in trouble, he would have sent her his wedding ring."

He glanced down and I realised I was fingering mine, for I was again feeling guilty about failing to let my wife know I was breakfasting elsewhere. Despite his plausible explanation for her calling me "James", I was still not entirely happy about leaving her in Anstruther's hands. Holmes's tendency to suspect everyone was clearly contagious.

Then I had an idea. "Holmes, I have only been married a few months, yet already it would require an effort to remove my wedding ring. You remember what John Douglas said about his? It would have taken a file to get it off. St. Clair could not remove his either. Not that I see how his sending a signet ring instead signifies anything anyway."

"You make an excellent point, Watson," said he with an approval that made my heart sink, for I knew what was coming. "Of course you have missed the point as usual. We shall return to that presently. As for why he could not have sent her his wedding ring, it tells us a separation seemed imminent. He feared to do so, lest she read it as a final confirmation this was so. She would suppose it signalled he had determined to commit suicide or disappear. She was to collect his life insurance and bring up their children alone."

"This is quite fantastic, Holmes," I complained, for he had always to dive down for the darkest of all possible diagnoses. "You have no reason to suppose he was sleeping anywhere but at the Cedars. Or have you deduced some secret mistress?"

"Not a mistress, Watson. He was sharing a bed with a man."

"You don't mean . . . ?" I had just recalled how Holmes had said my associate Wilde had visited the Bar of Gold. I had assumed he meant out of idle curiosity.

Once again Holmes read my mind. "Why, Watson, you are warm, as the children say. Not your bosom friend, Wilde. Did I not mention Kernahan's theory that Boone and St. Clair were lovers? He, too, had nearly hit the mark. Now wind up that ingenious mechanical toy adorning your shoulders. Think! Hugh Boone did not exist. What use would an imaginary man have for a bedroom? And yet he rented one at great expense and considerable risk at the Bar of Gold. The reason is obvious. He did not sleep there, but St. Clair did."

I would not give up. "Mrs. St. Clair said that on the morning of the day he disappeared, she sensed he had cut himself in their bedroom. He confirmed it himself when he confessed all. The finger St. Clair held up for our inspection had been cut and bandaged over just where he must have been wearing his wedding ring. That strengthens my argument, don't you see? It would have been doubly difficult for him to remove the ring. He would have had to remove the bandage as well as prying it off."

"Perfectly true. Except you are forgetting one thing. If Mrs. St. Clair really had hurried up to her husband on sensing he had cut himself, she would certainly have insisted on bandaging it at once. But Boone held up an unbandaged finger to display a cut that he claimed had been reopened as he was opening his window. If we suppose that it had been cut hours earlier, then it would still have been bandaged and that would have soaked up the fresh blood. In fact, it was a fresh cut only bandaged up when he was taken into custody. Now, think, Watson. Had Boone, whoever he really was, habitually worn a ring, let alone a wedding ring, they could hardly have failed to notice a paler band or two of skin upon his finger where those rings had been."

I had spotted the flaw there. "Not at all, Holmes. He could have dirtied his hands to conceal any paler skin. In fact he must have done. Otherwise he would hardly have dared to hold his finger up for them to inspect."

"Excellent, Watson! Except that you have forgotten he refused to wash his face."

I wondered whether I was missing something. "What does his face have to do with it?"

"What, you do not see? If the most obvious clue to his true identity had lain in his hands, he would not have permitted them to wash those either, yet he made no objection to that. No, that particular Boone never wore rings, lest the pale bands give him away. St. Clair, by contrast, need not have worried about that, as you shall see. On the other hand, so to speak, I doubt St. Clair had ever cut his finger at all."

"But Mrs. St. Clair said he cut himself in their bedroom!"

Holmes proved to be pedantic as ever. "No, Watson, she only spoke of '*the* bedroom'. She could not bring herself to speak of '*our* bedroom', besides which it was not their old bedroom where the injury was sustained. Nor was his finger wounded. Remember that right-hand man? He, or some other confederate, may just have come off the morning shift."

171

This was too much. "Holmes, you cannot be serious. Do you now intend to conjure up an entire society of amateur mendicants that took it in turns to don a red wig and play at being Boone? All on the basis of the absence of a single pale band on a ring finger? There are trifles and trifles." I helped myself to some more to illustrate the point.

"No, no. Had I removed that plaster from St. Clair's upraised hand in his cell, the wedding ring would have been discovered and nothing else besides. Imagine how St. Clair must have congratulated himself when I failed to do so! 'You slipped up there, Mr. Holmes, clever as you are, for if you had chanced to take off that plaster you would have found no cut underneath it.' That was the thought I read between the lines of his sadly furrowed brows. As if I would commit such a blunder after the Birlstone fiasco of 1888!"

I realised Holmes was wilfully overlooking one thing, though I could not imagine why. "But the fact Mrs. St. Clair said her husband had cut himself just as Boone did proves they were one and the same person. You must see that."

"No. It proves she meant me to deduce as much. You recall she said she was not the fainting kind? She spoke the truth. She only feigned that swoon when blood was found on a sill in Boone's rooms. While seemingly unconscious, she attended as Boone held up his bloody ring finger. She saw how she could use that to direct me towards the desired solution. That was why she withheld the signet ring she said was enclosed with the received note. I exasperated her by failing to ask to see the signet. I knew her, Watson."

"You knew her?" I hoped Holmes was not indulging in one of his puns. I was still anxious about her eagerness to have Holmes in her double bed. Nor had I forgotten his appallingly ungentlemanly act in snatching the note before she had so much as entirely withdrawn it from an intimate place of secretion.

"Yes, Watson, I knew her. I deliberately seized upon the note in that admittedly far-from-gallant manner that you so rightly disapproved of, but really I had no choice. Only thus was I able to confirm it was both warm from having nested in her cleavage for a very considerable time, and deeply scented with her person. The implication was clear. It had been secreted in her bosom long before and ready for production at any time. Do you not understand? That scene was not spontaneous at all. You recall how theatrically she posed at her front door? That was a *faux pas* on her part, for she would keep one hand decorously raised. I saw she had cut *her* ring finger immediately above her wedding ring. It was no accident, Watson. She had deliberately cut it before slipping on that signet to stain the ring with her own blood. She planned that I should inspect it and think

172

of Boone's cut finger. That was why she spoke of her husband's wound. I would conclude the blood was that of St. Clair and Boone. Then I would deduce they were not two men but one. It was so painfully obvious she wished me to study that ring that I declined to do so, and thus had an admirable opportunity to study her as she very professionally strove to conceal her frustration and annoyance. It was a first-class performance."

Being a *prima donna*, Holmes regards anyone who upstages him as a rival. "Really, Holmes, for one so Quixotic, you are not very chivalrous. She was deeply distressed at the disappearance of her husband. There is no reason to suppose she was acting."

Holmes gave me a look of admiration or contempt or maybe the two things went together. He put a pitying hand to my better shoulder. "You are a good man, Watson, and dissimulation is alien to your nature." Was this a compliment or a criticism? I was puzzled and could not quite tell.

"Every man's virtues are his vices and vice-versa, you see," he continued, as if to answer my unspoken doubt. "You are too naïve. You are too innocent. Of course she was an actress. No, I am employing no euphemism. I do not mean to brand 'Adventuress' upon so fair a brow. But do think about it. Did I not say as we approached the Cedars she was seated beside a lamp to catch the sound of our approach? Did she not seize that lamp and hurry off to greet us? Her professional instincts stopped her in time. She would turn her exit into an entrance. So once at the doorway she paused to position that lamp behind her, checked the letter was securely secreted in that splendid bosom I caught you admiring with a connoisseur's eye – do not deny it – and then peeked through a side window to watch us get down from our trap and walk up the drive to the front door. Only when we were almost at it did she fling it open to pose in a transparent gown through which that lamp's light shone to silhouette her superb figure, posing with one hand raised and quite motionless save for the heaving of her bosom as if after an energetic sprint."

"You exaggerate, Holmes," said I indignantly. "Her dress was not transparent. It was *mousseline-de-soie*. You slander an exceptionally beautiful and queenly lady in insinuating otherwise."

"Queenly? Ha! It depends which queen you have in mind. Cleopatra, perhaps? I doubt anyone would mistake her for our own monarch in black. *Mousseline-de-soie*, you say? Well, muslin, *mousseline*, Muslim casual, call it what you like, Doctor. She reduced herself to a silhouette more completely than you strive to do me in your brazenly hagiographic fairy tales. Nothing could have been more admirably contrived than that pose. As for her cry of joy on seeing me and her sob of disappointment on belatedly registering that I was not alone, those were just a little unconvincing, were they not? Did I say I believed her when she said she was not one of nature's swooners? There was a time when she swooned swanlike and on cue to rapturous applause night after night. It is my belief, Watson, founded upon my experimentation with the female type in three separate continents, that the vilest street walker of the East End does not present a more dreadful record of sin and shamelessness than does the smiling and beautiful retired actress hailing from the West End's theatreland."

"But she was so genuinely anxious for her husband," I pleaded.

"Oh, yes. The anxiety. The heroic stoic resignation. You recall how she pleaded with me to be frank and confirm her worst fears. She slipped up when she urged me to reveal what was in my 'heart of hearts'. The presence of the Dane in the Heart of Gold had put her in mind of those words. It was the actress speaking, you see, for she was recalling Hamlet's praise of his own dear Watson, who is every bit as exceptional a golden mean man in the street as mine, just before the travelling players enter onstage. In Shakespeare's day, you know, wandering players with no patron were classified as beggars. Conversely beggars played at being actors to escape being whipped. I think she must have attended one of my annual productions of *Hamlet* in Regent's Park. Ah, it was the last. You remember it? That was the one in which my Baker Street urchins played all the female roles. It was magnificent. Let us not speak of it. When Mrs. St. Clair sprang her trap and accused your humble servant, she was playing at being Portia. 'Then perhaps, Mr. Holmes, you will be good enough to explain how it is that I have just received this letter from him today?' Gentlemen of the jury, I rest my case. Please find the defence expert guilty. Ah, Watson, had she defended Shylock, he would have had his pound of flesh washed down with a gentle rain of blood. So would Mr. Moriarty for that matter. It is I not he who would now be running a crammer. But you see, she was putting me on the spot, the better to redirect the spotlight upon herself."

It was pointless to attempt reasonable argument with so dyed in the wool a misogynist as Sherlock Holmes. What use to cite my experience of wine, women, and roses as proof positive that none of them are capable of any deep deception? Truth is beauty and beauty is truth. Doubtless she had groaned at the doorway because she had mistaken me for her husband. He had reminisced to her on his acting days, and she naturally assumed he had returned to her in disguise.

But Holmes thinks the only woman to be taken at face value is a bruised corpse and such discolorations are more beautiful to him than the rosy hue of the most perfectly complexioned living girl. I blame De Quincey. In *On Murder Considered as One of the Fine Arts*, he wrote approvingly of Howship's admiration for "*a beautiful ulcer*". As an army surgeon, I will only say that sickness and crime are only beautiful in the eye of the degenerate. Maiwand lost was but marginally better than Maiwand had it been won. Of course, I suppose from the point of view of the enemy, it was.

Perhaps I could appeal to Holmes with facts. "You clearly imagine she knew of her husband's double life. That could not be so. It was by the merest chance she happened to glance up and see him at a window of the Bar of Gold. She was there by accident, having just collected a parcel from the offices of the Aberdeen Shipping Company in Fresno Street. She was looking around for a taxi to take her to the train station."

Holmes emitted a cynical humph implausibly conflated with a exceptionally sardonic sniff. There were no limits to the powers of that remarkable man, in whom the vilest things became becoming.

"There are precisely seven objections to that. Firstly, why could not a parcel sent from Scotland to London be posted or transported by train the extra seven miles from those offices to the Cedars? Secondly, if she meant to do shopping on so hot a day, why did she not avail herself of the carriage they kept at such great expense to take her into town and then from shop to shop? She could then have travelled home in it rather than walk from the train station beneath a stack of packages under a blazing sun while wearing a tight corset guaranteed to cause the average woman to swoon. Yes, Watson, like you, I did observe.

"Thirdly, if anxious to spare the wheels of their carriage and the soles of their groom's shoes unnecessary wear and tear, why did she not avail herself of a cab, rather than stagger like one fresh from a gin shop beneath an ever increasing burden of parcels, asking the cabbie to wait while she went into the aforesaid offices to collect that final parcel? Since she would only have paid the driver on completion of the journey to the train station or to the Cedars, there would have been no danger of his bolting leaving before she returned. "Fourthly, even if we suppose that her cabbie abandoned her, having seen an enemy pursued over the decades and determined as he was to avenge the love of his life, would she not have summoned another to take her home or to the train station once she was back in Fresno Street?

"Fifthly, what would have possessed her to plunge instead into Upper Swandam Lane, one of the vilest alleyways in the East End, and a place that the police dare not venture into alone? Did she really imagine she was more likely to find a cabbie in so impoverished and disreputable an area than in the more respectable Fresno Street? Or perhaps you picture her as an over-eager autograph hunter anxious to have the Ripper engrave his signature in her skin?

"Sixthly, she claimed the instant she heard a cry, she at once gazed upwards to a second-storey window of the Bar of Gold and so caught sight of her husband. Would not any ordinary person have first gazed all around them for the source of such a sound? Only after that would they think of looking to the heavens. Seventhly, and most important of all, her testimony is quite at odds with her husband's version of events."

It seemed to me that Holmes had made rather more than seven objections, but had cheated by combining some to satisfy his endearingly superstitious passion for the number seven. However, such an objection would have played into his hands and strengthened his argument that was lying. I therefore confined myself to questioning his final objection alone as the weakest link in his chain of reasoning: "Mr. and Mrs. St. Clair's accounts tallied exactly."

"Ha! Hardly. He told us he had gone to a window of his rooms in the Bar of Gold and on looking down was startled to see his wife standing directly below and already gazing fixedly up at them. At this he hid his face in his hands and darted out of sight. By contrast she claimed she only looked up in response to his cry of dismay and that far from attempting to conceal his face he had waved his arms in the air in just the melodramatic manner Hamlet advises actors not to do. Now, which sounds more likely to you?"

My friend was conveniently forgetting his golden rule. "Holmes, have you not told me again and again that when you have eliminated the impossible, then the improbability of whatever remains is irrelevant? It is impossible she knew her husband was in the Bar of Gold. Therefore, the improbability of his behaving that way is immaterial. He must have."

"Why was it impossible she was lying?"

"Because she knew nothing of his past life."

"No? You are forgetting those guest rooms at the Cedars. Deny if you wish that the bedroom suite we occupied was their bedroom. The fact that Mrs. St. Clair surrendered it to me when I might not need it at all implies she was able to sleep in a single bedroom elsewhere. Doubtless such rooms were reserved for house guests. That implies they entertained. Many such guests would have been old friends of St. Claire from his days as an actor and journalist. That writer Kernahan told me of a mutual friend who had been such a guest at one of their house parties. He and others would have reminisced on how he had once dressed up as a beggar and earned more in a day than in a week as a reporter. Of course, St. Clair would have changed the subject but too late. It must have piqued his wife's interest. If she had not done so already, she would certainly have perused his past articles with their description of the fictitious beggar who would one day be resurrected as Hugh Boone."

176

I began to feel uncomfortable, but consoled myself with the thought that I at least was in a far more secure position than St. Clair. Mary was determined to read all my past work, but fortunately, she knew nothing of my youthful contributions to the happily defunct *Holywell Street Journal*. Being a brief-lived and subscription-only publication, I lived in hope she would never learn of it. She was hardly likely to encounter the kind of connoisseurs who had subscribed to it. The only one who might have posted her copies out of spite was Stapleton, and he was at the bottom of the Grimpen Mire. It was best to shun such thoughts. I returned to the matter in hand.

"She may well have read his articles, I grant you, Holmes, but how could that possibly have led her to suspect him of leading a double life?"

"Women are not fools, Watson. You think me a misogynist because I know they are never to be trusted, but that shows I hold them in higher esteem than you do. You suppose them incapable of Machiavellian thought. I do not. And if they can deceive, then they can penetrate deceptions. Do you not see, then, that she must have asked herself how it was that her husband's handwriting altered so dramatically whenever he found it necessary to write to her, assuring her that all was well and he would soon return? I have already explained that from time to time he would have been incarcerated for days or weeks, lest the higher authorities come to suspect he was bribing the constables to turn the Nelsonian eye. How were such disappearances to be explained? Was he seeing another woman? Was he involved in some criminal enterprise? Or was he taking drugs? She had to know.

"She followed him and saw him enter the Bar of Gold. Having been an actress, she disguised herself and descended into its depths, but found no trace of him save perhaps for a Crucifixion print acquired by him years before. What proof had she that it was the very same copy he had once owned? She returned to the street and, masquerading as a beggar woman, waited for him to reappear. Instead out came Boone, the spitting image of the redheaded beggar St. Clair had described himself playing in those articles. She understood the awful truth. After that, it was a matter of unmasking him in such a way as to ensure he would have to renounce that life forever."

"But it was the purest chance he just happened to look out from a window of his rooms!"

"Chance? Pshaw! The Bar of Gold is the most infamous opium den in the entire the East End. Naturally Prince Pagan has visited it, though only to be able to boast to his Bohemian subjects he has done so. Your friend Oscar Wilde followed in the footsteps of Dickens to do research akin to his. I must confess, though, I had not really deduced from certain

177

tooth marks that the pipe I handed Kernahan was ever smoked by the inventor of the immortal Inspector Bucket. Never mind. The Bar can still boast of a clientele that includes such notable addicts as Isa Whitney, and then there are those regrettable characters sent to collect them. One can count on investigative journalists dropping in from time to time, too. You must see that over the years, dozens of men and women St. Clair knew have frequented the place. Is it likely he would have neglected to take the elementary precaution of keeping the shutters on his windows permanently closed? Worse, would he have invited discovery by gazing down from them for all the world to see?

"The implication is clear. Mrs. St. Clair bribed his cleaner to open those shutters contrary to his strict instructions that they should never be touched. On entering the rooms to tear off his too tight collar and necktie, he perceived this and in a fit of anger dismissed her. After that, he had no choice but to close the shutters himself. It was then that he saw his wife gazing steadfastly up at him."

"But if she meant to unmask him why did she not come armed with a sponge to wipe away Boone's face?"

"Oh, she might have done just that, had she not realised her blunder in time. Once she had forced her way into those rooms, only to find no sign of her 'husband', but in his place the beggar of St. Clair's articles sprung to life, she was certain at first it had to be him. Then she realised the thing was impossible. No actor could have transformed himself so completely in seconds. It had to be someone else playing that part. A consideration of Boone's teeth confirmed it."

That flew in – well – the teeth of all experience! That was what I had meant to say, but unfortunately I did not think of it at the time. "Surely you are joking, Holmes. Whoever heard of anyone identifying a man on the basis of their dentures?"

Holmes sighed. "Ah, Watson, Watson. Have you forgotten already? No doubt I am being uncharitable. You probably never remembered. Why, it was only last Saturday, please make a note of it, that we investigated the little matter of the Stockbroker's Clerk, which as you ought to recall turned on Hall Pycroft's observation that twin brothers shared the same gold filling. That perceptive prospector struck gold thanks to the briefest of glances into that black gap like the mouth of the Bar of Gold. It was in all the papers. To her credit, Mrs. St. Clair read between the headlines and detected mine as the unseen hand responsible for the apprehension of the villains, though predictably the police took all the credit. I am relying on you, Watson, to tell the public the truth.

"Having come to suspect her husband was the beggar Boone, she thought to prove it by means of the same trick. She would consider the beggar's teeth, always assuming he had any. In his case, it was easier since three of the Man with the Twisted Lip's front teeth were perpetually on display. They were in much better condition than one would expect of a beggar living off sugar and bread. They were still there.

"Contrary to her expectations, though, she soon perceived Boone's were *not* her husband's. Evidently he had managed to escape by the skin of his own teeth. Ha! Amusing, don't you think? No? Never mind. It was then she remembered my name had been mentioned in connection with that affair of those brothers with fillings as alike as two gold peas in a pod. She determined to use me to unmask her husband, forcing him to renounce Boone forever."

But I held my ground. "All that is very ingenious, Holmes, but aren't you forgetting something? We *know* St. Clair was Boone. You yourself unmasked him. That is final." I crossed my arms in a most forceful manner, for it seemed to me my logic was impeccable. I was surprised when Holmes appeared to be less than impressed. That was unreasonable of me. I ought to have known better after all these years.

"No, no, no. Not at all. After that leaden degenerate manager of the Bar of Gold had barred her way, Mrs. St. Clair reversed back out into the alleyway to fetch help. Her husband naturally supposed she would not stray from the entrance and would moreover barricade the Bar prior to storming it with reinforcements. Had he not assumed this, he would have attempted an escape during her brief absence. He need not have run out into the street. He could have used that trap door I mentioned leading from the Bar of Gold to the Thames. But he dared not do that for fear it was being watched. Is it likely, though, that he would have thought to change into Boone in the less than a minute of freedom he feared was left to him? It would have taken all that time just to deposit six-hundred and ninety-one pennies and halfpennies into the pockets of his coat prior to casting it out of the window and into the waters below. The calculation is a simple one."

"He might have managed it," I protested feebly. "He had only just begun to dress prior to leaving to catch the train back to the Cedars."

Holmes put on Number Three from his range of seven expressions for weary patience.

"The collar." he sighed. "The necktie." Another and a deeper sigh. Weary Patience Number Five.

"What of them?"

"Oh, nothing – save, of course, for the blindingly obvious. Ah, Diogenes, why did you waste the philosopher's lamp, searching for an honest man? You should settled for a man or a woman who could at least *see*. Mrs. St. Clair was evidently such a one, for she observed at a glance

179

he had not yet removed his coat but had already torn off his collar and necktie. Incidentally, that shows what exceptionally good eyesight she had, so don't try to explain away her cry of disappointment on perceiving I had brought someone with me to the Cedars by claiming she was so myopic she mistook you for her husband. No, do not protest, I assure you there is absolutely no need for her to offer up a prayer to St. Clare as the patron saint of eye diseases. The blind spot was your own soft one for blondes, my dear and besotted doctor."

"I never intended to claim any such thing," said I indignantly. "The path was narrow and winding and I must have been concealed behind you. That would explain it." Perceiving he was preparing to pounce like a tiger upon my poor defence, I hastily went on the offensive. "You have made a mistake, Holmes. He had not, as you suppose, only that second taken his collar and necktie off. On the contrary, he had just put them on."

Holmes gave me a look to wither a rose.

"Whoever heard of a man putting on his coat before his collar and necktie? But what are the first things a man removes with infinite relief the moment he returns home? An insufferably stiff collar and an accompanying necktie as constricting as a noose. It follows he was not preparing to depart. He had only just arrived."

This really was too much. Now was the time to wield the sturdy sponge of Common Sense to wipe the face of Truth clean of Speculation's clinging cobwebs. "Holmes," said I firmly, "not a single word you have uttered matters in the least! Poke about in the gloom with your philosopher's lamp and bury your nose in your pipe bowl, if you wish, but it does not alter the one indisputable fact: We visited Boone in his cell at Bow Street Magistrates" Court and you unmasked him before my very eyes! Seeing is believing and I know what I saw. Hugh Boone turned in an instant into St. Clair. Or are you going to tell me the face you revealed was a second mask? Am I to suppose it was you playing both those parts while some unsuspected twin sister of yours was masquerading as you? Was that why you refused to share that bed with me at the Cedars? Because you were actually her?"

Holmes looked at me in surprise.

"Ingenious! Very, very ingenious. Of course I would never employ so hackneyed a device as to have a twin sister impersonate me just so I might play at being St. Clair playing at being Boone. That really would be unpardonably lazy. But that notion of a mask behind a mask is really quite witty. Watson, you ought to have been a writer of fairy tales. You have certainly introduced intriguing possibilities. Why, that little black girl we discovered behind a yellow mask may not have been a little black girl at all. Why did I not think to wipe a sponge across her face? Think, too, of that creature Doctor Challenger claimed had escaped his clutches during his investigation of the island of Flores? Perhaps it was that refugee who was concealed behind those black and yellow faces, lest Challenger recapture him and put him on display. But enough of such nonsense. Let us think what my illustrious ancestor William of Baskerville would have done in a case like this. He would undoubtedly apply Occam's Razor. We shall do so and thus see past the trimmings. Why have two false beards when there is no need for one?"

I considered my friend with some concern. He had spent many hours alone inhaling those deadly fumes in that infernal opium den. Then he had resorted to *nicotiana rustica* while chewing on coca leaves. He had been without sleep for days. As his shaman's pipe gave another ominous crack, I wondered whether he had not reached breaking point too. I began rummaging in my black bag for my universal panacea. I would force him to take it.

Mr. Holmes swatted the spirit aside like a symphony conductor exorcising a whiff of broken wind.

"Brandy be damned! But come now, Watson, you have not thought things through. Perhaps you are unfamiliar with the architecture of Bow Street Police Station. The holding cells run along two sides of the building on the ground floor. Did I not say St. Clair took the elementary precaution of bribing members of the police to ensure he was rarely arrested and when actually detained at Her Majesty's pleasure was treated like royalty? In accordance with his wishes they did not touch him with their filthy hands. That cell in the cellar was reserved by appointment for Hugh Boone. You must see that. The beggar was arrested in the East End by a detective inspector from the West End who had no business being in the City at all. Boone should never have been taken to Bow Street in the first place, let alone incarcerated there contrary to all customary procedures. He ought to have been taken to a prison to await his trial. Do I have to spell it out to you? Police corruption is not a thing of the past. The wheel turns and the same bent spokes come up."

I was deeply shocked. "Is that why you express such contempt for Gregson and Lestrade? You think them dishonest?"

"On the contrary, when I call them incompetent I am but paying them a backhanded compliment. Their palms at least have never been greased. Conversely, why do you suppose I praised Inspector Barton lavishly for searching Boone's rooms so very diligently? Why, he even overlooked the box on the table before him. Mrs. St. Clair had to seize upon it to reveal the children's bricks intended for her son. Did you not perceive how I charitably shrugged off Barton's quite incredible failure to arrest Boone at once on the charge of murder – to say nothing of his letting his confederate the manager go scot free? After leaving them together and alone, should not Barton have searched the manager for any notes passed to him by Boone? Not that there were any."

Here was an example of my friend's own fallibility that might have taught him to be less critical of others. "Holmes, you are forgetting that letter to St. Clair's wife."

"Indeed? Why, then it is high time I abandoned law keeping for some sweeter pursuit. Beekeeping, perhaps. I forget nothing save by choice. Do you think such a man as that manager would have been entrusted with St. Clair's identity and address? Blackmail would undoubtedly have ensued. No, such a note could only have been passed on to someone unable to blackmail without being exposed himself. Can you not deduce who that was from the dirty thumbprint and the shreds of shag tobacco in the envelope?

"A sailor?"

"No, Watson. A detective. Those clues were too obvious. They were precisely what one would expect a competent if unimaginative inspector to supply me with. But the tobacco shreds were inside the envelope while the thumbmark was outside it. If the manager of the opium den left those shreds there, he did so before the envelope was sealed. Where would he have sealed it, bearing in mind that he was under police observation? In the opium den. Would there not have been a faint scent of opium clinging to the paper? There was only the scent of Mrs. St. Clair's perfumed breasts. No, no, Boone passed the note on to Barton and he delayed posting it to give the impression it was handed to some sailor who promptly forgot all about it. The one piece of real wit was to post it at Gravesend. A nice touch of gallows humour, that."

"But why did you not tell me you suspected Barton?"

"Lest we encounter him and you eyed him askance. There is no doubt in my mind he is one of St. Clair's insiders. Bradstreet may be another of St. Clair's men, for you may have noticed the inspector acted as if there could be no charge against him despite evidence enough he was guilty of the most outrageous case of serial begging in the history of crime. Did I say St. Clair's men? That is to assume St. Clair is not himself the instrument of some greater power."

"You cannot mean Adam Worth?"

"Well, it is certainly a possibility. Perhaps I mentioned that at the exact same hour you were celebrating your questionable friend Doyle's birthday last year, Worth's home was being raided by the police. I had told them to look beneath his bed for the Duchess of Devonshire wearing her hat at an infamous tilt. They found nothing. Not a thing, Watson. I realised my mistake too late. I had mentioned the intended raid to you and you in

182

turn told Doyle, who at once passed on the confidence to Worth, who acquired further information concerning it from his insiders at the Yard. No doubt Doyle shall be rewarded royally for services rendered. I should not be surprised if Worth arranges for him to receive all the royalties from your future work. I do not trust that artful conman Doyle."

I have long since learnt to patiently endure Holmes" professional suspicion of the best of men, even one as honourable as my occasional collaborator. Why, Conan Doyle has graciously consented to lend me his name as a *nom de plume*! The courageous fellow insisted upon it despite the very real danger to his own person. He was deeply anxious lest Holmes's enemies think to target me and my wife. Holmes, of course, interpreted such selfless generosity in the most cynical manner possible.

As for the police, they could not possibly be as corrupt as Holmes supposes. That he is prejudiced is understandable enough, though, since the Trial of the Detectives shocked the nation and happened to be just after Holmes opened his consultancy in Montague Street. It had left Scotland Yard in complete disarray and wondering who had exposed them. The question for a time was not whether a detective could go wrong, but rather whether there was a single Scotland Yard detective who had not done so. Men like Lestrade were recruited to fill the void left at the Yard, being thought so imbecilic as to be incapable of guile. Things have improved greatly since then, but Holmes will not acknowledge it. I have come to accept it is best to let his slanders pass.

"There again," mused Holmes, lost in his own reflections as I had been in mine, "Worth cannot endure forever. I am beginning to suspect someone is at work weaving a rival web against the day when the great man meets his Waterloo. Is Doyle working for Worth or for someone else? Or is he a double agent? Leave that for the present. The point is this: St. Clair was not playing Boone on the day the latter was arrested, indeed I doubt he plays him at all these days save for training purposes. It was thus a matter of his changing places with whomever was Boone at that time. The switch must have been made just before we came calling."

"Impossible!"

"It will cease to be so just as soon I have explained how it was managed. Obviously with an insider at Bow Street, which was the reason why it was essential Boone be kept there, it was the easiest thing in the world for the man playing Boone to remove his makeup and then walk straight out of the building. St. Clair took his place. In his case makeup was superfluous."

"You mean he took some special potion? Like Stevenson's *Jekyll and Hyde*?"

"Not Stevenson's. Mansfield's. You witnessed that actor's transformations when you and your fiancée attended a performance of the dramatised story at the Lyceum last year, did you not? It is a little thing called *acting*. Those who have mastered it have no need to paint an inch thick." Here was a touch of the familiar contempt for the greasepaint brigade of professional thespians, whom Holmes spurns as in his eyes only going through the motions of acting.

But I was incredulous. "Holmes, I saw the change! One moment there was the repulsive Boone and the next he had turned into the pale and delicate Mr. St. Clair. That had to be more than acting."

At that moment Holmes gasped and pointed dramatically towards the window. I followed his gaze but could see nothing. When I turned back he had vanished and I found myself face to face with Professor Moriarty, or rather with *The Strand* illustrator Sidney Paget's portrayal of him as based on Holmes's description. It is a curious thing, but although I at once realised this was Holmes achieving one of his lightning transformations, I was still horrified. I seemed to see how that noblest of men might have fallen had he been fully seduced by De Quincey's *On Murder Considered as One of the Fine Arts* and his equally infectious *Confessions of an Opium Eater*. Consumed in combination, they could have proved as fatal as a cocktail as morphine and cocaine. The next moment his Mr. Hyde had vanished and my very own Dr. Jekyll had been restored to me.

"Bear in mind, Watson," said he, with a smirk suggestive of self-satisfaction at having made my flesh creep, "that Boone's cell was subterranean. Moreover ours was an early morning call while he still seemed to be slumbering. St. Clair was wholly lost in the shadows of his cell. Do you not see how very easy that deception was? First he distorted his features. Then as I passed my sponge across his face he relaxed them and simultaneously shifted into a ray of light just then penetrating through the open doorway. That was the reason for the sudden and illusory paling of his face. It was well done, though I believe I could have managed it better. I presume I do not need to explain to you, a doctor turned writer, how easy it is to deceive the man in the street who is willing to suspend his disbelief? I say nothing of such a one's intellect, since as a general rule there is nothing to say anything about."

It pained me to hear Holmes speak in such extraordinarily cynical terms about the beauty of the world and paragon of animals. If there is one thing I have learnt from my medical career, and that I trust have brought to my literary one, it is never to abuse the faith of those put into one's care, be they readers or patients. Nor is it possible to over-estimate the intelligence of the British public. I concluded Holmes was projecting his own tendency to manipulate others onto me. He appeared to believe that

"Trust me, I'm a doctor" had become "Trust me, I'm a writer." Or perhaps he was toying with me.

"You are not serious. It is all very ingenious, to be sure, but you are contradicting yourself. You said earlier the murderer could not have escaped from the Bar of Gold since the police were watching it so carefully. If St. Clair had not changed into Boone, then he would have had to have been hiding somewhere in it. Where could he possibly have done so?"

Holmes bestowed upon me the sour look of a cat who has just been pecked on the nose by a parrot, safe behind the bars of its cage. "Have I not already told you that? Ah, but to hear is not always to attend. St. Francis preached to the birds but did they listen, any more than we do to the sermons of bees? Did I not tell you I glimpsed the murderer of St. Clair at the distant end of that den's long, narrow berth like that of a slave ship? The man was kneeling by a brazier and lost in self-pitying penitence until the very moment I made a move towards him. On discovering that the killer had been confessing his sins to that print of the *Crucifixion*, I naturally thought of the blessed St. Clare, founder of the Poor Clares, who as you know are the keepers of the crucifix that spoke to her friend, St. Francis. In illness, she saw the mass projected onto a wall of her sick room in the manner of those new moving pictures. She should really be made the patron saint of motion photographs. I must remember to suggest it to his Holiness the next time He requires my assistance. But you see that my thinking of St. Clare suggests even then I had begun to suspect who the murderer might be."

"And St. Clair?" I asked impatiently, for I saw now whom Holmes supposed was the penitent killer before the Crucifixion.

"Oh, he got away, of course, for I had assured the police they could end their watch on the Bar of Gold once I was in the den to await the concealed man's move. The murderer, as I still supposed he was, which was not so very wide of the mark since St. Clair would indeed do away with Boone soon enough, could not shift until the manager gave the all clear."

"And when did you definitely conclude the kneeling man was St. Clair?"

Holmes seemed troubled. "To be honest, Watson, I don't know. That raises intriguing philosophical questions concerning what knowing is and who does it. You know that the Descartes of legend concentrated his thoughts in the concentrated atmosphere of a stove? It was there that he deduced he must be because he thought he was. But what was it that thought he was? Sherlock Holmes exists, of course. There can be no question of that. But what is Sherlock Holmes? Someone or something perceived Hugh Boone and St. Clair were connected, but what part of Sherlock Holmes it was that did so is not entirely clear even to the aspect of that admirable gentleman that is speaking to you at this moment."

I was beginning to understand how Horatio must have felt chaperoning his exasperating friend the Dane of Elsinore. Oscar Wilde had quipped to me after attending one of Holmes's annual productions of *Hamlet*, "Is the chap really mad, or is he only pretending to be mad?" At the time I had assumed he meant the Dane. Later, I wondered whether he was actually speaking of Holmes. Or there again, he could have been conflating the two, as Holmes himself sometimes seemed to do.

Holmes suddenly burst out laughing, and not in his usual inhibited Diogenes Club way either. I could hear him loud and clear. "I'm sorry, Watson. What nonsense I do talk at times. All I mean is that just as Dr. Jekyll is not one but two, so the same may be said of Sherlock Holmes, and indeed of any man. That is not to begin to speak of women. Let us not do so. Something in me knew that St. Clair had created Hugh Boone, and told me so as I sat staring at that *Crucifixion* through the veil of opium fumes until it seemed to come alive. Then in came the person from Porlock and dissolved all into thick air. Your esteemed thinking machine knew something had been lost, and a little voice told him it could only be recovered by sitting Siddhartha-like confronting Bermejo's *Michael* and the devil in the bedroom of the St. Clairs while smoking *nicotiana rustica*. So he did so. Then it came to him. But to put it into words took much longer. I am not sure I can do it now. And yet I'll hammer it out. You remember what I said about the *Crucifixion* print earlier?"

"You observed that Jesus was being offered a sponge soaked in opium or some other pain killer."

"That was the superficial justification for its presence in the den. It seemed to excuse escapes from this world by means of drugs. If religion is the opium of the people, then why should not opium by the religion of the aesthetic elect? That is the view of Thaddeus Sholto and others who play at being Oscar Wilde, including Wilde himself."

It occurred to me that such witticisms suggested Holmes might almost be included among their number. "But you do not think that was its chief meaning for St. Clair?"

"Most assuredly not. What mattered to him was a god who took on human form, and was ruined and disfigured to hold a mirror up to those making faces at him that would have made Boone seem like a beauty. The wet and foul sponge thrust into the face of that crucified god has been likened to one wiped across his image by an iconoclast, you know, to leave something blurred, discoloured, inhuman and terrible. Precisely what I would have left had St. Clair as Boone really been wearing grease paint.

186

That was why I did it, though, knowing he would picture such a possibility. Then he would remember the transfigured and resurrected Christ. Such a remembrance would encourage him to attempt his own rebirth."

It is always unwise to divert Holmes with a technical question that can send him down a rabbit hole into some labyrinthine burrow, but I could not help it. "Are you sure St. Clair will keep his word? We do not even know he ever gave it, or to whom. He only said he had sworn to renounce Boone by the most solemn oaths which a man can take. What does that mean, anyway?"

My philosophical friend may not know who or what he is, or even what it is for him to be at all, but his biographer has no such doubts. His reaction to this little *caveat* was no more than what I might have expected.

"Do you think me such a dolt, Doctor, that I would accept the word of one who had lived a lie with his wife every day of their marriage, a man who was no more St. Clair than he was Hugh Boone, had I not witnessed him giving his word? What do you suppose he was doing, kneeling before that *Crucifixion*, beating his breast as passionately as St Francis himself must have done? Oh, to be sure, words without thoughts never to heaven go, But there was matter in his sighs and his profound heaves. They were what I attended to. You recall how Bradlaugh, that atheist fellow who founded the National Secular Society, was elected as a Liberal MP, only to be promptly imprisoned for refusing to take the religious Oath of Allegiance? There's a man whose word means something! It was only last year he was at last allowed to affirm instead of swearing, and just in time to support the matchgirls strike. Do you see now? St. Clair had been swearing to God he would dispose of Boone as surely as Jekyll had thought to exorcise Hyde. Those opium fumes took the place of church incense, and in the darkness of that den St. Clair might have been a monk in his cell. There were tears in his eyes. I confess I did not quite understand at the time. It is one thing to infer the possibility of a Niagara from a dew drop. To read a tear trickling down a cheek is trickier. Only after I had spent hours before the Bermejo did a lost intuition start to return."

"And then it was you went to the bathroom to collect the sponge."

Holmes had furrowed his forehead as if to squeeze his mighty brain dry of both perspiration and inspiration. "No. Not in that order. It was the terrible puzzle, Watson. I had felt a sudden and inexplicable urge to dowse my face in cold water. While I was at the basin doing so, I caught sight of my weary face in the mirror and so recalled how I had put on an even more dog-tired one for your benefit in that opium den, only to then smear a smile across it the better to observe the distortion to your features in response. Then I remembered: Seated before the *Crucifixion*, I had sensed St. Clair had been imagining the coming transfiguration of the ruined Christ. He had arrived at a turning point. He had come to a dead end beside a straight drop and, like Saul on the road to Damascus, he had to choose."

"Then you deposited the sponge in the Bellinger bag."

To my surprise Holmes looked perplexed. "That is the strange thing. I cannot quite explain it to you or myself, but I seemed to be moving in a kind of dream. Or there again, perhaps I was as close to an awakening as I had ever been. You recall the question I addressed to you immediately after my second *Eureka!* moment?"

"I'm afraid not, Holmes," said I apologetically. "I was still half asleep."

"Only half asleep? Ah, that is the question. My precise words were: 'Awake, Watson?' Actually, the question ought to have been addressed to myself as much as to you, though I could not comprehend that at the time. I was only half awake too. But let us not be distracted from our pressing superficial questions for now. The profound ones can keep, including the little matter of what it is to be really awake. Well, that travelling bag seemed to take me by the hand and lead me down the right path back to that heap of cushions before the Bermejo as nothing else could have done."

I did not quite follow that. "Surely, Holmes, a bag could not have led you anywhere."

"It led me to think of the gentleman it had been named after. You know how Lord Bellinger has a bee in his bonnet when it comes to spongers. He likes to rail they ought to be deported to Australia to lead honest lives of toil. His philosophy is if you donate a man a fish, you feed him for a day but if you teach him how to fish and make him do it, then you feed him for a lifetime. On one occasion he was with fellow house guests, all grumbling about how their sponges could not be packed without the dampness oozing out into the neighbouring linen. Bellinger seized a sponge, wrapped it in a towel, and proceeded to stamp on it furiously while crying out: 'You NONE of you KNOW how to PACK your SPONGE. The ONE way to PACK a SPONGE is to wrap it up in a bath towel and STAMP on it.' He would do the same to spongers given half the chance. And that brings us back to your primal problem."

"What was that, Holmes?" I had experienced so many puzzles I could no longer recall what the first was. I was not even sure there was one. It would make a good title, though.

"Well, you asked me why, having solved the mystery of St. Clair and Boone, I should then have returned to that cross-legged position before the copy of a Bermejo. You must see now it was to solve the deeper mystery of how I had stumbled upon the solution to the puzzle of 'The Man with the Twisted Lip'. The answer itself was nothing. To know how I arrived at it was everything."

188

"And now you know?"

"I think so, Watson. At least I glimpse it as in a glass darkly. I fear I must bore you now with my analysis of that Bermejo painting, but I have no alternative. It was seeing it through St. Clair's eyes that helped me to comprehend why that abominable *Crucifixion* print so moved him."

"Well, proceed," said I reluctantly, for though Holmes may have pigments in the blood, always supposing he had not fibbed about his ancestry, his obsession with rationality is definitely a distracting factor. He is so anxious to observe that he sometimes forgets to *see*.

Holmes shifted his gaze to consider his own reflection in his silver-plated coffee-pot. That surprised me, for he generally prefers to play the father confessor and confines himself to making windows into others' souls. As a rule, he is about as capable of self-reflection as a narcissist, and of soul-searching as a hibernating vampire, but for once I believe his introspection really was directed inwards. At the same time, I have no doubt he took in my reflected face, if only for purposes of comparison.

"Recall, then, that in the painting St. Michael is shown looking down at the Devil with a smile more of sorrow than anger and of pity as opposed to vindictiveness. The *coup de grace* he is about to deliver really shall be a stroke of pity. We might liken it to Christ striking down Saul on the road to Damascus, and enquiring of him why he persecuted him. Now tell me what the fallen devil sees."

"If I remember rightly, Holmes, it is gazing up at Michael."

"True, but let us be precise. His line of vision is to Michael's crystal shield. It is transparent, and he sees through it. He also sees his own reflection upon it. He sees what he was and what he has become."

"Why suppose he sees what he was?"

"The name 'Michael' means 'Who is like God?'. The unfallen Lucifer was the brightest of all the angels and so the most like God. The beauty of Michael therefore reminds him of what he had been. More precisely, he recalls what he was, and in an instant became as he assaulted the celestial sphere beyond which he could see the face of Christ. The hemispherical crystal shield stands in for that celestial sphere."

"Why suppose he is thinking of Christ? Why not God the Father?"

"Because Michael's head is adorned with heaps of pearls topped by a crucifix. The pearls signify skulls since 'Golgotha' means 'Place of the Skull'. His shoes are decorated with rubies that recall the stigmata."

"And you think St. Clair saw himself in the devil?"

"In a manner of speaking. Our calcified arachnid understands how he has fallen in striving to better himself. Now Michael will cast him screaming into the bottomless abyss. Nevertheless, it is not too late for him to repent as Saul did to become Paul. St. Clair understood that he, too, might be saved and regenerated. The first step was to take the place of his partner in that cell. The second was to permit me to unmask him."

"But why did you not insist he reveal all?"

"Because there was much more at stake."

"What do you mean?"

"Well, there were two related difficulties yet to be addressed. They were trivial by comparison with the perennial problems I was groping to bring into focus. Nevertheless they could not be ignored. Firstly, how could one man have acquired insiders at Bow Street Police Station? Secondly, could St. Clair as Hugh Boone truly have importuned seven-hundred pounds a year? Surely it beggars belief! If that were possible then there would have been no need for Jonathan Small to seek the Agra treasure, for with his wooden leg and the pygmy Tonga on tow, he ought to have acquired a sufficient hoard to cram the maw of the most all-devouring of dragons. He might have erected himself a tower beside Pondicherry Lodge from which to take pot-shots at the Sholtos far below. No, one man could not have solicited so much. A hundred might do so. Does that not suggest a solution to the difficulty? Have you not heard of the A.M.S.?"

"The Army Medical School?" said I uncertainly. "I was offered a teaching position there on the day I left 221b."

Holmes grunted his profound disapproval. "You did well to decline it. Please do not dignify that ramshackle crammer with so grandiose a title. The so-called 'Army Medical School' is in reality nothing but a disgraced mathematician and a cardsharp. Do not speak of it again. But you have not heard me speak of the Amateur Mendicant Society?"

"I never have."

"Well, they keep a low profile, to be sure. Literally. They hold court in a secret vault deep below the furniture store of Hamptons and Sons Limited between the National Gallery and Whitcomb Street."

I nodded. "I have passed it on my way to the Royal College of Physicians and Surgeons. It is a charitable society?"

"In a manner of speaking. Think of my Baker Street Irregulars. It is a kind of adult version of that. They are also known as the Poor St. Clairs, which may give you a clue as to the identity of their founder and president. I believe that as part of the initiation ceremony every new member has to play Hugh Boone for a day. That might explain why Boone's coat was cast out of the window into the Thames after being weighed down with coins to prevent it floating away. St. Clair would never have done that. He knew how swiftly bodies were hurried away by the current. Furthermore he was fully aware that in a few hours the tide would go out and then the coat would be revealed, at which time all the money in its pockets would speak

190

of the guilt of Boone. Money cannot be bribed into holding its tongue. I fear the Boone of that day will never be enrolled into the Red-Headed League, which is the Society's innermost circle."

I shook my head. "That hardly solves all the difficulties, Holmes. St. Clair could not have lived in such luxury, even as the leader of a gang of beggars."

"If that was all they were then what you say would be true. But perhaps you have forgotten that band of roaming constables from Bow Street that Mrs. St. Clair chanced to encounter as they wended their merry way towards Upper Swandam Lane in the East End? Curious, is it not? They claimed they were heading for their various beats."

"Why not really, Holmes," said I in some surprise, for I had imagined my friend would understand how dangerous parts of the East End are. "There are black spots where both police constables and angels fear to tread, save with comrades. And besides, if they were from the West End, they would have had no jurisdiction. Only the City of London Police can operate there, as I am sure you know." I felt embarrassed and confused. I was surely teaching my grandmother to suck eggs.

Holmes seemed puzzled and considered me as if I were a Neanderthal and he was wondering how on earth to demonstrate that two plus two make four. It was not such a simple thing to do.

"Watson, have you ever watched police constables disperse from Bow Street to the four corners of the earth? It is akin to the sight of foraging bees leaving their hive. I say the four corners, but of course the City is out of bounds to the Metropolitan Police. And they never proceed in a group. How could they possibly have done so, only to end up in the one area they had no business being in? Do you not see? With the single exception of Inspector Barton, who was a genuine if corrupt detective, none of them was a real policeman at all. That is why he had to be with them in case they encountered any City of London Police. He could then have explained they were on their way to a training conference or something of the sort, as indeed they probably were. Do you see? When the Amateur Mendicants were not begging for surplus coins, they were playing at being superfluous coppers themselves. If they were indeed on their way to a training session, it was in the Bar of Gold. As their chief and mentor, St. Clair was awaiting their arrival."

Like such police constables, I keep flat-footed upon the ground, and a good thing too or there would be nobody to prevent Holmes from floating away, never to be sighted again. "Perhaps you have overlooked it, Holmes, but there is a very simple explanation for their presence in Fresno Street. The City Police were doubtless overstretched and had requested the loan of a few constables to help them out." I was quite pleased with myself. Of course Holmes was less than impressed.

"Watson, as soon as Mrs. St. Clair had recovered from that feigned faint of hers, they escorted her home in a cab, presumably because she could not be trusted to take the train alone lest she succumb to an attack of brain fever as the horror of her situation came in its full force upon her."

Perhaps I was missing something. "Well, what of that? She was distressed, and her presence could have been no help to them in their investigations."

"No? You do not think it might have been useful if she had accompanied them to the nearest police station to give a sworn statement? But that would never do. In the first place she would ask them why they were taking Boone out of the City and all the way to Bow Street, and in the second it would mean a paper trail, to say nothing of setting the wheels in motion that had to result in Boone's transference to a prison elsewhere. No, no, those were counterfeit coppers intent at first upon stealing into the Bar of Gold. Then there was a change of plans. Their new aim was to steal away Boone."

"Impossible! How could they have done so unseen?"

"Ah, Watson," said he with a familiar shake of the disapproving head. "How many times must I repeat myself? The wheels turn, and yet the engine never really starts to work. Well, it is all a matter of elimination. Do away with all possibilities until you are left with only one. Let us grant first of all that a dozen constables could hardly have entered the Bar of Gold via an upper window, amusing though it is to picture them forming a human pyramid in order to do so. The front door was of course out of the question."

"The roof!"

"Good, Watson. But if the roof were feasible, then why did Boone not escape that way? What does that leave us with?"

I shrugged helplessly.

"Why, have you forgotten that trap door I told you of, the one occasionally employed for the disposal of corpses into the Thames on moonless nights? At least that was the rumour. I daresay one or two bodies have been dumped in the water that way, though it has far more important uses. Boone dared not use it, since he could not tell at first whether the police Mrs. St. Clair returned with were bogus or not. Copper-bottomed coppers would know of that trap door and watch it. As it happens, they were not the genuine article at all and had planned to sneak in that way via a rope ladder let down to the deck of the *Aurora* moored below."

"The *Aurora*!" I gasped. That had been the vessel Jonathan Small thought to use to outrun police launches and so escape with the Agra

192

treasure. "Are you sure, Holmes? Inspector Athelney Jones was certain its captain, Mordecai Smith, was quite unaware he was harbouring criminals on board."

Holmes's evil eye shot forth a ray to pin me wriggling to the wall like one of the lepidopterist Stapleton's specimens. I would be labelled "Simpleton" in due course. "Why, you are right, Watson. Jones is such a trusting sort of a fellow, always ready to give the benefit of the doubt. It took him all of five minutes to decide to arrest Thaddeus Sholto on suspicion of being suspicious. Curiously, though, when it came to Mordecai Smith, attempting to outrun a police launch, and bellowing at him to halt, it never occurred to Jones to wonder whether the captain of the *Aurora* really was both myopic and hard of hearing. No, Watson, it would not surprise me to learn that the mysterious Inspector Barton and Jones were one and the same man."

"But Jones is an idiot!"

"Or sufficiently intelligent to appear to be one. He was just a little too stupid even for a detective inspector. He overdid it. As for the *Aurora*, it was the fastest thing on the river, and the one vessel capable of speeding away from the Thames police. Do you not see? That was what it was designed to do."

"But to what end?"

"Ah. That raises interesting possibilities in relation to the work of the Amateur Mendicant Society. Let us indulge in a pleasing speculation. Suppose you had just relieved a bank of a few thousand gold napoleons. As a criminal mastermind, what would you do next?"

"I would dispose of them."

"Brilliant, Watson. Though perhaps just a trifle easier said than done. First you have to conceal them. If you are wise, you will then convert them into to some other form. After that, you would do well to ship them straight out of the country. The last place the authorities would look for such French gold would be back in France. Observe now how useful such Poor Clairs would be to you."

"I'm afraid I don't."

"Really? You do not perceive that those impostor constables would constitute the ideal guard as you transported your treasure to that secret vault beneath Hamptons and Sons? Oh, delicious irony, to have all those Napoleons melted down practically in the shadow of Nelson's Column! Once converted into busts of Napoleon they could be transferred to the Bar of Gold to be passed down through that trap door to the *Aurora* and thence to France. *Voila tout.* And mark my words, Watson, should we ever find ourselves investigating such a robbery, you can expect Jones to make an appearance. That is, he will do so if he is working for Worth or someone

193

ambitious to be his successor. Whoever that mastermind may be I am convinced he means to make the Amateur Mendicant Society his equivalent of my Baker Street Irregulars to go everywhere and see everything and be observed by nobody. It is really quite flattering. But I have a loose thread in my hands now, Watson, and I mean to follow it to the heart of the web."

"What thread is that, Holmes?"

"Why, Mr. Neville St. Clair. He is contrite, but he is in too deep. That was why Mrs. St. Clair needed me to unmask him as the only hope she had of releasing him from the clutches of whatever mastermind is intent upon replacing Adam Worth. I am sorry to say it may already be too late for that. Despite his revolt on the road to Damascus, it will take more than a swift baptism in St Paul's wharf to change him in the twinkling of an eye. Besides, his family might follow him through that trap door into the Thames. To save them, he may have to pay a heavy price. Perhaps the painting of St Michael vanquishing the devil prior to casting him into the bottomless pit may prove to be prophetic."

"How do you mean, Holmes?"

"Only that final problems often require last bows. I and that master actor may meet again some day to re-enact the scene in the painting for our unknown Napoleon's entertainment. I have in mind the ideal place to stage it."

Anglo-French School – *"The Wilton Diptych"*

The Adventure of the
Gaslit Detective
Continuing "The Blue Carbuncle"

There was a rush, a clatter upon the stairs, the bang of a door, and the crisp rattle of running footfalls from the street.

"After all, Watson," said Holmes, reaching up his hand for his clay pipe, "I am not retained by the police to supply their deficiencies. If Horner were in danger it would be another thing, but this fellow will not appear against him, and the case must collapse. I suppose that I am commuting a felony, but it is just possible that I am saving a soul. This fellow will not go wrong again. He is too terribly frightened. Send him to gaol now, and you make him a gaol-bird for life. Besides, it is the season of forgiveness. Chance has put in our way a most singular and whimsical problem, and its solution is its own reward. If you will have the goodness to touch the bell, Doctor, we will begin another investigation, in which also a bird will be the chief feature. But halloa! Belay that order, Doctor, for this is surely the Duchess of Morcar come in answer to my note. She is much before her time."

The next instant Mrs. Turner had opened the door to pompously announce the lady herself, who entered at that celebrated stately step she had adopted at the funeral of her fourth and final husband and had not departed from ever since. She was clad from head to foot in widow's weeds as quite the tallest woman I had ever seen. The black ostrich feathers in her bonnet bowed respectfully low since she absolutely declined to do so while passing perilously straight-backed through our doorway. Of her face I can say nothing, for it was entirely concealed by the heaviest of black veils. That brought to my mind tales of vitriol hurled during one of the many attempts to seize her beloved blue carbuncle. I thought I could guess who the victim had been. It was said she always dined alone so no soul would ever glimpse what passed for her features. Queen Victoria had reportedly dubbed her "the woman in black" and sternly condemned her mourning as excessive. The Duchess had retorted that Her Majesty reminded her of Queen Gertrude in *Hamlet*, whose period of grief was scandalously brief.

Holmes rose, bowed, and then to my utter amazement began to flap his arms about like a demented bird of prey. I was still more astounded when her grace proceeded to do likewise, so that together they resembled nothing so much as a pair of fowl engaged in a bizarre mating ritual.

Somewhat embarrassed my first instinct was to withdraw. Then I recalled how, on passing by the Diogenes Club one day, I had caught sight of Holmes and his brother Mycroft seemingly roaring with laughter over some joke while gesticulating in just that curious manner. I later learnt that since silence is the first and last rule at that club-library, the brothers had mastered a semaphore method of communication. Moreover, so that they might breakfast together while sharing jokes they had learnt how to laugh heartily but in utter silence. They can also munch toast noiselessly. I have never ceased to be amazed at the extraordinary powers of those two very remarkable men.

So now I saw the explanation for this behaviour. The Countess was a deaf mute. Rather unfairly she had been blackballed from membership of the Diogenes – not because of her sex, for it is the only club in London to permit both men and women if of sufficient intellectual calibre – but as too taciturn even for that society of anti-socials.

"Light the lamp, Watson," said Holmes as he reached for the precious gem he had left on the mantelpiece, and which he had rewrapped but not yet returned to his safe. "There is no need for dramatic lighting now that the thief Ryder is departed."

I should explain that at the time of the Baskerville affair Holmes had been intrigued by the villain Stapleton's innovative use of a unique fluorescent paint that made his monstrous hound turn bright blue in the dark as if on fire. Needless to say Holmes had salvaged several tins of it found in Stapleton's home and had been experimenting with it ever since. The need to terrify Ryder into confessing to the theft of the blue carbuncle supplied Holmes with the excuse he had so longed for to perform a psychological experiment. The fluorescent lighting had given to his interview with Ryder something of the atmosphere of one of my friend Conan Doyle's séances and had ensured the carbuncle shone forth with a cold, cruel light.

As Holmes observed later, presentation is everything. When the Koh-i-Noor diamond was first displayed at the Great Exhibition, it met with universal disappointment while seen by natural light. When this was changed for artificial lighting and the stone was placed upon drapery variously described as anything from shocking pink to imperial purple, disinterest gave way to wonder.

In the case of Ryder, the lighting worked rather like the colour filters that had assisted that gem of an actor Richard Mansfield in his transformation from Dr. Jekyll into Mr. Hyde. Holmes had explained that by such means, different faces or facets of his character could from moment to moment be turned to the light. Well do I remember how my fiancée had clung to me at the crisis of Mansfield's alteration, perhaps because she recalled absurd rumours that he was the Ripper. I wondered at that moment whether Plato's beast that rises in the sleep of reason might not exist in us all.

Do I need to add that an ingenious use of lighting when combined with my friend's incomparable acting convinced Ryder he was in the presence of a necromancer, one able to see into his very soul? That was just as well. Holmes afterwards confessed there had not been a shred of evidence against the scoundrel. My friend had been bluffing as only he could.

I lit the gas lamp and its flickering, pale-greenish light filled the room. Holmes solemnly handed the Countess the little black package containing that gem so tiny that, had it not been wrapped, it might have been blown away by a gust and lost forever. As she eagerly and yet reverently unwrapped that most precious of stones, more precious to her than the ring of Lucy Ferrier's enslavement had been to her lover Jefferson Hope, I awaited with bated breath the gasp of joy and wonder that must burst forth from her mute mouth at the sight of it. Instead, it was I who gasped.

She never did. Instead there came a long moan such as I shall never forget. I hear it now. It was full of pain and incredulous horror and a deep grief. I saw the reason for it. Where that unique blue carbuncle ought to have been there was nothing but a plain red garnet. Inexplicably, impossibly, the gems had been switched.

The look of appalled bewilderment upon my friend's face is seared onto my mind's eye. The unthinkable implication was clear to him. While Ryder had been clinging to my friend and begging for mercy with tears in his eyes, he must somehow have pocketed the carbuncle and left with that red stone. Holmes had evidently been so distracted by the vile gropings of that rat-faced coward that he had absent-mindedly wrapped up the new stone without so much as glancing at it. Then he had told the repulsive creature to leave his sight. Like myself, my friend must now have been picturing Ryder turning a corner out of Baker Street only to burst out laughing at having done the world's greatest detective. I burned with indignation at the thought.

"Impossible!" Holmes muttered. "He could not have managed it. He must have done. No! He could not have done it. Impossible!"

The veiled lady had turned her unseen face towards the mortified detective. Was she asking herself whether Holmes had stolen the gem? Not knowing him as I did, I could hardly blame her if she suspected as much. He had borrowed the stone from its discoverer, the commissionaire Peterson, without troubling to ask his permission. It did seem incredible that an amateur like Ryder, no professional thief but a mere hotel upper-attendant, could actually have outsmarted the great Sherlock Holmes. Yet when one has once eliminated the impossible, then whatever remains must be the truth. It was absurd to suppose Holmes could have stolen it. Therefore Ryder had. That possibility was the lesser of two evils and I settled for it. Now I could only empathise with my friend and share in his humiliation and shame.

It is at such times that blue blood shines through. Though the lady swayed dangerously, and I feared she might faint, still she recovered herself with a magnificent display of true aristocratic steel. It is for such *sang froid* that the ancient nobility of Transylvania is rightly famed. Though I pictured her mask of a ruined face beyond the veil as now contorted into a horror beyond horror, still she concealed her grief. In response to Holmes's semaphored regrets, she gestured as gracefully as the ghost of Hamlet's father. A chequebook appeared and I gathered a compromise of sorts had been agreed upon. The generous lady, understanding that the commissionaire Peterson had been building castles in the sky with the promised thousand pounds reward, had with Christian charity offered to pay a hundred pounds for that comparatively insignificant red garnet. At least Peterson would not go away entirely empty-handed. I rejoiced. I knew Holmes could not.

The kindly old lady departed, and Holmes lapsed into a chair and a sullen silence. I averted my eyes from him and gazed out of the window at the Countess as she climbed into her carriage. She could not have been alone, for as she punched the air with both fists I heard a man's voice translate that cryptic sign for the benefit of the coachman: "Drive on! Drive on! It is ours! Go! Go!" Instantly the driver lashed the steeds and a moment later nothing remained but dust and dung where the carriage had been.

That was the last we and the world ever saw of that good and great lady. Neither she nor the blue carbuncle were ever heard of again, and I gather she collected the twenty thousand pounds the gem had been insured for.

As for Holmes, I could see at a glance he was now beyond reach. To attempt communication with him would be like trying to speak with Socrates during one of his trances. I wished him the belated compliments of the season, neither expecting a reply nor receiving one, and left.

Having forgotten to visit Holmes on Christmas Day I was determined not to let his birthday slip too, so I returned to 221b on the feast of the Epiphany bearing the only kind of gift he was sure to appreciate: A puzzle, which took the form of another battered hat. My occasional collaborator Conan Doyle had very kindly lent me his father's for the detective to make such deductions from as he might. As an added bonus, Doyle had supplied an interesting theory regarding how Ryder had managed to switch gems without Holmes ever noticing. Conan Doyle believed that, aided by the mesmerising power of the gem itself, Ryder had hypnotised us just for the time it took to exchange gems. I was unconvinced, though I did recall having been spellbound by the stone. I had not considered the possibility that I was literally so.

By the time I arrived at 221b, I had decided against showing Holmes Charles Altamont Doyle's hat, having recalled how my friend had read my poor late brother's watch and deduced his unhappy history from it. He might do as much with the headpiece of Conan Doyle's father, whom the son was curiously reticent to speak of. It was not worth the risk. I left the hat on the hat-stand. Mrs. Turner was no longer at 221b, so I was free to ascend the stairs unguided with only my own headpiece in my hand.

When I entered his rooms, I was surprised to find that the shutters were drawn and the room in darkness save for a pair of candles to the sides of a portable altarpiece propped up on the chair Mr. Henry Baker's beggar's crown had been hung upon a few days earlier. The candles had been placed on the chair's seat together with an ingenious microscope of Holmes's own design. To my great surprise, the scientist himself was kneeling before the diptych with eyes closed and hands folded together. I had always suspected Holmes had intended at one time to enter the Church. This seemed like proof positive of a secret pious streak.

I cleared my throat but he did not stir. I thought discretion was called for. "You are at your meditations," said I, and made to leave.

Suddenly his eyes jerked open like those of a sentry awakened in the alarm. "Not a bit of it, Doctor! I am delighted you have come. I was merely performing a little thought experiment. Remove your stethoscope from your hat and hang them both up. A thousand apologies. I see from the state of your headpiece that Mrs. Hudson forgot to light the stairway. You see I have found it." He gestured towards the two-framed altarpiece.

"Gracious heavens, Holmes. The stolen Wilton Diptych!"

Holmes had been commissioned by the Earl of Pembroke, the most handsome politician in England, to recover that priceless work after the police had entirely failed to do so. They had searched the house of the undoubted thief not once but twice and with absolutely no success. Holmes had assured me they did not know how to look. Clearly he did. I had never doubted it, and indeed was only surprised it had taken him so long. I could not help wondering whether he had been delaying its recovery until today so as to make of it an apt birthday present to himself.

"Well, Watson, what do you think of it? I know you have a connoisseur's eye for beauty. She is a beauty, is she not?"

She certainly was. No one could have denied that this was a flawless gem of painting. That at least was my first impression. But beauty is not everything and when dealing with religious works spirituality comes first. This was undoubtedly a fine depiction of the Adoration of the Kings, and yet something about disturbed me, though I could not say what. It was reminiscent of the uneasiness I had felt when first I met Jack Stapleton, although I had no reason then to suppose so innocuous a fellow was in reality a series murderer.

Then there was the problem of historical accuracy. I am myself a stickler for this as readers of my accounts will know. It offended my sensibilities that the adult John the Baptist featured in the left-hand panel with the Three Kings at a time when he was only six months old. The right-hand panel was a little better, with the Virgin and Child and a band of angels correctly depicted save for a couple of unfortunate blunders. One of the angels was bearing a banner with the red cross of Christ's resurrection, which should not have been flown until after Jesus' death and return. A more glaring blunder was that all the angels sported badges bearing white harts. Of course, they should have featured lambs since St. John Baptist declared Jesus the Lamb of God at the Baptism. John was shown holding such a lamb in the other panel. The one other minor error was that there were only eleven angels. There ought to have been twelve. Perhaps the artist had run out of ultramarine paint for their robes.

"You expected to find me still licking my wounds after that fiasco of the blue carbuncle, did you not?" said he with a grim little smile.

I confessed that I had.

"Well, that is not my way. Instead I have been giving my mind a thorough reset by plunging into a chemical analysis of the pigments in this painting. You see that figure in the left-hand panel holding the ring with the huge spherical gem to it? He used to be a study in pink and red. See how the colour has entirely drained away. Those twelve badges borne by the kneeling youngest king and the angels had Richard II's white hart set in silver that would once have shone brilliantly be candle light. Sadly, they are black now. By contrast, the ultramarine is pure lapis lazuli from Afghanistan and as dazzling as the day it was applied. It would be worth a war or two to ensure a continuing supply of it. Incidentally, there is clear evidence that Richard II never had gas laid in."

I laughed. "You are joking, Holmes!"

"But in all seriousness. Note how the candlelight ripples and dances just as intended upon the stippled gold! You know I am a theatre man, Watson, so I must needs marvel at how proper lighting can transform what might otherwise be a static work. Or rather it appears static. Even at a chemical level you see this painting is changing even as we speak, though at a glacial pace."

202

I thought to ask Holmes why he had been kneeling before the altarpiece if not to pray. Somehow quite different words came out. "But how did you locate it?"

"Oh, it was simplicity itself. The police were hunting after a painting and not a book. They failed to consider that its dimensions are those of an illuminated manuscript and that it folds up like a closed tome. I turned my attention to what I knew they would ignore. It was on the bookshelf. That, I fancy, is not the question now preying on your mind."

It is best to be direct. "To be honest, Holmes, I had never thought of you as a practising believer. I was surprised to see you praying to this image." I tried to keep the disapproval out of my voice. Holmes's ancestry is Catholic whilst mine is Protestant.

"Oh, not praying – meditating," said he with a little chuckle. "I was putting myself in Richard's red shoes, or rather slippers, or say rather in St. Edmund's, since the boy wore those for his own coronation. I wished to see the work as Richard II had done. The exercise may not have been a spiritual one, but it was instructive nonetheless."

I was becoming confused. "You keep speaking of Richard II, Holmes, but surely this is a depiction of the Adoration of the Kings. What has Richard to do with it?"

"Why, do you not see that St. John the Baptist is introducing that youngest of the kings as he kneels before the Virgin and Child? As you must know, the feast of the Epiphany is both the feast of the Adoration of the Kings and the feast of the Baptism of Christ, so you see that both are alluded to here. There can be no doubt about it. Richard's favourite saints were the canonised kings Edmund and Edward, to which may be added the Baptist. They are all here with their attributes. Edmund was slain by an arrow and he bears it as if were his heavenly sceptre. Edward holds the ring he gave a beggar – in reality St. John the Evangelist – who shared my passion for playing parts. You know the fairy tale? The Evangelist handed it to pilgrims in Jerusalem with instructions that it be returned to Edward as a sign he would soon exchange an earthly kingdom and crown for heavenly ones. I am sure you remember Edward was said to have died on the eve of the feast of the Epiphany in 1066. Richard was reportedly born on the feast day itself, though I don't believe that. It is quite extraordinary, is it not, how the great and the good acquired quite a knack for being born and dying on feast days that signalled the hand of Providence as at work in history. Are we really to believe Shakespeare was born and died on St. George's Day?"

I longed to point out that Holmes himself had been born on the feast of the Magi. Did that not foretell he was destined to be a modern magus?

203

I decided not to tempt providence. "If this is Richard and he is playing at being one of the Three Kings, then where is his gift?"

"In plain sight, save to those who have eyes and see not. Come now, my dear fellow, is it not obvious? He has just passed that banner to the Virgin and the Christ Child is blessing it prior to its being returned to Richard as its steward. Do you not see how his hands are open as he plays the beggar to receive it?"

I did not see that at all. "This flag is the red cross of Christ's resurrection, Holmes. It cannot signify England. And what makes you think Richard has just given it to the Virgin and Child at all? Confess it. That is guesswork. Besides, should you not be devoting your energies to the recovery of the blue carbuncle before it is cut and sold in pieces?"

He shook his head. "That can never happen. It was smaller than a bean, so splinters of it would be useless for jewellery. It is thought to be unique, so no jeweller would ever accept it. Let it keep until after I have defended myself against your slander.

"You accuse me of guessing? You know I never guess. This is both the banner of resurrection and the flag of England. There is a parallel being drawn between the transfigurations of Jesus and Richard. Jesus renounced the kingdom of heaven to be born and to die and to be resurrected. Richard plays a game here of abdicating at his coronation, for you see he is a boy here, as he had been when he was consecrated king. He passes the banner – he is the custodian of to the Virgin and Child, so signifying that although this angel and those eleven angels all bear the badge of his house, it is actually the House of God. It is to be blessed and returned to him. At his death it shall once more be returned to Jesus and the Virgin. Then Richard shall be resurrected and given a new kingdom and have stars in his crown. Do you see now why you found me kneeling when you entered?"

I thought of how Holmes had sat by the side of the pit at the time of the Musgrave Ritual and imagined himself as Rachel Howells considering her treacherous lover down in it. "I suppose you wished to see through Richard's eyes when he had knelt in like manner."

"And when he thought of the day he would be unable to kneel, but would have this altarpiece placed at the foot of his deathbed. Try it yourself, Doctor." He gestured for me to kneel beside him, which I was not about to do. I had only just come from a patient's deathbed. I would be visiting another presently. I could do with a respite.

"The truly spiritual, Watson, will not avoid the call to something higher," he continued thoughtfully. "What kind of cesspool might not our poor world become if they did not? But is this not in reality an attempt to make the childish appear childlike? Is it not a puerile fraud?"

Ever since he encountered the King of Bohemia dressed like an actor playing at being a monarch, Holmes has been critical of blue bloods. He has vowed to devise a Holmes Test to reveal such blood as in reality a very ordinary red. "How do you differentiate between the childish and the childlike?"

"Why, it comes down to Jesus's warning that only those who make themselves like little children can enter the kingdom of heaven. Were we two ever happier than when playing that Christmas game of a wild goose chase? The blue carbuncle was then to us of no more significance than a bon-bon found in a Christmas cracker. By playing the game for its own sake, we became like little children on a Christmas Day morning. How different from that is the game of 'Seize the Crown' played by Richard and Henry Bolingbroke in the abdication scene of Shakespeare's play! I suspect Shakespeare was thinking of the game the boy Richard is playing here with the child King of Kings, in which Richard makes a Christmas present of what Jesus gave him and it is playfully returned. As depicted, that is a childlike action. In reality, it is an attempt to find a loophole by which to pile up treasures on earth and in heaven. When Bruegel painted the Adoration of the Kings, you know, he made of his monarchs fawning courtiers intent on bribing the palm of a newborn emperor so as to receive places near his throne hereafter. That is generally nearer to the truth."

I suddenly understood that for all his cynicism, Holmes was a prodigy who had never grown up. He was still with Don Quixote tilting at windmills in his personal world of make believe. He always would be. He had begun to speak again, though as if to himself.

"And yet the criticism is a valid one. How can we know that this flag signifies England? A drop of water. That is what we need. Where is a drop of water from which the ideal reasoner might deduce a Niagara?"

"A drop of water, Holmes?" My mind went back to Holmes's eccentric article entitled "The Book of Life", in which he argued for sermons in stones and books in brooks. As William Blake could see worlds in grains of sand, so Holmes would see them in the drops of dew.

"Why, yes. Let me see, let me see . . . ." He paused and I perceived he was rifling through the lumber room of his memory. "Ah, here it is: *This little world, this precious stone set in a silver sea...is now bound in with shame, with inky blots and rotten parchment bonds.*" It is wonderful, is it not? You as a storyteller ought to appreciate it as much as I can as a chemist."

I recognised the image from Shakespeare's play *Richard II* and could happily acknowledge it made my heart swell with pride to be an Englishman. I could not see how chemicals came into it. "Chemistry, Holmes?"

205

"Or alchemy, to speak more properly in the language of that time. The philosopher's child, or stone, you know, turns base metal to gold. The Christ Child would turn men's hearts to gold and so bring about a truly golden age. Now, what would the antithesis of such regeneration be? Come, I have just supplied you with it! Watson, what is the opposite of lead turned to gold? Be quicksilver in your thoughts. Come, come, the silver sea! Shine, my good conductor, shine!"

He considered me earnestly and I cudgelled my brains. Then quite unexpectedly I had it. "Why, silver turns black!"

"Bravo! You see? Shakespeare first likens England to a precious gem set in silver. What happens, though, when men cease to put their faith in the Book of Life and instead trust entirely in the book of reckoning of Mammon with all its debits and credits? The silver sea turns black with all those inky blots and rotten parchment bonds. It is the crisis we find ourselves in today, my dear Watson. Think of Blake's dark Satanic mills. Is the nightmare not being realised? Oh, for an east wind to blow the smoke away!"

I was certain that was untrue, for though our great industrial revolution has brought with it many problems progress is ever upwards. However, there is no point in trying to prove to Holmes that his glass is half full. He only starts wondering whether the half that has been drunk was poisoned. "That is all very fine, Holmes, but there is no silver sea in this picture. It is no use your saying there must be if there isn't."

"You should have more faith," said he sternly. "I say there has to be, therefore there is. Just because we cannot see it does not mean we cannot deduce it. Happy are those who have not seen, and yet believe.

"So let us reconsider Shakespeare's John of Gaunt prophesying England's doom on his deathbed. You know my methods. I search for precedents. What is the most obvious precedent in English history for such a prophecy? It is surely St. Edward's deathbed vision. He died making it on the eve of the feast of the Epiphany in 1066. Therefore, we might begin our search for a precious stone in a silver sea with Edward here."

I could see where this was going. "You are grasping at straws, Holmes," I sighed. "I grant you Edward is holding the ring returned to him just before he died. It is not set in silver, though, but gold. It can have nothing to do with Shakespeare's image."

"What if Shakespeare perceived a parallel between the return of the ring and the return of the banner here? And yet why should he, unless some image has been included to confirm that this flag of resurrection is England's? Thus there has to be a second stone."

"But there is no second stone!"

"There has to be! Come, now, we shall find it. What do we know? The stone must be spherical like the gem in Edward's ring, since Shakespeare has likened England to a '*little world*'. We can perceive no silver sea here, so it must have turned black in the very way Shakespeare describes. It has to be found with the banner to identify the flag as England's. Where, then, do we see just such a black orb when we turn to this banner?"

I saw it. "Well, there is a black ball atop the banner," said I sceptically. "You can hardly make of it a vision of England."

Holmes was not paying attention. He had a magnifying lens of his own invention at that orb and was examining it with absolute absorption. "Yes, I believe I can just make it out. There are vertical white streaks that could signify a castle on an island and the sails of a ship. Take a look, Doctor. I would value a second opinion."

I did so. Certainly there were such marks. However, I remembered how Holmes had once likened a cloud to a single feather from a gigantic flamingo and I had at once seen it transformed thus and as if through his eyes. Was he again causing me to see as he saw now? "Well, you might be right, Holmes," I conceded uncertainly, "but if this was once a silver sea that has turned black, we can never prove it, let alone restore it, so it does seem like rather a waste of time. Cannot we at last return to the problem of how Ryder switched that blue carbuncle for a red garnet?"

"No, no, this sheds light on how Shakespeare always thought in stories. We can relate it to the image in *Macbeth* of bloody hands turning a green sea to one red. In fact . . . ."

And then it was that my modern Socrates seemed to turn to stone. He was still gazing with the utmost intensity at the Virgin and Child, who might themselves had been a statue that had come to life. "What is it, Holmes? Have you seen something?"

"In my mind's eye, Horatio," he muttered darkly. "Gaslighting."

"I beg your pardon, Holmes?"

"Gaslighting. Could it be that simple? Yes, by heaven, I think I have it! Oh, I have been as blinkered as a colour-blind Pingelapian! She came at a crisis, Watson. As clear as day that is the solution."

"I'm sorry, Holmes. Who came? What crisis?"

"Why, the so-called Countess of Morcar. As for the crisis, it is akin to the one that coincided with your Christmas visit to 221b. Tell me, Watson, do you recall what colour my dressing-gown was at that time?"

"You mean the one your brother Mycroft had given you as a present and that you so disliked?" I asked shrewdly.

Holmes looked surprised. "What makes you think that?"

I chuckled. It was good to see that from time to time I could still amaze my master with my deductions and in doing so demonstrate how well I understood him and his brother. "It is simplicity itself," said I, without a hint of smugness. "You were striving to overcome your dislike of it. That meant it had been given to you by one of the few people you are friendly with. Who more likely than your brother? It might have been Mrs. Hudson, but then you would not have risked removing it when she might appear at any moment."

"Removing it?"

"Why, yes. Did you really think you succeeded in distracting me entirely? You urged me to study Henry Baker's hat with your lens and the instant I began doing so you whipped off that purple dressing-gown and put your old blue one back on."

Holmes seemed relieved. He smiled and shook his head. "No, Watson, on my word of honour no. I swear to you on my French grandmother's grave that there was only one dressing-gown."

"You mean you turned it inside out? Whatever for?" I knew the answer. Holmes had been "gaslighting" me, if his curious expression meant what I thought it did.

Holmes laughed. "Ah, my dear fellow, I promise I was not playing tricks on you. That is not it at all. Now do think back. Do you remember what struck you the instant you entered 221b?"

I pictured the scene. It really had been a study in scarlet. "I remember thinking it uncharacteristically charitable of you to permit Mrs. Hudson to change the décor to make it more Christmassy. I was surprised you would tolerate that garish red light."

"Mrs. Hudson had not yet returned from her family and friends. As for Mrs. Turner, she and the painter of *The Fighting Temeraire* are unrelated. She has no understanding of such things, beyond the art of peering through keyholes. It was I, doctor, who introduced that red light, and not because I wished to change professions and hang up a red lamp to compete with yours. I had been experimenting with different colour filters. Infrared produced excellent results when it came to photographing this diptych. While you proceeded to peruse that headpiece I removed the filter so you could see it clearly by normal gas lighting. You concluded your investigations and looked back only to surmise I had switched from a purple to a blue dressing-gown. It was the same blue dressing-gown it had always seen but no longer bathed in a red light. It was the red light that had turned it purple."

It was beginning to dawn on me what Holmes was so audaciously suggesting. "Holmes, you are surely joking! You cannot tell me the blue carbuncle turned into a red garnet just because the lighting conditions had changed. I grant you your fluorescent blue lighting to scare James Ryder made the stone look bluer than ever, but why should ordinary gaslighting turn it red when that old lady paid a call?"

"Old lady? Ha! We were the dear little old ladies to be deceived not once but twice! That was probably the same actor who thought to trick us at the time of the fairy tale you entitled *A Study in Scarlet*. Perhaps we should re-title it *A Study in Blue Scarlet*. And yet it may not have been him. I wonder . . . . 'Morcar' is suspiciously close to 'Moriarty', is it not? Could that bean counter really have been playing the Countess? No, it is too far-fetched even for one of your fantasies, though only just. I know you have been tempted to suppose I and Conan Doyle are one and the same person, simply because we never appear together in the same room. As if I would wish to be found in such company! But as for the present 'Study in Scarlet', the answer is to be found in elementary chemistry. You have heard of vanadium?"

"Never."

"Well, it is quite a recent discovery. I produced it by reacting vanadium chloride with hydrogen only twenty years ago. Of course, I never received any credit for it. What can you expect in this world?" Holmes spoke with some bitterness, still resentful that his Holmes Test had been ignored by criminologists. He had dismissed my accidental discovery that his reagent was precipitated by Mrs. Hudson's strawberry jam as well as by haemoglobin on the grounds that his test could not be wrong, and therefore there had to be blood in the jam. Ever since then, he has treated his landlady with greater respect. He no longer spreads her jam on his toast.

"I know nothing of vanadium, Holmes," said I at last to end the sullen silence. "What has it to do with your theory that a blue carbuncle can turn into a red garnet?"

Holmes opened his mouth to speak, paused, put a pipe in it instead, and lit it. "I will blind you with science, Doctor. Trust me, I am a chemist. If the garnet contained vanadium, then it would have appeared blue by natural and fluorescent light and red by incandescent light. We first saw it by daylight when Peterson brought it to us and it was blue. We saw it a second time when I used fluorescent lighting to frighten Ryder and it was again blue. When the Countess arrived, we introduced the incandescent gas lighting and it turned red. I suppose you might say that our blue garnet was a myth akin to that of Lady Robert St. Simon. Technically there had been no such person, and you might say the same of the blue carbuncle. Of course, you could also say that of your mythical Sherlock Holmes in his deerstalker bespattered with beeswax and with a magnifying glass in place of a monocle permanently glued to one eye."

I turned a blind eye to such base ingratitude. Boswell probably had to suffer as much from Dr. Johnson. "If what you say is true then it was the merest chance that you chose to employ that fluorescent lighting with Ryder. Had you not done so, then it would have turned red then and you might have had time enough to deduce the cause before the veiled lady, or veiled somebody, appeared."

Holmes spat a "Ha ha!" "Coincidence? Speak not to me of coincidences! There were far too many coincidences, as I shall show. Forget coincidences. Ryder was in on the plot, as was the so-called plumber Horner. Do you suppose I would have left the latter languishing in his prison cell over Christmas had I not known that? Really Watson, his involvement ought to have been obvious from my slippers."

I was befuddled. "Your slippers, Holmes? What do you slippers have to do with anything?"

Holmes sighed. "I put on slippers the moment we entered 221b with Ryder. That should have told you two things. In the first place, I never had any intention of holding Ryder. Had I meant to I would have kept my shoes on in case he took flight."

"Well, that is simple enough," I conceded, "but what have your slippers to do with Horner's guilt?"

"You mean you do not see? The *fire*, Watson. Or more precisely the *grate*. I stretched my slippered feet so pointedly towards the fire to draw attention to the grate there, meaning Ryder to realise his earlier crass error."

I must have looked stupid. He sighed resignedly.

"Ryder had told the police he had called in the plumber Horner to solder the second bar of the grate in the Countess's room. As one of my aliases, I occasionally adopt the role of a plumber called Escott, so I have a decent knowledge of plumber's rockets and grates, besides which grates are one the first things I investigate at crime scenes. All grates are cast. If you wish to amuse yourself for an afternoon, why not spend it striving to solder cast iron? The thing cannot be done. Neither Ryder nor Horner knew this. Hence we may safely conclude they had to have been working together. Horner was no more than a decoy. There was no evidence against him and the police knew it. Referring the case to the Assizes was the merest ruse to play for time in the hope he would confess to his true role in a bigger plot. Why else would they have referred a London case to the counties?"

"But what was Horner's role in the affair? Surely if the police doubted he had stolen the gem, they would have suspected Ryder of falsely accusing him to divert suspicion from himself. Why run that risk?"

"Horner was necessary for one reason and one reason only. Cannot you perceive it?"

Predictably I could not.

Holmes paused and then proceeded to superfluously repeat the question: "Why was Horner, Jack Horner, little Jack Horner, little Jack Horner the plumber . . . Oh, very well. The name, Watson. He was used for his name, as was the profession chosen for him. It was to make me think of the nursery rhyme, the better to plant in my mind the idea of the blue carbuncle like the plum that little Jack Horner plucked from a Christmas pudding. And what do Christmas puddings do when fulfilling their ultimate destiny? Picture yours."

I did so. "Well, Holmes, they are borne in with the lights out, and with the brandy flaming all about them."

"You have it. And the flames are blue, like those of the fluorescent paint upon that hound in the Baskerville affair. How did you describe it to me? '*The huge jaws seemed to be dripping with a bluish flame.*' Was that not identical to the flames upon a Christmas pudding? Now, I believe every human being is not two but one, and that there is a second brain able to process information that the conscious mind is unaware of. The intention was to set my second brain to work. It was to encourage me to wish to achieve an effect comparable to that of a Christmas pudding by employing Stapleton's fluorescent paint."

I thought of Holmes alone in Baker Street on Christmas Day and suddenly felt guilty. Why had I not invited him to partake of our own feast? He would not have come, but I ought to have done so. Someone had understood that, although outwardly he would not have felt unwanted and discarded, yet a part of him would wish to have shared an experience remembered from childhood. Those blue flames dancing upon that blue gem were indeed his compensation for being denied a simple Christmas pleasure. And yet, who in the world could have understood Holmes so well, so much better than I did, so much better than he did himself, to have perceived that secret craving?

I shook myself free of pointless speculations. "This is too fantastic, Holmes. That would require some unknown mastermind who was aware that you had stolen – *borrowed* – Stapleton's fluorescent paint after the Baskerville affair was over."

"Watson," said Holmes gravely, "do you suppose Jack Stapleton, clever though he was, could have invented that quite revolutionary liquid? What if he had done? Are we also to believe he could have bred a hybrid hound of so demonic a nature? No, no, he had to have turned to some criminal agency for assistance. That agency was also behind the carbuncle affair. How could it not be?"

211

"I don"t see the necessity."

"Why, the theft of the garnet was nothing. Of course, it was the most transparent of insurance frauds. That subsequent Christmas party game of a wild goose chase was to entertain the troops, and I mean by that both those who were never unsuspected and others who all unsuspectingly assisted our mastermind over the year just past. Someone was for a time playing the game for its own sake and I thank him for it. Evidently, then, that mastermind supposes I inadvertently helped him fulfil his plans. The highly convenient deaths of Irene Adler and Birdy Edwards come to mind, which I appeared to make possible by encouraging them explicitly or implicitly to flee the country, only to be lost at sea."

"But who was it?"

"I have my suspicions. Now that I have forced Mr. Moriarty into premature retirement in London, someone must fill the resulting vacuum. Do not forget your Newton. Every action requires an equal an opposite reaction. If there is a consulting detective, there must be a consulting criminal. The universe requires it so that a deeper balance may be maintained."

By now I was becoming prey to a growing paranoia. "Holmes, if Ryder and Horner were both instruments of a higher power, then whom can we trust? Can we be sure that the man who called himself Henry Baker was anything of the sort? You really should have asked him to try on that hat."

"The Cinderella Test?" Holmes asked with a chuckle.

"Well, he had a large head, but I cannot swear it would have filled that colossal hat."

"It would not have done. That is why I did not ask him to try it on."

"Holmes!"

"Did I not say there were hairs adhering to the lower lining owing to the use of lime cream? Do you suppose an inebriate would have wasted money on lime cream that he might have spent on gin and lime? And why do you suppose there were no hairs higher up? He had padded the upper area with newspaper pages that fell out when it was knocked off. That hat was never made for him. He picked it up out of the gutter outside his former club."

"How can you possibly know that?"

"Because it was once Mycroft's. Mr. Henry Baker was a member of the Diogenes Club prior to his decline. Then he moved to the Reading Room of the British Museum, which is the poor man's Diogenes. At one time I made extensive use of it myself. As for how I knew the hat had been padded, Peterson picked up the paper and brought it to me with the hat and goose."

212

"You never showed it to me," said I resentfully.

"Because I have too high a regard for your common sense. You would at once have suggested we place an advertisement in that same paper as the one Baker would have been most likely to read."

"But why didn"t you?"

"Watson," said he with a rueful smile, "do you not see that Peterson, being a stickler for the law, would have informed the police that it was Baker who had broken a shop window while defending himself from some roughs? What would the regaining of a goose have been compared to the cost of repairing that window? I wasted two days deducing so much from his hat to distract from the real means by which his location might very easily have been ascertained."

"But how?"

"Oh, it was hardly a difficult task. A drunken man bearing a goose is seen staggering down Tottenham Court Road at four in the morning on Christmas day. Obviously he had to be living nearby. Now, how many Mr. and Mrs. Henry Bakers do you suppose live within easy walking distance down Tottenham Court Road? I will tell you. One. Add to that his tipsy state and the likelihood is the nearest tavern would have identified him at once. But of course, I knew precisely where he lived the instant Peterson came through the door."

"Holmes!"

"Oh, yes, I did. You must remember that when first I set up shop as a consulting detective, I lived in Montague Street opposite the British Museum. For two years I was in the situation Henry Baker is in now. I economised on heating and lighting by spending much of my time in the Museum, where I honed my skills by deducing the histories of artefacts and their past owners. There is no difference between reading the ancient crown of England or a battered billycock. Naturally I spent countless hours in the Reading Room. Occasionally Baker would visit it too, though he was on the rise as I was falling. He took pity on me and treated me to the occasional meal. I have no doubt there were times when as he saw me shuffling back to my cold dark rooms, he must have muttered to himself: "There, but for the grace of God, goes Henry Baker." When I moved out of my old apartment, he moved in. He is there still."

"But if you knew each other, why did you not say so?"

"Shame, Watson. Shame. He was heartily ashamed of his fall from respectability. Had we been alone, it would have been a different matter, but not with you present."

I was disappointed. "And so all your deductions from his hat were false? You knew all about him already?"

Holmes smiled mischievously. "I must confess that though some of what I said was true, I entertained myself with concocting the most fantastic supplementary deductions simply to play for time. My reading of those tallow stains on his hat, for example, was the merest fairy tale. You must admit it was ingenious."

"Very! But then how did those stains get there?"

"Well, obviously my explanation was nonsensical. You remember what I proposed?"

"That he carried his hat upstairs at night and that tallow from his candle fell upon it."

Holmes laughed and as he did so I found myself laughing too as together we pictured the absurd scene. "Yes, Watson, you see how ridiculous that would be. We are to suppose that on entering his home he at once took off his hat, presumably to hang it on the hat-stand, then forgot to do so and furthermore neglected to put it back on his head. He then groped his way upstairs, or rather would have done had not both his hands been full, unless we are to suppose he carried both hat and candle in one and the same hand. If he did not, then we must picture him holding the candle directly overhead his hat to ensure the tallow dripped down onto it."

"Then how came the tallow onto the hat?"

"You recall I deduced his misfortunes had been brought about by drink. I offered no evidence in support of such a claim, but I knew you would accept it unthinkingly in view of your unhappy brother's demise. He did drink, but not quite as heavily as I had suggested. Consider what state he would have been in at four in the morning on Christmas Day had he been a genuine alcoholic. He would not have been able to bear himself up, let alone the goose. He would have been drunk in a gutter or at best crawling along on all fours."

"But the lack of foresight! Surely that was the result of drink."

"Was he not taking the goose home as a peace offering? He had been planning that propitiatory gift for an entire year. And could a drunk with no foresight have managed to choose between an extra drink or a further payment of a few pence towards that goose week after week? That demonstrated extraordinary will power and quite exceptional foresight."

"But his face was red and his hand trembled!"

"You observed that despite the freezing weather he had nothing on beneath his coat. You would be trembling, Doctor, would you not? The reddening of the face was due to that and to his embarrassment. He drank, certainly, but that was as a *result* of his failure. It was not the *cause* of it."

"And what was the cause? How did he fall so far despite his evident intelligence?"

"The tallow stains, Watson. You have forgotten the tallow stains."

"How do those help us?"

"Think of the simplest explanation and ninety-nine times out of a hundred that will be the correct one. When does one find tallow stains from candles upon a saucer, say?"

I thought about that. "When one has put a candle onto it."

"Very good. And so why might one find tallow stains on a hat? Obviously when it has been performing the same duties as a saucer might."

"Holmes!"

"Holmes me no Holmeses, Watson, but ask yourself when a man might put candles upon his hat. Is it not obvious? When he needs to see in the dark as he works. But the dust on that hat was of the indoor variety. Why could he not have placed the candle on a table? Because he was at a window and sketching or painting some outdoor scene, for example the night sky. The man had become an artist, Watson, and probably an *avant garde* one whose art would not be in demand. The tallow stains confirm it."

"Why?"

"Aside from the fact that a prosperous man would employ beeswax candles, there is the inspiration for those candles about the rim of his hat. He had doubtless heard stories about a certain unsuccessful *avant garde* Dutch painter in France who has resorted to the same trick. Baker thought to imitate him by way of paying homage. Such sentimentality is also evident in his initialling his hat "*H.B.*""

"Why is that sentimental, Holmes? Surely it was eminently practical."

"Of course it wasn't," said he impatiently. "He ought to have written his name in full. No, it was another tribute of sorts. Who do those initials bring to mind?"

I thought of one of my heroes. "Henry Beecher?"

Holmes tut-tutted impatiently.

I gazed about and my eyes fell upon the Wilton Diptych. "Henry Bolingbroke!"

"Good! But not good enough. Think of artists who tend towards satire and caricature."

"Hieronymus Bosch?"

"Better, but let us stay close to home. Our Henry Baker was evidently an admirer of the political cartoonist known in his lifetime simply as "*H.B.*" It was his way of doffing his cap to him. Incidentally, that is why I permitted your partner Conan Doyle to have the first edition of *A Study in Scarlet* illustrated by that execrable illustrator his father. "*H.B.*" was John

215

Doyle and your collaborator's grandfather. Thinking of that made me recall poor Henry Baker. After that I could not deny the request."

I was relieved at the revelation Holmes had a heart. "So Ryder and Horner were the only ones in on the plot."

"Oh, there was one other. That was Breckenridge, the gentleman at the sham poultry stall in Covent Garden."

"What made you doubt him?"

"Covent Garden is a fruit, flower, and vegetable market. The stink of dead birds would not have been tolerated."

"Except at Christmas, Holmes."

"I might grant you one stall as an exception to disprove the rule. Breckenridge assured us, though, that there was a second stall nearby. That I cannot permit. Nor was there the least sign of any bird at his. No, he was gambling I would not check and see if the other stall even existed. He was also betting I would not investigate the address he gave for the supplier of those geese."

"What makes you think that?"

"Because I have an encyclopaedic knowledge of London. He gave Mrs. Oakshott's address as 117 Brixton Road, which would have put it at the corner of Blackwell Street."

"Well, what of that?"

"Only that Blackwell Street was until very recently called Baker Street and is still so marked on most maps. Do you not see the joke? A man called Henry Baker is duped into setting us forth on a wild goose chase from Baker Street to Baker Street – to say nothing of its taking me back to my very beginnings as a detective in Bloomsbury. Had we thought to visit Mrs. Oakshott, I"ll wager we would have found nothing but a manufactory of artificial kneecaps for geese that have lost their goosestep. And by the way, that story of two identical white barred-tailed geese had to be pure nonsense."

"Why should it be?"

"Because the only white barred-tailed geese are the Pink-footed Geese of Greenland and Iceland. They should by rights be found in Denmark, since they are as rare as Hamlet's one honest man picked out of ten-thousand. To find one would be remarkable. To find two together in those countries would be beating odds of a hundred-million-to-one. The chances of finding a pair of them in a backyard in Brixton would be incalculably miraculous. That second one did not, then, exist. As for the bird switched with Baker's while he was in his cups, think of that black ink he applied to the tallow stains on his hat. I have no doubt that a little spirit of wine would soon have demoted that goose and stripped it of its bars. And then there is the trifling difficulty of its crop."

I thought this pedantic. "I know that geese do not have proper crops, Holmes, but I think we can forgive Peterson for his imprecise English."

"Granted. That is not the problem. The difficulty is that Ryder claimed he could feel a gem smaller than a bean entering the crop of the goose. Setting aside the impossibility of such a feat, do you not think it curious that he should have committed precisely the same linguistic error as Peterson?"

"That had to be a coincidence. How could he have known Peterson had done so?"

"Do you recall, Watson, how when you arrived at 221b, Mrs. Turner insisted on taking you up to your old rooms? Do you suppose Mrs. Hudson had not told her you lodged with me for seven years? What was the result? When Peterson burst in crying out that his wife had found the gem in the crop of a goose, she could hardly have failed to hear it. She was a spy, Watson, and reported back everything we said. I used her and now she is gone."

I fell into the armchair that I had just sprung out of. "All this for a simple Christmas game? It is incredible!"

"Well, the game was an incidental entertainment to close the affair before our mastermind collected the twenty-thousand pounds insurance money. However, that gem had already served a far more serious purpose. Tell me, Watson, have you ever heard of Cecil Rhodes?"

"Never." In fact, I knew perfectly well who Rhodes was, but it occurred to me that future readers might not. And besides, Holmes had once pulled my leg that he had never heard of Thomas Carlyle.

Holmes stretched out towards his bookshelf for a battered tome that I recognised as his copy of Winwood Reade's *Martyrdom of Man*. It was signed by the author and was apparently very dear to him, though for myself I confess I tried to read it and gave up after the first page. It was much too daring for me. He turned the pages as if preparing to read from it, though I suspect he had memorised his favourite passages long ago.

"When I was young, Watson, I confess to feeling a little lost and alone in this commonplace world of commonplace people. The individual is no doubt capable of moments of wakefulness but *en masse* mankind is simply a herd. Then in 1871 I read Darwin's *The Evolution of Man* and it left me wondering whether man had any future at all. Fortunately, a few months later Reade's book appeared, and I saw he might have.

"Now listen to this: '*The religion which I teach is as high above Christianity as that religion was superior to the idolatry of Rome.*' Stirring stuff, eh? And that is just the start. He goes on to prophesy '*a heaven in the ages far away*'. a heaven moreover filled with worlds colonised as the Americas and Australias of the future!

217

"Later Rhodes and I both read the preface and conclusion of James Moriarty's *The Dynamics of an Asteroid*. In the preface, the professor deduces an asteroid caused the sudden extinction of the dinosaurs and predicts that another shall one day lead to the extinction of mankind on earth. In his conclusion, he quotes from Reade and argues with him that our only long term hope is to travel to the stars."

Holmes had that dreamy look in his eyes that he always gets when he is talking nonsense, particularly after he has added one or two more puncture marks to the "*V.R.*" he is tattooing onto his left arm. Personally, I prefer happiness now to happiness a few million years hence, but I knew better than to argue. I waited patiently for him to get to the point.

"Reade, you see, believes that the martyrdom of man over millions of years must ultimately be rewarded. He shall be '*raised towards the divine power which he will finally attain...our faith is the perfectibility of man ... the extinction of disease, the extinction of sin, the perfection of genius, the perfection of love, the invention of immortality, the exploration of the infinite, and the conquest of creation*'. Put simply, man shall one day become his own god."

And Holmes accuses me of writing fairy tales! So, we shall all live happily ever after. "That is all very fine, Holmes, but what has it to do with the blue carbuncle?"

The dreamy look left his grey eyes as my human voice awakened him out of his fantasies. "Reade would be the John the Baptist of a new religion," he continued more crisply. "Rhodes would be its messiah. He means to lay the foundations for the realisation of Reade's dream by reuniting the British Empire with the United States so that our race might rule the world. To fund his enterprise, he needs power and power requires money. He intends to make De Beers Consolidated Mines the richest, the greatest, and the most powerful company the world has ever seen, controlling at least ninety percent of the world's diamond production. The old East India Company is his model, being as it was the world's first global commercial organisation and possessing at its height an army twice the size of that of Britain. Rhodes plans that his Consolidated Mines shall dwarf that Company and serve a more than merely commercial purpose. With Rhodes, money means power, and power is but a tool."

"But the carbuncle!" I persisted.

"Yes, yes," said he, impatient with my impatience. "You know Rhodes came to London last year and proceeded to seduce all and sundry with his vision including, I am afraid to say, my brother Mycroft, who has since betrayed disturbing signs of stirring out of his accustomed somnolence. Heaven help the world if that great brain should ever turn itself to any serious purpose! He and others were particularly impressed by Rhodes's plan to form a secret society of exceptional men who would work behind the scenes to pull the strings of the puppet masters. It is not too much of an exaggeration to say that such men would sometimes *be* the governments they would seem to serve."

Holmes held up his hand to silence my next protestation. "Patience, Watson. To answer your question, that blue carbuncle was but bait. I have said that Rhodes means to control the world's supply of diamonds. The stir caused by that tiny garnet could not but trouble him. Where there was one, there had to be others."

"What makes you suppose that?"

"If there were none, then there would have been no need to conceal the garnet's place of origin. That story of its being discovered by the Amoy river was the most transparent of deceptions. There is no such river. A river in Androy in Madagascar is the likelier location. I am merely speculating. Rhodes was desperate to know for sure where such precious gems were to be found."

"And who was behind the ruse?"

Holmes seemed both thoughtful and troubled. "I cannot say. It may have been Moriarty's successor, whoever that is, now that I have plucked him down. I know from brother Mycroft that Rhodes naturally wished to see the author of *The Dynamics of an Asteroid*, the man whom he rightly regards as having successfully supplemented Darwin's theory of slow evolution with his own hypothesis of sudden mass extinction. Moriarty could have introduced him to his *protégé* at such a meeting."

"Could it not be Moriarty himself?"

"No, no, he is a spent force. His coming to London proves that. Did you not say of this city it is a cesspool into which all the loungers and idlers of the Empire are irresistibly drained? Besides, at most Moriarty was never more than a criminal consultant advising the real players. No, whomever was behind the blue carbuncle is far more ambitious. He means to seduce the master seducer and make Rhodes' secret society his own personal instrument."

I thought back to the case of the Noble Bachelor and of how Holmes had expressed the hope that the Stars and Stripes might one day be quartered with the Union Jack. Suddenly I felt uneasy. "Holmes, forgive me for asking, but were you not yourself tempted to become part of such a society? After all, you have as much as admitted that its dream is very much like your own."

"No, Watson," said he seriously, thought after a moment's hesitation. "I never was. Well, only briefly. Then I reminded myself that when once men begin to speak of an end that justifies the means, then the means must start to determine the nature of that end. After that, it was simply a matter of putting myself in Rhodes' shoes to determine precisely what his means might have set in motion.

"You know how I proceed in such cases. I gauged his intellect and saw that it was almost as exceptional as my own. Then saw the world through his eyes. You recall how I gazed into the depths of that blue carbuncle? I was imagining myself as Rhodes, sitting on the edge of the de Beers mine at Kimberley and looking down at the blue diamondiferous ground, reaching from the surface, a thousand feet down . . . and reckoning up the value of the diamonds in the "blue" and the power conferred by them. In fact, every foot of blue ground means so much power to him. To do what? To turn this precious blue stone that is our world red. To bring all under the sway of the British Empire. Tomorrow the world and the day after tomorrow Mars! To make man a god! It seemed like a fine dream until I applied the Holmes Test. Then I saw that this earth of ours is but the devil's pet bait, and all the pink upon the world map suddenly turned to a dull, dirty crimson."

He had been gazing out of the window at the street below, with its endless streams of human consciousness flowing unendingly to and back. Suddenly he shook himself and seemed to awaken with a start from a reverie. "I see an extraordinarily beautiful politician at the doorway reaching for the doorbell. It is undoubtedly the Earl of Pembroke come to collect his diptych. Be a good fellow and hand me the pink wrapping paper."

NOTE

A note to collectors of Sherlockiana: Bekily blue garnets, aka "blue carbuncles", can be purchased from Moriarty's Gem Art. Showroom: Crown Point, Indiana (around the courthouse square). Address: 126 S. Main St, Crown Point, IN 46307 U.S.A. Website: *moregems.com*. Telephone: +1 (219) 662-1390.

Agnolo Bronzino – "*Allegory with Venus and Cupid*"

The Adventure of the
Worm That Turned

Continuing "The Speckled Band"

" ...Having once made up my mind, you know the steps which I took in order to put the matter to the proof. I heard the creature hiss, as I have no doubt that you did also, and I instantly lit the light and attacked it."

"With the result of driving it through the ventilator."

"And also with the result of causing it to turn upon its master at the other side. Some of the blows of my cane came home, and roused its snakish temper, so that it flew upon the first person it saw. In this way, I am no doubt indirectly responsible for Dr. Grimesby Roylott's death, and I cannot say that it is likely to weigh very heavily upon my conscience: *'For 'tis the sport to have the engineer hoist with his own petard'*. Besides, Doctor, does not the Bard wisely caution us that *'Conscience does make cowards of us all'*? As for that same serpent I do repent, though heaven has pleased it so, for its entombment is sadly reminiscent of a certain Brunton's demise. No, that is for another time. Let us speak instead of the slaying of Polonius, if you please, for I am at present wrestling with the problem of enacting *Hamlet* in the Park again this summer."

I should explain here Holmes is a keen amateur-actor manager whose annual Shakespeare productions are always well received, and that despite their ascending to such rarefied heights of pure art that it is said there is no man in the literary press capable of criticising them. One female reviewer has praised his Baker Street Irregulars as *"the best amateur theatrical company in London, either for tragedy, comedy, history, or pastoral, but never the commonplace."* When Oscar Wilde accompanied me to Holmes's *As You Like It*, which he did with the express intention of demonstrating he was more artificial than anything in the play, he confessed himself enchanted by Holmes's Baker Street boys in the female roles. He quipped it was indeed as he liked it. Wilde was clearly taken with the lovely boy who played Rosalind, the heroine who disguises herself as a lad and is then called upon to play at being herself. Presumably that was why Wilde identified with her.

How could I tell him the truth? It was entirely in keeping with Holmes's somewhat perverted sense of humour to have cast Billy in that part, for my friend had deduced from signs too subtle for me to observe that he was a she. Street Arabs are every bit as misogynistic as Holmes and never permit girls into their gangs. Had her fellow Irregulars discovered the truth, she would have been expelled on the spot.

Holmes, though, prizes genius in any form. He therefore imitated Horatio Nelson when he extended his telescope to read an unwelcome flag communication: He turned a blind eye to his magnifying glass and entirely failed to perceive Billy's true sex. It was after all hardly the only irregularity he winked at in the gang. That was just as well, for without an instantly available troupe he could never have staged the little scene by which he strove to deceive Irene Adler in the affair I have chronicled as "A Scandal in Bohemia". Nor would it have been half so convincing had he not acquired experience in staging outdoor performances. But then Holmes is ever the dramatist in real life, as I was reminded the next moment.

"Here is my pocket Bard. But do not move an inch. What's this in an English train compartment? No! The Giant Rat of Sumatra? Who would have thought it? Stay perfectly still, Watson. Your life depends on it. Dead, for a ducat, dead!"

Each "Dead!" was accompanied by a lightning thrust of his cane at the seating not an inch above my shoulder. His aim was, I assume, superb, which was as well for me since it was the shoulder struck and shattered at Maiwand. His action startled me into attentiveness. I had been introspecting on the death of Dr. Grimesby Roylott, for if Holmes suspected Hamlet of premeditated murder in the case of the old counsellor Polonius, I harboured like suspicions concerning my fellow lodger's dispatching of that equally beastly man. At that moment, though, I felt as one who awakens and feels he is in a dream. "Holmes!" I cried. "Have you gone mad?"

"'*My pulse as yours doth temperately keep time, and makes as healthful music,*'" said he with a chuckle. "'*I essentially am not mad, but mad in craft.*' I aimed to make my point economically and regain your full attention. If this was madness was there not method in't? Did I not score a palpable hit? Confess it."

I probed the rent to the seating. Would that I could probe the mind of Sherlock Holmes as easily! I decided against pointing out he had himself told me Hamlet's temperate pulse after killing Polonius was evidence of moral insanity. "Bear in mind, Holmes, it is less than two years since the Balcombe Tunnel Mystery. I don't relish being involved in another such incident. What point was that? I assume you are not referring to this hole."

"You have just been privileged to experience something like the shock of Shakespeare's audience when their hero cried '*Dead, for a ducat, dead!*' as he stabbed the unseen Polonius through the arras for the very first time. Oh, come now, please forgive me. My aim is superb. You were never in any real danger. And you an old campaigner! Really, you should thank me."

I regarded my friend with all the seriousness of Horatio considering his friend the Prince after the fiasco of the play-in-play *The Mousetrap* – at least if Holmes's *Hamlet* of 1882 was anything to go by. Nor was I willing to acquiesce to so easy a change of subject from a real killing to a fictional one. What was Polonius to me or me to Polonius that I should weep for him? Not that I could weep for the monstrous Roylott either. Yet wretch as he was, he still had the right to be tried and convicted by due course of British law. Holmes represented that law, certainly, but he was not its incarnation and he could not trump it. This is not yet America. Over there I gather they look upon these things in a different way: Apparently the President had recently shot his mistress on Fifth Avenue with no repercussions. Of course that may be fake news and I do not know all the alternative facts.

The more I thought about it, the harder it was for me to blindly accept Holmes's assurance he had killed that perfect brute by pure accident. And yet was my strange fellow lodger really capable of murder? I had only known him for a little over two years. I still understood so little about that walking book of life and death.

A dawning comprehension was evident in Holmes's eyes. "Ah. I see, Doctor. You are recalling, are you not, the dire warnings of our mutual friend Archie Stamford concerning your perverse fellow lodger. What has he been saying? 'Holmes poisons guests he invites to tea!' 'Holmes beats female corpses with a stick!' Being a former army surgeon, you are broad-minded, of course, and would give your heart a winking mute and dumb to either sadism or necrophilia as the eccentricities of genius. But the two in combination? That is too much! This same stick that spanked Roylott's serpent into a towering passion has caned many a sleeping beauty no trumpet save for the last can awaken. Two mornings ago, you found me looming over your sleeping form. Were you in danger of a fate worse than death? You could have sworn you locked your door."

I sometimes wonder whether Holmes's more tasteless jests are not intentionally provocative. I remembered that rude awakening. I confess to a moment of real apprehension on seeing a cadaverous face looming over mine. Admittedly that was partly because the previous night I had fallen asleep over Baring-Gould's *Book of Werewolves* at the point where one of the virgins opens her eyes to find Elizabeth Barthory contemplating her as the next involuntary blood donor.

It was also perfectly true that deeply concerned friends had persisted in hinting at Holmes's less salubrious foibles. He engaged in self-abuse, they said, injecting himself with dangerous mind-altering drugs. One acquaintance thought he had seen Holmes about to enter an opium den but could not be sure, for where the detective had seemed to be a moment before, there was then only an old man shuffling down step by painful step at a funeral pace as if to his own mausoleum. True it was too that Holmes disappeared from time to time into the most miasma-ridden regions of the great cesspool that is London to pursue crimes, or commit them, or both. I was not sure he knew the difference or really cared. If, as Winwood Reade apparently says, the individual man is an enigma, what was I to make of one as cryptic as Mr. Sherlock Holmes?

He was a genius, of that there could be no doubt, but should that reassure or disturb me? Professor Lombroso has conclusively established all genius is allied to madness. Auguste Dupin's biographer Poe surmised his subject was possessed of a brilliant but diseased intelligence. In view of such modern discoveries, it had seemed only prudent to heed the caution of Stamford never to drink from any bottle Holmes offered me until he had done so himself.

Stamford was equally dogmatic as regards the death of his beloved dog, insisting he had died of the latest organic alkaloid Holmes fed him by way of a scientific experiment. He had gloomily foretold my bull pup's days at 221b were numbered as surely as would be those of a monogamist living among the Mormons. Predictably he took a melancholic pleasure in saying he had told me so after she passed away of natural causes within a week of my arrival. To set his mind at rest, a careful autopsy was performed and revealed nothing amiss, yet that failed to dissuade him. He chose to believe the poison was a new one for which no test existed. When, by pure coincidence, Mrs. Hudson's dog turned poorly just as Holmes happened to be in desperate need of a subject for an experiment, Stamford took that as the final proof. It did not help that Holmes was decidedly annoyed with the dog for inconsiderately failing to drop dead the first time the experiment was performed. I now know that was just Holmes, but at the time it left a bad taste in the mouth reminiscent of almonds. If Holmes had been living in an earlier age, he would certainly have been burnt as a necromancer. Had he escaped such a fate, it would only have been by being hung as a grave robber first.

For all Stamford's dire forewarnings of the "You'll be next" variety, when Holmes summoned me to accompany him on a second adventure more thrilling than the Jefferson Hope affair, I could not resist the siren call to arms. Such was the spell that charismatic man had cast over me. I followed him even as Hamlet did the spirit that assumed the form of his dead father. The Prince did not know whether it was a heavenly father or a father of lies. It made no difference. Even so did I go with Holmes into the darkness, knowing full well it might be to my death. Better that than the comfortless, meaningless existence he had rescued me from. Does the reader of penny dreadful tales of horror insist their author reveal in advance what is to happen next? He expects and desires to be taken by surprise. Holmes needed a witness for when he took the murderer red-handed. That was enough for me. I would be useful to him. I could ask for nothing more.

It was only after the event I began to have doubts. Holmes had observed that when those of my profession go wrong, they are the first of criminals. But what of the detective gone wrong? That thought led to another: Had Holmes ever really meant to take Roylott alive?

The best way to conquer a fear is to confront it. I had to speak out.

"Holmes, I pay absolutely no heed to the vile rumours spread about you. At the same time, I have to say your taking only indirect responsibility for the death of Dr. Roylott does seem a little disingenuous."

Holmes raised eyebrows like a pair of guardian birds taking to the air to bar the way to the windows of his soul. But I pressed on.

"Suppose you came upon a man clutching a smoking gun while standing beside a freshly bleeding corpse. He says he has just apprehended the pistol red-handed. Would you let such a Smoking Gun Defence stand? Now look at Roylott's death. The moment we discover his corpse, you seize that snake coiled about his head and throw it into a safe, slamming the door shut. You claim it was the snake that killed Roylott, and technically you are correct. Still, it would not have done so had you not struck it and forced it to return in a rage through that ventilator and straight at the face of the villain. Was the snake not your smoking gun? Can you really say you entirely inadvertently used it to remove a Goliath? I only ask because of the rumours in Stoke Moran."

"Rumours? What rumours?" asked Holmes with all the innocence of a calculating man. He seemed surprised and even mildly interested.

"Holmes, we were *seen*! Roylott's death shriek aroused the entire village, so naturally everyone in the inn we were staying at across from the Roylott's was up and about. There were frightened faces at every window. The innkeeper never for a moment believed your claim we were just popping out for the night to visit some village acquaintance whose name you could not recall. Everyone there suspected we were involved in Roylott's death. When we were seen clambering back through the wall of the Roylott estate, all their worst suspicions appeared to be confirmed. Fortunately, they were too terrified to attempt to apprehend us. I think they noticed the bulge of my Webley No. 2."

Holmes was mildly amused. "Dear me! But does it matter what they thought? You care far too much about public opinion, Doctor. Besides, I took the precaution of giving false names at the inn. Let the rumours fly.

It will give the parents there something with which to scare their children at night."

"I only went with you because I supposed you needed a witness for when you made your arrest," I grumbled. "I had not realised you were indifferent to whether you took Roylott dead or alive."

Holmes ran a long and thoughtful finger along the parietal fissure of his cane's skull head. It was carved into the same shape as one excavated by Dr. Challenger on the island of Flores, which some surmise was the true place of origin of the escaped specimen Tonga and also of the so-called giant rat of Sumatra.

"I am quite intrigued, Doctor. Are you perhaps implying something more? Do you have any reason for supposing I wished Roylott dead?"

"It was that cane," said I, eyeing it nervously and cursing myself for neglecting to bring my own sturdy Penang lawyer with me in case I required it for my defence. It was dignified, solid, and reassuring. To speak plainly, it was lead-filled. "You laid it on the bed and sat down beside it near the ventilator. Had you meant to take Roylott alive, you would have stationed yourself with me near the door. Moreover, you would have brought a gun and not a cane for defence if you had meant to arrest Roylott. To speak frankly, Holmes, an English jury might find you guilty of murder in the first degree."

Holmes seemed quite impressed. "Not bad. Not bad at all. You are coming along, Dr. Watson. I may use you again. But that does raise another question, does it not? What do you intend to do about it? As a law-abiding citizen, can you in all conscience do anything other than inform the authorities?"

"I am sure that won't be necessary, Holmes," said I nervously. "I know you will do the honourable thing and inform them yourself. There were extenuating circumstances, after all. Many would say you ought to be commended for ridding the world of a foul and venomous beast. Your sole crime was taking the law into your own hands."

"And if I do not give myself up?" he enquired indifferently, idly switching his cane backwards and forwards presumably to test its weight. It too was probably lead-filled.

I swallowed but saw it was my duty to stay firm. "Well, then I give you my word, which I hold dearer than my life, I shall be obliged to inform them myself."

Sherlock Holmes reached across the train compartment and shook me by the hand. "That's what I think. You are a brave fellow, Watson. It took courage for you to stay with me in that pitch darkness with no idea what I intended. It took still greater courage to warn me you were prepared to arrest me without even drawing your Webley No. 2. You pass every test.

Now here's what I shall do. I will reveal to you all the true facts of the case concerning the murder of Dr. Grimesby Roylott, for you are right and it was murder. Two murders to be precise. I was only guilty of one of them. You shall be my judge, jury, and executioner, and there is not a man I would rather be sentenced to death by. Judging from my pulse, I should say our rate at present is fifty-four-and-a-quarter miles-an-hour. If the verdict is guilty, I shall assent to whatever sentence you wish, be it to leap from this train to my certain death. Agreed?"

I nodded, for at that moment I could not speak.

"Very well, then. And let me first say that I confess to the murder by torture of what you mistook for a foul and venomous beast, though a more charitable description would be poor, helpless worm. Moreover, I am sincerely sorry to say it was no swift though terrible death but a slow and lingering one. That could not be helped. Now let us begin at the beginning, which in this case and hopefully in many cases to come must be the appearance of a client at 221b. You recall that vision of a woman in black seated in our sitting-room window? I mean Grimesby's daughter, Helen Roylott?"

Fortunately, I had found my voice once more. "*Stoner*, Holmes. She was Roylott's *step*-daughter." Holmes's blunder was a curious one and I made a mental note of it. Had he indeed been experimenting with transcendental drugs, and could they have resulted in temporary insanity? I docketed the possible plea. "As for her appearance, I shall remember it to my dying day. It was nothing if not dramatic."

"Ah, 'dramatic'," said he, savouring the beloved word. "Yes, it was that. The woman was an amateur actress once, you know, like myself. Once an actress, always an actress. I was tempted at first to suppose her appearance a recycling of Holbein's painting of Christina of Denmark in widow's weeds. It was only indirectly so, for Shakespeare drew upon that work too. Ah, Watson, had the Dane turned to Ophelia for consolation after the death of old King Hamlet, they would have cast off their mourning weeds to be redressed both as bride and groom and as king and queen. Happily, he did not, or there would have been no tragedy. Of course you understand Miss Roylott – *Stoner* – was still in mourning for her recently deceased mother and her twin sister, Julia?"

"No, Holmes," said I in some surprise at this second slip. "Her mother died eight years back, in a railway accident near Crewe. Her twin sister Julia died two years ago."

"So long? Oh heavens, died two years ago and not forgotten yet? And slanderer's tongue persists in hissing o'er the world's diameter frailty's name is woman! So you doubt her deep mourning proclaimed by the heavy veil?"

229

"She wore a black veil to protect her complexion," I explained. "That is the correct solution."

"Indoors at half-past-seven on an April morning in foggy London?" Holmes seemed sceptical.

He had a point. I thought about it. "She was seated in the window and the shutters were raised. She was scanning the street to see if her stepfather had followed her."

Holmes did me the justice of thinking about that. For less than two seconds. "Possible. It is true one would have expected an exceptionally agitated woman to be pacing up and down, up and down, as she impatiently awaited the arrival of her last hope. Except . . . We will come to that. As for her veil: Being an actress, she lifted it as if it were a theatre curtain being raised upon some tragic scene. You know what inspired that? It was my Prince's first appearance.'

Here was an egotist indeed! "'It could not have been, Holmes. Yours was an outdoor performance and only the backdrop was black."

"True, but my Hamlet entered onstage at a funeral pace and in the all-encompassing black robes of an Elizabethan mourner for a late king. His head was bowed low as if to seek his noble father in the dust. It was concealed by his huge hood. He seemed like the ghost of an old Blackfriars monk still haunting the stage built there after the dissolution of the monasteries. Then when his mother asked why his father's death seemed so particular to him, he flung his hood back with a cry of '*Seems, madam? Nay, it is!*' only to reveal a young man playing at being prematurely aged by grief. There can be no doubt about it, Doctor. Miss . . . *Stoner* – attended a performance of my *Hamlet* last year, doubtless concealed behind that self-same veil. She saw me, but I could not see her. You recall I played the gravedigger. Nobody else could have done it. My height meant I was perfectly visible to all, even when I stood in that deep grave."

Where a detective's diagnoses end, the doctor's must sometimes begin. "Holmes, Helen Stoner was shaking with terror. Why else would she have been seated by the window on so cold a morning if not to watch for her stepfather? That was the only reason why she had her veil down."

For so superb an actor, Holmes was singularly unsuccessful in his valiant attempt to gulp down a yawn unobserved. I suppose he thought I was not playing the game. My explanation was plausible but boring. I heard once of a certain aristocrat deeply offended with an abstruse and expensive Harley Street specialist who diagnosed theirs as a commonplace case of measles. Such was the irritation I read in my friend's eyes. "No, Doctor, her father – forgive me, *stepfather* – could have had nothing to do with it. She timed her entrance onto our stage with exquisite care. I checked your *Bradshaw's*. The first train left Leatherhead at 7:22 and arrived at Waterloo at 8:11. She was safe for at least an hour. Besides, even if Roylott had taken that first train, he must still have wasted precious time hammering on the door of my old lodgings in Montague Street first, for that was the address supplied by Mrs. Farintosh in the old letter Miss Stoner – for I must remember to call her that – left behind for Roylott to discover."

"You altered the time on my mantelpiece clock before you woke me up?" I was indignant at the childish parlour trick. "It said a quarter-past-seven! Now you tell me it was actually nearer nine?"

"I never touched your late father's old timepiece, Doctor," said he with amusement. "The hour was correct, unless by means of the dark arts I had altered the fall of its shadow too. Newton, you know, taught himself as a boy to tell the time to the quarter-hour from the shadows in his home, though I'll wager the trick never saved his life as it once did me mine. No, Miss Stoner was lying when she said she had travelled to London that morning. She actually left late the previous night and stayed at a private hotel in the Strand. The variety of London mud on her shoes was quite unmistakeable both by sight and smell. As for the still damp soil that speckled the left arm of her jacket, that is easily accounted for. She opened the door of her cab on her way here. It could not have been so perfectly fresh had she acquired it at least an hour ago.'

"But she cannot have lied!" I cried. "That would be to bring into doubt her entire account of the previous night! Besides, she was still clutching half a return ticket. And what makes you think she deliberately let Roylott know she was coming to 221b? And why else seat herself in our window? And why – "

Holmes held up his hands to signal his craven surrender. "You are the Maxim Gun of interrogators," he laughed. "Your questions come at me in bullet swarms."

"What is a Maxim Gun?" I asked in puzzlement, for despite my military contacts at the club, I had never heard of any such device.

"The future," mused Holmes dreamily. "A gleam in the imperial eye, or so I am informed by my – my informant. Now to take your first question first: Of course she was lying. She was a woman, was she not? I am told you are one of London's leading experts on that peculiar species, Doctor."

I did not rise to the bait. Even at so early a date, I had learnt how fatal and futile it was to encourage so confirmed a misogynist. "Well, what of her being seated in our window?"

My friend paused to refill his travelling pipe with the cheapest shag that money could buy, as painstakingly as if it were the genuine Bradley's Arcadian mixture. Holmes has absolutely no appreciation of tobacco. This has always pained me, for I would dearly have liked to share the secret of the Arcadian mixture with him. But a promise is a promise. My friend Barrie the cricketer had been peculiarly delighted with my repetition to him of Holmes's vision of the two of us flying out of our bow window hand in hand, then gently removing the roofs to peep in at the queer things going on inside. In his gratitude, he had confided in me his precious secret on the understanding that I would tell none unworthy of it where it might be obtained. Sadly, then, I cannot take upon myself the responsibility of introducing Holmes to Arcadia.

"Here is a tip, my good fellow," said he at last, having paused for so long – not, I think, because he had been puzzled by the difficulty of my question, but rather because he found it hard to explain what in his eyes was the self-evident. "When there is a seemingly insurmountable obstacle to understanding, strip that obstacle of its trimmings, and seventy-six times out of seventy-seven it shall turn out to be the solution in a cunning disguise. Why should a woman who has just come shivering out of a nipping and an eager air enter a room with a crackling fire and avoid that blaze like the plague? Why should she not warm her toes at it, and prefer instead to secrete herself in the very coldest niche she can find?"

"It makes no sense," I confessed.

Another and more pregnant pause. A sigh.

"Watson, I tell you how to find the answer and you pig-headedly shun my excellent advice. No, that is unfair to the discerning nature of pigs. Let us think rather of truffles cast before the common herd of mankind. I can only say again that when there appears to be an insuperable impediment in the way of your goal, do not neglect to consider whether that obstacle might not prove to be the very means by which you may ascend to what you seek. Why should she choose the spot that was coldest when she was shivering with cold? So that she might continue to do so! Do you see now how the solution becomes self-evident and is contained within the question? Therefore, the next question to ask is why she wished to persist in her uncontrollable trembling."

"You feel she was influenced by the works of Sacher-Masoch?" I knew of that gentleman, owing to my contributions to the *Holywell Street Journal*. It would not have surprised me to discover my friend was a secret subscriber. Holmes's diagnosis seemed like wishful thinking on the part of a suspected necrophobe. "You think that false bell-pull was installed in the bedroom for purposes of recreational restraint?"

Holmes burst into silent and yet hearty laughter. I discovered much later that, like his silent toast-munching he had mastered the art the better to converse with his brother Mycroft while breakfasting at the Diogenes near St. James's Square, a club library founded by Thomas Carlyle where all auditory communication is banned. "Ingenious! Highly ingenious, Doctor. But I think we may cut the Gordian Knot and select the simplest solution instead. Did you by any chance catch a faint metallic sound like something being shut just as we were about to enter the sitting-room?"

I thought back. "Why, yes, I did. You think she was closing your safe?"

Holmes sighed. He has made a special study of sighs. He claims that the sighs of Hamlet, Claudius, and Ophelia are the overlooked highlights of the play.

"The window, Watson. She was closing the window."

"You mean she was signalling to someone outside?"

"Of course not. She was inhaling that bitter and eager air to set her teeth chattering away. The one puzzle is why, having achieved her aim, she did not put the finishing touch to her little cheat by hastening over to that blazing fire before we entered. The answer is simplicity itself: Had I found her trembling by the fireplace, I could never have supposed she was shaking from the cold. I would have surmised it meant she was terrified. By remaining by the window, she meant to guarantee my seemingly faulty diagnosis. Then she discomfited me further still by raising her veil to reveal a damsel with grey hair, a ploy inspired, as I have said, by my own Hamlet's childishly theatrical gesture. It was admirably done." Holmes bowed his head as if to acknowledge a splendid adversary and an excellent actress.

This was perfectly preposterous. "But Holmes, why should she wish to make you think you had blundered? I know how touchy – I mean, I am sure that making anyone look foolish would not be the best way to ensure their cooperation."

"As a matter of fact, I was not deceived for a moment," said he frostily. "It was charity on my part to permit her to think I was. That was all. Besides, I was intrigued by her determination to intrigue me. She promised me horrors I was to have the pleasure of translating into cold facts. As for her desire to make it appear I had failed to deduce her true state at the very outset of our interview, her aim was to exacerbate my urge to shine. I had no choice but to proceed to make brilliant deductions based on the clues she so kindly and prodigally supplied. For example, I appeared to play into her hands when I deduced she had travelled to London earlier that morning."

"So she had," I protested. "You are forgetting that half-ticket still clutched in one hand."

"I forget nothing, save by choice," said he with a touch of brittle asperity. "You really are very slow, Doctor. Must I explain that when I said I 'played into her hands', a pun was intended? Do you imagine she would have held onto that half-ticket all the way from Waterloo? She would have put it in her pocket. She must have thought I slipped up badly there, for had I insisted on inspecting the ticket I would soon have confirmed it was not what it appeared to be at all. Nor was she. Do you not see? She knew if she asserted she had taken a fictitious train an hour before the first left Guildford, even a Lestrade would have smelled a fellow rat. By permitting me to deduce it for myself, and then gasping with awe at my unrivalled brilliance, she hoped to flatter me into trusting to my own faulty judgement. She thought to play upon me like a pipe, Watson, as women always do. They are snake charmers all."

I think there was grudging respect behind that sneer. I later discovered that one of Holmes's many redeeming features was an unfeigned admiration for a worthy opponent. I was reluctant to disillusion him. "I don't think she was as manipulative as you imagine, Holmes. Her grey hair testified to her distraught state. She was only thirty."

Holmes kindly bestowed upon me a look of the most pitying contempt. "Watson, do you really understand anything at all of the unfair sex? You remember everything of course, but you learn nothing. A woman intends to escape the clutches of a sadistic swine through marriage. Would such a one not strive to look as attractive as possible to the opposite sex? It is inconceivable she would not have dyed her hair? Now, once we have eliminated the impossibility that she did *not* dye it, then what remains? She dyed it. Therefore, she dyed it *grey*. It was but another ingenious ploy by which to reel me in."

"Holmes!"

"Why the indignation? Would you condemn a rosy-cheeked lass for pinching those cheeks to make them still extra rosy? Would you spurn a redhead who coloured her hair as the grey began to appear? Where is your patriotism? Think of Elizabeth I. Then why should it disgust you with all of female nature if Helen Stoner made herself as piteous as possible to guarantee my services? Accept the truth, Doctor. Womankind adheres to the precept that the best way to be a part is to act it."

I had come to understand how pointless it was to engaging in verbal fencing with this hybrid offspring of a rapier and a scalpel. I tried a different tack. "Well, I grant you she may have resorted to a little charming feminine duplicity to recruit you to her just cause. In return, Holmes, will you please grant me that hers were snow-white lies. She excused her stepfather's murderous tendencies as due to an inherited criminal strain. She stressed how, even after receiving a stiff prison sentence, he at once returned to his medical practice. She played the devil's advocate by concealing from us his one motive for murder. She never mentioned her mother's will that would have deprived him of much of his income should his stepdaughters marry.

"And I don't know if you noticed, Holmes, but she kept nervously tugging down her right sleeve, lest we glimpse those five little marks that the tyrant had impressed upon her wrist when he gripped it. The man was a maniac. Why, only last week he almost murdered the local blacksmith. That ought to have opened her eyes at last to the danger she was in. She might then have breathed a sigh of relief at the thought he would be incarcerated, at least until after her wedding. What did she do instead? The landlord of our inn told me in the strictest confidence he had heard she pawned her wedding dress to pay his bail! You will not believe it, Holmes, but seems she told her friends and relatives that as wedding gifts, she would rather receive cash than all the candelabra and butter dishes in London so as to fund his defence at the coming trial. That speaks of her credulous innocence and her blind devotion to him."

Holmes snorted. "The credulity is entirely yours, Doctor. You must see that since he had ceased to be licensed to kill following the murder of that butler, he could hardly have returned to practice, save as a back street abortionist or a criminal consultant specialising in untraceable poisons. As for why she was so very anxious to stand bail for a convicted murderer and abusive father, that ought to be obvious. The attack on the blacksmith was a godsend. Naturally that blacksmith swore he would play the revenger should Roylott be found not guilty at his trial. Such black oaths were of course recalled after Roylott's mysterious death. Nor was he the only suspect she took care to supply. By informing us that Roylott had murdered his native butler in India and escaped the noose, she raised the possibility the dead man's family had at last taken their revenge. Finally, she craftily introduced a pair of exceedingly sinister strangers into the neighbourhood only hours before Roylott's death. True, they had behaved in all ways as exemplary members of society – with the one exception that they were probably paid assassins."

"I saw no such sinister strangers."

"That is because you did not know where to look. Have you forgotten the two men masquerading as architects who gave false names at the Crown Inn opposite the Manor House, stepped out on the night of the murder there, returned soon after it, and then vanished without trace? As you said, Watson, they were *seen*.'"

Was Holmes playing games with me? Was my modern knight in truth a *condottiere*, a contracted mercenary, a hired assassin well pleased to slay a dragon to save a damsel in distress? Had that entire melodramatic opening scene been staged to deceive me in case I was needed to give evidence in a court of law? I shook the thought off as unworthy of a gentleman. "She never even considered others might wish Roylott dead. She was incapable of thinking ill of others. Helen Stoner was determined not to so much as hint that Roylott could have murdered her sister and would target her next."

"You really do not see it, do you?" said he wonderingly. "Is it possible you still do not understand? By stubbornly refusing to accuse him while giving in evidence against him, quite unknowingly of course, she was ensuring we would not doubt he was still the born killer he had first revealed himself to be in India. Now, had she begun by stating point blank that Roylott had killed her sister and would kill her next, it would have raised the possibility that everything she said sprang from her paranoid bias. The more she seemed pathetically and loyally determined to conceal what a murderous monster he was, the more I would interpret the evidence just as she meant me to. She made it almost insultingly easy to perceive the truth."

At last I began to understand! Holmes was not quite as inhuman as I had been led to believe. "For all her grey hairs, she was very pretty," said I slyly. "She was quite attractive, was she not?"

Holmes frowned with evident annoyance. He seemed to think that insulting. "I am a human being, Dr. Watson. I have never denied it. Regrettably, there is no escaping one's humanity. As regards your sentimental insinuation, though, I will grant you no more than this: When damsels in distress come calling and appeal to my quixotic streak, urging me to slay dragons on their behalf, I confess to experiencing a peculiar feeling akin to wellbeing whenever I do agree to play the knight in shining armour. Why should that be? Some chemical is released into the brain when one engages in altruistic behaviour. The moral and philosophical implications are immense, for if that is so, then unselfishness might actually be selfish, since those who habitually do good are perhaps nothing more than addicts who must have their next release of that particular chemical."

"That is a little fanciful," said I doubtfully. I did not like the idea that good and evil might be nothing more than competing drug addictions.

"Well, my experiments in this area are still in the early stages. The fact remains she lied in the expectation we men would enjoy being lied to. Her lies were to create the impression she was more concerned to protect her father than herself."

"Her stepfather, Holmes." Why did he persist in making that slip? As his possible future biographer, I made a note of that. Did it relate to something in his past?

Holmes shook his head. "Her father, I say, though should you one day have your account reprinted in one of the more respectable family

236

magazines, you need not mention it. You recall she insisted that hereditary madness in the family was passed from generation to generation, but only along the male line? Now, if there was such criminal insanity, it would have been present in the females as well as the males. Why was she in denial on that point? She did not wish to admit she had inherited it too. It was quite evident to me she had. But her chief reason for asserting he was not her blood father was once again to create the impression she was striving to mitigate his offences. She falsified the time of her mother's death for the same reason. Mrs. Roylott died months rather than years ago. That was obvious."

"But how?"

"Without explicitly revealing that Roylott had a monetary motive for wishing his daughters dead, she dropped a very broad hint by promising to reimburse me *once she had married* and thus become financially independent. Of course, that implied her mother had left her a tidy sum in her will. I do not expect you to keep up with the latest changes in the matrimonial law, Doctor. As a confirmed bachelor without prospects, why should you? The Married Women's Property Act received its royal assent on 18 August, 1882, and by it a married woman may possess property of her own as opposed to being her husband's: She no longer requires her husband's consent to draft a will.

"But Roylott had a stroke of good fortune. His wife was badly injured in a train collision at Crewe the month after the Act was assented to, on 30th September to be precise, and so became her devoted husband's resident patient."

The miscalculation was a simple one. "That would have been after the Act was passed!"

"Ah. I have a confession to make. I was so impressed by Helen Roylott's trick in preserving that half of a return ticket in her hand I could not resist playing a like one on you. That was why I returned to 221b, ostentatiously clutching a paper bearing mathematical hieroglyphics to defeat a Mor – a more than mortal wit. You recall how I told you I would walk down to Doctors' Commons to acquire the relevant data? The statement was perfectly correct, only I carelessly misplaced a word. I ought to have said, 'I shall walk down to the Commons, Doctor,' but somehow it came out as, 'I shall walk down to Doctors' Commons,' which was of course impossible, since that famous establishment where marriage licenses and wills were once kept was demolished in 1867. The precise sums in Mrs. Roylott's will were immaterial. All that mattered was firstly that such an inheritance would have been sufficient to make Helen Roylott financially independent, and secondly, the date after which her mother could have bequeathed it to her. In the Commons library and archives I

237

ascertained that the Act only came into law on 1 January of this year. I cannot prove Roylott murdered his wife. Let us be generous and say no more than that it would have been quite exceptional incompetence on his part had she remained alive under his care until after that New Year's Day deadline. Hence the deep mourning weeds of Helen when she visited us."

"But then where was the motive for murder?"

"Why, do you not see? It was there with a vengeance! It was not Roylott who would have benefited from the death of Helen, but Helen from the death of Roylott, and to a far greater extent. By neglecting to save his wife, he had merely secured the third of the income from his wife's investments that might otherwise have gone to the daughter. Now consider the current situation of his grieving daughter. She shall inherit that entire income plus his estate, being the sole known surviving member of the family. Of course, Roylott might have cut her out of his will, but that would have been too risky. He had to play the loving husband and father, lest the already suspicious authorities conclude he had murdered both wife and daughter. They would then have pressed for a conviction at his coming trial for murderously assaulting the blacksmith. This time he would have been put away for life."

I was far from convinced either as a doctor or as a serious student of the fairer sex. "I cannot believe she would be so mercenary, Holmes. You saw how sickly she is. She has not many years to live."

"You are right about the sickness, Doctor, though not for the reasons you suppose. She shall indeed be dead in a few years, of that I have no doubt. She only wished to avenge her mother and sister first. The money was incidental."

Men of genius sometimes miss what is blindingly obvious to lesser intellects. They spend so much time observing that they forget to see. "That cannot be true, Holmes. Had Roylott not died when he did, then as a repeat offender he would have received a pretty stiff prison sentence breaking stones on Dartmoor for almost murdering the blacksmith. Would that not have been revenge enough?"

But he was adamant. "Ha! That would never have happened, though what if it had? He would have been out of Princetown within hours. A man who can twist steel pokers into knots could have parted the bars on his cell window in seconds. That is immaterial, since he would never have been sent there. He would certainly have been found criminally insane and so sent to Broadmoor, not Dartmoor. Life there would have been comparatively comfortable. More to the point, the daughter would not have been out of reach of the father, but he out of hers."

238

"He did deserve to die," said I uncomfortably. "You saw those finger marks he imprinted on her wrist. Father or stepfather, either way he was a degenerate beast."

"A beast, certainly, though as it happens he was innocent of those lesser marks. But as for her repeatedly tugging at her sleeve as if fearful lest they be detected, that was to *attract* my attention and ensure I located them myself. Depend upon it, Doctor, women only ever conceal their bodies to attract the male eye to what is screened."

How little Holmes understood the modesty of the female sex! "No, no, she sincerely wished to hide them. You saw how she blushed violently when you pushed back the frill of black lace that fringed her right hand. She was mortified you had discovered her terrible secret. I thought she would die of shame."

"Do not exaggerate the symptoms, Doctor," said he coldly, and I thought of how my teachers had chided me thus in my undergraduate days. "You always do that. You thought I turned chalk white at the appearance of the snake through the ventilator, yet you only saw me by the yellow flare of a single match that you supposed had so blinded you as to render invisible a snake spitting and writhing upon the bell-pull. She merely blushed with pleasure at the success of her little act. She thought she had deceived the world's finest detective."

I considered digressing to mention most authorities thought the great criminologist Bertillon worthier of that title. It would have been pointless. Once he knew it, he would have done his best to forget it. It was best to press home my winning argument. "All that you say is by-the-by. The facts condemned Grimesby, so absolutely she hardly needed to point an accusing finger at him."

Holmes chuckled. "Did she not? Did she not? Well, let us reconsider the death of her twin sister, Julia. You do remember all the circumstance? Please summarise them to refresh both our memories."

I referred to my shorthand notebook. I had learnt Pitman for writing prescriptions speedily in the heat of the battle. I shall paraphrase what I then read aloud, asking my readers to excuse the police report style.

"Shortly before her murder, Julia, on being almost overcome by the noxious cigar fumes her father had been blowing into her bedroom through the newly installed ventilator, left there to visit her sister in hers. There they passed some time chatting until Julia supposed the smoke had to have have cleared from her own bedroom. As she was leaving, she asked her sister whether she was in the habit of whistling at night, for she had heard such a sound herself. On receiving an answer in the negative, she then left and Helen heard the sound of her key turning in her lock. Hours later, Helen was awakened by a terrible scream and went out into the hallway, where she found someone had lit the lamp there. By its light she saw Julia stumble out of her room before collapsing in agony. With a cry of 'It was the band! The speckled band!' Julia had pointed towards Roylott's bedroom door. Then she lost consciousness, slowly succumbed, and at last died. But Holmes," said I, suddenly anticipating his argument, "it was Julia who pointed that accusing finger, not her sister. Do you doubt Helen's word for that? You have no reason to suppose she was lying."

"Oh, it is quite impossible she was not lying. Or if she was speaking the truth about the pointing finger, which I doubt, then she was lying. You recall Helen asserted that afterwards her sister's clutched hands were forced open, and within the fists were found concealed a burn-out match and a matchbox? I regret nobody thought to inspect the contents of the latter, for it may well have contained a truly remarkable worm. Now, she might just conceivably have clutched a matchbox in case she needed to strike another light, but why continue to hold onto the used match? Moreover, one holds a match between one's forefinger and thumb, so why was it found concealed inside her clenched fist?

A thought had struck me. "And how could she have unlocked her door?"

"What makes you think she ever locked it?"

That was what I would call elementary. "Helen heard a key turn in the lock soon after Julia left her. That proves she did."

"On the contrary, it strongly suggests she did not. Consider that Helen testified she only heard the key turn in the lock once. Now, if the inhabitants of the Manor House really were afraid that the wild beasts roaming the grounds outside might break in and murder them in their beds, would she not have unlocked and then relocked her door when she crossed over to Helen's room? As a matter of fact, the beasts could not have broken in since they had to have been on long leashes and kept apart in different areas of the grounds. We will come to that. What matters here is that Helen ought to have heard the key turn twice as Julia first unlocked and then relocked her door once again. Since Helen only heard it turn once, it follows that Julia never locked it at all. She might have secured it to keep out her father, but what would have been the point? He undoubtedly had copies of keys to every room in the house. No, there was only one person who had the strongest motives for keeping his room locked at all times, and that was Grimesby Roylott. It was he who had unlocked *his* door, for having heard Julia leave her bedroom for Helen's, he would have been anxious, lest she decide to sleep with her sister that night. Therefore he would have tiptoed out to peep through Helen's keyhole to ensure she was alone. I am sorry to deprive you of your childish locked room mystery, Watson, but you must see that was purely for my entertainment."

240

"Entertainment!"

"Obviously. My dear doctor, did you not perceive in her a fellow teller of fairy tales? Think of her description of Julia's door opening so very, very slowly in the best traditions of melodrama, only to then have Julia burst forth like a jack in the box and reeling like a drunken woman? As a theatrical effect, the contrast between that agonising slowness and her abrupt appearance was entirely justified, but in terms of real life it was practically a contradiction. No, Helen Roylott's aim was to weave a fine little puzzle in the most dramatic terms. She meant to guarantee my intervention, to say nothing of my eventual assistance in the concealment of her crime."

"But the mystery was there! She had no need to change the facts."

"Oh, it was there all right, though not in the way you think. It was the behaviour of the police and not the criminal that fascinated me. Is it customary outside those cheaper forms of fiction you so love for the police to search for secret recesses in the walls and floor of a crime scene? Was it because the Roylotts were undoubtedly an old Catholic family who had concealed priests in their time? Somewhat ironic, that, given the Roylotts were of royal blood. When he framed himself in our doorway, the resemblance of Grimesby to Holbein's Whitehall Mural Henry VIII was quite unmistakeable. Henry sowed his royal oats, you see – hence the change of name: 'Roylott' is hardly your typical Anglo-Saxon moniker. It began as an insult and became a badge of pride, as well as something of a shield. It was why they escaped comparatively unscathed during the persecution of the old faith."

"Well, that's as may be, but you are wrong about the house, Holmes!" cried I, seeing at last a chance to wash away all those ephemeral sandcastles in the clouds. "The house was but two centuries old. It was built long after the persecution of the Catholic Church in England had ceased. There could have been no priest holes."

"Oh, she was probably lying when she told you that. But for precisely that reason we may eliminate so obvious and hackneyed a device from our consideration. On the contrary, knowing it would be the first thought of policemen who had been told tales as boys of Roylott secret tunnels and suchlike tricks, the villain took care to kill Julia in a room where he supposed there could be no such priest holes. Not that the police were looking for any. They were searching for something much smaller."

"What do you mean?"

"Well, it is evident from the fact that they examined the walls between the bedrooms and yet they entirely ignored the ceiling. You must have seen how low the latter was. Rather too low, don't you think?"

"Why, no. Surely low ceilings were quite normal at the turn of the last century."

"You are still assuming the house was only two centuries old. Let us suppose it was. It would have been built, then, at about the time that the wealth of the Roylotts began to be squandered. The old house would have been demolished and an extravagant new one erected in its place with no expense spared. Such country houses were intended to impress and the rooms on the ground floor, which included the ballroom and dining room, had high ceilings precisely because humbler homes had low ones. Those very low ceilings tell us it was built much earlier, though even then they have to be accounted for. The answer is obvious. There *was* a priest hole in the space between the floors, though ironically Roylott never suspected as much. Nor did the police."

"How can you possibly be so sure?"

"Because I had expected there would be one. A consideration of the dimensions of the house merely confirmed it."

"My dear Holmes!"

"Oh, yes I did. You have heard of Stonyhurst College? It has long been Roman Catholicism's strongest English citadel. Its Long Gallery is impressive, but its ceiling is five feet lower than it ought to be, just like those of the rooms on the ground floor of Stoke Moran Manor House. It did not take me long to discover the priest hole beneath the floor of one of the bedrooms above the Long Gallery. Of course, since the Morans and Stoners were both ancient Roman Catholic families, little Grimesby was sent there for his education. That was why the police searched the bedroom so very carefully for superfluous apertures."

Here was further evidence Holmes was a lapsed Catholic. I jotted down a note to that effect. It might be worth visiting Stonyhurst one day. What a find it would be were I to discover the young Sherlock Holmes's diary concealed in such a priest hole! But no, that would be dishonourable. Chiding myself for such a thought, I swore inwardly never to investigate Holmes's professed past without his express permission, despite the fact that the little he had told me concerning it did not seem to be entirely trustworthy.

"But Holmes, if the police knew Roylott had been at Stonyhurst College as a boy, and that explains their search, why do you insist they were not looking for priest holes?"

"It was not Stonyhurst itself that stimulated Roylott's imagination so profoundly. It was the precedent he was supplied with while there. Who do you suppose inspired him to create that wildlife sanctuary? Have you not heard of Charles Waterton, the fellow who influenced Wallace, Darwin, and Challenger? At Stoneyhurst, they still speak in awe of his

242

ascent up the sides of the school's towers. He was before Roylott's time, but his fame lives on."

"Why, Holmes," said I, "I do believe I have heard of the man." A memory of Tadpole Phelps's face looking pleadingly up at me as I prepared to dip it into the toilet swam into ken. To my great shame, I had thought by such petty acts of cruelty to win the official prize for School Bully of the Year. To make matters worse, I only came third. "Was there not a police inspector Phelps bitten on the nose by a rabid dog back in 1838 whom Waterton cured with curare?"

I smiled to see Holmes so startled and not a little displeased. I was about to explain that I had known a distant relative of that gentleman at school when I saw him smile back and knew there was no need. He had found something to criticise.

"You have been misinformed. The inspector died before Waterton could administer the cure. I give you the curare, though, for it was he who introduced it into England. There was a golden opportunity missed! So long as a poison is unknown, there can be no test for it. The authorities evidently suspected Roylott had thought to do what Waterton ought to have and did not. Do not look so disapproving. Please understand I speak only from an aesthetic point of view as a connoisseur of murder. They were searching for any orifice through which he might have employed a blow dart to kill his daughter in her sleep."

"But then why did they not take note of that ventilator grille?"

"Because they did not observe it, any more than you did when we visited Roylott's bedroom. We will come to that. Suffice it to say, for now that the means by which he thought to conceal his guilt unintentionally revealed to me the full extent of it. A confessional screen can sometimes disclose the sins of the father confessor, though I can tell you from experience it is unwise to demonstrate as much. Let us not speak of that, but pass on. For the present, we are only concerned with establishing the guilt of Helen – what was it – *Stoner*.

A reminder was necessary here. "We agreed, Holmes, it is *you* who are on trial for the murder of Grimesby Roylott. You can hardly expect to gain my sympathy as your judge and jury by attempting to make a scapegoat of your client."

"But you misunderstand me. I am not suggesting she should take my place on the scaffold. I am merely observing that if and when Mr. Justice Watson passes sentence on Mr. Justice Holmes, he might consider doing so on both me and her. She was certainly as guilty as I. Cannot I tempt you with a scene you could then supply your more romantic readers with? You could have us take the drop together, locked in each other's arms. It would double the readership of *Doctor Watson's Baker Street Journal*. It might even break into three figures."

I was far from happy with all this, though I stowed away Holmes's cynically sentimental image for future use. "I am sorry, Holmes," said I firmly, "but I think yours a most unwarranted accusation."

"Really?" Holmes spoke with the smug assurance of a man who is habitually incapable of contemplating the concept of defeat. "Let us re-examine the crime scene in our mind's eyes. Recall what we found when we visited the Manor House and scrutinised the bedrooms of Mr. Grimesby Roylott and the late Julia Stoner – for if we must, let us continue to call her that by courtesy. Her chamber supplied all the clues required to reveal how her murder was managed. Roylott had certainly sent his calculating adder through the dummy ventilator and down the dummy bell-pull to sting Julia as she slumbered."

"That is not to be doubted," said I with decisively crossed arms.

"We are agreed then. But, in the case of Roylott's bedroom, an obstacle arose just as soon as Miss Stoner had escorted us there."

I was mystified. "Surely not, Holmes. He had not even bothered to lock his door."

"That is the obstacle I was referring to. Like most laymen, you suppose a locked room more of a mystery than an unlocked one, whereas in cases such as the present one it is the unlocked room that is the real difficulty. I have already said that the only inhabitant of the Manor House with a clear motive for locking his door was Grimesby Roylott, and it was his key turning in the lock Helen heard after Julia left her on the night of the murder. And do you imagine it was his habit to leave his room wide open every time he was absent from home? He was often away for weeks on end while roaming with his gypsy friends. It is hardly very likely, is it?"

"But he must have done," I pointed out shrewdly. "She had no key, and assumed when she took us there that the door would indeed be unlocked."

"Then she knew it was open because she had herself unlocked it earlier. She had a copy of his key."

This was too much. "Really, Holmes, you are too cynical. When your glass is half-full you assume the worst and suppose it was poisoned. Why should you suppose such treachery? Surely there is a simpler explanation. He had visited his daughter's bedroom early in the morning and discovered her gone, and an old letter from her friend Mrs. Farintosh on the bed. He read it and came across your name and address. In his fury he stormed off to London and quite forgot to lock his door. It was carelessness, no more than that."

"Then why did she not cry out in surprise and express her amazement that he had blundered so badly? And, having discovered his door unlocked upon his return from seeing Holmes the busybody, would he not have deduced I had ignored his advice and broken in? Do not forget that on the merest suspicion that his butler in India had been stealing from him, he had beaten the man to death. That was in the days when he was still comparatively sane. His rage against his daughter on discovering his room had been penetrated would have been more murderous still. Besides, even if he had charitably blamed himself and spared both the housekeeper and his daughter his blows, are we really to suppose he would not have taken the greatest care not to repeat his howler on the night of the intended murder? You recall that when we eventually went to his room to discover his corpse, the door was once again unlocked. No, Helen had been in the room, and had departed from it just before we arrived there. The saucer of milk upon the safe proves it."

"But Roylott had poured it out to give to the snake."

Experts can be exasperating and Holmes was particularly so. "Serpents are not partial to milk. Nor are cats, for that matter, though they welcome cream for its fat content. As an enticement, water would have been infinitely preferable in this case. No, that milk was left there by Miss Stoner as a clue to the contents of the safe. It was a hint that it imprisoned a serpent whose venom congealed blood in seconds."

I could not help smiling at so fantastic a notion. "Why should a saucer of milk suggest that?"

"Not to you, perhaps, but as I say she was an amateur actress who had been deeply impressed by my revolutionary outdoor production of *Hamlet*. She was thinking of the poisoning of Hamlet's father. The spirit tells the Prince that though the official story was the old Hamlet had died of a snakebite '*the serpent that did sting thy father's life now wears the crown*'. A fine image, that, which she drew upon for the *denouement* as we shall see. But do not distract me. The poison used for that murder '*doth posset and curd, like eager droppings into milk, the thin and wholesome blood*'. That is the action of the Russell's Viper, which as I am sure you know can turn a saucer of blood to jelly in mere moments. I surmise the action of the Roylott's adder is similar."

"But how could she possibly have known he kept a snake in his safe? Or do you picture her spying on him through that ventilator grille?"

I had meant it as a joke. Despite myself I found myself picturing her doing just that. The ceiling was so low that even she could have reached the grille, provided she stood on a chair. Despite myself, I felt a touch of guilty pride when Holmes nodded his head approvingly.

"Why, Watson, you excel yourself. That is criminally good. Only you have it the wrong way 'round. It was Roylott who initially introduced that grille in order to spy on his daughters. He was not so foolish as to overlook its potential as a two-edged sword. The solution was simple enough and one that you must have observed when we investigated his bedroom. Think back. What was the one feature of that room you entirely failed to observe?"

I did so. Suddenly it struck me. "Holmes, there was no sign of that ventilator grille! How could I have missed it? "

"The same way the police did when they probed the walls for concealed orifices. Roylott have hidden both sides of it behind paintings at the time when the police came calling. You recall that copy of a Bronzino *Virgin and Child* in her old room? It was hanging over the grille during the police investigation. You remember that painting in Roylott's room I identified as a satirical representation of King Henri II of France and his mistress Diane de Poitiers, their relationship idealised as akin to that of a mother and her son? It was concealing the grille. Since it portrayed Venus and Cupid engaged in an incestuous kiss it, spoke to me of the sexual proclivities of Grimesby Roylott, which is precisely why you averted your eyes from it in some embarrassment. You saw but chose not to observe it. You could never be a detective, my dear fellow. "

"I remember now," said I, frowning deeply. "It was an obscene version of the original in the National Gallery."

Holmes seemed perversely amused. "Actually no, it is the National Gallery original that has been doctored, and to the pure connoisseur of crime is therefore the vandalised one. Just as I cannot believe a true account of our last adventure will be published in my lifetime, so the National Gallery concluded their acquisition could not be put on public display uncensored. Perhaps some facts should be suppressed, or one might say repressed. What we saw in Roylott's bedroom is the painting as it once was, complete with erect nipple between Cupid's fingers, with his quiver scatalogically targeting his nether regions, and with her tongue in his mouth – or with his in hers. If the latter were indeed the case, then he would indeed be the serpent his lover Psyche feared he was, for it would resemble a snake's. That would be apt enough. Since Cupid is armed with arrows dipped in honey, he was a flying serpent, bearing in mind that bees were so classified in medieval bestiaries. "

I was growing increasingly uncomfortable. "Really, Holmes, is it absolutely necessary to leave no stone unturned? Must one expose all the worms beneath them? "

Holmes was contrarily contemptuous of my moral disapproval. "It is absolutely necessary, particularly since one of those worms is the

246

'Hispaniola Serpent', as the complaint is sometimes called to this day. Our client was concealing rather more than those five little spots upon her wrist, you see. I patted her forearm to confirm my suspicion, and as I anticipated, she flinched. It was partly because my action put her in mind of abuses suffered at the hands of her father. It was also out of real physical discomfort. As you said, she does not have many more years to live. That picture confirmed my diagnosis."

I realised I had been gaping in amazement. Since my mouth was open, I thought I might as well use it. "Holmes, you cannot be saying that the painting could tell you that! Or are you saying the figure clutching its head in the background is a depiction of a syphilitic?"

"No, it merely personifies love's sufferings. Come, in a picture of Venus where would one expect to find an allusion to venereal disease? Venus herself, of course."

I considered that alabaster form in my medical mind's eye. "Holmes, she was perfect! Pygmalion's statue come to life could not have been whiter. She bore less blemishes than the Knidos *Venus*."

Holmes produced a degenerate chuckle. "A most pertinent comparison, given the legend of how one of that statue's more ardent adorers came to leave his mark upon her. Now recall that cheerful child with the bells of a fool or a leper upon one ankle. He is about to hurl rose petals upon Venus, as if at a wedding. We have much to fear from such flowers. Like the smiling and beautiful countryside, they too can conceal worms in the bud."

"What do you mean?"

"Consider the other foot of that stupid boy. I call him stupid because it is pierced through by a rose thorn, but the pain signal has not yet travelled from his foot to his brain. His cry of triumph shall turn into a scream of agony when the signal's journey is accomplished. His foot shall swell until it is as gigantic as that lion's foot of the monstrous sphinx girl beside it. Now picture this blanched beauty covered with rose petals. Do you not see the visual pun? Oh, come now, you are an army doctor. You know what happens when Venus encounters Mars. Syphilis was once classified as a venereal leprosy. As for those rose petals, they will supply her with the image of the syphilitic roseola rash to transform her into a speckled blonde. It was such a rash that Helen Roylott concealed from us. She directed us towards those finger imprints, the better to ensure we did not inspect further afield."

I was aghast. "Holmes, you know not what you say. No father would be so selfish as to infect his own daughters with syphilis, no matter how perverse his passion for them."

247

"In his case, love and selfishness went together. Besides, as a quacksalver, he had a spurious justification for it: '*Diseases desperate grown by desperate appliance are relieved or not at all.*' You are doubtless aware of the superstition of the army camps that one can be cured of syphilis by sleeping with a young virgin? Thus Roylott could tell himself he was merely seeking to cure himself of his complaint. By that means, he craftily excused his unnatural practices."

"Her own father!"

"Her stepfather, Watson. I thought we had agreed upon that polite fiction."

"A Catholic!"

"An unholy father. How do you think he justified his leering at his daughters through that grille? He cast himself as a father confessor at his screen making windows into their souls. Besides, the devil can quote scriptures, and he could always refer to the pragmatic sacred incest of Lot's daughters with their drunk father as a precedent. Doubtless Lot and Roylott alike employed inebriation as an initial excuse until they could make scapegoats of their daughters. But to understand his feelings towards her after his crime, one must look to the rape of Tamar by her brother Amnon. My Biblical knowledge is a trifle rusty I fear, but you will find the story in the first or second of Samuel. Let me see, let me see . . . '*Then Amnon hated her with exceeding great hatred, for the hatred wherewith he hated her was greater than the love wherewith he had loved her.*' When once one has committed an abominable crime, one must choose between damning oneself or one's victim."

I recalled how Miss Roylott had spoken admiringly of Holmes as one who could see deeply into the manifold wickedness of the human heart. For the first time I understood just how deeply he had descended into the filthiest slums of the soul. It horrified me. I shook – or rather, shuddered the revelation off.

"It is unthinkable!"

"Then the problem is solved. Do not think about it. That was the choice the authorities made – hence their failure to properly examine Julia Roylott's corpse for puncture marks, despite their suspicion she had been injected with a hypodermic by the defrocked ex-Doctor Roylott of herpetological celebrity. They saw, but chose not to observe, the leprous mark he had left upon her. Had they made public the fact she was suffering from syphilis, but was so desperate to escape her abusive father she meant to wed and so infect her new husband, her sister Helen's life would have been ruined too. Out of charity they thoughtfully averted their eyes. They did so again when they discovered that grille in his bedroom after I had removed the painting that concealed it. Once the heard about the snake in

Roylott's safe, they understood how Julia's murder had been managed. They supposed he had tried to repeat the trick, but that his snake had revolted. Their verdict that he had died 'playing with his snake' was something of a euphemism, though, and expressed their undoubted disgust at his Peeping Tom practices. They were right that violent delights have violent ends."

Would I not be better off away from this dangerous resident patient of mine who infected me with all manner of sickening thoughts? The question was at that time an academic one, for I was then a poor man and my older brother had inherited the entire estate. Until his unforeseen death five years later, I would receive none of the income. It was best not to think of such things. I determined to distract myself with technical questions.

"Well, if Helen did not learn of the snake by spying on him through that grille, then how could she have done?"

"You forget, Watson, that Roylott was frequently away with his gypsy friends for weeks at a time. That snake could have survived a day or two in his safe, but no longer than that. Who was he to entrust it too? His introduction of a housekeeper provides us with the answer."

"But she was old and her mind was going."

"Who better? Or so it seemed to him. It was merely a matter of terrorising her into doing his will. As an army surgeon you know it is a sergeant major's task to make his men fear him more than they do the enemy. His was similar. He made her fear him far more than she did the wild beasts entrusted to her care. But as the days of his disappearance turned into weeks, her fear of an absent Roylott faded and was finally outweighed by her dread of her present charges. Then we may picture her on her knees before Helen, begging her to take on those onerous duties, and above all never to reveal her treachery to Roylott. Thus did she confide in Helen the secret of the snake in the safe and supplied her with the combination to it. Helen soon discovered documents in it that revealed exactly why Roylott have every reason to dispose of his engaged daughter and then his wife. It is true that Julia could not have inherited anything had Mrs. Roylott died before the change in the law, as indeed she did, but Roylott had the foresight to see that the change to the status of women was inevitable and realise it would be far less suspicious if she died before it came about. Of course he might have murdered his wife first, but he had no way of justifying that to himself. Like Amnon, he could more easily bring himself to hate the daughter he had raped for being his great temptation."

"Monstrous."

"Human. Of course the distinction is often an artificial one. So it may be in the case of Helen's desire for a vitriolic act of vengeance. She milked

249

the snake of its venom. I realised that when I saw the saucer of milk on the safe. By a simple association of ideas the milking of the serpent caused her to think of the spirit's likening of the effect of the poison poured into old Hamlet's ears to that of eager droppings into milk. Since she only thought of that play because she had seen my production of it, she rightly supposed I would make the same association in the manner I suggested earlier."

It saddened me to see how determined Holmes was to transfer the blame for Roylott's death from himself to that poor, innocent girl. "Holmes," said I firmly, "you know full well it was *you* who killed him. You were the one who forced that snake to back track up the bell-pull. Don't you dare to deny it. I saw you do it. I also witnessed the results of your handiwork. Shall I ever forget that horrible tableau? When I die I shall still see that vision of Roylott seated with the recoiled snake about his brows, like one of the damned enthroned in hell. No mortal hand could have posed him thus in the few minutes that elapsed between that ghastly shriek and our discovery of the corpse. The blame for his death is yours and yours alone."

"Really? And what of those singular silences in the night-time?"

"Silences? What silences? There were no silences. Why, Roylott's shriek raised the entire village. You remember when we crossed from the manor house to our inn afterwards, there were faces peering out fearfully at us from every window. I was surprised they let us back in."

"True enough. But what of the long silence that preceded the cry? From our rooms at the inn, we observed Roylott's return home. We saw him shake both his raised fists at the lad who fumbled to open the manor gates. The man was apoplectic with rage."

The point was a fair one. As a doctor I could supplement it. "Miss Stoner said a sudden inexplicable change for the worse came upon her father after he had already served a prison sentence for murder. That could be explained as the onset of tertiary syphilis, you know. I believe he was going mad."

Holmes nodded. "He was certainly a very peculiar mixture of the professional Machiavellian and the untameable ape. He was a cunning fellow, but one who was losing his mind. Only the onset of insanity would explain his folly in bursting into 221b to so perfectly confirm Miss Stoner's depiction of him as a homicidal maniac. Now, bearing in mind his complete inability to control himself – what might you have expected from him when he encountered Miss Stoner that night? He knew she had drawn me into that affair. He had tried to browbeat me into dropping the case. Surely his next step ought to have been to browbeat her into writing a letter informing me my services were no longer required. When she resisted, would he not have resorted to more forceful methods of persuasion?

"If he meant to kill her, he would not have touched her, Holmes. Given your involvement, he had to assume there would be an autopsy. He could not afford to leave signs of physical abuse."

"Granted. He was not to know that those marks on her wrist already seemed to give in evidence against him. They were her insurance policy, lest her deep plots did pall. At least if she died, they would convince the authorities he had been abusing her. They would then have passed the sternest sentence upon him for his assault on the blacksmith. He would have been incarcerated as a lunatic for the rest of his days. But Doctor, you must see that while he might have feared to mark her visibly, he could still have lashed her with his all-too-toxic tongue. Yet we heard nothing until that scream."

"You forget, Holmes, we only saw one light, showing that she retired early, pleading a headache, just as you had advised her to do."

"My dear Watson, is it likely that this incestuous – this sadistic beast – would have charitably consented to postpone either a verbal or a physical assault because she had a headache? Had she called out to him from behind her locked door that she would appreciate if he put off beating her to a pulp until she felt up to it, would he not at least have screamed at her that she would regret it all the more once his hands were about her throat? Actually he would not have done so, for as I say he undoubtedly had keys to every room in the house and the power besides to lay an axe to her door with a cry of 'Here's Grimesby!'"

"But the light!"

"Ah. The light. Singular, was it not? It went out at nine. It never passed from room to room while someone made for his or her bedroom. It just went out. No light ever appeared in their rooms, or indeed in any others. Take that with the silence and is it not obvious why that should be?"

"I was myself groping in the dark. "What was he doing, Holmes?"

"Nothing. Absolutely nothing. She had doubtless left a drugged bottle of brandy by the door to greet him upon his return. Then, when he was helpless, she injected him twice with the snake's venom."

I was thunderstruck. "No! How could she ever have acquired a hypodermic?"

"She took the hypodermic from his old doctor's bag. That would also have supplied her with whatever drug she employed to debilitate him. It need not have rendered him entirely unconscious."

"Why suppose that? And why on earth suppose she injected him twice?"

"You recall how when we found him he appeared to be staring up at that Bronzino painting covering the ventilator grille? It had to be replaced, lest we see the light from the open dark lantern through the grille. Best not to mention he seemed to be considering the picture should you publish an account. Have him stare aimlessly up at a corner of the ceiling instead. Of course at the time of his death, he was not gazing at either."

"Then what could have mesmerised him so?"

"His daughter's malignant face as she gleefully injected him with venom. She had to do so twice so that the authorities would suppose a snake had bitten him. Afterwards she posed him to make it seem as if his eyes had been opened, and in the painting he now saw both his sins and the wages he would be paid for them."

It was clear to me Holmes as the accused was being deliberately obtuse. He knew his theory was nonsense. It was time to remind him of certain inconvenient facts he had chosen to overlook. "You forget, Holmes, we both heard Roylott scream the instant we returned the snake through the ventilator. He died when it assaulted him, which it would never have done had you not struck it and so forced it to retrace its steps in pain and fear and anger all mingled and expressed in one dreadful hiss. You ought to do the decent thing and take responsibility for your crime."

Holmes did not look particularly penitent. "Have you ever seen a snake go backwards, Watson? If I struck it as it was descending that bell-pull, it would have had to do so. And if my striking out at it had indeed enraged it, why did it not fly at me as the cause of its suffering? Did I not tell you that it hurled itself at the first person it saw? How could Roylott have been that person if it returned backwards through the ventilator and was still facing its true assailant? Besides, do you not see that the incident as stated is physically impossible? A rope-climbing snake I can accept, but a rope-climbing snake that can reverse direction? A worm may turn, but it cannot like the crab go backwards. That would be asking too much."

Holmes likes to condemn me for seeing without observing, but in this case seeing was quite enough. "I am sorry, you cannot expect me to deny the evidence of my own eyes. I saw it return through the ventilator. That is final." I crossed my arms again to signify as much.

Holmes waited.

"Well, possibly I did not precisely see it *per se*, so as to speak, but it must have done. I certainly would have seen it had you not blinded my eyes with the flare from your match. But I saw everything else as clear as day, so it must have been there. The snake was blinded too. That explains why it did not fly at you and did assault Roylott. It had just then recovered its sight. The fact it could not see you lashing out at it surely goes to show just how dazzling that match must have been."

252

"The only reason you did not see a snake," said Holmes thoughtfully, "was because I neglected to tell you to. Had I warned you in advance that a serpent would enter the room in that séance-thick darkness, then in your mind's eye you would soon have imagined it crawling up your trouser leg and so cried out in terror long before things came to a crisis. '*In the night, imagining some fear, how easy is a bush supposed a bear!*' As for myself, I deliberately entered fully into the part I had to play, and so I am pleased to say I saw precisely what I intended to see. It was an adder of the mind, a false creation, proceeding from the heat-oppressed brain. I deliberately permitted myself to become confused. Having performed one or two trifling experiments with hallucinogenic drugs, I had besides considered the possibility that Roylott would introduce an ordeal poison into the room via a rubber hose. He could thus have caused Julia to die of fright, thinking in her delirium the hose was a snake. I half-expected such an illusion. When I saw what appeared to be a snake emerging from the ventilator, I doubted for a moment whether it was real or not. For a few seconds I did not know what to believe and what not to believe. My beating at the bell-pull may have been a case of real panic. The snake, or the dummy snake, had by then been hauled back through that screen, but once I had started I could not stop. Besides, it all happened in an instant. It was attached to a string, you see. Once it was safely back on the ledge behind the painting, the string was yanked away from it."

"But the scream!" I shrieked. "You have forgotten that scream! That had to have been Roylott! Therefore, that tableau could not have been the work of a human hand! It was proof of a higher power at work!"

Holmes waited until my ejaculation was accomplished before removing his hands from over those curiously elongated and slightly pointed ears of his. "Illogical, Doctor. Is it really necessary for me to remind you that I forget nothing, save when it is expedient to do so? But perhaps that is what you are insinuating. Let me assure you, then, the very things that seem to you to prove my guilt and her innocence actually demonstrate that she must have murdered Roylott. Whether she was working as the god of justice's instrument, or as that of the devil, or both, is really beside the point. But to begin with that *tableau vivant* – or rather *nature mort* – I suggest we drop by at Tussaud's later to experience its Chamber of Horrors, just as Miss Roylott did shortly after she paid us a call. She doubtless posed Roylott with a mind to seeing him immortalised there at some future date. Speaking of immortality, remind me to suggest they employ Oscar Meunier to produce my likeness."

"What a fantastic idea!"

"Is it? My fame is growing. The only danger is I may become a legend. Tussaud's draws the line at those who can never die. However, as long as I do not actually rise from the dead, I ought to be safe. What of it if I did? Then their likeness of me could be used for target practice. You look puzzled. Oh, you meant my suggestion that the tableau was posed. Well, one might accept Roylott would have been in his dressing-gown over his nightshirt to rush out into the corridor later and encounter the housekeeper as if he had just left his bed. One cannot grant him those heelless Turkish slippers as the very worst footwear when handling a poisonous snake, given the precedent of Achilles. No, it was all too well staged-managed. I could not have done it better myself. Was not that dog lash on his lap just a little too like a sceptre? And that serpent about his brows too like a coronet? Why do you think you could not help thinking of that notorious Ottoman tyrant Abdul the Damned, whom cartoonists delight in depicting as Faustus being dragged away by Mephistopheles down to a seat reserved for him in hell?"

It was true. I had thought of Abdul Hamid II, 34th Sultan of the Ottoman Empire, perhaps because I had read somewhere that he kept a pet snake and big cats in his youth. He might easily have been one of Roylott's role models. "That's as may be, Holmes, but it does not follow she posed him thus."

"You are overlooking one blindingly obvious fact, my dear doctor," said my occasionally irritating detective friend. "We were meant to suppose Roylott had just passed the snake through the screen in the wall. We had to imagine him standing on a chair to observe its descent. And yet we found him perched on that chair beside a table at some distance from the screen. Are you telling me that while screaming his serpent-choked head off, he calmly descended from that chair and carried it to the table before seating himself upon it? Bear in mind we are first to imagine the snake launching itself backwards through the air at Roylott prior to recoiling itself about his brows. Would he not have done well to have dropped the dog lash so as to devote his remaining moments to clawing in vain at the snake in an attempt to remove it before treading it under those heelless slippers? But I will grant you this: It is just possible I may unintentionally have co-authored that admirably theatrical tableau. It would be quite fitting if I did so, for a *tableau*-style painting of an execution by an ancestor of mine may have inspired Madame Tussaud to set up shop in Baker Street the year after it was exhibited to great public acclaim. I have said too much. Forget I told you that."

I have dutifully done my best to do so, particularly since Holmes later informed me that his grandmother was a Vernet, which does not seem to have been true. It is possible he only asserted as much because it permitted him the alliteration of claiming Vernet was in his veins. Such doubts only arose later though. At that moment, I only wondered how on earth Holmes could think to take credit for that awful scene. I expressed my incredulity with my eyebrows, but he quickly matched them and browbeat them down with his own.

"Remember, Watson, that the Roylotts lived in London for a while. Doubtless Grimesby dropped by at the Zoo in Regent's Park from time to time to glare back at the slithery, gliding, venomous creatures with their deadly eyes and wicked, flattened faces. Where were his wife and daughters? They were elsewhere in that same Park. They were privileged to witness a moment of dramatic history as *Hamlet* was performed just as it had been in Shakespeare's day, beneath an open sky. There you have one of Helen Roylott's sources of inspiration for that tableau."

Here was egotism run wild! "What could possibly make you think that?"

"Well, the shape in the form of Hamlet's father tells him that the latter was murdered in his garden and that *'The serpent that did sting thy father's life now wears his crown.'* Do you not see how she turned that image on its head to crown Roylott with a serpent? We did not find him in a garden, I grant you, but we did make our way through a fallen Eden to him. Waterton, who was descended from the author of *Utopia,* had tried to recreate paradise in the form of a wildlife sanctuary. Roylott had thought to do the same and failed."

So Holmes the dramatist in real life would take credit for the work of providence! The thing was absurd and I could prove it.

"Holmes, it is impossible anyone could have coiled that deadly snake about Roylott's head. Even if they had succeeded in doing so, by the time we arrived it would have uncurled itself. No, it must have just finished encircling that brute's brows at precisely the moment we appeared on the scene."

Holmes shook his own wonderfully swollen head. I waited with some amusement to see how he could surmount such impossibilities. Nor did he disappoint.

"In the first place, the worm you saw was totally innocuous, and not only because Helen had milked the Roylott's adder of its venom earlier that day. It was not that snake. She had simply painted her own innocent pet to make it resemble the Roylott's speckled band. She had of course drugged it lightly to make it manageable. The poor, helpless worm was only just beginning to awaken when we saw it slowly start to feebly raise its head."

That could not be true. "Holmes, even if that were so, you could not have supposed it inoffensive when you first saw it. You must have supposed it had killed Roylott, as no doubt it had. And besides, you would not have assured me that Roylott was dead ten seconds after it had stung him unless you had definitely identified it as an Indian swamp adder. Would you have shut it up in that safe if it had not been harmless?"

"As for knowledge, Watson, you really should have suspected Miss Stoner had murdered her father the instant we discovered Roylott's door was once again unlocked. She had only just left the room, and in great haste lest we intercept her, as we would have done had I not deliberately paused until some time after the screaming had stopped. But that bedroom door was not the crucial clue. It was far more important that the door of the safe had been left ajar."

"Why, what of that? If Roylott had intended to return the snake to the safe, he would hardly have shut it again. He had to keep both hands free to manage that deadly creature."

"Precisely! Do think that through. He opens the safe wide to remove the snake. He leaves the safe door open. What does he not do? He does not begin to shut it again and then have second thoughts just as he has almost completed the action. Why make extra work for himself by nearly closing the door, thus introducing the need to reopen it fully first? No, Miss Stoner had left it ajar for effect."

"How absurdly simple!"

"My innocent and honest friend, I happily acknowledge simplicity is your department, as it could never be mine. I therefore bow to my master in that field. But to continue. If as you suppose I was the murderer of Roylott, then I needed to delay our entry into his room until the serpent's venom had done its work, lest your doctor's soul tempt you into attempting to save his life. That was why I took care we should not leave Julia's bedroom until some minutes had passed. Moreover, I rather ridiculously knocked not once but twice on Roylott's door as if expecting him to politely invite us in for tea. It was another delaying tactic."

"That is pretty damning, Holmes," I confessed with a sigh.

"Not at all. Once in the room, it was certainly my aim to prevent you from examining either the corpse of the snake. But why? I told you he had died within ten seconds of being bitten. Why, the scream we heard lasted longer than that. I had to convince you an examination of Roylott's corpse was pointless. Had you ignored my injunction and taken his pulse, you would instantly have realised he must have died hours earlier."

"And the snake?"

"Can you ask, my dear Watson? Do you imagine I have no respect for your medical talents? You, who spent months as an army surgeon in serpent-infested India? I knew you had been taught to identify all the Indian snakes and could tell the poisonous from the harmless ones. At four yards those painted spots might deceive you. Had you approached any nearer, you would have recognised the poor creature as perfectly

256

innocuous. Therefore, I quickly popped it into the safe and slammed the door shut. By the time the authorities finally manage to force the safe open it, I am very much afraid she will have died of asphyxiation. *Mea culpa*."

So that was the meaning of Holmes's confession! He meant he had murdered a mere snake! I sighed with relief mingled with exasperation that he should think to play such tricks upon his friend. Nevertheless, some lingering doubts remained. "If the serpent we saw was not the Indian swamp adder, how did you know that was what Roylott kept?"

"Actually, I knew with certainty it was no such thing for the simple reason that the Indian swamp adder is a myth. There is not, and there never has been, any such serpent. Consequently it shall never star in a Tussaud tableau. I invented it. Obviously, I could not name a real snake, since you would have raised objections. As for the actual and rather remarkable worm Roylott used on Julia, it was until recently quite unknown to science. That was the point. You have heard of Dr. Lamson, have you not?"

The name did seem vaguely familiar. "Was he not some fellow hanged a year or so ago?"

"There but for the grace of God goes Dr. Watson. It was at Newgate on 28 April of last year, to be precise. He thought he was safe because his poison of choice was the toxin aconitine, which is hardly ever resorted to by murderers. Since each poison has to be tested for individually, he was sure it would never be detected. Lamson was arrested on 8th December, 1882, but it took months of mechanical slog by Auguste Dupre of Westminster Hospital – a brilliant man if one accepts the mediocrity's definition of genius as nothing more than mindless hard grind – to at last identify the vegetable alkaloid. He suspected it was administered out of malevolence rather than a spirit of scientific enquiry. Injected mice produced excellent results, though I myself prefer to deal in dogs. They all died. To do Dupre justice, he fearlessly tasted the corpse's residues on himself. He noted a burning, tingling kind of numbness that even I found it difficult to define when placed on my tongue, though it was oddly redolent of Mrs. Hudson's jellied eels when prepared by her while engrossed in your risqué reminiscences as serialised in the *Holywell Street Journal*."

"You think Roylott inspired Lamson? But the latter entirely failed to evade the law."

"Lamson's poison was merely singular. What was required was not the unusual, but the practically unknown. I learned at the British Museum that Roylott was a recognised authority on the medicinal use of singularly obscure venoms, and that his name has been permanently attached to a certain serpent which he had, in his Indian days, been the first to describe.

It is now thought to be extinct, as indeed it probably will be in a very few hours."

This was all very ingenious – save for the minor difficulty that it was all rubbish. "Holmes, why do you still persist in overlooking the one key fact? Your beautiful theory is quite exploded by a single undeniable truth: The hundred villagers of Stoke Moran can bear witness we did not imagine Grimesby Roylott's awful death shriek. Since we heard it immediately after you sent the snake back through the screen, that had to be the cause of death, and you had to be the one responsible. You murdered him."

Holmes shook his head. "It is you, my dear doctor, who have quite forgotten the evidence of those five little finger marks upon Miss Stoner's wrist. Is it possible that with your unrivalled knowledge of sensational literature, you still cannot grasp their immense significance? They not only prove that Roylott was long dead when the scream rang out, but tell us who actually shrieked – and why."

Holmes's sarcasm was quite uncalled for. "You know perfectly well I have no encyclopaedic understanding of crime as you do. I cannot refer to precedents. As for those cruel finger imprints, there can be no doubt whatsoever they had to have been made by Roylott. You saw how massive his hands were, and how easily he turned your poker into a snake just as carelessly as Aaron did his wand."

"Oh, but you do know a great deal of sensational history, as you revealed when I told you not that long ago what my true profession was. Think back to then. And concerning his massive hands, I quite concur that just as Hercules was known by his feet, so Roylott might be identified by his mighty paws. But had we compared those marks on Helen's wrist with the fingers of the late Roylott, it would at once have been apparent he could not possibly have made them. Oh, come now, Watson, what precedent must spring instantly to mind?"

"How should I know," said I irritably, for it really was too bad of Holmes to play such games. "I say again I know nothing of the history of crime."

"You know your Poe. Think of his 'Murders in the Rue Morgue'. Were not just such marks imprinted upon the neck of a victim? That charlatan Dupin proved the hand that made them was too massive to have been a man's. It had to have been the hand of an Orang-Utan. Now, in this case we are faced with the opposite difficulty. Those five little spots were clearly made by a small yet exceptionally powerful paw. Conclusion?"

"Holmes! I whispered. "A child has done this horrid thing."

"A child of sorts was involved, to be sure," said he with a chuckle. "You recall that creeping creature which scuttled across our path in the garden? First it seemed to have a kind of epileptic fit, and then it sprinted

258

off as fast as its two legs could carry it. I told you it was an Indian baboon once it was safely out of sight. I could not let you suspect the truth. You were right to diagnose tertiary syphilis in the case of Grimesby Roylott. That deformed, unfinished thing sent before its time into this breathing world scarce half made up was his handiwork. It was afflicted with congenital syphilis. So to give him his due, Roylott need not have been eliminating his daughters for his own sake alone. In his deranged state of mind, he may have dreamed of making that creature his heir."

"No, no," said I uneasily, not wishing to believe any of this. "It was the baboon."

"How could it have been? Did you not see the state of the walls about the estate? It would have escaped in an instant. The baboon had to have been kept on a long leash."

"But the cheetah! We heard it mewing outside the window."

Holmes considered me with amused impatience. "Doctors who do not go wrong can make excellent detectives. Sadly, Dr. Watson, you will never make either a first-rate criminal or a first rate detective. You have even forgotten the first lesson you were taught at the start of your medical training. When you hear hooves think horses first and zebras second. Do you know why its mewing was so like that of a domestic cat? Because it *was* a domestic cat. As for that sound like a kettle you later supposed a snake hissing, it is just as easily explained. I knew before ever we set foot in Roylott's room that night we would find a kettle smoking there."

"My dear Holmes!"

"Oh, yes I did. You know my maxim, even if you must obstinately persist in misquoting me for the sake of sensationalism. It is never possible to eliminate all possibilities – save for one. Therefore, identify which is the least improbable of them and regardless of how weary, stale, flat and unprofitable it might be, it is the likeliest to be the truth. Thus, when a thing looks like a kettle and sounds like a kettle as a general rule it is a kettle. Only rarely does it turn out to be a deadly serpent disguised as a kettle, and intent upon tempting a Mrs. Hudson into eating forbidden apples. As for snakes on the prowl, they are as silent as the grave until threatened, and the more harmful the snake, the less likely it is to hiss. Moreover, you yourself observed how pleasing and soothing that hissing sound was, being as comforting as a cup of tea on a cold night. The hissing of a snake neither is nor is intended to be placating. That would rather defeat the object of the exercise, which is to terrify and intimidate potential predators."

I was growing increasingly suspicious. "And I suppose, Holmes, you are about to tell me that the marks on Helen's wrist were made by the baboon! Have you made a special study of the fingerprints of anthropoids?"

Holmes took this in one of his long strides. "As it happens, I have. I was called upon to authenticate a recovered Leonardo recently. I did so by detecting the fingerprints upon it – of one of the artist's privileged favourites – who had left his marks there while the paint was still wet. Leonardo kept a pet monkey, you see. Now consider that Miss Stoner must have been confident her painted snake would achieve the desired effect on the baboon when it was needed. On some previous occasion, by chance or as a deliberate test, that baboon had been confronted by Roylott's snake – or Julia's own – and in its terror had clutched at her wrist leaving those marks. If it was an accident, it was one she profited by. The result you know."

I was mystified. "I don't, Holmes. The baboon played no part in the affair. Not once did it do anything in the night-time."

"No, not once. Twice. Those were the curious incidents. The first time was when you seemed to scare the life out of it as we were crossing the grounds of Stoke Moran at night. I have explained that. It was not the baboon. The second was when we heard that terrible scream. And yet, unlike every cat and dog in the village, it failed miserably to echo that screech. Can you not see why that was? Come, I know your methods. Eliminate what you suppose impossible and the solution should become apparent. There is no reason why it should not have cried out – therefore it must have done so. But only *one* scream was heard. Therefore, it could not have been Roylott. Therefore, it must have been the baboon crying out as it was being tortured by Miss Stoner. Had you examined her wrists afterwards, you would have found not five but ten little spots on her wrists. The scream that impossibly combined pain and fear and anger was the combination of the anthropoid's and hers as she also cried out in her agony and rage. That explains why it was both human and inhuman, and how it could have been expressive of pain and fear and anger all at once."

"But then where was the baboon?"

"Once it had done its work, Miss Stoner stuffed a banana in its mouth and chucked it out of the window. It may be long gone by now, and I fear that the superstitious villagers will club it to death as a monster. Whack! Whack! Whack! Ah, what crimes are committed in the smiling and beautiful countryside! There again, since authorities claim Roylott died playing with his pet, we are perhaps meant to picture him spanking the monkey."

I was busy jotting all this down. I might introduce it into some other account, for it was clear I could never reveal the truth about the murder of Grimesby Roylott to the general public. When I looked up from my notebook, I saw the accused smiling across our compartment at me with insufferable complacency.

"Well, now, Watson, let me remind you I am your prisoner. It is time. You are the British jury, and I never met a man I would more wish to be sentenced to death by. You shall be my judge too. First let us comply with the formalities. Do you find me Guilty or Not Guilty?"

I was about to speak the words "Not Guilty" when I saw in Holmes's eyes his absolute confidence I would do so. There was not the slightest trace of guilt. I gulped and in doing so found that I had swallowed the word 'Not', for to my surprise only the word "Guilty" left my mouth. After that I was speechless, while Holmes gaped like a baby bird that had expected to receive a worm from its mother and instead finds its mouth filled by a particularly repulsive red leech.

After that he puffed on his pipe for a time and then seemed to come to a decision. Once more he leaned across the carriage and shook me by the hand. "I was testing you yet again, Watson, and still you ring true. Well, it is a great responsibility that I am laying on you, but you are worthy of it. You are right, of course. Though I only murdered an innocent snake, I confess I also slew Roylott in my heart as surely as in his mind's eye Hamlet *shish-kebabed* his mother and uncle in the incestuous pleasure of their bed."

I made a face that Holmes misread as bewilderment. Actually, I was picturing the scene and thanking the Bard it was never staged.

"You do not understand? Perhaps the allusion was obscure. Turkish warriors often skewered meat on their swords before roasting it, so '*shish kebab*' means 'skewered roasted meat'. The Dane would have made the incestuous pair one flesh prior to posting them together into the flames of Hell. What is done in imagination is done in the soul too."

"Thank you, Holmes, but in fact I understood only too well. What I do not quite grasp is that responsibility you say you would burden me with. Are you saying you wish me to be your conscience? And yet, earlier on you appeared to quote Hamlet approvingly where he says that conscience makes us cowards."

"He was a coward when he said that. It was the same moral cowardice that caused him to exorcise his Ophelia from his soul as a devil disguised as an angel of light and embrace instead the real devil in the pleasing shape of his dead father. He was seduced by the promise of a holy crusade. How delightful to know you are on the side of good with *carte blanche* to fight evil! You may then do what you please, knowing the end justifies the means. No, Watson, it cannot be enough for you to become my Horatio and tell my story. You must also be my Ophelia to whisper in my ear that I, too, am mortal when I ride in my victory chariot."

I must have looked doubtful, for I was not at all sure Holmes would hear me above the public adulation he clearly anticipated he would receive in the very near future. I thought of his own interpretation of the deafness in one ear of Shakespeare's *Julius Caesar* as signifying as much. Nor had I forgotten the first bow I ever saw him take to acknowledge the reverence of an imaginary audience at our first meeting. But I perceived it was my duty to do my best. In the meantime it would be tempting providence were I to speak my misgivings aloud. I therefore thought it best to redirect my doubts where they would not cause offence.

"And do you suppose that if Grimesby Roylott had taken his daughters' hands and made them his guides he would never have slain his butler? Surely the man was born bad in his bones. He had inherited a criminal strain and so could never have escaped his fate."

Holmes's eyes took on that distant look they always had when he was at his most introspective. On this occasion, and perhaps uniquely, I sensed such reflection was upon his own nature as a good guide to the manifold wickedness of the human heart.

"I accept your scepticism, Doctor, yet consider what lay at the heart's core of his evil – and perhaps his daughter's too. Theirs was a fundamental blunder. Neither had a contempt for the law. Far from it. They both possessed an absolute faith in it. Think of Roylott's first great crime. He had believed human laws that ran contrary to those of God would cheat him of the life of a thieving butler. He could not permit that. Accordingly, he acted as God's scourge and minister to pass sentence and execute it. You see how that explains his outrage in my case? He saw in me a mercenary usurping his authority as the one true instrument of divine justice. It was an understandable enough mistake, for like Roylott I must confess I sometimes prefer to stand and act above the law."

"But his wife and children!"

"The operative word is 'his'. Dr. Roylott was brought up in a world only now passing away, in which wives and children were the legal property of men and made to know, love, and serve the latter as created in the image of God the Father. Now human laws are starting to change, and duties may make way for rights. In Roylott's eyes, such a brave new world devoid of a slave caste would necessarily verge on the blasphemous. That is why Helen Stoner behaved as she did when first we met."

"How do you mean?"

"She supposed all men like her father and sought to play upon me accordingly."

That seemed absurd to me. "But she appealed to you as a modern knight who fights for justice and defends the innocent!"

"Precisely so," said Holmes, not entirely managing to conceal his pleasure at such a portrayal of himself. "She came to me as if I imagined myself to be the last court of appeal, and so as certain as Roylott of my special election as one born to personify the law. Think how she eulogised me as one uniquely able to penetrate the dense darkness in which she had cloaked herself. So I did. She came so choked in black and so heavily veiled it seemed like darkness visible. She also flattered me I could unfold the darkest tales in the hearts of men, rather as Roylott convinced himself he could see it in his daughters when observing them through that ironic confessional screen. But let me be honest with you, Watson: I rarely trouble myself with the so-called hearts of men, women, or children, any more than a heart surgeon should do. A surgeon as a surgeon should only concern himself with the muscular organ that pumps blood through the body. I solve crimes and deliver the perpetrators to justice. Why should I go beyond good and evil as defined by the law? Like the surgeon, I wash my hands of the rest. Where the philosopher ends, the detective begins."

"And you believe she was working to tempt you on?"

"Undoubtedly. And I might easily have succumbed. Perhaps next time I shall. That is why I hereby appoint you as my good angel to save me from such false ones. Every Othello should have a Desdemona to cling fast to as his protection against the Iagos of this world. And speaking of Shakespeare, I think we may now dismiss the affair of the Roylotts from our minds and go back with a clear conscience to the curious problem of the killing of old Polonius in *Hamlet*. You do remember all the circumstance?"

I was reluctant to do so. "But do you really think Miss Stoner was such a false angel of light? That is surely a little unfair."

Holmes had relit his pipe and was clearly equally intent upon changing the subject to return to the more pressing problem of how to stage his next production of *Hamlet*. I could not prevent myself sighing resignedly, for it was hardly a subject I wished to discuss. He perceived it. He kept his Red Indian composure, and keeping in character puffed out five smoke rings in rapid succession that signalled his annoyance. Perhaps if I made clear my lack of sympathy for his approach to the play, which I sincerely believed was fundamentally flawed, he would soon drop the idea of discussing it with me.

"I am sorry, Holmes," said I apologetically, "but you do tend to treat that play as a murder mystery with Hamlet as the detective. It is rather more than that, you know."

"I am entirely in agreement with you on that point. But you misunderstand me. It is not I who make the mistake of treating the affair as a murder mystery, but Hamlet. And yet, your point is an interesting one.

It is possible that Miss Stoner drew upon the Spirit as well as the Prince as sources of inspiration in her attempt to seduce me into unwittingly playing the revenger on her behalf. The Spirit works to turn the Dane into an agent of the dead letter of the law, one who regards prayer as nothing more than a legal loophole, and views the murderer as if he were a stage villain – hence beyond redemption since incapable of repentance. She meant to ensure I regarded Roylott in that manner. The only difference is she appealed to my scientific side by suggesting his damnation due to a criminal strain in the blood. I am really very indebted to you, Doctor. You have stumbled upon something truly new."

I was pleased that I had helped Holmes in some way, though I could not imagine how. "I don't quite follow you, Holmes. Surely the similarity is very slight between the ghost of Hamlet's father urging him to avenge his murder and Helen Stoner pleading with you to be her modern knight and slay a contemporary dragon?"

Holmes chuckled. "A modern knight, am I? Upon my word, Watson, you really are a poet. You could turn the safe of a blackmailer into the open maw of a dragon to swallow up the reputations of damsels in distress.'

I can now, thought I as I jotted down the image in my notepad. I recalled Holmes has said Hamlet is a modern man who finds himself forced to play a medieval revenger. I think he uses the play to hold a mirror up to himself, for he was ever the Quixotic knight ready to tilt at submarine periscopes mistaken for the long necks of prehistoric sea monsters.

"But you were asking how Helen Stoner," he continued, "and wondering how she could have imitated the Spirit urging Hamlet on to a holy crusade, were you not?"

"I think so," said I doubtfully.

"But it is perfectly simple. It turns on both the Spirit and Stoner being examples of St. Augustine's angels of darkness masquerading as angels of light. It is a matter of how they played on their victims' virtues to turn them into their worst vices."

Here was yet more reason for suspecting Holmes had once seemed destined for holy orders in the Catholic Church – hence his tendency to treat clients as if he were a cross between a doctor and a father confessor. "I am sorry, Holmes, but I must confess I am not *au fait* with Augustine's works."

This revelation did not appear to surprise him. "His theory is well worth understanding as the key to grasping much that is most seductively evil in the world. Shall I summarise?'

"Please do."

"In essence, then, his argument runs as follows: Most men are so easily seduced by the devil that he must regard them – rather as I do the majority of mundane criminals – as hardly worthy of my attention. Be one a detective or a devil, the game of discovering the predictable evil in the mundane man is a game that is hardly worth the candle. The common herd may be taken with pet baits such as love, fame, power, and so on. But there are a few nobler beings – and I include Hamlet and myself among these – who are quite immune to such lures. How, then, is the devil to take those more challenging souls?"

I thought about this. 'I cannot imagine."

"Well, the devil has never tempted you. Unless, of course, he has made an attempt to do so in my person, in which case he and I have apparently met our match. Augustine's angels of darkness appear as angels of light to promise the good and pious man a holy crusade in which the end justifies the means. He calls on such heroes to sacrifice themselves and others to the sacred cause. So appealed to, they follow him when he likes and where he likes, into the mouth of Hell if need be.

"That was how the spirit seduced Hamlet. But it was sly. It knew a philosophical young man fresh from that theological power-house, Wittenberg University, would suspect it of being a father of lies rather than his heavenly father. Therefore, it first supplied Hamlet with a technical problem to solve. Was it speaking the truth about the murder? Obsessed with that question, the Dane supposed once it was answered, he could proceed with his revenge. He quite forgot that morally it was the least important difficulty. The real problem was whether revenge was justified at all."

"And you think Helen Stoner was working on you in that way?"

"Most certainly. She provided me with a tantalising locked room mystery and a villain whose damnation was a foregone conclusion. She worked to convince me a throne was reserved for him in Hell, just as surely as there is a prime spot awaiting him in the Chamber of Horrors. Armed with such certainties, I would send a snake with his name on it to him without a qualm. She was a good classicist."

"How do you mean?"

"She had read her Aristotle. His theatre is nothing but a latrine for relieving killing machines of compassion prior to their appearance upon the field of Mars. He decreed, you see, that the purpose of tragedy in the theatre is to exorcise all effeminate feelings such as pity and fear, so as to prepare the soldier for the theatre of war. That is what Hamlet means when he complains that conscience makes a man a coward. It is the Prince's conscience and not the King's that is taken in *The Mousetrap*, that play in which the murder of old Hamlet is re-enacted. The Dane incorrectly

265

identifies the murderer as the revenger, and so imagines he is witnessing a perfect revenge as the mirror image of the act avenged. Then he identifies that revenger as himself and takes him as his model. That is in accordance with Plato's warning that we imitate the heroes and villains we see onstage. Thus freed from all moral restraint, he may proceed fearlessly with his mission. Let he who is without conscience cast the first stone."

"You are speaking of a less civilised age, Holmes."

"Ha. Think of the Indian Mutiny and its aftermath. First the British soldier was made to weep at tragic tales of the atrocities committed by the enemy. Then he went out and committed the like atrocities himself. He did not do so with a clear conscience. He did so with no conscience at all."

"I assure you, Holmes," said I indignantly, "that the British soldier seeks death before dishonour."

"'Death before dishonour' is an admirable maxim, no doubt, but one that the Maxim Gun may shortly bring into question. Well, that is for the things to come. May we have bowed out long before that cleaner, better, stronger, and braver new world dawns."

"I think, Holmes," said I, rather more perceptively than is my wont, "that it is you who are reading Hamlet in terms of your preconceptions, and not Hamlet who is misreading the villain as hero in the play within the play. He cannot bring himself to kill Claudius at prayer because his conscience will not allow it. He is making excuses when he says he will wait until he catches him about some damnable act and then act so swiftly that the King will not have time to cry out to God to receive his soul."

"No, Watson," said he with a smile, crushing my confidence beneath the weight of his own. "Your Hamlet is like your Sherlock Holmes: Both contradict themselves regularly. Your Holmes will doubtless achieve a kind of immortality not unlike that of the Prince, for contradictions make such creations seem as enigmatic as real human beings. But the difference between Hamlet and your Holmes is this: Your Holmes contradicts himself because you unthinkingly record what I, the real Holmes, say and do without any attempt at explanation, and so the contradictions remain. But Shakespeare takes care to give us a character whose apparent contradictions, if carefully considered, can be seen to be no contradictions at all. That is, every apparent contradiction actually involves a kind of explanation."

"These are but wild and whirling words, Holmes!" I gasped. "Whatever do you mean?"

"Take the fact that Hamlet fails to kill Claudius at prayer, and the next moment slays the unseen Polonius concealed behind an arras to eavesdrop on the interview between the Prince and his mother. Now, if Hamlet had only been making excuses in the case of Claudius, then on hearing what might be Claudius behind the arras, he would again fail to act and as it happens rightly so. But he was not making excuses. Hence unexpectedly given an opportunity to kill Claudius up to no good, and without giving him a second to repent by running him through without so much as drawing back the arras first to face the doomed man, he acts at once and without thought. The first scene makes possible the second, for it leaves him frustrated and desperate for a chance that is unlikely ever to come again. Thus an apparent contradiction actually makes perfect sense. In the first scene he thinks but does not act. In the second he acts but does not think. But the second would be impossible without the first. The first explains but does not excuse Hamlet's blunder, for in his heart he had recognised the cry for help was that of the hated old Polonius, but did not care which of them he killed."

"But do you have any reason to suppose he knew Polonius was behind the arras?"

Holmes smiled as at some private joke. "There was that peculiarly deadly reference to a rat. I cudgelled my brains over why Hamlet should have cried out that one word just before he slaughtered Polonius. Any ideas, Watson?"

"He could have been mocking the high voice of the old man," said I doubtfully. "But Holmes, the voice must have been muffled when heard through the arras. He might still have mistaken it for the King's, if that was what he wished to believe. Besides, his mother tells Claudius the cry proved her son's madness and so exonerated him of the crime. He really did believe it was a giant rat."

"Denmark is not Sumatra. There was more to it than that. Hamlet is an incurably witty fellow who loves a pun, even when it betrays his innermost thoughts. He has just returned from Wittenberg University in Germany. He knows the German word 'rat' can mean 'council' or 'counsellor'. Polonius was the King's chief counsellor, so the pun is obvious. By it Hamlet reveals he knows full well he is killing Polonius."

"Holmes," said I, suddenly suspicious, "you would damn Hamlet based on a pun. But what of yourself? When I caught sight of Roylott with that snake encircling his brains, I recoiled speechless at the horror of the thing. You, though, at once launched into a little sermon full of Biblical and Shakespearean allusions concerning those hoist by their own petard. I checked your allusion to Ecclesiastes and it was nothing if not apt: '*He that diggeth a pit shall fall into it, and whoso breaketh an hedge, a serpent shall bite him.*' And you spoke of violence '*recoiling*' upon itself, as if you had anticipated that sight of the snake coiled about Roylott's head. It was almost as if you had prepared your speech beforehand."

"Why thank you, Watson," said he innocently. "It is always good to have one's extempore wit acknowledged."

"Was it extempore. Holmes? I do believe you knew what Helen Roylott was up to from the very start. Except how could you have done? No, it is impossible."

"And your method requires that one eliminates the impossible, does it not? Or the unthinkable at any rate, which for you is the same thing. But come, I see our train is drawing into London. If we hurry, I think we may be in time for one of Mrs. Hudson's splendid breakfasts. Since, though, we have already supped full with horrors, remind me to stipulate that there be no jellied eels."

As a postscript I may add that in place of the eels, Mrs. Hudson supplied us with an alimentary paste in thick cords between those of macaroni and vermicelli. However, when Holmes came to raise the cover of the dish placed before him by an uncharacteristically demure housekeeper, he found nothing but an extravagant cheque, an emerald snake ring, and a telegram that read simply: "*Julia safe.*" I was confused, but Holmes chuckled and explained it was a play on words. Miss Stoner had recovered her pet snake Julia out of Roylott's strongbox, safe and sound after all. The ring with a serpent biting its own tail was a symbol of prudence and recalled that of Catherine de Medici, which her enemies assumed contained poison. They asserted her motto was "*Hate and Wait*". Holmes took the view that although that was pure slander in her case, in spirit Helen Roylott had adopted it as her own. She had always wanted to be the first of the stoners.

I also noted he smiled with some satisfaction on receiving that brief missive. Stamford insists it was owing to the size of the cheque, but that could not have been true. He returned it to Helen Roylott with the peculiar request she supply him instead with those reproductions of Bronzino's *Venus and Cupid* allegory and his Virgin and Child with saints, which she was more than happy to do. I think she had meant to burn them. The former work now hangs in Holmes bedroom as part of his rogues' gallery, and on the opposite side of the same wall the latter daub decorates my room, rather as they had once been hung back to back concealing that fatal ventilator.

A strange enigma is Mr. Sherlock Holmes! For his pleasure at receiving that cryptic telegram was, I think, at learning he was not the murderer of a poor, helpless worm after all.

Joseph Wright of Derby – "*An Experiment with the Air Pump*"

The Adventure of the
Rule of Thumb

Continuing "The Engineer's Thumb"

"**W**ell," said our engineer ruefully, as we took our seats to return to London, "it has been a pretty business for me! I have lost my thumb, and I have lost a fifty-guinea fee, and what have I gained?"

"Experience," said Holmes, laughing. "Indirectly it may be of value, you know. You have only to put it into words to gain the reputation of being excellent company for the remainder of your existence. That's your true line in life, sir, and you may take the word of one who knows something of tellers of tales. You have made a start already, as I understand."

A curious look came into Victor Hatherley's expressive blue eyes that a layman might easily have mistaken for fear. Of course, my doctor's eye instantly diagnosed it as nothing but shattered nerves and the inevitable delayed reaction to his terrifying ordeal.

"Who has told you that?" he asked with a nervous laugh. He looked quite anxious.

"Oh, nobody. You say that for two years you have sat at your desk awaiting clients who never came while your clerk did the same. It is inconceivable you did nothing but stare at your copy of Joseph Wright of Derby's painting '*An Experiment on a Bird in the Air Pump*' on the opposite wall month after month. It is still less likely you kept a clerk twiddling his thumbs at another desk without at least giving him something to do. You busied yourself with reading Wilkie Collins, Mary Shelley, and of course a certain Dr. John H. Watson's 'Reminiscences' as published in that inestimable magazine the *Holywell Street Journal*. I cannot be any more precise than that. What I do know for certain is that you also wrote stories of your own. Nobody could have told so extraordinary a tale so very convincingly who was not a practised storyteller of the first water. You were always destined for the printing press, Mr. Hatherley, not the hydraulic press. Would you not agree, Watson?"

Victor Hatherley had been staring with an ever-wider mouth and dangerously bulging eyes at my friend in perfect amazement at this series of impossible deductions. He slowly rose from his train compartment seat, remained standing for a few seconds and then fainted. Bestowing a reproachful look upon Holmes, I rummaged about in my bag and quickly found my medicinal brandy. With this I proceeded to lubricate the hydraulic engineer's throat. Clearly the swoon was obviously the result of excessive blood loss from the amputation of his thumb. As if to confirm his growing delirium, he whispered a name to me a couple of times that made no sense at all. After that came a curious semi-whishing sound from his throat and then a puzzling stertorous wheezing.

"What did he say, Watson?"

Holmes had been observing all this with clinical curiosity. "Nothing. He was raving," said I curtly, for I was more than a little annoyed with my friend for unnecessarily disturbing the man so. "You should not have excited him, Holmes, with your foolish deductions, if that is what they really were."

"Doubtless you suppose he fainted from blood loss."

"I know he did. I am the doctor."

"And I am the detective. What was the word he whispered in your ear?"

"A name."

"Isaac?"

"Holmes! If you heard it why ask me?"

"I did not hear it. I did not need to. As for the accuracy of my deductions, these shall be confirmed soon enough. We had best take him to his rooms in Victoria Street near your own." And after that he ceased to speak, but instead sat stock still like Socrates struck dumb by a thought. If it was not a cataleptic trance, it was a wonderful impersonation of one.

Before readers pick up their pens to write letters complaining that I have changed my address yet again I should explain that by this time I was indeed living near Victoria Station and not in the vicinity of Paddington, as stated above. I had thought it wise to supply false addresses in view of certain threatening letters received from my more unreasonable female readers. It seems that some of them have taken offence at my supposed abandonment of my wife from time to time to accompany Holmes on his adventures. I can only say that what they could not know is that she "abandoned" me just as often as I did her, and by cheerful mutual agreement.

My medical duties meant I was not always available to partner Holmes, and at such times, Mary made an admirable substitute. In fact, if anyone had reason for being jealous it was I, for Holmes did not conceal his admiration for my beloved Mary as possessed of a natural genius for detective work that I frankly admit I lack. I always admired her for it. One day I may publish her personal accounts of her own wonderful adventures with my esteemed friend Mr. Sherlock Holmes.

I should make one further point. For some months after our marriage we lived very happily with Holmes at 221b in an absolutely Platonic *ménage a trois* that nonetheless might easily have been misrepresented by our enemies. In some ways, I would say that this was the happiest time of my life. That, too, is a subject best left for future discussion.

Our train pulled into Victoria Station and Holmes recovered from his trance, whether feigned or real. Mr. Hatherley was only semi-conscious. We soon hailed a cab and within twenty minutes had him in his bed. I administered more medicinal brandy before giving his heart a thorough examination with the stethoscope I always keep in my hat. Having done that, I joined Holmes in the engineer's consulting room.

It was mildly irritating to discover he had been right and there was indeed a copy of Wright's *"Experiment on a Bird in the Air Pump"* on the wall opposite the engineer's desk. A moment's reflection reassured me that his seemingly brilliant deduction was not witchcraft, though, since no picture would more obviously suit the rooms of a hydraulic engineer. It was as predictable an item as the print of Fildes' '*The Doctor*' soon to be purchased for my surgery.

Next, I turned my attention to Hatherley's bookshelf to see what writers had contributed to his style. It was with an amalgamation of pride and annoyance I observed he possessed bound volumes of the *Holywell Street Journal*, sandwiched unsurprisingly between sensation novels by Wilkie Collins and Mary Shelley. I was of course happy to see he was one of those few men of discernment acquainted with my serialised reminiscences. I would have preferred it if he had not been introduced to them in a publication which, despite my contributions, was still of a somewhat questionable reputation.

Nevertheless, I was delighted to discover that the latest issue lay open on his desk at that scene in "The Adventure of the Big Dog of the Baskerville Family", as it was originally entitled, where Miss Stapleton urges me to fly the Moor. I wondered if Hatherley's recounting of a similar warning he had received a few hours earlier from an equally mysterious and beautiful woman had been influenced by my account. It occurred to me that if ever he did turn his account into words on the printed page, as Holmes had advised him to do, I should receive some of the credit for it. A simple acknowledgement would suffice.

"And yet he seemed never to have heard of you. Does that not strike you as just a little queer?" Holmes had evidently been eyeing me quietly the better to impress me with his old mind reading trick.

"Embarrassment, Holmes," I explained, colouring a little. "If I do say so myself my reminiscences have raised the tone of the *Holywell Street Journal* considerably, but it is not yet a magazine to be seen with in polite society."

"Ah, yes. I read your 'Confessions of a Wayward Stethoscope' series of reminiscences on your experiences in three continents with great interest. I particularly enjoyed 'The Adventure of the Mahratta Minister's Sister (and Her Pig)' – a story, I feel, for which the world is not yet prepared. But I can think of another reason why our budding author might not have wished to admit that you were a principle influence on his style. You are quite correct that his account of that encounter with the Beautiful and Mysterious Woman in the Old Dark House was borrowing liberally from your very similar description of your meeting with Miss Stapleton last year."

"Only as regards style, Holmes."

"*He* only stole your style – or rather that of those you had yourself borrowed from. There is never much honour among writers. The content was pocketed by whoever plotted Hatherley's tragedy.

"Next note that Wright picture. I heard your humph, Watson. It was the sound you invariably make whenever something strikes you with the benefit of prophetic hindsight as absurdly simple. And doubtless you understand now why Hatherley muttered 'Isaac' just before slipping into unconsciousness."

"How in the name of Jehovah did you know that, Holmes?"

"But that, too, is absurdly simple. The demonstrator playing at being another Isaac Newton in the painting is performing a sacrifice to science. He has borrowed the pet bird from those little girls and asked them to trust him to return it to them intact. They should have more faith. The impassive man with the watch shall signal to the showman when he should let the air back into the pump to resurrect the bird. It is, you see, a new sacrifice of Isaac. It is a test of faith in the new religion of science."

"But why suppose Hatherley would have thought of this picture at such a time?"

"Because in that hydraulic press, he had become like that bird. And just as an angel appeared at the last moment to save Isaac even as Abraham had raised his cleaver to bring it down on his neck, so the Beautiful and Mysterious Woman materialised miraculously to deliver Hatherley out of that Chamber of Doom. She probably had a watch in her hand to time that deliverance to the last possible moment. I daresay Hatherley felt as if he was trapped in one of his own sensational stories. Actually, he may have been trapped in someone else's. Perhaps we are too."

I have employed capitals the better to communicate the world of sarcasm in Holmes's allusions to The Woman and other features of this affair. Perhaps it was his revenge on me for "The Scandalous Bohemian Prince and the Beautiful Opera Singer", which had just appeared in my own subscription-only *Baker Street Journal*. Holmes has no appreciation of poetic licence. His objection that he hardly ever alludes to Irene Adler as "The Woman" is particularly petty.

"What do you mean, Holmes? I am not a character in someone else's story. I think, therefore I am."

"Hmm. Perhaps. But do you not see that he was chosen, just as you once were, for his exceptional ability as a storyteller? No, I am certain of it. There is a peasouper of a plot in progress, and the brew still thickens in the cauldron. I feel a second finger above his on the pen."

I could see now what Holmes was doing. Mycroft Holmes put it well when he observed that his brother had to be the dramatist in real life – hence his greatest fear was that he might actually be a character in a story written by another. He was like those conspiracy monomaniacs who believe a grey eminence sits motionless at his desk and secretly pulls the strings behind the scenes. That would explain this fantastic new theory that Hatherley was somehow part of a plot that revolved around him. I sometimes think the only reason Holmes refused to accept the Copernican astronomy was that he needed to place himself at the centre of his universe.

Was his use of transcendental poisons to pierce the veil the cause or the effect of his paranoia? It was probably both. He wished to go beyond what he called "the land of mist", to arrive at the ultimate truth, but in the attempt he lost himself in a still thicker fog. Or so I thought.

Little did I know there really was a master plotter at work whom Holmes would soon have to confront. Having no inkling of that at the time, though, my chief aim then was to find some way of convincing my friend his fears were groundless. That meant getting him to understand the adventure of the engineer's thumb was just as it had seemed to be, with no plots within plots and no evil masterminds directing our every move. It had been a simple case of coiners whose stamping machine had developed a minor fault, so requiring the services of an engineer who proved to be a little too inquisitive and so had to be stamped out.

The problem was Holmes was able to read my thoughts before I could do so myself. "Ah. You think it is the cocaine talking, do you not, Doctor? You are starting to regret deserting your resident patient for a wife. Well, well, since you insist, let us reconsider the facts of the case *de novo* and see which of us is right. But it must be *de novo*, Doctor. Keep in mind that had Hatherley's amputated digit lengthened an inch for every lie he may have told, he would not have needed to make that thirty-foot leap to safety he spoke of. He could simple had slid down his severed Pinocchio thumb instead."

I nodded. It seemed superfluous to speak. Anything I said would already have crossed his mind.

"Then let us begin, my Boswell, where Hatherley shall do, should he take my advice and devote himself to the printing press in future, though that has its own dangers and is just as capable of crushing a man to death as the most powerful hydraulic press in the world. Let us start with his appearance in your surgery at some time before seven this Sunday morning. Your maid tapped on your bedroom door and reminded you that the two men from the station were still waiting for you in your surgery. Then she scurried away before you could call out "Come in" so you might question her as to the nature of the case, and also ask for hot water to wash your face and hands. She was evidently a very proper girl who had come across reminiscences concerning your varied and colourful gynaecological experiences. That you were in bed with Mrs. Watson was no guarantee that she would have been safe."

Holmes had paused. I was not about to dignify his aspersions with a reply.

"Well, Watson?"

"Well what, Holmes?"

"I am waiting, Watson, for you to note the first difficulty."

He had stressed the word "waiting". Knowing his methods, I instantly understood that this was a clue. "But surely, Holmes, you cannot think it sinister that the maid did not ask them to wait in the waiting room. That is easily explained."

"Of course it is. She never had the opportunity to do so. Having picked the lock from the inside, your railway guard poked his head out of your surgery to ask her to tap on your door just in case you had fallen asleep again. She naturally assumed that you had happened to be downstairs in your dressing-gown when they had come calling. You had let them in, unlocked your surgery, and left them in there while you returned to your bedroom to get dressed."

"Holmes, how did you know that I always lock my surgery door before going to bed?"

"As a qualified doctor licensed to kill, you keep medicines and implements in your surgery that in the wrong hands could prove fatal. The idea that a maid so prim and proper – she would not even think of entering the Watsons' bedroom so you might question her further would have been so irresponsible as to have let in two unknown men without your permission is absurd enough. It is still more ridiculous to imagine that even if she had mastered the art of picking locks, she would have left them alone in your surgery behind closed doors, and free to perform heaven knows what operations. It never occurred to her that they could have broken in via the window, only to then demand you summon the master."

I felt myself falling at the first hurdle. "This is all too fantastic. Mr. Muircheartaigh, the railway guard who brought Hatherley to me, suspected his charge might try to escape. That is why he insisted on going with him. He installed Hatherley in my surgery intending to stand guard outside the closed door until I arrived. Surely there is nothing sinister in all that."

"If he was afraid Hatherley might try to escape he would never have left him alone in your consulting room. He could have exited via the window. And besides, this Mr. Muircheartaigh only left the room when he heard you descending the stairs. His purpose was clear. You said he closed the door tightly behind him, did you not?"

"I did. Very tightly."

"What did you mean by that?"

It was so curious a question that I had to pause for thought. "Why, I meant he held onto the door handle very tightly. It was because he was afraid his charge might have a fit of hysteria and attempt to bolt."

"He thought might climb out of your window?"

"The door, Holmes," I corrected him. "Muircheartaigh could hardly prevent him from escaping through the window simply by closing the door!"

"Of course. And might he not also have been afraid that in a fit of despair Hatherley would use your surgical instruments and your poisons upon himself?"

I paused for thought. "Hmm. There's a flaw there."

"Indubitably. The best way to ensure Hatherley did not attempt suicide would be to keep him under watch. The best way to guarantee he did not climb out of the window was not to leave him alone in that room. Therefore – he did not shut the door to keep Hatherley in. He did so to keep you out. Do you not see that what he was actually doing was preventing you from entering until whomever was still inside your surgery had completed whatever operation they had come to perform prior to leaving the way they had come?"

"No, no, Holmes. The guard had placed Hatherley under arrest in all but name. Perhaps I should have mentioned that Mr. Muircheartaigh had been a station master in the west of England until an – ahem – painful and lingering disease had forced him to resign from that post. I used mercury to cure him of it. He dreams of redeeming himself in the eyes of the authorities. He saw this as his last chance."

"By abandoning his duties?"

"By bringing a murderer to justice. You remember the Balcombe Tunnel Mystery of 1881?"

Holmes closed his eyes tight and brought his spider-legged hand to his bulging spider-bellied brows in an absurdly exaggerated attempt to retrieve the memory. Perhaps it was impertinent of me to ask the question, given the importance of the case. *The Daily Telegraph* had printed an innovative drawn portrait of the murderer Percy Lefroy Mapleton, and Holmes had hung it on one of his bedroom walls. It was besides only the second-ever murder on the national railways. I deduced Holmes required me to humour him.

"About three months after our investigation of the Lauriston Garden murder – "

"Try to be precise, Watson. It was on Monday, 27 June, 1881."

"As I was saying, at a station – "

"Preston Park Station, Brighton. And be succinct. No poetry. You are not describing the death of Ophelia. Incidentally, she committed suicide."

I took a deep breath. "A man got off a train covered in blood. He claimed that he had been the victim of a murderous assault. The railway guard Thomas Watson was suspicious. He noticed that a chain was hanging out of one of Mapleton's shoes and pulled out a watch. However, Detective Sergeant George Holmes – "

"The blundering fool!"

"As I was saying, Holmes, he did not share Watson's misgivings. Mapleton was put into his care but he gave Holmes the slip."

"Incredible imbecility!"

Holmes had sprung up from his seat and was shaking his fists in the air in inexplicable rage. He seemed to be taking the folly of a brother detective remarkably personally. Noticing my amazement, he sat back down and gazed detachedly into the distance as if nothing had occurred. "Continue."

"Anyway, a body was found in the Balcombe Tunnel with one thumb almost completely severed. It was surmised Mapleton had not been the victim but the assailant. He was hanged."

"29 November, 1881. Had the eugenicist Galton's recommendations been put into practise Detective Sergeant Holmes would have joined him on the gallows. Well, well, there but for the grace of God, I suppose. What is your point, Doctor?"

"Why, it is simple enough. Muircheartaigh saw Hatherley leaving a train hugging a bloody hand and his mind at once went back to that second railway murder. When Hatherley claimed he had been the victim of a murderous assault, Muircheartaigh wondered whether he was not trying Mapleton's trick. There was his missing thumb in support of his protestations, but in his desperation to evade the gallows he might have improved upon Mapleton's story and cut it off himself. Muircheartaigh brought him to me because I am acquainted with you. If you unmasked Hatherley, he would receive due credit and be reinstated as station master. That explains why Hatherley had heard of you, but evidently knew nothing of our past partnership. Muircheartaigh had concealed it from him lest he bolt. I published in the *Holywell Street Journal* anonymously, you know."

Holmes nodded approvingly, which was as good as applause to me. "Very plausibly argued, Watson. Quite ingenious. Yet I did not quite follow your explanation as to why this Muircheartaigh didn't perform his primary duty of reporting to his superiors that a desperately wounded passenger had evidently either committed an assault or been the victim of one. Can you really think of no other reason why that guard might have thought it necessary to play the guard indeed with Hatherley? No? Well, well, we will ponder that difficulty in due course. But now I would trouble you with another question. I am not, I confess, quite the household name you had assured me your accounts would make me."

"I have done my best, Holmes," said I indignantly. "Perhaps I haven't mentioned it before, but my efforts have cost me a pretty penny. My reminiscences of experiences abroad were profitable enough when published in the *Holywell Street Journal*. They positively refused to publish the account of the Lauriston Garden affair until I committed myself to supplying further personal reminiscences free of charge."

Holmes looked startled. "But surely when you reprinted in *Beeton's Christmas Annual*, they paid you something?"

"Paid me? Surely you are joking, Holmes! I had to pay them. My collaborator Conan Doyle managed to knock them down to a payment of twenty-five pounds. He waived his agent's fee on return for his name alone appearing on the cover, which was fair enough since his was the only original material."

"And your very own *Baker Street Journal*?"

"Has always run at a loss. Besides, it is by subscription only and few read it. Fortunately, Conan Doyle has just managed to negotiate a reprinting of *The Sign of the Four Men Who Stole the Agra Treasure*. The title and one or two other minor details will have to be changed. I've left all that up to him, including choosing my *nom de plume*."

"Hm. I think I can deduce what *nom de plume* he will choose for you. Watson, you are far too trusting. But let us press on. My point is that it is odd Hatherley should have heard of me when so few have, and yet he knew nothing of you. That is particularly queer since as I noted earlier he is a reader of your reminiscences."

"I told you, Holmes, I originally published anonymously, for obvious reasons."

"Ah, yes. Strange bedfellows that your tales shared sheets with. Well, let us continue. When you entered your consulting room, what did you find there?"

"Hatherley was seated at the table dressed respectably enough, and with a handkerchief spotted with what I took at first to be a strawberry pattern wrapped about one hand. He had put his soft cloth cap atop the books on the table."

"Books?"

"Reference books. For my writing – Poe, Gaboriau, Wilkie Collins. All the standard classics. I jot down notes for my accounts during surgeries and write them up last thing at night and first thing each morning."

"And do you not lose any patients?"

"My practise is never very busy."

"I was thinking of prescriptions written while preoccupied with tales of strychnine poisonings. What did you deduce from his hat?"

"From his hat?"

"Precisely."

"You are surely joking, Holmes. Of course, I know that you can read a man's history in an old hat based on the stains and so forth. But his was brand new. It had no history at all. Hence you could not have deduced its owner's story from it. Sometimes, you know a hat is an adornment for the head."

"And the head an adornment for the shoulders as mantelpiece. You really saw nothing worthy of note about it?"

"What should I have seen?"

"What a blind man would have. The fact that it was there at all. Have you forgotten what happened later? When asked to accompany the diabolical Colonel Stark to inspect the hydraulic press, Hatherley said he supposed he had better put on his hat. He was told it was unnecessary since the press was upstairs. As the murderous assault followed hard on the heels of that inspection, he never had a chance to recover his cap. How was it, then, that he still had it?"

I could only look confused. Things were not going as well as I had hoped. From such unimportant details, Holmes was perfectly capable of concocting major conspiracies. He was regarding me with smug satisfaction at my discomfiture.

"Never mind, Watson. What of the rest of his attire?"

"You cannot object to that, Holmes! He was quietly dressed in a suit of heather tweed. You cannot tell me you traced a scarlet thread of murder in that too."

Holmes chortled. "Nothing of the sort! That was the difficulty. It ought to have been as hard to find such a thread as to locate one particular

280

needle in a haystack sized heap of needles. You recall Hatherley said he had awakened after the amputation to find his sleeve drenched in blood? Even that handkerchief ought to have been soaked through instead of merely resembling Desdemona's strawberry-patterned one."

"You liken the handkerchief to Desdemona's," I grumbled, "but I might liken you to jealous Othello reading too much into trifles. I know where you are going with all this. You are about to say he only lost his thumb seconds before I saw him."

"Why should you suppose that, Watson?" asked Holmes innocently. "Let us not jump to conclusions. Reconsider that amputation, then. I bow to your specialist knowledge. You were an army surgeon. You have severed arms and legs enough in your time."

"And a head once, but that is a long story."

"A chicken, no doubt. Or perhaps a Scotland Yard detective. What was your impression when you inspected that thumbless hand? Did it seem to you like a clean cut?"

I shuddered at the memory. "Horrible! Horrible! Oh, horrible! It looked as if it had been hacked at or torn out of the roots. Perhaps both. It was not clean at all."

"Torture, Watson. It was no surgical strike. And yet in Hatherley's account, it was a blow so mercifully swift he barely registered the blow. What do you make of that?"

I am a realist with no time for fantastic fairy tales. "Really, Holmes. Are you trying to tell me it was ripped out on my doorstep and then transported back to Eyford for a fireman to find it perched on a window sill of a burning house? The thing is impossible!"

"Not in the least. Forget your doorstep. The operation must have been performed on a window sill in your surgery to have left no trace of blood in the room As for your other objection, it would have been easy enough to bribe the fireman to claim he had found it there. Whether the one he showed us was Hatherley's is, of course, quite another question."

As the facts slowly evolved before my own eyes all my clarity was making way for increasing confusion. Each new discovery seemed like a further step descending to utter bewilderment. I could only cling to the certainty that I had examined Hatherley and he had not. "You forget, Holmes, that when I first saw him he was deathly pale from a dreadful loss of blood. That proves it cannot have been a recent amputation. He must have been bleeding profusely for many hours."

"Really. Then how do you account for the fact that you told me he had been 'blushing hotly'? Could a man suffering from excessive blood loss have been blushing hotly?"

281

I made a mental note to alter "blushing hotly" to "pale-looking" should I manage to have my account reprinted in America, where I gather editors are more pernickety. In this country, I am glad to say, "Trust me, I'm a doctor" still counts for something. But I had to confess that Hatherley did seem to make a remarkably swift recovery once I had administered some medicinal brandy.

Holmes raised his eyebrows. "I think 'miraculously' is the word you were searching for."

Not to be outdone I raised mine. "That is surely an exaggeration, Holmes."

"Is it? Would you, a doctor, have consented to take him to me at once rather than prescribing an hour or two in bed had you not been entirely confident that he was up to it? All told, he would seem to have made seven journeys within a space of twenty-four hours and with very little sleep, yet this man who had almost been crushed to death by a hydraulic press, had been deprived of his thumb, had fallen thirty feet from a homicidal maniac, and who had had no rest save for a few hours while unconscious as his life blood drained away, showed no signs of fatigue after that initial performance in your surgery until the time he fainted dead away in our train compartment."

This would have been easy to explain to a fellow surgeon. "You see, Holmes, even a dying man can display extraordinary resilience when desperate enough. That hysteria of his renewed him, even as it guaranteed his collapse in due course."

To my surprise, Holmes seemed quite amenable to this notion. He nodded thoughtfully. "You may have hit upon it. The dying Jefferson Hope was a case in point. You recall he had only hours to live, and yet he almost overpowered three men, one of whom was myself, and that despite his being handcuffed. The monomaniac was on a quest. He had a mission to fulfil, and even after he had accomplished it, the high lingered. Is it not clear that Hatherley was equally driven? He had a deadline to meet. He had twelve hours. Oh, and it doubtless helped he had been injected with a pretty high percentage of cocaine. I think I know the signs."

So do I, thought I to myself. "He certainly knew the clock was ticking if that gang was to be apprehended. That was why he was so eager I should take him to see you."

"And yet he did not think to inform the police at Reading. Do you recall his reaction when he first laid eyes upon me?"

Holmes is quite vain. "He had a look of awe as I recall."

"No, it is not vanity, Watson," said he in answer to my secret thoughts. "And that was no awe at the sight of a great man but quite the contrary. He was disappointed to find I was not the elongated matchstick of your accounts. Having read your serialised "The Adventures of Dr. Watson and the Case of the Mormon Murder" in the *Holywell Street Journal*, he had naturally supposed I was the thinnest man in the world, and as tall as a long jump Oxford Blue. He had imagined me flattened out in that hydraulic press. He found it was the printing press that had transformed me into your two-dimensional character, one able to fit comfortably inside brother Mycroft. That was why I was unsurprised by his account of that ordeal under the hydraulic press. I had been expecting something of the sort."

"Oh, come now, Holmes!"

"I speak the truth. Sometimes one must mind read deep enough to perceive processes unsuspected by the very consciousness being probed. Let this case serve as an example."

"Well, I am a sceptic," I confessed.

"Let us see if I cannot convert you. It is my contention that the thought of what he had imagined I ought to be insinuated itself into his account without his realising it. You recall how he portrayed Colonel Stark as the thinnest man he had ever known? He was still thinking of your 'Sherlock Holmes' and imagining how I might be he after a session beneath the hydraulic press. Only now it was Hatherley who was creating a caricature of a real man by imagining it had been the Colonel who had been flattened out in that terribly strange room."

I made a tactical withdrawal. "I admit I may have exaggerated your skeletal appearance to make you more interesting, Holmes. Hatherley was doubtless doing the same in the case of the Colonel. It hardly follows nothing he said was true. He was honest enough when it came to admitting that his career had been an absolute failure."

"His career servicing the hydraulic press. His career serving the printing press may have been rather more fruitful. But let us consider that official profession. Why do you suppose that after two years he had not built up a clientele by word of mouth?"

"You yourself struggled at first, Holmes," I ventured to remind my friend.

"As the world's first and only personal consulting detective. It was an entirely new niche. And I had no choice. Corruption at the Detective Department was rife and had to be exposed. After that, of course, there was no question of their ever accepting me at Scotland Yard."

I realised Holmes was alluding to the Trial of the Detectives of 1877. I nodded.

"But the world will always need hydraulic engineers. Why then did it not need Victory Hatherley?"

"I suppose because his old employers Venner and Matheson did not recommend him."

"Or advised its clients to avoid him like the plague. The latter is far more likely. Consider his performance in the case of that particular hydraulic press. He was invited to inspect its chamber with care, and yet he failed to observe there were no signs of the fuller's earth it was supposedly compressing while there were traces of metallic deposit. He really ought to have inspected the trough with the greatest care since there was a possibility that fuller's earth might have entered the mechanism and caused the problems. Yet he was so unobservant that the Colonel had to absent-mindedly forget to lock the chamber door and abandon Hatherley later to wander where he would so he might return to the press and make that belated discovery."

"Oh, come now, Holmes!"

"I am perfectly serious. Next, Doctor, think of how he diagnosed the difficulty. I appreciate that you as a doctor cannot examine the heart of a patient save with your trusty stethoscope. He did the equivalent of that when he attended to the whishing noise the machine made. But unlike you, Doctor, he could have peered into the heart of the machine had he thought to do so. Instead, he noted no more than that an india-rubber band had shrunk and needed to be replaced. It never occurred to him to point out to the Colonel that since the ceiling of the chamber was nothing more than the end of the piston which was housed the next floor up, he ought to have been taken to inspect that first. Studying the empty chamber was a pointless waste of time, save as an opportunity to discover that the fuller's earth story was nonsense. Such an examination was akin to a veterinarian entering a carriage to attend to the sounds of the horse harnessed to it as the basis for his diagnosis. And then there was the question of the engineer's ear."

As a doctor I knew that to apply a stethoscope to a patient's heart is of course not quite the same as cutting the patient open to examine that organ first hand. Nevertheless, I was defiant. "Nine times out of ten to listen to a patient's heart is good enough, Holmes."

Holmes tapped his ear knowingly. "Provided one has reasonable hearing, which it seems Hatherley had not. You recall he said he knew the house he was taken to had to be deep in the countryside because of the absolute stillness? Since when was the countryside absolutely still? Let us suppose that the building was in reality a moated castle. Still there ought to have been the sound of the wind in the trees and the occasional distant hooting of an owl. He heard absolutely nothing. He was evidently a little deaf."

"No, Holmes, you are wrong," I cried, determined to defend our new friend. I was perhaps a little too gleeful, as I cannot help being whenever I can remind Holmes of his human fallibility. It is good that at times I can play the role of the slave on the triumphal chariot whispering into the conquering hero's ear that he, too, is mortal. "He heard the ticking of an old clock in the passage."

"He could not," said he coldly. "How did he know that the clock was old? Only if he had already have seen it. He only imagined that he heard it. Or he imagined both the old clock and its ticking. Either way it shows how unreliable his senses were. Remember how even with his limited German he could see that the books on the table were works of German poetry and science? Yet when the Beautiful and Mysterious Woman addressed the Colonel, he could not tell whether they were speaking German or some other language despite the fact that the Colonel replied to her query with a monosyllable: '*Nein*', or something of the sort. No, his hearing was clearly poor, yet he relied on it as the chief means by which he made his all-too-swift diagnosis. No wonder if, after two years he had no clients at all. Indeed, I do not doubt his sloppiness as an engineer was as important a factor as his outstanding ability as a storyteller in the decision to employ him for that very special job."

"But you are wrong, Holmes," I corrected my friend. "What they particularly valued in him was his uprightness. The Colonel trusted him to keep his word and tell nobody about his mission."

Holmes shook his head with a smile. "Hardly. If he had been so very honest, he would never have agreed to be party to a swindle, nor would the Colonel have claimed that his aim was to cheat his neighbour out of land rich in fuller's earth. A completely honest man would rather have starved than work for a self-professed villain whose absolute lack of trust in others clearly signalled he could not be trusted himself. But a man who loved stories and telling stories would have been excited at the atmosphere of mystery and danger that the Colonel worked so hard to create."

I could not help thinking of Holmes's delight as he had shared with me details of how he had cheated a poor broker out of his Stradivarius. It seemed to me that the act of swindling the man had delighted him more than the Stradivarius itself. A strange enigma is man! To take pride in one's wrongdoings! Do thieves rejoice and exult in their criminal pursuits? I prayed that I might never be exposed to such temptations. The thought made me shudder. "Could we move on, Holmes? My wife may be wondering what has happened to me."

Holmes bestowed upon me a reproachful look as upon a listener who shows impatience with a great storyteller. "Oh, well of course if you have more pressing business to attend to. Let us hasten on then to Hatherley's arrival at Eyford. There was a nearly full moon that night. Mark that, Watson. He left the train station and discovered a carriage with the Colonel lurking '*in the shadow upon the other side . . . .*'" His eyes had lightened to Mycroft – grey as he repeated the words one at a time, '*in – the – shadow – upon – the – other – side*'. Hmm. Those were his exact words. What do you make of that?"

"How can I make anything of it, Holmes, if you do not tell me what shadow and the other side of what?"

"A very reasonable grumble, Watson. Sadly, Hatherley neglected to say either what cast the shadow or what lay between those two sides, though I think we may deduce both with ease. No ideas?"

"The other side of the street?"

"Perfectly correct! Now, if there was a nearly full moon then shadows would hardly have been thin on the ground – unless, that is, the moon was behind those houses where the carriage was parked. In that case it would have been entirely lost in their gloom. But in that case, how could the Colonel have been concealing himself in 'the shadow'? He had to be keeping himself out of some light source and that must have been responsible for the particular shadow in which the villain had cloaked himself. What light source would that have been?"

"A street lamp?"

"I have already explained why I do not believe that the Colonel really was the world's thinnest man. We may discard the notion he was concealing himself in the shadow of a lamppost. What remains? Come now, he was standing by his carriage."

"A sidelight!"

"Excellent! He was standing in the shadow cast by one of its sidelights. We are making progress."

But I was dissatisfied. "Wait a moment, Holmes. That makes no sense."

"No?" Holmes frowned. "You perceive some difficulty? I should be glad to hear it."

"Why, it may be nothing," said I hesitantly, starting to lose my nerve. "It is the most trivial thing. It is surely nothing. Let us suppose the Colonel was hiding himself in the shadow cast by a sidelight on his carriage. I see that. What I don't understand is why the sidelight was lit. Surely he would not have needed to hide himself in the shadow it cast had it not been lit in the first place."

Holmes beamed his approval. "You have it exactly, my dear Watson! Either he wished to engage in a spot of lurking – hence he had to supply himself with both a light source and the consequent shadow it cast to conceal himself from that very light – or all that lurking was intended to ensure Hatherley did not suspect the light was actually lit to guarantee the engineer he saw something else."

"That seems a bit devious."

"But it must be so. Had the Colonel's sole aim been to conceal himself, he would have remained seated in the carriage. There was no need for him to have got out of it at all, save to lurk. Now, what do you suppose he meant Hatherley to see?"

"But there was nothing for Hatherley to see."

"You are forgetting one thing: The carriage."

"The carriage? Why should the Colonel have wished Hatherley to see that?"

"Not the carriage, Watson, but the carriage *horse*. He wished him to note that it was fresh and unused."

"Preposterous, Holmes!"

"Why so?"

"The last thing the Colonel would have wished was for Hatherley to see the horse had just been collected. It would have told him their destination had to be nearby. Then he would have guessed the old dodge of driving so many miles out and then doubling back was being employed."

"Right! Absolutely right! And from that what follows?"

I suddenly understood. "Holmes, you are being absurd! You cannot be suggesting it was a double bluff. The secret mansion had to have been that house at Eyford that we saw burning later."

"We will come to that. I admit, though, that it might have been a triple bluff, so we must not yet rule out the possibility that the burning house was indeed the one Hatherley was taken to. And there again," he added thoughtfully, "it could have been a quadruple bluff."

I thought of the game of "even and odd" described by Holmes's precursor, Auguste Dupin, in which one must guess whether the number of concealed marbles is even or odd and if one guesses right one wins them. The skilled player is able to deduce whether his opponent shall suppose a double, triple, or quadruple bluff and so on. Suddenly I thought I understood. "Holmes, do you suspect Moriarty is behind this?"

He smiled sadly. "No, Watson. I regret to say that the dark rumours I spread about him have been entirely successful. I saw him last month at the First International Congress for Experimental and Therapeutic Hypnotism. We were both disguised, of course. He was a broken man. I daresay that the once famed author of *The Dynamics of an Asteroid* shall soon follow your example and naturally gravitate to London, that great black hole into which all falling stars are irresistibly sucked." Holmes heaved a great sigh as a saner and less brilliant man might have done for a bereavement.

"You have no reason to suppose the carriage did not double back," said I, chiefly to turn Holmes's mind from thoughts of his loss. As a doctor, I know that work is the best antidote to sorrow.

"Well, there are certainly some facts that would suggest it was a double bluff, though I admit that they would also be consistent with a triple or quadruple bluff. You recall Hatherley's arrival at the Old Dark House?"

"He was hustled into it and then left alone in a room with a circular table and a harmonium."

"Yes, we will come to that. Note first that the instant he was through the door, the carriage left. That could have been to return the hired horse and carriage to Eyford."

"But it need not have been."

"If the driver had been a gang member, then he would not have left assuming the Colonel would have preferred to keep Hatherley under guard. Moreover, if the carriage was the gang's, then it would have been used for the later escape, assuming that the flight was genuine. Why should they have travelled atop an open cart with several crates full of coins if there was a safer and more comfortable alternative? But there are at present too many 'if's'. For now, we can only follow Hatherley into his labyrinthine mansion or castle and tread those stone floors worn down by centuries of soldiers. It does sound rather like a castle, does it not?"

I nodded. "That would make sense, Holmes. The gang would hardly have chanced installing a hydraulic press exerting a force of many tons two or three storeys up unless they were sure it could bear such punishment. It was like repeatedly striking at it with a vertical battering ram. They would have placed it in cellar."

"Or the old torture chamber, aptly enough. Your deduction is impeccable, but is also an example of the art of seduction. I heard a lecture on that subject given by one Mr. Gruner at that Congress I spoke of."

"What do you mean, 'the art of seduction'?" I was interested.

"Well, in this case that your reasoning is irresistible, but could be entirely erroneous. Let us suppose that Hatherley was seduced by such pleasing reasoning himself. Being an engineer, he would have understood very well that only an ancient and very thick stone floor could have borne that press. So he deduced the floor simply had to be made of stone, as he told us it was. But just suppose for the sake of argument that it was not. In that case, we might arrive at a very different conclusion. What if that press did not exert tons of pressure at all?"

"But it had to, Holmes. How else could it have crushed a man?"

"It could not have done. So now we have two possibilities. According to the first, that citadel was an almost indestructible castle. According to the other it was nothing of the sort, in which case that hydraulic press must be suspect. It was not counterfeiting but counterfeit. Now think of that familiar bleak stone staircase you ascended at St. Barts on your way to our first ever encounter."

I found myself fidgeting nervously. "Ah. That."

Holmes chuckled. "No need to feel embarrassed, Watson. I know it was a little white literary lie. Had you ever passed under the hospital's magnificent gateway to enter the building by the conventional means, you would know that the main staircase is exceptionally handsome and decorated with murals by Hogarth, though personally I would have preferred it had they used his 'Four Stages of Cruelty'. So please do not feel the need to blush so."

"I followed Stamford blindly."

"Of course you did. The devil knows best what he said to persuade you to ascend a ladder to one of the upper windows."

"He said he had a peculiar taste in these matters," I mumbled with some embarrassment. "'It's a joke, my good sir – a practical joke, nothing more.' He promised me it would startle the life out of you."

"I understand," said he sympathetically. "I know you never suspected that your encounter at the Criterion Bar was no happy accident. Of course, had it been me, I would have realised at once some game was afoot. Would Stamford have trudged from Barts to the Criterion for his lunch hour only to at once consent to go with you to the Holborn instead? But you are the most credulous of men, Doctor, which is quite endearing, but does mean men take advantage of you."

"Not only men," I thought to myself. Holmes smiled and I regretted the thought. He saw it and taking pity on me he continued.

"Stamford was an agent for whatever higher power had plotted our meeting. Whomever selected you was a man of true discernment."

I was flattered but unconvinced. "Why me?"

"Because like Hatherley you are a born storyteller. That was the chief qualification in both cases. Let us not digress. My point is that just as there was no bleak stone staircase such as you imagined at Barts, so Hatherley's grim stone floors need not have existed either. You visualised yours because it just felt right. He deduced his because as an engineer he could not conceive of anything more lunatic than to locate your vertical battering ram upstairs, save on a stone floor several inches thick. The alternative explanation never occurred to him."

I consoled myself with the thought that I was in good company. "I can see no alternative, Holmes."

"There is always an alternative, Watson. In this case, it is very obvious indeed: Hatherley deduced that the floors had to be stone since nothing else could have survived such a hammering. He could just as easily have deduced that since they were *not* stone, they never received one. No? Well, I must give you time. Here is a hint. Ask yourself what conceivable use a hydraulic press exerting tons of pressure could be to a gang intent on stamping out counterfeit coins that would not have required a hundredth of such force. Cudgel your brains over that while we proceed. Where were we?"

"With Hatherley in that castle."

"We may pass over his inevitable encounter with the Beautiful and Mysterious Woman urging him to go back. I believe you observed that copy of the *Holywell Street Journal* on his desk open at your meeting with the beautiful and mysterious woman on the moor. Coincidence? I think not. But we need not concern ourselves with wondering whether he plagiarised that entire incident from your account or only the style. Instead, let us proceed to his inspection of the chamber of horrors."

"You mean the hydraulic press."

Holmes shrugged. "Same difference. The Colonel unlocked it, described how awful it would be if anyone were to start the machine while someone was inside it, and once that pointless inspection was complete, absent-mindedly forgot to lock the door to it when they left. Hatherley then listened to the press in action and instantly diagnosed the difficulty. He neither thought to ascend to the piston on the next floor, nor was it suggested he do so. It did not occur to him to offer to correct the very minor fault. Now, Watson, if Stark meant to ensure that Hatherley should learn as little as possible, what would you expect him to have done next?"

"Why, pay him and hurry him back to the railway station in that carriage with the frosted windows."

"But that was impossible. The carriage had disappeared the instant Hatherley was through the front door. Besides, the Colonel had insisted the engineer stay the night there, so hugely increasing the likelihood he would at the very find some window in so vast a mansion that was not shuttered and barred. How guard against such a possibility?"

"Lock him up in his bedroom and keep a guard on the door."

"And what did he actually do?"

"Why, Holmes," said I in surprise, for it had never occurred to me before. "The Colonel left him unguarded to wander wherever he desired. That was foolish, especially since he had forgotten to relock the door to that chamber."

Holmes chuckled gleefully. "Yes indeed. How very remiss of him. Unless, of course, he had intended all the time to put the machine to the use it was designed for, which was no more to stamp out coins by the thousands than to compress fuller's earth into bricks."

I was bewildered. "What do you mean, Holmes, 'the use it was meant for'? What other use could it possibly have had?"

My friend smiled. "Ah, Watson, all great villains have a sense of humour. I mean all the true artists. Colonel Stark revealed his wit when Hatherley demanded he know what the exact purpose was for which the machine was designed."

"What, you mean it was to dispose of unwanted guests?"

"No. It was a torture chamber. The only real question is whether it was intended to inflict physical or purely mental suffering."

"You horrify me!"

"I incline to the psychological," continued Holmes in his most coldly clinical manner. "First the psychological and then the physical. The amputation of the thumb was the icing on the cake. As for the inspiration for that chamber of horrors, we have it before us."

Holmes had directed my attention back to the Wright painting "*An Experiment on a Bird in the Air Pump*". "One of our criminal mastermind's agents doubtless visited Hatherley for a consultation and then reported back on the décor. Our mastermind decided to put the engineer in the situation of that bird. The showman in the picture has degraded what should have been a course of lectures into a series of stories. Our mastermind used that particular story as the basis for his little murder-room drama. Why else would that so-called 'press' have descended at a snail's pace? It was clearly meant to do so. The slower the better if the aim was not to compress the body but rather to depress the mind and oppress the spirit."

I felt myself growing disillusioned at the thought of such senseless cruelty. "But why, Holmes? Was it torture for the sake of torture? Was it nothing but the cruel jest of some devil playing at being God?"

"That may have been part of it," said he thoughtfully. "I speak from personal experience when I say that to have the power of life and death is quite intoxicating. It is why I became first a scientist and then a detective."

I thought of Holmes's experiments on my bull pup.

"I think I mentioned earlier that I was at the First International Congress for Experimental and Therapeutic Hypnotism a few weeks ago. The truly intriguing talks were the unofficial ones at the fringe of the Congress. Bertie Rucastle, a quite remarkable child prodigy he, mesmerised us with a perverse but instructive lecture on the systematised vivisection of cockroaches for fun and profit. He reminded me of that boy there gazing up in wonder at the expiring bird in Wright's painting. One can imagine he will soon start experimenting to see how long it takes mice to suffocate in corked bottles."

"And you think whomever devised that bogus press was just as sadistic?"

"That was not what I had in mind. So monstrous a child as Bertie Rucastle is not the product of cruelty alone, but also the absence of its opposite. Consider Wright's picture again. The most significant figure in it is the one you cannot see."

I scanned the painting in vain to identify whom Holmes meant. "I'm sorry Holmes. I can't see who you mean."

"The table, Watson."

"The table, Holmes? What can that tell us? It has been recently polished. That robs us of all our data. Now, if it was scratched, then I have no doubt you could read between the lines to learn the histories of all those present. But it is a perfect mirror. Why, that seated introspective old man could see his face in it."

"Yes, Watson. So might that father figure, who is so anxious to ensure his distressed daughter observe the experiment that he forgets to attend to it himself. Were he to catch sight of his own reflection in that table, he might learn to know himself. Now, who do you suppose ensured it was transformed into a spotless mirror?"

"It has to be the father, Holmes."

Holmes gave a bitter laugh. "The father? That is very likely! He was so thoughtless it did not occur to him to spread a cloth upon the table before permitting this philosopher to put his equipment upon it. You can see how his instruments have permanently scarred its surface."

I scrutinised it. "You are mistaken, Holmes. My eye detects no scratching."

"But my mind's eye does. The instruments that have made the marks conceal them."

"And I suppose your mind's eye perceives the person who is not there," I grumbled.

"Why, of course. When one wishes to investigate the properties of a thing, one does so by removing it from the scene. Then one notices what happens in its absence. That is what has been done here. Come now, which member of the family is absent?"

"The mother!"

"She is the Copernican sun whom all the other household members orbit. Her place as heart and hearth is usurped here by that vacuum in which that bird is expiring. It is meant to put us in mind of the Dove of Wisdom by which the Virgin conceived the Light of the World in her womb. Now imagine that this was one of your sentimental stories, Watson.

292

Would you not have her burst in through that mausoleum style doorway into this crime scene to dispel the darkness with a lamp held high?

I could not help doing so. I was recalling Mrs. Hudson's horror on discovering Holmes dancing about an experiment that had ruined the breakfast table. "I see your point, Holmes. She would surely be unhappy to discover the damage done to a prized piece of furniture."

"Ah, but that would be nothing to her horror at the scarring of her children. Can you not picture her dashing the showman's hand away from that pump to let in the air? Would she not play the exorcist and cast out this sham wizard in his dressing-gown who so perfectly proves the truth of Wisdom's warning in the Bible, that those who hate her love death? And can you not see her daughters rushing to her arms? The son would not. He would curse her for ruing the tragedy before it could reach its climax. The seeds of a lifelong love of vivisection have been sowed. Now do you see my point? The absence of such a mother is as important as the presence of such a father. And that raises the difficulty of Moriarty."

"Moriarty? But I thought you said he could have had nothing to do with Hatherley's adventure."

"Oh, he did not. It is impossible. That is what is so intriguing. It troubles me and gives me hope for the future."

"You have lost me, Holmes."

"You see, whomever introduced that woman as Hatherley's saviour revealed a sentimental streak they themselves probably could not acknowledge. It is the same with Moriarty. It is what has puzzled me about him ever since I examined his study. Why should one of society's tigers have a painting of a Greuze girl cuddling a lamb hanging behind his desk? And what is the connection between that and this Wright painting?"

"Why, whatever makes you think there is one?"

"The Professor has written a privately circulated monograph on Greuze and his influence on English artists. In it, he notes that three years before this Wright was painted, Greuze planned to produce a vision of a happy family with children playing, women working, and men engaged in experimental physics. It was thought the project had been abandoned, but Moriarty claims he came upon the picture in the hands of a Jew broker in Tottenham Court Road and purchased it for fifty shillings. He has no shame. Then in 1765, Greuze painted his famous image of a girl mourning over a dead canary. Moriarty contends Wright was inspired by those pictures to paint the Air Pump. Incidentally, as one might expect of the author of *The Dynamics of an Asteroid*, he also owns a copy of Wright's 'A Philosopher Lecturing on the Orrery'."

"The what, Holmes?"

"The orrery. A working model illustrating the Copernican heresy. Moriarty's is unique. His only features the sun, earth, moon, Mars, Jupiter and the minor planets. Most remarkably of all, two of those minor planets are shown leaving their orbits to strike the earth. He claims one of them was responsible for destroying the dinosaurs and the other shall destroy man."

"Now that you have told me that I shall do my best to forget it," I muttered. "Some facts should be suppressed, or at least a just sense of proportion should be observed in treating them."

"A quote, is it not? Baxter, I think. Those who declined to review his magnum opus agreed. But the point is this: Moriarty clearly saw the work of Greuze and Wright had collided unexpectedly, and that the Air Pump was the unforeseen result. It cannot be a coincidence Hatherley just happened to have a Wright too. The odds would be astronomical against it being a coincidence. And that torture chamber was just the kind of toy that might have interested Moriarty. Yet I repeat that the Professor is finished. So, did the sorcerer have an apprentice? Is it such a new mastermind we are dealing with? Ah, well, one can but hope. What is certain is someone was using Hatherley as the subject in his own series of experiments. And they were originally inspired by that Air Pump painting."

"But why suppose that?"

"Because Hatherley tells us the first thing the Colonel did once they were in the Old Dark House was to deposit the engineer in a room with a round table at its centre laden with German books of science and poetry. That was clearly meant to make him recall Wright's painting with its round table recalling the Lunar Society's."

"'The Lunar Society'?"

"A group of scientific enthusiasts that included Erasmus Darwin, the grandfather of Charles Darwin and Francis Galton. The introspective gentleman in the picture who has taken off his spectacles to gaze at the questionable shape in the flask and imagine it is a skull may be Erasmus Darwin. He is asking himself if this is really an experiment at all rather than an entertainment for men who cannot put away childish things. The Lunar Society met when there was a full moon and liked to call themselves the Lunatics as a piece of ironic wit. They believed in the enlightenment. But the full moon in Wright's picture is suggestive of moonshine, for there was clearly no reason why this sham experiment had to be performed at night. Nor could anything new have been learnt from it."

"Why, Holmes, what a coincidence! There is a nearly full moon just now!"

294

"No coincidence, Watson. That, too, was expected to lead Victor Hatherley to think of this painting and imagine himself as that bird having the life squeezed out of it. As for those books on the round table intermingling poetry and science, they were intended to encourage a sense of the Gothic horror of Victor Frankenstein's experiments as described in a work published fifty years after this picture was painted. Mary Shelley was born the year Wright died, you know."

I could see Holmes was still determined to believe some dramatist in real life equal to himself had stage managed everything. It was too fantastic. "You cannot believe, Holmes, just because there was a full moon and a round table and some works of Romantic fiction that it was all part of some secret plot?"

"And the harmonium, Watson. You are forgetting the harmonium."

"What harmonium?"

"Hatherley tells us that the Colonel put his candle down on top of a harmonium. Now, those criminals had to be ready to leave at a moment's notice, hence that harmonium had to be a portable one. It is one of the few instruments that can be played using only one thumb. Do you see? Someone could not resist including it as a piece of black humour. It was prophetic of the fate planned for Hatherley all along. That same black wit was in evidence when Hatherley's guard jerked his thumb towards your consulting room to signify where the engineer had been deposited. Someone was playing on you both as upon a pipe."

"But to what end?"

Holmes continued to gaze meditatively at the painting. "It could have been a case of what your new acquaintance Wilde likes to call art for art's sake. I have a dark namesake in Chicago who is at present constructing a murder castle based on the disassembly lines of the city's slaughterhouses. His victims shall go in by one door and their skeletons shall leave by another to be sold to doctors and hospitals. The medical profession, Watson, is a most valuable institution, if you only know how to use it. It can be a licence to kill. Now, assuming our criminal mastermind does indeed have a somewhat perverted sense of humour, he may have contracted Mr. Holmes as a criminal consultant to advise on the architecture of the castle Hatherley found himself in. The chief innovation is that the latter citadel was chiefly intended to be a place of mental torture to make the mind more pliable.

I was quite relieved. "So it was more than just as cruel jest? There was some point to the exercise?"

"Oh, yes," said Holmes indifferently. "Our mastermind may be a devil, but he is not a god. He had a very definite purpose. It was to get me out of London. Moreover, he began preparing for this action at least a year ago, for it was at the time of that ear-severing affair that those advertisements appeared in all the papers. You know, the ones concerning the missing hydraulic engineer alluded to in the argument between the Beautiful and Mysterious Woman and the Transparently Sinister Villain just before Hatherley supposedly had his thumb cut off – hardly likely to be a coincidence. Doubtless the case of the severed ears was the inspiration behind that severed thumb."

I was incredulous. "Holmes, you cannot seriously be suggesting that those advertisements were fictions?"

"They had to be. They said no more than that the missing engineer 'left his lodgings' without thinking to give his address. That is because he had none. He did not exist."

"But the argument – !"

" – Was staged. Hatherley noted that the Colonel and the lady both spoke in English instead of their own native language. They had not done so previously. It was for his benefit."

"But to what end?"

"That is the point. It was intended to convince me of the truth of Hatherley's story. Those advertisements must have been intended for *my* eyes. Someone knew I keep all the advertisements from all the key newspapers in London. I would recall that particular one and take it as proof positive that Hatherley's tale was gospel truth. Fortunately, I do not believe in gospel truth."

"And you think the woman was to release him from that press at the last moment?"

"Just like the bird in the air pump resurrected when the showman's assistant signals to that entertainer to do so. It really was the most ridiculous locked room mystery. Of all the secret doors we have ever encountered, the one at the back of that hydraulic press chamber was surely the most contrived."

"Well, Holmes, you may be right, and then again perhaps you are not." Then I remembered. "But the thumb! Surely you cannot deny the evidence of the thumb found on the window sill. That is final."

"I do not deny it is final. What it is evidence of is quite another matter. The crucial problem is whether to believe it was amputated when and where Hatherley said it was. I maintain that it was not."

"Do you have any reason to doubt it?"

Holmes blew a smoke ring through his pipe. It was green, which suggested he was combining tobacco with one of his transcendental poisons. "Hatherley described the Colonel's assault as 'Very murderous indeed'. Would you agree?"

"Undoubtedly."

"Then why did he not aim for the head?"

I considered this as a doctor. "So you think he only meant to prevent Hatherley's escape?"

"By cutting off a thumb while he was using it to cling to the window sill? Rather counter-productive, don't you think, since it guaranteed that he would lose his grip? No, Watson, it never happened."

"But Holmes, his thumb was discovered by a fireman on that very window sill after the fire had been put out."

"I tell you again that it was not his thumb. I examined it. I am certain of it."

I could not help laughing. Holmes was being particularly preposterous. "It resembled nothing more than one of our new cook's burnt sausages! Not even you could have made anything of it."

"It was a sausage with a fingernail, Watson, and I have told you again and again that there are few things as suggestive as fingernails. You must have observed it had been filed into a curve following that of the finger. But that was not the crucial point. Did you happen to note any discolouration?"

"None whatsoever," said I firmly. For once I was determined not to see what Holmes expected me to see. I felt with some pride like Aristotle declaring that he loved Plato dearly but more dearly than Plato he loved truth.

To my surprise Holmes nodded approvingly. "Precisely. There was absolutely no discolouration. None whatsoever. After such a roasting, there ought to have been and yet there was none. It was unnaturally natural."

At first this sounded like Holmes's usual perversity. Then I thought of a lady I had known in her boudoir painting her nails. I noticed that it was to reinforce the natural skin tones, as is quite fashionable these days. "Why, Holmes, I think I understand!"

"Yes, Watson, you see it. Normally such colouring would be quite invisible, but in this case it was apparent because of the discolouration to the rest of the thumb. This tells us that though its owner's corpse shall soon be discovered in Whitechapel, she was not one of its denizens. By the way, remind me to send a telegram to the Yard reminding them to be on the lookout for a limbless and headless trunk"

"Why, Holmes," said I with a nervous smile, "you almost make me think that the theory you and the Ripper are one and the same person is correct. How else could you know that?"

In an instant Holmes had vanished and in his place was Mr. Mansfield's hideous Mr. Hyde grinning hideously. It was not only his face that had been transformed into a devilish mask. His body had grown hunched and his right hand was crippled by rheumatism. For a moment I swayed and was on the verge of fainting. Then the monster began to laugh uncontrollably. "Ah, Watson! Your face is one I could not have managed myself. Please do not worry that I have stumbled upon Dr. Jekyll's potion. Jack the Ripper is a myth invented to increase the circulation of *The Star* newspaper."

"Very funny, Holmes," I said indignantly, "but if cocaine has not turned you into a homicidal fiend, how can you know all that you say you do?"

"Oh, there is no mystery to it at all. It is pretty elementary class stuff, provided one has an encyclopaedic knowledge of crime. On this occasion you really shall be quite entitled to cry out that it is absurdly simple once it has been explained. You know what anniversary it is today? I mean apart from its being the first anniversary of the launch of the Peral submarine, which brother Mycroft assures me shall make naval warfare impossible for a year or two to come."

I frowned. Then I snapped my fingers. "Of course! The first six Football League matches were played last year to the day!"

"And you think that might relate to a corpse missing three-quarters?"

With an effort I restrained myself from pointing out that a "three quarter" is not a position in football. There would have been no point. Holmes's knowledge of sports is about on a par with his understanding of the motions of the planets. "Then I am at a loss, Holmes."

"It is, of course, the first anniversary of the discovery of Annie Chapman's mutilated body in Whitechapel. When the trunk of another woman is discovered a day or two from now and the death estimated as having occurred on this Sunday, then naturally everyone will assume it, too, is the Ripper's work. As for the absence of limbs, the police will suppose it is purely to prevent her identification. It will never occur to them that it is also to conceal the previous removal of a thumb."

I had just been struck by a dreadful thought. "Holmes, you don't think that it could be the corpse of that beautiful and mysterious woman? Perhaps she was in one of the cases on that cart!"

"Admirable, Watson. The trunk in the crate. You are developing a distinctly pawky if disturbingly ghoulish sense of humour that the authorities would do well to take note of. Banish that thought from your mind. There was no trunk in the crate because there was no crate in the cart. There was no crate in the cart because there was no cart on the road. There was no cart on the road – "

"Holmes! You will leave me with nothing! Please tell that at least what I saw was real! I saw that pillar of smoke from that burning house at Eyford! Do not deny that too."

Holmes shook his head sadly. "My profound apologies, Watson. I fear I must indeed deprive you of it. But let us take it slowly so that you have time to adjust and mourn. I grant you that the burning house was real. It does not follow that it was the house Hatherley was taken to, for as I have already demonstrated the freshness of the horse proves nothing. Nor can we assume that the lamp left in the hydraulic press chamber would have caused that fire. If the floors really were of stone, then a fire could not have spread so swiftly. And if as I suggested to Bradstreet the chamber was used for amalgamating molten metals, then the idea that its walls were wooden becomes just a trifle problematic. But let us first consider the evidence in support of the claim that the burning house and the old dark house were one and the same."

"It is surely conclusive. There were the footprints left by the woman and the little Englishman when they carried Hatherley from there to the train station. That alone proves he must have been there."

"Interesting. Whose were the gigantic footprints? You recall, Watson, that one set of prints were those of someone with remarkable large feet and the other set were exceptionally small."

"Why, the small ones were the lady's and the large ones were the little Englishman's."

"That would be to avoid the rule of thumb in such matters. You recall that at the time of the Lauriston Gardens Mystery, I explained how one can deduce the height of a man from the length of his stride? I was of course lying."

I was stunned. "Lying?"

"I must confess I was not entirely unaware you were already serialising your reminiscences. It was the chief reason why I was keen to have you as a fellow lodger – so that you might record my cases. But I had no intention of sharing all my secrets with Scotland Yard, so I supplied a deliberately misleading method."

"But then how did you know the height of the man?"

Holmes raised one foot and tapped the sole of his shoe. "With one very notable exception, a person's foot is about fifteen percent of their body height. Under normal circumstances, we would be forced to conclude the small footprints belonged to the fat little Englishman and the large footprints were those of the statuesque lady, who may have been the goddess Athena in disguise. It is hardly very likely, Watson. Remember how Hatherley stressed the excessive thinness of the Colonel. He would surely have obsessed on the gigantic stature of the lady and the dwarfishness of the Englishman."

"Then whose were they?"

"Oh," said Holmes with a smile, "that is obvious enough. The tall ones belonged to the King of Bohemia and the small prints were those of Tonga the cannibal dwarf. His body was never recovered from the Thames, and if he died of our gunshots, then he ought to have floated. He is probably feasting on the roasted leg of that Whitechapel lady even as we speak."

"What an amazing coincidence!" I cried. "Why, it was only last month that I agreed to the reprinting of *The Sign of the Four Men Who Stole the Agra Treasure*."

"Best shorten the title. My dear fellow, I was joking. No proper gang is complete without a gigantic thug, so the big man is no problem. Nor was a dwarf involved. I said that the rule of thumb had an exception, and this is it. We are dealing with a case of lotus feet."

I frowned. "An Oriental malady, Holmes?"

"In a manner of speaking," said he grimly. "In Japan, the feet of women can be bound for aesthetic effect and to restrict mobility."

I was aware of my friend's interest in Japanese culture, but this seemed like wishful thinking on his part. "Come now, Holmes. Do you have any reason to suppose a Japanese woman was involved in this affair?"

"The footprints were those of a lady shuffling along, taking tiny steps. They were not the footsteps either of a normal child or of a dwarf. I cannot be mistaken in this. And besides, it confirms the true reason for that amputation. There is a second rule of thumb in this case, you see."

"For heaven's sake, Holmes, what do you mean?"

For answer Holmes held up his little finger and bent it back as if he meant to break it. "It is the smallest finger that grips tightest on the hilt of a sword. Therefore, as an act of atonement, it is the top of the left little finger that is amputated in Japan to make the amputee more dependent on his boss. Possibly Hatherley had fingered some member of the gang. The fact that this was not the little finger, but the thumb, tells us our mastermind is not himself Japanese, but is interested in Japanese culture. Just as Bartitsu is an adaptation of jiu-jitsu, so our mastermind has modified another practise to suit his own needs. Heartless though he may be, he is a man after my own heart."

It was time to inject a healthy dose of commonsense. "Well, that is very ingenious, Holmes, but it hardly counts for much. All it means is that Hatherley was not borne away by the lady and the Englishman. He could still have been carried off by others."

"True. But you recall, I said I failed to discover the least clue there to suggest where the gang had gone. There were no tracks, you see. Not only were there none to support the story of the cart, but no carriage tracks either, which casts serious doubt upon whether Hatherley could ever have been brought there from the train station."

"But Hatherley's house had so much in common with that one," I urged.

"Roses and gravel drives? I wonder how many thousands of homes in England have roses and gravel drives. Consider, too, Hatherley told us that at no time during his journey did the carriage ever go uphill, yet the burning house was atop a hill. That it was burning and so fiercely argues against the identification too, particularly if you still accept that the citadel was of stone floors and presumably capable of withstanding a medieval siege involving catapults hurling fireballs. At the very least, you must accept the house we saw had to have been set alight long after Hatherley's ordeal, for Hatherley waited at the station for an hour before he took his train to Reading. During all that time did he hear, smell, or see any sign of that inferno? Did he catch cries of '*Fire!*'? There were none. No, it was probably set alight hours later to conceal the evidence. Or perhaps I should say – to conceal the *absence* of evidence, since there was no sign of those counterfeit coins or of that hydraulic press."

"But there was that immense tail of smoke rising up to the heavens, Holmes."

"Was it not too immense? Doubtless that twister of dust was shot up into the air when the smoke from the funnel of our train was spotted. It would have been then that the explosives were detonated."

"Explosives? Dust?"

"Explosives to launch the dust. Fuller's earth to be precise. It is far lighter than normal dust and hangs in the air for much longer – hence is ideal for spectacular effects. One day your accounts of my adventures shall be projected onto screens as a series of moving images. Then that pillar of smoke like the twisters of Kansas shall be reproduced with fuller's earth and nobody will guess the original was nothing more than that. Did you not feel your eyes itching when we visited the burning house? I observed every one of those firemen rubbing their eyes. It is an irritant, you see."

"But Holmes," I protested, "Hatherley detected not the smallest trace of fuller's earth in that chamber."

"Precisely," said he with his usual perversity. "And in this case the *absence of evidence* really is the *evidence of absence*. Did I not say that a man as cunning as the Colonel would hardly have invented so fantastic a tale as that fuller's earth was being pressed into bricks for no reason at all only to then fail to sprinkle a little of it in the chamber where it was supposed to be compressed? It was a double bluff. He made the claim so that when none was seen it, would be assumed that he had to be lying. There were actually huge stockpiles of it. Once its intended use was out of

301

the question and it had to be destroyed, it was put to that dramatic use instead."

"Intended use? What intended use?"

Holmes shrugged. "There we enter the realms of speculation where even great detectives fear to tread. Still, it is always pleasing to speculate purely as an intellectual exercise. The London dockers strike shows every sign of concluding peacefully, despite all previous fears to the contrary. Trade unions shall now be viewed as an alternative to revolution and so to be welcomed. Now, our criminal consultant could have been commissioned to commit some terrorist act to be blamed on the dockers to discredit their movement. The fuller's earth would be used to make the act far more spectacular, since seen from miles away. Then it is perceived that trade unions might be integrated into the *status quo.* The action is cancelled. So our criminal consultant decides to put all that fuller's earth to good use by putting on a fine show to convince me to extend my sojourn out of London."

"That hardly discredits the theory that the press was being used by a gang of coiners," I pointed out. "You do yourself an injustice, Holmes, by disregarding your own brilliant explanation to Inspector Bradstreet on how the hydraulic press was used as a furnace for amalgamating the molten metals to create the German silver used in the counterfeit coins. It was a master stroke to stamp them while they were still cooling."

"And the wooden walls? Would molten metals have been poured at a temperature in excess of two-thousand degrees into a room with wooden walls?"

"Well, of course every theory has its initial difficulties," I explained. "But a fire would only have been started if some of the metal splashed out of the iron trough. It was just a matter of pouring the metals with care."

Holmes nodded. "A little like using Prussic Acid as a gargle – provided that one does not swallow it, there is no danger whatsoever."

"Exactly. And when you add the overwhelming evidence of all those crates full of counterfeit coins, your earlier explanation surely holds water."

"Just as a wooden container might hold molten metal."

I could not understand why Holmes was being so sarcastic about his own explanation. "Well, really, Holmes, I do think you are being a little unreasonable. Not a single coin was found anywhere among the ruins of that house. That proves the coiners must have taken them all with them. Therefore they had to have been in those crates on that cart seen speeding towards Reading."

"Brilliant, Watson! But there is one thing I still don't quite understand. If that cart was burdened with several travellers and a number of crates full of counterfeit coins, how is it that the peasant claimed it was travelling at such speed? It ought to have been crawling along at about the same rate as that hydraulic press descended to stamp all that white-hot metal."

"But the evidence, Holmes!"

"Ah, the evidence! There were absolutely no signs of coining, which proves how cunning the gang were. The cart vanished on reaching Reading, which was a further demonstration of the gang's genius. But might there not be another possible explanation for why none save for that one poor peasant ever saw a cart? Rather than imagine thousands of coins, will not a single coin do? I am referring to the sovereign that peasant received for telling his story."

"Holmes," I protested indignantly, "you agreed with Bradstreet's theory it had to be a gang of coiners since the hydraulic press could not have been put to any other use."

"I did not agree with him," snapped he peevishly. "He agreed with me. The difference is crucial. If you recall, he said there was no doubt as to the nature of the gang and it was I who at once concurred that they were coiners using the hydraulic press as a furnace. Bradstreet, you will remember, at once nodded his head approvingly as if I had taken the words right out of his mouth. When he repeats them to his superiors, I promise you I shall disappear from the scene as miraculously as that fictitious cart."

"Oh, really, Holmes."

"There is no 'Oh, really' about it, Watson, save for the fact that he really did get promoted after that affair of the man with the twisted lip by taking all the credit due to me for cracking the case. He shall look very foolish when he tries to argue that a highly flammable hydraulic press was used amalgamating metals at a temperatures in excess of two-thousand degrees Fahrenheit, particularly since no trace of the copper and zinc essential to the production of what is termed 'German silver' were found in the ruins of the building. I very much doubt we shall be seeing Detective Inspector Bradstreet of the Yard again."

I was shocked at such uncharacteristically petty vindictiveness on my hero's part. "Holmes, you cannot mean it. Would you damage a man's career simply because on one occasion he stole the credit from you? Think of his family."

"Family?" Holmes frowned. "I did not know that detectives could have families. Lestrade . . . Jones . . . Hopkins . . . Gregson . . . Baynes . . . MacDonald . . . Dupin . . . No, no, we are not the marrying kind. Which reminds me. In view of recent events at Cleveland Street, I had best ensure my street urchins do not congregate before 221b for some time to come.

But as to your insinuation that this is pure spite on my part, it is quite untrue. Bradstreet is a bad apple. He took bribes, you know."

"Surely not!"

"Oh, he was not alone. I wonder how many coppers that beggar Hugh Boone dropped into constable's helmets in his role as President of the Amateur Mendicant Society to ensure blind Justice looked the other way. Why do you think Boone remained in custody at Bow Street contrary to all customary procedures and was never required to wash? Now that Bradstreet is at the Yard, I have no doubt he has been receiving bigger bribes from the current Napoleon of Crime. Do not look so shocked, Doctor. How else could Adam Worth have operated with impunity for so long?"

"But if you do not trust Bradstreet, why did you take him with you to Eyford?"

"Because I do not trust him. It was to prevent him from informing the local police we were on our way. Do you seriously imagine a gang could have continued operating undetected for so long without police cooperation? To bribe bent coppers with suspect coins would certainly have been amusing."

Here was Holmes's little trip. "Then you admit they might have been coining!"

"Oh, it is always possible our mastermind was also involved in coining as one among many activities. If so, was it was to help finance his move to London. But that press had nothing to do with coining. Surely you must see that now."

"In that case, Holmes, whatever possessed you to stress it was their one activity?"

"I knew as well as our mastermind did that a year ago, a gang of coiners had passed through Reading on their way elsewhere. It was a useful cut-and-dried story with which to warp my mind. I saw through it, but used it to warp Bradstreet's. You recall I deduced Hatherley had to have a reproduction of that Wright painting in his office. Wright's travelling showman is playing at being an Isaac Newton, just as Bradstreet plays at being a Sherlock Holmes. That gave me the idea."

I must have looked blank.

"But surely, Watson, you must know Newton was an alchemist, though he had to perform his philosophical investigations discreetly, just as my own into spiritual telegraphy have to be out of the public eye. Image is important. By the way, should I appear to perish prematurely. I am trusting to your wife, whom I gather regularly communes with the spirit of her deceased mother, to communicate with mine, if that is possible."

"How did you know Mary is a medium?" asked in some surprise. "I had thought it best not to tell you. I had no idea you would be sympathetic."

Holmes chuckled. "Why, you recall how distressed she was when she learnt her father had died many years ago? She had not seen him since she was a child sent away from India to be brought up in Britain. She was so very upset because she had long sensed his presence and so assumed that he was alive. In fact, that presence meant he was dead and desperately striving to communicate with her. But that is a subject for another time."

I thought it best to change the subject to the less controversial of the two available. "Well, what has alchemy got to do with coining?"

"Surely that is obvious. The one is the antithesis of the other. Coining is sham alchemy. Naturally, then, Isaac Newton hated coiners like the devil, particularly after he was put in charge of the Mint. So you see now why thinking of this counterfeit Newton engaged in sham alchemical experiments turned my thoughts that way."

"But a showman is not an alchemist!"

"No, but alchemy works by repeatedly killing and resurrecting its materials. This showman is reducing that white bird to the alchemical 'crow's head', which is to say to inert matter, and is about to resurrect it to demonstrate his godlike power over life and death. Of course, in reality he is just a foolish old man who does not perceive he is soon to die. In all his getting of knowledge, he has neglected to get wisdom."

"All that is well and good, Holmes," said I impatiently, "but there was a gang and it did escape. It could not have just vanished into thin air. Where did it go? Where is it now?

"In general terms that is self-evident. The chief aim of this entire business was to get me out of London. Therefore, that is where they are now. Why it was so vital to have me away from a labyrinthine metropolis of six million souls I will admit I do not as yet comprehend. As for how they left Eyford, that is too obvious for words."

"Not to me," said I meekly.

"Why, I have established that the true headquarters of their organisation could not have been the burning building, but must have been somewhere else entirely. But in that case, why should they have deposited Hatherley so near to the train station? Clearly to ensure he travelled back to London from there. Of course, they would be on the same train."

"But the porter never saw anything."

Holmes smiled condescendingly. "Does it not strike you as odd, Watson, that the same sleepy porter whom Hatherley witnessed yawning and rubbing his eyes at the end of a long day when he arrived at Eyford at eleven was the same sleepy porter he saw again an hour before the first

305

morning train drew in? You might say, though I know you will not, that he had just taken up his post when Hatherley first saw him. You will not say that, Watson, because I know you will apply the test of the fresh horse. If he had just taken up his pointless post, then he would have been wide awake rather than acting like a man worn out after a long day. The conclusion is obvious: Either he was a member of the gang, or at the very least he was in their pay."

I shook my head. "That is impossible, Holmes. Even if Hatherley was not in such bad shape as he later claimed, he must still have been badly shaken. If the porter was a gang member, he would have offered to take him to Dr. Becher's house a short walk away. Hatherley would never have suspected he was being returned to his tormentors."

"The porter would not have done so if the plan was to make Hatherley believe he had escaped, only to retake him just as his train was approaching London. I have said that this was something of a scientific experiment, and Hatherley was the laboratory animal. First he was traumatised in that chamber of doom and by subsequent events. Finally he underwent physical torture in your surgery as his thumb was torn out at the roots. They probably used your instruments and medical supplies to do so. It was then placed in a saline solution and before they left via the window. He was informed it would be sewn back on provided he completed his mission in time. He was told he had twelve hours. But I fear, Watson, those twelve hours are due to expire."

Even as Holmes spoke, there came a terrific crash from above as of breaking glass and splintering wood. Holmes leaped to his feet, his eyes afire.

"Ah, I should have known! Quick, man, quick, or we shall be too late!"

With the spring of a cocainised cheetah, Holmes had bounded out of the room, and then I heard him ascending the stairs three steps at a time as he made up the pathetic rear. I found him in Hatherley's bedroom, standing motionless as a statue before the broken window and gazing out at the street below.

"A ladder!" he muttered. "I might have known it. Borrowed from your account of the Jefferson Hope affair, I'll be bound! For all we know the very same ladder Stamford used to sneak you into St. Barts. Well, well, I should not begrudge Hatherley his digit. If he is in time for it to take, then I wish him joy of the worm. Come, Watson, I am panting for 221b. Save for Simpson, my Irregulars shall be scattered to the four corners of the metropolis forthwith in search of the gang's new headquarters. Fly, you beauties, fly! My bones tell me it has to be near my lodgings else why all that trouble to have me out of the city? And every cloud has a silver lining, even one composed of fuller's earth. The quest will be a great adventure for my Baker Street urchins, and should quell their calls for a pay rise in solidarity with the dockers. A bob a job indeed! I cannot have them picketing 221b, not in view of that Cleveland Street business and your new acquaintanceship with that fellow Oscar Wilde."

"Holmes! I cried indignantly. "I dined with him once by chance at the Langham, along with some highly respectable gentlemen and an American publisher. That hardly constitutes an acquaintanceship." Yet I saw the wisdom of his precautions. Our enemies could easily misrepresent our use of my detective's boy scouts. Had not Holmes brought down Moriarty by spreading dark rumours about his proclivities on the basis of that Greuze painting of a pubescent girl?

We took a cab back to Baker Street. When we found our way blocked by no less than four removal vans before the empty yellow house opposite 221b, Holmes leaped out and dived into the traffic, quite heedless of the risk to life and limb. A whistle brought his boys to him from every corner and even a manhole. An instant later they had their instructions and were dispersing to the four corners of the metropolis. If the gang was above the Thames and below the clouds they would find it.

I entered what had once been our rooms to find Holmes already bent over a map of London like a bird of prey, circling above a jungle and attentive to every rustle that might mean his next dinner. He had drawn a circle with 221b at its centre and was perusing the area through a powerful magnifying glass, tapping at each point of the compass in turn with his famously elongated forefinger. I watched him as one mesmerised until a fortunate flash of light from a window of the vacant Camden House across the road broke the spell. I could be of no further assistance. It was time to return to my wife. I bade him farewell, but I suppose he did not hear.

The removal vans were gone and I easily hailed a cab. The traffic was moving freely once more. Sunday. Our cook would be serving sausages. I winced. Doctor though I was, I could not stop thinking about that cooked finger.

If Holmes was right, then somewhere in London the engineer's thumb was being sewed back on. I started as a cry of pain rang out. How foolish! I had thought it was him. "Pull yourself together, Watson," I chided myself with a chuckle. "What you need is a medicinal brandy."

It had been him. The reader should not reprove me for failing to realise it. Holmes himself never dreamed that the new spider of the city would brazenly locate his web's nerve centre in Camden House straight across from 221b. It was a perverse little joke. Holmes would scour the city to the north, south, west and east and never think the trick he supposed played on the police at Eyford was being played on him. As he considered that map through his glass, a new and more deadly Colonel was gazing through his famous airgun's telescopic sight to follow the detective's every move. That trembling finger on the trigger was stilled only by the paternal hand upon his shoulder of the future Napoleon of Crime and a reassuring word whispered in his ear: "Soon, my friend, but not quite yet."

William Hogarth – "*Marriage a la Mode: 1 The Marriage Settlement*"

The Reappearance of
Lady Diana Spencer
Continuing "The Noble Bachelor"

"**H**is conduct was certainly not very gracious."

"Ah, Watson," said Holmes, smiling, "perhaps you would not be very gracious either, if, after all the trouble of wooing and wedding, you found yourself deprived in an instant of wife and fortune. I think we may judge Lord St. Simon very mercifully, and thank our stars that we are never likely to find ourselves in the same position. Draw your chair up, and hand me my violin, for the only problem which we have still to solve is how to while away these bleak autumnal evenings."

I sprang from my easy chair, in my heat upsetting the seat I had been propping both my aching legs upon. I could have struck Holmes with his precious Stradivarius, so outraged was I at that thinly veiled allusion to my fiancee's inheritance lost at the bottom of the Thames. It would have been worth the loss of a Stradivarius to dent that frontal development of his and set his organs of humanity to work. If the thinking machine had any. How could it, if it could so cynically insinuate I secretly meant to dredge up her jewels from the sea bottom? I would never so much as told my love had not the treasure been lost. Better to forfeit my angel forever than risk being called a gold-digger. (That Agra treasure chest is today filled with real treasure, for I use it to keep her communications with me from beyond the grave via Lady Conan Doyle. It is as precious to me now as the tin dispatch box beneath it crammed with notes on cases shared with Sherlock Holmes.)

I thought I saw the meaning of my friend's snide remark that though Hatty Doran had been in London for the Season, she could never have fallen in love with a man during all those months. Of course, Holmes had not forgotten how I claimed to have fallen in love with Mary Morstan at first sight. Or second sight, to be honest. He was slyly insinuating he did not credit my claim! That was it. He was warning me against our whirlwind romance. He was foretelling we reap as we sowed. We would inherit the whirlwind.

"I must get back to Baskerville Hall," I muttered. "You were right, Holmes, I should not have deserted Sir Henry's side even for a few hours, fiancée or no fiancée. I assure you I shall not do so again." I was gone, slamming the door behind me.

311

One pain drives out consciousness of another. So hurt was I that I quite failed to notice the pain from my jezail bullet wound had vanished the instant I announced my return to Dartmoor. Much later it occurred to me it had returned earlier at the very moment I had declared I ought to pay a lightning visit to my fiancée to see how she was battling with the seating arrangements for our wedding. The chief difficulty had been where to seat Holmes. It would not be a problem now.

During the whole of my train journey back to Baskerville Hall, I mulled over what to do next. It was not Holmes's fault. It was in his nature to be unfeeling. I had to choose between him and Mary, that was clear. A clean break was best. Once this affair was over, I would shake the dust of 221b from off my feet. There was no point in seeing Holmes again. He had his pipe, his cocaine bottle, and his violin. He did not need me. I did not need him now.

So preoccupied was I with these miserable thoughts I quite failed to register that the queerly comical Italian priest who had shared my compartment on the journey down now accompanied me on my return to Dartmoor. I faintly recall glimpsing his face reflected in the window grinning at me as at some private joke. It never occurred to me that we would ever meet again.

The truth was, though, that like Shakespeare's *Antony* I could not renounce Holmes any more than Antony could his Cleopatra. Age cannot wither him nor custom stale his infinite variety. I was unable to bring myself to speak of how he had hurt me, though – hence I never raised the difficulties I had had with that affair of the eponymous Noble Bachelor until he happened to speak of it himself just before the case of the disappearing bridegroom began. It was immediately before the arrival of the client in the absurd Georgiana Spencer hat that he revealed the truth. He had known Lord Robert St. Simon was intent upon poisoning his bride Hatty Doran slowly but surely over the course of several married years. The Spanish serpent would have been a slow as the Roylott's adder was swift in that earlier affair of the Speckled Band – not that St. Simon meant her any ill.

I should mention that I write these words only for the serious and discreet student of Holmes. In popular versions of my accounts alterations and amendments were deemed necessary. So, for example, in *The Strand*, "A Case of Identity" opens with a brief excerpt from a far longer and more philosophical dialogue concerning the merits of fact versus fiction. That excerpt closed with Holmes offering me a pinch of snuff from a baroque snuffbox of old gold. Neither of us takes snuff and Holmes strives after a Spartan simplicity in all things. More to the point, few actions have ever given my friend more perverse pleasure than his absolute refusal to receive

312

any gift from the King of Bohemia for attempting to recover photographic evidence of a secret wedding. It would have given Holmes still greater joy to have sent back whatever later present the King might send him. The humiliation of His Majesty would have been absolute.

However, once the detective had declined to accept His Majesty's hand, to say of nothing of the ring in it, Bohemian pride required that something be accepted by Holmes whether he liked it or not. A later offer of a knighthood was snubbed. Holmes would not kneel before a man he insisted was on such a different level from himself.

At least His Majesty had the good sense to see he would require the services of a still greater detective to ascertain how to make Holmes an offer he could not refuse. Accordingly, he had contacted the government and from Mycroft Holmes had learnt of one snuffbox his brother would certainly cherish. Unfortunately, it was unavailable. A copy of it existed, though, one that legend had it was produced under the supervision of the original artist. Some even believe it was the work of the painter himself. It was to be auctioned by the so-called Duke of Balmoral following the failure of his second son's wedding to the American heiress, Hatty Doran.

Holmes had fallen in love with the works of the artist Hogarth during his time at St. Barts, for during his time there he had passed by the latter's murals upon the grand staircase every day. I have never seen them myself, since for reasons it is unnecessary to go into here, I have only ever entered the hospital by a back door. Nevertheless, Holmes assures me they are magnificent. A snuffbox by Hogarth could hardly fail to delight, quite aside from its slight associations with the Holmes family.

The snuffbox was of course a painted one. I do not mean it was akin to those painted snuffboxes distributed by the Emperor Napoleon when he visited England in 1855. His six Napoleons had adorned six snuffboxes. No, the snuffbox Holmes could hardly refuse was the one featured at the start of Hogarth's tragedy in six scenes entitled *Marriage a la Mode*.

Holmes had good reason for coveting that series, for having consulted the National Gallery records, he had confirmed it was mortgaged by one John Fenton Cawthorne M.P. to a Mr. Holmes by 15 June, 1795. Then it was auctioned at Christie's on 10 February, 1797 and acquired by the great collector John Julius Angerstein. His collection was purchased by the government in 1824 to form the core of the National Gallery collection, which first opened its doors to the public that year.

Holmes deduced this Mr. Holmes had to have been one of his ancestors. Unsurprisingly, therefore, the sitting room at 221b had long been adorned with prints of those six scenes. I think I may have mentioned in passing that when St. Simon entered, he had glanced to left and right taking them in, though at the time I failed to realise as Holmes evidently had he was eyeing them with the greatest suspicion.

What did surprise me on returning to Baker Street at the time of "A Case of Identity" was that those prints had blossomed into colour, and the old gold snuffbox in the first scene now shone forth. Since my previous visit, the prints had been replaced by the Balmoral copies of the original paintings.

"Take a care not to reveal this series is in my hands, Watson," said he, and I saw he was but a shade paler than the average Londoner. He was flushing with pride. "A certain presiding Napoleon of Crime might be tempted to acquire them to complement his portrait of Georgiana Spencer, given allusions to that family and to the Balmorals. Speak of the King's gift as a real snuffbox rather than as that empty one Lord Squanderfield is using to mime the taking of snuff as he practises before that mirror there. He has been in the Hall of Mirrors at Versailles, you see. You can tell that from the red heels to his shoes, which are *de rigeur* at the French court. I must remember to purchase a pair against the day I shall accept the Legion of Honour. Judging from Squanderfield's condition, it was not the only palace of fantasies he frequented in France, though elsewhere the mirrors adorned the ceilings. You see that, like Lord Robert St. Simon, he bears the scars from Cupid's poisoned darts."

"Syphilis?" I asked in some surprise. "Surely not, Holmes. I can see a black patch on this Lord's neck, but it covers signs of scrofula. He must have died a consumptive. And as for St. Simon, I grant you he was prematurely aged, stooped and bent his knees as he walked. There was also some early hair loss. It is possible he consorted with infected women. It is just as likely, though, that he was consumptive too."

"No, no," said Holmes with his usual undue confidence. "I blundered badly in the case of that corpse found at Birlstone. I should have peeped under the sticking plaster on the chin of what had once been a face. I am not about to make the same mistake twice. Our Lord Squanderfield there will one day have a face just as ruined as that corpse if the sickness is allowed to run its course. So will St. Simon, which is why he is still a bachelor in his forties. No Englishwoman would have him."

I could not help laughing. "Oh, really, Holmes, do you claim to have the eyes of a lynx, that you can see through walls and beneath that painted patch?"

"In a manner of speaking," he answered calmly. "I can do so with my mind's eye. Consider that the patch is not flesh coloured but black. It attracts attention. His beauty spot complements it. Now, if that patch concealed signs of syphilis, one would expect an attempt to make it inconspicuous. But scrofula would encourage some degree of sympathy.

Therefore, the choice of that black patch would suggest that, as you say, it is scrofula. Yet even if it were the king's evil, as it was then called, one would not expect it to be advertised quite so blatantly. The first Lady Diana Spencer, you know, had just such signs of scrofula on her neck and died a consumptive. Efforts were made to conceal it. No, no, this is syphilis, but we are meant to suppose it is scrofula. That father of the bride minutely studying the marriage contract to ensure every "*I*" is dotted is missing the point. Either that or he chooses to make the black patch his blind spot."

"Wonderful!" I cried. "I am not sure I agree with your reading of this painting, Holmes, but there is so much to see here. It just goes to show life cannot compete with art."

"On the contrary," said my friend with determination. "It demonstrates quite the opposite. Do not think that Hogarth was inventing the story here out of thin air. Think of it. He began painting this scene in 1742, the self-same year the legend of the Hound of the Baskervilles was penned by one Hugo Baskerville. Do you imagine theirs was the only family accursed down the generations? That was also the year the notorious wastrel Johnny Spencer sold the paintings at Althorp. Lady Sarah Churchill, Duchess of Marlborough, the de facto head of the Spencer family, had previously cut him off, along with her other heirs, save for her favourite, Lady Diana Spencer, to whom she had meant to leave her vast fortune and huge properties. But Lady Diana died young and a reconciliation with Johnny took place. He would get everything if he married but nothing if he did not. Legend has it she presented him with an alphabetical list of candidates, and he chose the one at the top of the page to save time. Since the wedding took place on St. George's, Hanover Square, on a St. Valentine's Day, that was untrue."

"How so, Holmes?"

"Why, the story is a piece of pawky humour. It recalls the St. Valentine's game of picking names out of a hat, the same game Hatty Doran was forced to play at the behest of her father. I cannot see how else she should have hit upon St. Simon. With his legendary wealth, Mr. Doran could easily have purchased a duke."

"But what makes you believe Hogarth was thinking of Johnny Spencer?"

"Given his outrageous lifestyle, it was practically inevitable he would be afflicted with venereal disease just like Lord Squanderfield here. But Hogarth is unfair. It would seem that, despite his dissolute nature, Johnny's wife loved him dearly. Of course, a satirist like Hogarth did not worry about that. You see those chained hounds before the bride and groom there? Convicts chained together were said to be 'wedded'. Ah,

Watson, when I saw how St. Simon reacted to my Hogarth prints, I became more determined than ever to bring about his separation from Hatty Doran, lest history repeat itself yet again."

I was now thoroughly confused. "I don't understand, Holmes," I confessed meekly. "I was under the distinct impression you did no more than ascertain after the event that Hatty Doran had fled from the wedding breakfast to answer a summons from her true husband by an earlier secret marriage. How can you say you brought about a separation if the second marriage was bigamous?"

"Because her first marriage would hardly have been recognised in any court of law, to say nothing of the religious authorities. Incidentally, she was never married to Francis Hay Moulton."

"But you told St. Simon you had it on the best authority that they were," I objected indignantly. "How can you argue against those overwhelming proofs you yourself supplied?"

Holmes frowned disapprovingly. "One of the capital errors is an appeal to authorities. You a doctor, and yet you unquestioningly accept my assurance? Have you learnt nothing from me, Watson? There was not one shred of evidence. Where was the marriage certificate?"

"Of really, Holmes, that is nit picking. The man was taken by Apaches. He was lucky to escape with his life. All his papers would have been scattered to the winds."

"And the witnesses to the wedding?"

"Killed by Geronimo."

"And the priest?"

"Scalped."

"How very convenient. And yet, I had it on the best possible authority that a wedding was performed. Clearly a willing suspension of disbelief is not restricted to official works of fiction. By the way, Watson, I seem to recall the Apaches surrendered in 1886, a full two years before Moulton tracked the Dorans down to London. How do you explain why he waited so long before informing his wife he was alive?"

I frowned. Then I snapped my fingers. "Amnesia!"

"Amnesia. How elementary! But then of course all your solutions seem absurdly simple to me once you have explained them."

I suspected Holmes of sarcasm. It would have been beneath my dignity to enquire. I appealed to reason instead. "Well, if there was no evidence to support their assertion, why did St. Simon accept it without question?"

Holmes nodded approvingly. "Now, that is an intelligent question – or rather, it would be if you were framing it as one, which of course you would not think to do. Let us ask another. If he did accept they were

316

secretly married, why did he not at once charge Moulton with inciting his wife to commit bigamy? Why not threaten to take the matter to court unless he retained the alimony? You see that whether he accepted the assertion or not, his passivity seems inexplicable. So explain it, Watson. Use my methods."

"Obviously something must have happened between the disappearance and reappearance of the bride to cause him to change his mind."

"What could that something be?"

"Had he seen someone?"

"Ask rather whether his daughter had seen someone aside from Moulton."

"Why, she had seen no one other than Flora Millar."

"Ah, yes, the lady friend of St. Simon whom he feared just as the King of Bohemia did Irene Adler, and for the same reason. They had it in their power to prevent the weddings from ever taking place. How do you suppose Miss Flora Millar might have made St. Simon's marriage to Hatty Doran, or anyone else for that matter, quite impossible?"

"I cannot fathom it."

"Flora Millar was actually Lady Flora St. Simon."

"Holmes!"

"Oh, it is perfectly true. Poetic justice is the best revenge. St. Simon married Flora Millar in his youth. How delicious to work with the bride to convince the world that she, too, was secretly married! Of course, St. Simon knew her tale was a fantastic one, but he was powerless to object for fear that Lady Flora would reveal the truth about their own secret marriage. Beautiful, is it not?"

"Criminal."

"Some crimes are beautiful."

I knew a specialist who took as much pleasure in a well-developed case of gout as another man might in a moss rose. There is no accounting for taste. Besides, at that moment I had other concerns. "Holmes, you told me you deduced she could not have fallen in love with any man in the few months she had been in England. You said she had to have had a lover or husband in America."

He had detected a trace of resentment in my tone. "My dear Watson, I did not for a moment mean to cast aspersions on your painfully sincere passion for Miss Morstan. As for my claim that Miss Doran could not have fallen in love with any man during her sojourn in England, I assure you I spoke the absolute truth. Nor could she have done so in America. But surely that is obvious."

"Not to me."

"Well, it should be soon enough." Holmes slithered down lazily into the depths of his easy chair. "It is safe to reveal the truth to you now, though of course you must never reveal it. As with all your popular accounts, Watson, your intention ought to be to misdirect the public far from the truth. Now let us review the ostensible facts of the case and see if you cannot deduce that truth for yourself. And to make your task a little easier I shall provide you with a clue in the form of the final solution: Poison. A poison, I might add, the recipe for which has been handed down from father to son of the Balmorals for generations. It is, moreover, the same poison by which Lord Squanderfield over there ruins his bride in Hogarth's little tragedy, so you see that the Balmorals was one of the families the satirist had in mind."

"What, you would make of St. Simon another Grimesby Roylott?"

"Say, rather, that Grimesby Roylott slipping a serpent into his daughter's boudoir was but the shadow of this crime. Now recall the instant Hatty Doran turned round at the altar and saw Francis Hay Moulton seated in a pew reserved for the families of the bride and groom. Are you imagining that?"

"I can see it."

"Good. Picture the moment preceding it."

I thought for a moment. "That would have to be when her father left her to take his seat in the pew reserved for him."

"Now tell me why she glanced towards the front pew where Moulton was sitting. Which was it?"

"Why, I suppose Moulton must been sitting in Doran's pew. Doran would have hesitated when he saw Moulton there. That was why the daughter turned around."

"I always look for precedents, Watson. In this case, the one that most readily comes to mind is Macbeth seeing the ghost of the murdered Banquo occupying his place at the feast. Would you not agree?"

I hesitated to do so, remembering that one of my friend's most cherished precepts is that when one has eliminated the impossible, then whatever remains, no matter how improbable, must be the truth. What Holmes was proposing was clearly impossible, since a man like Doran would surely have had the intruder thrown out of the church. I therefore cudgelled my brains for some suitably improbable alternative. Then I had it. "Holmes, Mr. Doran was blind. He had to be. To all those present, it would have seemed as if the father led his daughter up the aisle, but in reality it was the daughter who led the father. She had to turn round at the altar to guide him to his place. She sat him down next to her secret husband without his ever realising he was not alone. Nobody thought to ask

318

Moulton to leave since they assumed he was with Doran. That explains everything, does it not?"

To my very great disappointment, Holmes seemed amused rather than impressed by my brilliant suggestion. "Better late than never, Watson," said he with a chuckle. "Of course, it was the first possibility I considered, though needless to say I instantly rejected it. We are getting ahead of ourselves, but you recall her wedding dress was found in the Serpentine recreational lake not far from the Doran's home? Before the police set to work dragging it for corpses, they naturally asked Doran to identity the dress and the wedding ring recovered with it. They also showed him the note discovered in one of the dress pockets."

"Which proves he was blind!" I cried triumphantly. "He would have recognised the handwriting as Moulton's! Besides, if he was not blind, how could he have failed to see Moulton writing that note while seated beside him?"

"Excellent, Watson! But you are forgetting that the note was initialled *'F.H.M.'* He would surely have mentioned to the police that those were the initials of Hatty's former fiancé. No, no, either he was lying, or Francis Hay Moulton was not the gentleman's true name, or both. As I say, we are getting ahead of ourselves, but please docket that. In the meantime, I will grant you this: Perhaps Doran was indeed blind, and so failed to see Moulton seated beside him, but if so it was a wilful blindness. Or say, rather that he *chose* to see but not observe."

"Well," said I reluctantly, "I suppose the blind theory has some holes in it. And yet wait a moment – need Doran have known anything about the presumed death of Moulton? He could not have done, which would explain why he could have been no more than irritated to discover the former fiancé taking a seat in his reserved pew."

"The paper!" cried Holmes in triumph. "To be sure, he knew the secret lay there. Remember, Hatty Doran claimed she fainted dead away on reading a press account of the Apache attack in which Moulton died. Picture her father finding her on the ground still clutching that paper in her hand, muttering Moulton's name as she would hundreds of times more over the coming months of her delirium. Once Doran had finally succeeded in wresting that paper from her, he would have read every word with the keenest attention. Surely he found that reference to Moulton's death at the hands of Geronimo's Apaches."

"That cannot be, Holmes," I protested. "If he had thought Moulton dead, he would have cried out in amazement on seeing what he would have thought his ghost. Why did he not do so? Why did he not scream, 'Keep him out! For Christ's sake, keep him out!'?"

"Because he knew full well Moulton was not dead."

319

"He was in contact with the Apaches?"

"There were no Apaches. Did I not say they surrendered in 1886? Can you think of no precedent that would explain this?"

I dredged my memory for references to other Indian atrocities. "I believe that the Mohawks were falsely accused of perpetrating the Boston Tea Party."

"To be precise, the actors in that tragedy masqueraded as Mohawks. What, then, if those Apaches were not Apaches but men in the pay of Doran? They had been ordered to murder him. Instead they enslaved him. I believe you erroneously described Moulton as sunburned. Our lights were low. He was of mixed race. That made his enslavement an easier matter."

"Ah. Was his mixed race the real reason Moulton declined to consent to the match?"

"Oh, Miss Doran was never interested in Moulton. Her heart belonged to quite another and does still."

That could not be right. "But she was sick for months after the announcement of his death!"

"Crafty sick – at least it was after a time. The horror of the news brought home to her the ruthlessness of her father. Plus Doran was determined to marry her to some English aristocrat. For her, marriage to any man would have been a fate worse than death, and had he understood why, he might well have tried to kill her too. Feigning sickness was her way of putting off the evil day, but the pretence could not continue forever. She had to be permanently free of so dangerously violent a father, whom she now knew was a robber baron in the most literal sense."

"How do you mean?"

"American slang is very expressive," said he thoughtfully. "You recall she told us her father struck a rich pocket? In mining parlance, a 'rich pocket' refers to the discovery of a mass of gold or any valuable mineral deposit, but with my knowledge of criminal underworld, I understood her real meaning. She had hinted at it when she said the richer her father became, the poor Moulton was. Robber barons are very aptly named. You see now what she meant when she whispered to her confidante Alice that someone was guilty of claim jumping?"

"But we know what she meant, Holmes," I reminded my friend. "She was damning St. Simon for committing bigamy."

"No, no, claim jumping implies a knowing guilt. She could hardly accuse St. Simon of bigamy if she was the guilty party. Her father had picked Moulton's rich pocket. That was why the man who may once have been Doran's partner desired revenge."

320

"By humiliating him? Then why did he not speak out in the church and declare the wedding bigamous?"

"Setting aside whether it was, revenge is a dish best served cold. Besides, Moulton was hardly the only one seeking revenge. We will come to them. You recall what happened next?"

"She glanced over at Moulton a second time and he put his finger to his lips to signify she should proceed with the ceremony. The third time she looked over at him she saw him writing a note that was obviously intended for her. It was the one instructing her to come when called. He slipped the note to her while she and St. Simon were leaving the church."

"Too fast, Watson, too fast!" Holmes cried, signalling frantically with his upheld hands for me to slow down. "Do you not recall that St. Simon said they were heading towards the vestry at the time when she dropped her bouquet?"

"Perfectly well."

"And that it was while she was passing along the front pew that she dropped her bouquet into it?"

"Certainly."

"Note the subtle shift from the 'we' to describe their movement towards the vestry to the 'she' when describing her walking along the front pew. Do you not see the implication of that?"

I slowed to a snail's pace as instructed to consider this. "I can only suppose, Holmes, that she and St. Simon became separated. They would presumably have been arm in arm and then she slipped out of his and began moving in the opposite direction. St. Simon said she hated it when he gave her his arm. She even refused to allow him to lead her into the breakfast later."

"A trifle, but a trifle of the most vital importance. Now consider the sequence. The couple ought to have turned about to walk down the aisle and out of the church. Instead of that, St. Simon began heading for the vestry with the clear intention of slipping out by the back. Tell me, Watson, why do you suppose His Lordship, with his aristocratic respect for ancient tradition, should choose to adopt so innovative a course?"

I had not forgotten, as Holmes evidently had, his dread of the danseuse Miss Flora Millar. "That is easy. He was afraid his former mistress was lurking in the laurels to hurl vitriol at the bride, or perhaps to flourish evidence of his breach of promise, or worse. That was why St. Simon had those policemen in plain clothes stationed at the church."

Holmes shook his head. "There never were any Yard men. Lestrade would have known of it. They were private detectives, though in view of their duties, St. Simon thought it prudent not to admit as much to me. But what makes you think they were stationed at the church?"

321

It was a strange question. "To prevent members of the public and Flora Millar in particular from entering uninvited."

"Then how was it that Moulton not only slipped in, but was able to sit in the front pew reserved for Mr. Doran? Even under ordinary circumstances that would have been impossible. The usher would have insisted that he leave. How do you explain that?"

"I cannot."

Holmes chuckled. "It is simplicity itself. One of the detectives was to take the place of the usher. The other was to stand guard outside. On the day they were nowhere to be seen. Thus there were no security measures whatsoever. But where were they, Watson?"

He looked keenly at me. I did not wish to disappoint so thought long and hard. "I suppose," said I, "that if they were not at the church, they must have been somewhere else."

"Excellent! No, no, I speak without irony, for there is nothing wrong with stating the blindingly obvious as the first step taken towards the truth. They were somewhere else. So where were they?"

I shrugged my shoulders. That was beyond me.

"At the last minute, St. Simon received a warning that the lady – that Miss Millar – meant to post incriminating material to the police and the press if he went ahead with the wedding. The detectives were therefore redirected to seize Flora and force her to reveal where the evidence was concealed. She misdirected them and escaped. They rushed over to the church and signalled frantically to St. Simon not to leave by the main entrance. He panicked and headed for the vestry. The bride separated from him and so was able to toss Moulton the bouquet."

"Not toss it, Holmes," I corrected him. "She dropped and it fell into the front pew."

So annoyed was Holmes with himself for having committed so crass an error that he dropped his pipe to the floor, where it scattered ash this way and that. I did not imagine Mrs. Hudson would thank him. He soon recovered himself, though, and stooped to pick the pipe up. He froze, though, while clutching it but before raising it and looked towards me quizzically. "Tell me, Watson, for I was distracted. At what angle did my pipe fall to the ground just now?"

I was not surprised by my friend's question. He had never been very good at grasping Newtonian physics, and to this day is uncertain whether the earth rises or the sun falls down. "It fell vertically, Holmes. That is how gravity works, you know."

"I confess I did not. Assuming you are correct, if Hatty Doran had dropped her bouquet where would you expect it to land?"

"Why, at her feet."

322

"You would not expect it to swerve off course and fall inside the front pew?"

"No," said I confidently, "that would be quite impossible, Holmes."

"Then you would not advise me to write to the author of *The Dynamics of an Asteroid* to suggest a subject for his next work? But in that case, how do you explain that when St. Simon turned round he saw Moulton handing the bride back her bouquet?"

I had to confess I found myself perplexed. I was sure Newton was right.

"But it is so simple. The superstition is that when the bride throws her bouquet, whomever it strikes has to marry next. It is traditionally hurled at the ladies, but I do recall St. Simon informed us she had been a tomboy, devoid of the least respect for the mores of civilised society. But for the present that is by-the-by. The real question is why she threw it at Moulton at all."

"Why, that is obvious, Holmes. It was so that he could slip that message to her instructing her to come when he called for her."

"He wrote that note before entering the church?"

"No, no, she saw him writing it when she glanced over at him."

"For the third time. And yet neither St. Simon nor any of those in the bridegroom's family's pew notice her repeated glances towards Doran's adjacent pew, nor did they see the intruder seated next to Doran scribble any note. No, it was written earlier and never passed to Hatty at all. It was already in the calling card holder in the pocket of the wedding dress presently to be fished out of the Serpentine. Do not make the face of the fish that discovered it, Watson. It is perfectly straightforward. The important thing was to put that hotel bill it was written on into my hands. Not that Moulton was ever in any hotel. Ah, the catfish face. I say he was never at any hotel. Do you really need me to explain?"

"I fear that you do," I muttered apologetically.

Holmes sighed resignedly. "Ah, well, let us start with the note. He initialled it. Now, Dr. John H. Watson, please suppose you have been kidnapped by the Montmartre Apaches and are presumed dead. You return in time to attend the remarriage of your wife. During the ceremony you slip her instructions to elope with you afterwards."

"Holmes," said I indignantly, "I would do no such thing. I would stand in the shadows at the back of the church to see if she seemed happy or not. If she did then I would slip away. To do otherwise would not be love but selfishness."

"Yes, yes," said he impatiently, entirely missing the point. "But let us suppose, having been half-scalped, the organ of selflessness had become detached. For the sake of argument, then, you pass her such instructions.

How do you sign them? '*Yours to the end of time*'? '*Sincerely, Hamish*'? Or would three '*X*' marks for kisses suffice? Let us suppose that for once you heed my injunction to cut the poetry and the superfluous romanticism. Presumably you initial it '*J.H.W.M.D.*' in case she fails to recognise your handwriting. Ah, but I was forgetting. She saw you writing it."

I began to understand. "It's curious."

"Now, John H. Watson, do you really suppose it was pure coincidence Francis H. Moulton, as we shall continue to call him, just happened to have the same initials as Flora H. Millar? Of course not. That message was to be her alibi."

This was nonsensical. "An alibi, Holmes? How could something that cast suspicion upon her as a possible murderer be an alibi? Lestrade was sure it proved she had done away with Hatty Doran." I hastily closed my mouth before Holmes could accuse me of more fish impressions.

"Oh, but that was deliberate. Once Miss Doran was known to be alive, then Miss Millar would be forgotten and her real role in this business never so much as suspected. Now let us consider the hotel bill on the back of which that pointless note was scrawled. Was there anything odd about it?"

I pictured the bill, the top and bottom of which had been torn away leaving only the date and the itemised list of expenses for 4 October, 1888. "Nothing at all, Holmes. It could have been a bill from any one of a score of the most expensive hotels in London."

"Just so. That is the point. And why could you not tell which hotel it was?"

"Because the name of the hotel had been torn away, as had been the name of the customer being billed."

"Curious, Watson, is it not? To keep hold of a bill for five days that had been so torn that nothing remained of it, save for the date and the prices? Hardly very likely, is it? So very convenient that the names of both the hotel and the customer had been removed. A little too convenient, was it not? Consider, too, that we are to picture Hatty Doran not simply slipping that note into her pocket, but carefully placing it in her calling-card holder. And of course, it occurred to neither her nor Moulton to check the pockets of the dress before dumping it in the Serpentine. No, my dear Watson, that note was never meant for Miss Doran. It was meant for *me*. The name of the hotel was torn away so that no Yard inspector would think to call at it. The name of the customer was removed because it was not Francis Hay Moulton. Of course, it is obvious whose bill it really was."

"Not to me."

"No? It should be. It was *yours*."

If I gaped this time it was as a landed fish that had been pumped full of laughing gas. "This time I know you are joking, Holmes!"

For once he admitted it. "Well, I am, I confess it, but to make a point. It was not literally yours, but it was that of your unsuspected doppelganger. Do you not see, Watson, that it must have been your twin? I am surprised we have never encountered him before. You really should introduce him into one of your fairy tales."

"Well, explain the joke."

"Consider that the price of the breakfast was the same as for the lunch and that there was no dinner. The bill was for only one day. Surely you can put yourself in this customer's position without any adjustment for the personal equation. We are dealing with someone who was shocked at the cost of the first meal of the day and strove to economise on the second, which ought to have been far more expensive. Then they made up their mind to leave the hotel, before the day was out to lodge in some less pretentious and less expensive domicile. On leaving the hotel, they threw that bill into the gutter in disgust and Moulton picked it up."

"But how do you know that it was cast into the gutter?"

"Why, because of the consequent staining."

"But that was due to the effects of the water seeping into the calling-card holder after the dress was dropped into the Serpentine."

"Precisely what we were supposed to think. It was left in water so that the soiling would not be thought significant. At the same time it had to be recovered before the water entirely obliterated the message and the itemised bill. That was why Moulton left it at the edge of the Serpentine where discovery would be almost immediate."

I was incredulous. "You mean all that business with the bouquet was just to make it appear Moulton had slipped her a note, when in fact it was already in her calling-card holder and the holder in the dress?"

"Oh, no, not for that alone. You are forgetting the ring. She had to pass it to him before she left the church. Did you not recall earlier how she took the greatest care not to allow St. Simon to recover her arm afterwards? It was not just that she cringed at the touch of a – *the* – man. It was also lest he see the ring was gone. It had to be cast into the Serpentine with the wedding gown. It had to be found with it to ensure that nobody would doubt that was the dress she had worn."

"But the dress was hers!"

"Oh, do think, Watson?" said he impatiently. "How could it have been? Do you suppose she undressed in the park? Or do you imagine that after they had made their escape, Moulton travelled all the way back to the scene of the crime, so to speak, at the very time when that park was crawling with official searchers, to say nothing of the eager public? Her dress was burnt. The one the police fished out was a duplicate made at the same time as the original. Or do you suppose she threw hers out of her bedroom window for Moulton to catch quite unobserved by the passers-by? And I suppose that when she left in that ulster, she was dressed in nothing but her underwear beneath it."

Holmes helpfully waved his pipe towards a Delaroche reproduction of *The Execution of Lady Jane Grey*, which shows that unhappy girl so attired for her death. I assume this was intended to assist me in imagining Hatty Doran in such a state. I averted my mind's eye from the scene he had conjured up.

But now I found myself floundering in waters that were growing ever deeper and dirtier. "This is beyond me, Holmes!" I cried. "Are you seriously suggesting he dropped an identical dress straight into the Serpentine before ever they sped off in his cab? And at the very edge of the recreational lake? Surely he would at least have rowed out and thrown it in after weighing it down. It had to have drifted to the bank later."

"It could not have done. It was discovered with the ring. Had they not been together, the ring would have been lost as surely as that Agra treasure Jonathan Small emptied into the Thames. The dress could have drifted away in time, but not the ring. They had to have been left together and where the discovery would be immediate. You must see that."

"Well, when do you suppose the substitute dress was cast into the Serpentine?"

"We know that, Watson," said he impatiently. "No sooner had Moulton signalled to Miss Doran to leave the breakfast, than he at once left the cab in which they were to make their escape and headed off into the park. He went there to dispose of the twin dress. What possible reason could he have had for going there otherwise? Do you suppose he felt an overwhelming desire to feed the ducks? Was he planning to conceal that ring in some goose's crop? Once Miss Doran had left the house, every second counted, for they could not know how soon her presence would be missed and the hunt on."

I thought about that. My friend was right, of course, but that raised an obvious difficulty that both of us had overlooked. "Holmes, how did she ever manage to leave the house unobserved? I know that she threw a gentleman's ulster over her wedding dress, but surely that would have made her more conspicuous, not less. It would not entirely have concealed the gown, and a runaway bride in a man's ulster would have attracted attention. Besides, there were those two detectives. And remember, Holmes, she had her maid Alice pack her a bag, I suppose with basic toiletries and a change of clothes. The footman would at once have tried to relieve her of it to bear it out to one of the carriages outside. He must already have seen her running upstairs. Why did he not see her run down too?"

"Ah, that is where our *danseuse* played her vital part. They had much to hope from Flora. She burst into the house and made – or played – the most important scene of her career, leading the footman, the butler, and those two detectives a merry dance as she strove to burst into the breakfast room. We know that she tried to do so since the butler was obliged to leave the feast to assist in her restraint. While she was scratching the footman's eyes out, Miss Doran was able to slip away. As soon as Miss Millar saw she had done so, she abruptly terminated the struggle and seemed positively eager to be expelled. She had to join Miss Doran, you see, so that their presence together would be witnessed and reported. Murder would be suspected. Lestrade would come to me with that note. I would solve the mystery."

"This is fantastic, Holmes," I sighed. "Why go to so much trouble, even if, as you say, someone desired revenge of some sort on St. Simon or Doran or both? Why so contrived a plot?"

"Nothing else would do if part of the plan was the public humiliation of the fathers," said Holmes firmly. "At another time, a less spectacular fiasco would have made the headlines with ease, but after the police released their poster of Jack the Ripper with its facsimile of the '*Dear Boss*' letter on 3 October, desperate measures were called for. That is why the hotel bill was collected the next day."

"So let me get this straight. They were never at the hotel? They were always at those lodgings in Gordon Square?"

Holmes's smile was a cross between the Pickwickian and the Milvertonian, at once humane and sinister. "Ah, Watson, you will never learn, which is part of your charm. There are no lodging houses in Gordon Square. Do you recall how I once followed your thoughts as you studied portraits of your heroes General Gordon and Henry Ward Beecher?"

"Well well. It was amazing at the time, though simple enough once you had explained it."

"Humph. We shall see. Did you notice that just before I named the location of their lodgings, I glanced over at those pictures?"

I frowned. "No, I can't say I did."

"Well, you should have. You should also have read my thoughts if the trick is so very easy. Yet you entirely failed to consider that the name of the one man who condemned the Plymouth Church for vindicating your hero Beecher concerning his sexual indiscretions was Francis Moulton. For his pains, Moulton received a miniature coffin with his own name upon it written in blood. That inspired your friend Conan Doyle's ominous messages from his mad Mormons and also the word '*Rache*', also written in blood, above gangland murder victims in New York back in 1880. Well, let that pass. But for you to have failed to realise I was searching for some

327

address for their lodgings at the very moment my eyes fell upon Gordon's image? That was unpardonable."

I stared at Holmes. I could not believe he would ever deceive me so. "You mean that you chose Gordon Square entirely at random?"

"No, not entirely. Remember that when first I came to London, I lived in Montague Street, which is a mere stone's throw from Gordon Square. There was no danger you would trip me up with questions concerning the location. I knew it too well. But really, Watson, you ought to have realised what I was doing, given that I glanced over at Gordon not once but twice. Oh, come, do not look so puzzled. Surely you remember I also did so when suggesting to Lestrade he drag the fountains in Trafalgar Square?"

I thought long and hard. "I do. And yet why should I?"

"It is so simple. You had been complaining you would miss the unveiling of a statue of General Gordon between the fountains on 16 October, which was only four days away. You must unconsciously have realised I was thinking of it as I made that suggestion to Lestrade. And yet you still failed to see I had invented the address of the mysterious millionaire and the runaway bride." Holmes wagged a disapproving finger at me while smiling his most irritating smile. "Too bad, Watson. Too bad!"

"But why claim he had left the hotel at all?"

"Well, I thought it would be wise to ensure we got our story straight before Hatty recited it. I needed those four hours for that, you see. I am afraid she still managed to slip up once. She claimed that Moulton took her straight to Gordon Square, but in the story, we had agreed upon Moulton only booked out of the hotel the day before I went there. It was foolish of me not to alter my own account once she had blundered."

"So you were in on the plot from the beginning," said I sadly. "Or was it from before the beginning?"

"Oh, come now, Watson, you know it was," said my friend with what I felt was unreasonable impatience. "Did you not perceive how, when first I met St. Simon, I began to refer to Hatty Doran as 'the young lady' and hastily corrected this to 'your wife'? Surely you should have understood from that I knew full well subsequent events would make it appear the wedding had been invalid."

"But you explained that, Holmes," I reminded him. "You were able to deduce the correct solution from the newspaper articles I read out to you."

"Was I? I placed the greatest significance upon the fact that her early years had been spent in a mining camp. None of your papers made any reference to that. And can you really imagine I thought it inconceivable she could have fallen in love with some handsome fellow on the sea voyage to England or during the Season and after it? I confess I am no romantic, but with your own example before my eyes, such a failure of imagination would be inconceivable. I was talking nonsense, and you of all people ought to have realised as much."

I felt thoroughly ashamed of myself. How could I have imagined that Holmes's dismissal of the possibility of love at first sight was a sneering allusion to my own instant attachment to Miss Morstan? I saw now how unworthy my suspicion had been.

"Yes, it was, but I forgive you," said Holmes, who had correctly interpreted my blushes. "What is less pardonable is that you failed to recognise the significance of the fact that a gourmet feast for five consisting of four normal diners and my brother, who just happened to drop by to discuss the reunification of the English-speaking world the moment St. Simon had bowed out, was delivered less than an hour after I had departed in search of the missing bride."

"It was certainly very efficient of the shop," said I approvingly. "I suppose the provender must have come from Fortnum and Mason. Only they could have supplied so delicious a supper at such short notice."

"And not asked you to sign for it?"

"That was an oversight," I agreed with a disapproving nod. "And yet, who else could have selected those comet vintages for you? I deduced they were ancient," I added proudly. "They were concealed beneath a century or so of cobwebs."

"And you assumed Fortnum and Mason have a giant Sumatran rat spider on their payroll? Since when did any shop you know of sell cobwebbed bottles? And besides, how could I have known for sure that the runaway bride was not boarding a ship at that very moment? Would I really have squandered the first hour of my quest dithering over vintages before determining who might be available to attend the feast? There is such a thing as counting one's omelettes before one has caught one's chicken. How, then, could you have failed to realise those bottles came from a private cellar and were selected by quite another hand?"

"A private cellar? Whose?"

"Why, Lord St. Simon's, of course."

I was shocked. "You stole them from St. Simon's own cellar? Holmes, you went too far!"

"Hmm. An amusing idea," said Holmes thoughtfully. "Yes, I am sorry I did not think of it. But no, I was referring to the *real* Lord St. Simon. The one we met was a myth. He never was and probably never will be any such person, given his self-poisoning."

I was stunned. "You mean the fellow was an imposter?"

"Doubly so. We may call him a gentleman by courtesy, but he was really nothing of the sort. As for that title, of course only his older brother had the right to call himself Lord St. Simon. It was easy enough for the spare to deceive Mr. Doran at first, though, for as an American he had no understanding of the subtle niceties of English titles. He thought he was getting a future duke, though I have my suspicions concerning Balmoral's title too."

A thought struck me. "Holmes, do you recall that neither St. Simon's father nor his older brother attended the wedding?"

Holmes considered me keenly. "You have an idea?"

"Well, just one: If St. Simon was using his brother's title to bag himself an heiress, it might have been resented by the true Lord St. Simon. The father might not have approved of such blatant claim jumping either."

Holmes applauded me. "Brilliant, Watson! You are on sparkling form today. And your most astute observation might also help to explain Lord St. Simon's desire for revenge as a dish best served cold. That *pate de foie gras* was the aristocratic equivalent of humble pie. The sight of those bottles from his brother's cellar must have left a particularly nasty taste in Lord Robert St. Simon's mouth. I am surprised I did not think of it myself."

I hope one day to learn to be on guard against my friend's envenomed rapier wit. But I was not yet ready to concede. "I think you are being a little uncharitable, Holmes. Doubtless he tired of forever correcting Americans who would insist on introducing him as Lord St. Simon instead of Lord Robert St. Simon. As for the impression he was heir to the dukedom, that was probably perpetrated by hostesses when including him on their guest lists. It is surely inconceivable, though, that if St. Simon had tricked Mr. Doran into thinking him the true heir the latter would have proceeded with the marriage, once he had learnt the truth."

"Unless he had foreseen that certain unfortunate events would presently elevate St. Simon to the dukedom."

"Holmes!"

"Oh, do not sound so shocked, Watson. Some robber barons really are robber barons and worse. I have said that those Apaches were not really Apaches and were used by Doran to remove Moulton after he had first fleeced him of his gold. Do you suppose Doran meant to stop there? Balmoral and his oldest son might shortly have met with unhappy deaths at the hands of Apaches of the Montmartre variety. Not that St. Simon would have enjoyed his title for very long – he might have been thankful for that. The Hispaniola serpent's poison will instead guarantee him a slow and lingering death. At least I have spared Miss Doran the same fate. She and her true love may live together safe from slander's tongue and the world that would condemn them."

"But why should the world disapprove of her marriage to Moulton?"

"Oh, good heavens, she had no interest in him. Surely you see who her true love was?"

"I have no idea. I suppose that just as in detective stories the murderer is the one person who is never suspected, so you are going to reveal to me he was the last person I would ever think of."

"And who is that?" asked my friend, grinning mischievously.

"Holmes! It was you!"

Holmes roared with laughter. It was some minutes before he covered. At last he wiped the tears away and continued.

"Well, Watson, if you cannot see who it was, then perhaps it is better if I do not say. I will only remind you of the evidence. If you still cannot or will not apprehend the truth, then who am I to force it upon you? To begin, then. You recall how St. Simon described her as a tomboy devoid of any respect for the mores of society, and yet rigorously and courageously true to her own moral compass?"

I nodded approvingly. "An all-American girl of true grit and brim full of the pioneer spirit. St. Simon spoke of her wandering amid the hills and woods about a mining camp."

Holmes snorted. "His Lordship did indeed make Deadwood sound like the Lake District. One had the distinct impression she spent her time prospecting for golden daffodils. The truth would have been rather different, I fancy. Such a girl would have had to be as tough as nails if she was to grow to womanhood without being raped. If she played cowboys and Indians, it would have been with real guns versus real arrows. Now square such a one with the creature she described to you fainting away on reading a single and thoroughly unreliable account of Moulton's death at the hands of the Apaches, to say nothing of her ensuing delirium. Hardly very consistent, was it?"

"It is certainly curious," I conceded.

"But that is not the half of it. The Hatty Doran that St. Simon praised would never betray her principles. She was quick to perceive how to act rightly, and resolute in doing so. Utterly independent, she would not permit him to take her arm. And yet the Hatty Doran of her account was the feeblest creature imaginable, instantly to be enslaved by whichever man happened to be in the room with her at the time. When it was Moulton, he had but to command her to wed him and she did so, though the result was she had to live a lie with her father for years. Yet when that father instructed her to marry a man, she felt nothing, and she did so. Do you not see, Watson, that the Hatty Doran she described was an American's idea of the feeblest of wilting English roses? All her talk of doing her duty with her husband was entirely at odds with her innate American belief in rights. No, no, Watson. That Hatty Doran was a myth. There is not, and there

331

never could be, any such person. I doubt there ever will be such a pathetic creature outside the pages of your little fairy tales."

"Then who was it that her confidante Alice helped her to fly to?"

"Hmm. Perhaps you should ask your friend Oscar Wilde to tell you something about the birds and the bees."

It was my turn to smile, for Holmes clearly knew nothing about Wilde. Holmes smiled back. I suppose he imagined the joke was on me.

"Well, Watson," he chuckled wickedly, "I shall say no more. Only consider that St. Simon could not understand the curious intimacy that existed between Miss Doran and her so-called servant Alice. He put it down to an American informality as displayed towards menials. I assure you, my dear fellow, in the land of the free no self-respecting American would dream of going into service if they could avoid it, for who would kowtow to an equal? But perhaps this is a tale for which neither you nor the world is yet prepared."

I had no idea what Holmes was talking about. I knew better than to persist, since the more I did so the more he would tease me with hints that gave away nothing. "Well, Holmes, if you will not answer me that then at least explain this: You said we should judge St. Simon very mercifully, yet you clearly believe he was the real gold digger. How can you be so very charitable, particularly since you think he would have infected his bride with syphilis? To my mind, his conduct was unpardonable. What excuse did he have?"

By way of answer, Holmes gestured towards the six scenes of Hogarth's *Marriage a la Mode*. "These are the witnesses for the prosecution." Then he pointed once more with his pipe stem at the reproduction of Delaroche's *Execution of Lady Jane Grey* over the mantelpiece. "And that is the witness for the defence. Take the Hogarths first. You recall I said St. Simon took note of the presence of my Hogarth prints when first he entered 221b? Well might he do so, and not just because his father was about to auction these self-same copies. He knew that when Hogarth painted the originals, he was thinking of particular families: The Spencers and the Churchills, of course, but the Balmorals too. Ah, Watson, the old curses are the best! Hogarth began to paint these in 1742, the very year that a certain Hugo Baskerville first penned his account of the curse of the Hound. Well, these pictures glance at the curse of the Balmorals and families like them. You see the bride and groom there? Which of them is the victim in your eyes?"

I did not need to think twice. "The bride, obviously. You can see how miserable she is. The groom is too busy to notice. He thinks of nothing save for his reflection in that mirror."

"Well, as a satirist Hogarth condemns everyone. Now, another artist might blame no one. Do you see how Delaroche has stolen from Hogarth to create his own vision? And do you understand how in that vision there are nothing but victims?"

I could not for the life of me see any connection between the Hogarths and the Delaroche. More to the point, I could not understand why Holmes supposed Hogarth must have had real families in mind. I said so. "Even if he was thinking of the Balmorals and the Spencers and the Churchills, he could hardly have alluded to them specifically. He would have been haled to a court for wounding their characters. Besides, you can see that the Earl of Squander is pointing to his family tree, which grows out of the loins of William the Conqueror. Surely no real family could ever claim as much."

Holmes chuckled. "Think of the Duke of Holdernesse, whose true ancestors were cattle rustlers. My own family is said to go back to William the Bastard's sister Adeliza, and so to Charlemagne. But you really should brush up on your anatomy, Doctor, for if you look more closely you will see the tree here grows not out of the Bastard's loins, but rather out of his stomach. The distinction is a pertinent one."

"I don't see how," I grumbled, feeling that Holmes was trespassing upon my territory. "Stomach or loins, what is the difference? I don't suppose any family would claim direct descent from the Bastard's stomach either."

"Ah, but the Squanders do," said he with a cunning smile. "The Steward of the Conqueror was one Robert Despenser, so named since as the head of the household he had dispensed the food from the pantry. Now, 'to dispend' also meant 'to squander', so the pun is an obvious one. Moreover, the Despensers boast that this Robert was their ancestor, and both the Balmorals and the Spencers regard themselves as branches of the Despenser tree. So you see that Hogarth is taking aim at them all."

"That may be so," I conceded, "but it is very general. It is not as if he included portraits of recognisable celebrities of the age. How could he, since they would have sued him for slander?"

"Ah, but he has! Consider the portraits of the Earl and his wife here."

I was bemused. Certainly there was the portrait of the Earl of Squander as a great warrior, ridiculously adorned with The Order of the Golden Fleece, but there was no other portrait I could see. "I think you are mistaken, Holmes," I had the temerity to suggest. "There is no woman portrayed here."

"No? Look again. Follow the furtive gaze of the Earl and it will lead you to his admired and rightly feared better half."

I did so and realised this modern Perseus was peeping askance at a copy of Caravaggio's Medusa upon Minerva's shield. "Oh, come now,

333

Holmes – now I know you are joking," I laughed. "You know perfectly well that is no portrait."

"No? We shall see. Let us begin with the portrait of the Earl. Does he have any distinguishing features?"

"He has the Order of the Golden Fleece, which is the highest Catholic order of chivalry. What English Lord would be awarded that? Surely it is a joke."

"Oh, undoubtedly. If the Earl of Squander came into possession of it, he could only have done so as a robber baron fleecing corpses upon a battlefield. We might conclude that he had struck a rich pocket. But I think a satirist of Hogarth's calibre might have been wittier than that. I reminded you the Holdernesse family were once cattle rustlers. They would have stolen sheep from the Spencers too, whose flocks were among the greatest in the kingdom. Other ancient aristocratic families could trace their origins back to great military achievements. The Spencers alone owed their rise to efficient animal husbandry. The irony here hardly needs stating. The Squanders are striving to restore their fortunes by means of very bad husbandry indeed. They would wed a son infected with the French disease to a bride suffering from the English malady – which is to say that melancholy peculiar to women. It is a marriage of sicknesses. It is hardly an injection of fresh blood on either side. Now think of the Balmorals and their haemophilic strain. You see those two hounds chained together, where convicts so chained are said to be 'wedded'? They are so similar as to suggest an incestuous union. Are not the real unions of the Balmorals dangerously incestuous too? That is the real curse of the hounds they ought to fear."

"Well, I grant you that the portrait of the Earl might glance at the Spencers and Balmorals and their origins, but you cannot seriously suggest the Medusa he is considering so timorously could be any real woman."

"No? You recall how St. Simon described Hatty Doran as 'volcanic'? He was thinking of one of his more distant ancestors. Sarah Churchill, Duchess of Marlborough, was dubbed 'Mount Aetna' for her fearsome eruptions. She was regularly likened to the Furies, whose special duty it is to avenge wronged mothers. She was notorious for cutting off her heirs to spite her face until all she had left was her granddaughter, Lady Diana Spencer, whom it is said she attempted to match with the Prince of Wales. Being the wealthiest woman in England, she promised a fortune if he would wed her. Her assumed aim was simple. She had been the adored favourite of Queen Anne until they fell out. As such, she had been the power behind the throne and was dubbed Queen Sarah. If she could have installed Diana beside the Prince, then she might have made puppets of them both. She would *be* the government. You have heard of the

334

Kensington system? It was intended to make the child Victoria entirely subservient to her mother so that the latter would be the real power once Victoria was enthroned. Sarah was just such a string puller."

This was too much. "Holmes, what you say is quite absurd. Sarah Churchill was a strawberry blonde and renowned as a great beauty. How can you possibly imagine that Hogarth could represent her via this image of a serpent-haired Medusa?"

"Ah, but Medusa was a great beauty once. You know her estranged daughter Henrietta was praised as 'the learned Minerva'? That deity bears the face of Medusa upon her shield. It was why Sarah spoke of Henrietta as having once been so fair to then turn so foul, thus likening hers to Medusa's fall. Besides, the frame of this Medusa painting is topped by a crown."

"Well, what of that?"

"But surely you know that 'Medusa' means 'Queen'? And you must recall from your religious education that Abraham's wife was called *Sarai*, which means 'discord' or 'strife', but she became *Sarah*, meaning 'princess', after she bore Abraham an heir. Sarah Marlborough became a princess when her husband was made a prince of the Holy Roman Empire. In the eyes of many, though, she was transformed from a princess into a breeder of discord, just as the once beautiful Medusa was turned into a monster so terrifying that to look upon her save in a mirror was to be turned to stone. You know that story of Sarah's metamorphosis? It is said to have been one of the inspirations behind Pope's poem *The Rape of the Lock*."

"I am all ears."

"Well, Sarah was an ardent Whig. Note that, Watson. The story goes that her husband wished to achieve reconciliation with a Tory adversary and so invited him to dinner. Knowing that his wife would never consent he put off telling her. At last he steeled himself to do so while she was combing her long hair before her mirror, doubtless so that he might avoid her direct eye. In a clumsy attempt at appeasement, he complimented her on the beauty of her golden locks. Thinking this condescending, she petulantly cut them off. The story goes she then had Kneller – a fine painter, Watson – immortalise the incident by depicting her clutching them like a long snake in one hand. I have seen the painting. In fact, the object she clutches may be a boa of the feathered variety. Besides, the painter could hardly have immortalised the incident if the story is true that her husband secretly gathered the locks up and stored them away as more precious to him than the Golden Fleece. She is said to have discovered them after his death. As for that political opponent, I doubt he ever existed. He was probably introduced for the sake of a pun on 'Whig' and 'wig'."

335

As always, I was spellbound by my friend's ingenuity, though as was often the case I was also a little incredulous. "Forgive me, Holmes, but your interpretation of this painting ignores one crucial point: The face of Medusa is gazing down in pity and horror at the poor bride here. That hardly suggests your Sarah as a brain-fevered Fury."

"No? Think of the story of Perseus, who saved the chained Andromeda from a hideous sea monster and then used the head of Medusa to turn her fiancé Phineas to stone, so saving her from an undesirable arranged marriage. That story is ironically recalled here. The face of this Medusa glares down upon a bride so pale we feel she is being turned to stone. Instead of saving her, this Medusa is dooming her. As for her serpentine hair, that foretells the fate of the girl. She will be infected with the Hispaniola Serpent – which is to say syphilis – just as Hatty Doran would have been had she wedded St. Simon. You know the story of Cupid and Psyche? She was tricked into believing her unseen lover Cupid was a serpent. In this present story, the bride's lover is just that. The fruits of their union will be the hideous distorted child of writhing limbs who is revealed in the final scene of the series."

"And you believe Hogarth had in mind some specific cash-for-coronets marriages?"

"I mentioned the first Lady Diana Spencer. After she died young, Sarah had no choice but to bequeath her vast fortune to her grandson Johnny Spencer as the one child she had not become hopelessly estranged from. He was a wastral sick with venereal disease who, in the year Hogarth began this series, mortgaged the paintings at Althorp, just as in our day a Balmoral has been forced to auction his. Sarah's one condition was that he marry. Legend has it she presented Johnny with an alphabetical stable of prospective brides and to save time he chose the first on the list, one Georgina Carteret. I do not believe it. They married on Valentine's Day, so the joke is clear. One Valentine's Day game is to pick a name at random out of a hat. Perhaps that is how Hatty was forced to select St. Simon, for there was nothing to recommend him. With his purported fortune, Mr. Doran could easily have purchased a duke."

"Holmes!" I cried. "I begin to understand what you were striving to do in the case of Miss Doran. Tell me if I am right. Were you not attempting to break the wheel and put an end to the endless repetition of such crimes?"

Holmes nodded grimly. "That was my aim, but one girl saved will not suffice. The Juggernaut's wheel turns on and the curse is renewed from generation to degeneration. The real problem is that while we think we learn from our mistakes, what we are actually learning is how to repeat them. We are sure we will get things right the next time."

336

My friend will always be a misfit in our age of optimism. "Holmes," I gently advised, "your problem is when you find your glass half-full, you suspect it was poisoned. But you have not yet spoken of your witness for the defence. I cannot say I understand what you meant when you spoke of that Delaroche *Execution of Lady Jane Grey* as a charitable reuse of Hogarth's story. I can see nothing of that series in this painting."

"When I was a child," said Holmes, gazing farsightedly towards but beyond the execution scene, "I dreamed of finding some secret stairway up onto that stage so that I might plead with them to halt that tragedy. I could not for the life of me comprehend why all those playing their parts in that scene should seem so decent and intelligent and yet all have acquiesced. Why was not the executioner at least brutish? How could he be so thoughtful and gentlemanly? But since he was so, how could he fail to apprehend he was about to murder an innocent girl? And on seeing this, how could he continue? Consider that old gentleman taking so paternal an interest in a girl who might be his own daughter. See how graciously he conducts her little hand towards the block. Now contrast that with the final scene of Hogarth's tragedy in which the lady has drunk poison on reading of her lover's execution. Her father is holding back the arm with which she would embrace her lifted child, though with her eyes closed she probably imagines it is her hanged lover kicking in the air and striving to embrace her so they might go together into the new world. Why is the father doing this? He is an alderman or a London mayor, and as such stands for the law. She is a suicide and her property is forfeit. It is his sad duty to remove her wedding ring and pocket it. Delaroche took that theft and transformed it into a father figure guiding a girl previously forced into an arranged marriage. The blindfolded Jane has been as one playing a game of blind man's buff to take an unseen mate. Now she is led to the block as previously she was led to the marriage altar like a lamb to the sacrifice.

"As a boy, I could not understand this until I read Thomas More on Richard III. More likens the world to a theatre with scaffolds as stages within stages. Men fear to speak more than is set down for them, lest they mar the action of the tragedy. They make the mistake of Polonius in *Hamlet*, you see, who thinks that to be true to one's part is to be true to oneself. More's Richard as the all-licenced fool does what he pleases, knowing that those who believe in the system will never prevent him, once he has control of that very system."

"But surely, Holmes," I argued, "Sometimes men's eyes are opened and they do change. Think of Saul on the road to Damascus!"

"Ah, Watson, do you not see he was the exception that proves the rule? Reconsider this executioner witnessing the first Protestant martyrdom of Bloody Mary's purge. Is not Delaroche recalling Saul when he watched the stoning of the first Christian martyr? The death of St. Stephen sowed the first seed of doubt in his mind. But this executioner is a Saul who shall never receive a blinding revelation on the road. He dare not speak or do more than is set down for him, or the tragedy will be ruined."

I considered this. "Then women like Hatty, those who reject all tradition, might be our best hope for the future?"

"Perhaps. And yet consider what they are up against. The Spencers still name their daughters Diana. Why? Because they hold fast to the hope that their dream may yet be fulfilled. One day some reincarnation of that first Lady Diana Spencer will wed her Prince Charming. And what then?"

We both sat in silence for some minutes as Holmes still gazed upon that poor blindfolded girl. At last he spoke.

"Well, Watson, since the problem is a perennial one, we must leave it to the future to decide. The only one we need concern ourselves with is how to distract ourselves in this weary, stale, flat, and unprofitable world."

I reached for his Stradivarius.

"No, Watson, not the violin. For you a good wife. For me the hypodermic. Go to her, my dear fellow."

Titian – "*Bacchus and Ariadne*"

The Adventure of the
First Clue

Continuing "The Beryl Coronet"

"**S**ir, I cannot find words to thank you. But you shall not find me ungrateful for what you have done. Your skill has indeed exceeded all that I have ever heard of it. And now I must fly to my dear boy to apologise to him for the wrong which I have done him. As to what you tell me of poor Mary, it goes to my heart. Not even your skill can inform me where she is now."

"I think we may safely say," returned Holmes, "that she is wherever Sir George Burnwell is. It is equally certain, too, that whatever her sins are, they will soon receive a more than sufficient punishment."

With further profuse expressions of his undying gratitude, and the reiterated promise we would presently receive ample evidence of it, Mr. Holder hurried away. I managed to contain myself until he had closed the door behind him. Then I picked up the solitary boot Holmes had thrown into a corner and, springing from my seat, hurled it at the door after the banker as an expression of my disgust.

Thinking to spring to Mary Holder's defence proved to be an unwise action, for I had forgotten that Holmes's recent indoor target practice had temporarily lamed me in one leg. One of the bullets from my souvenir Jezail musket had ricocheted. In consequence, I sat back in my chair even more abruptly than I had risen. As I rubbed my leg, I ruefully eyed the "*V.R.*" composed of bullet pock marks and punctures that Holmes had tattooed so deftly into the wall, now further dented after Holder's earlier furious assault upon it. "If he meant to prove he is not ungrateful," I thought to myself, "he might at least have offered to supply something to cover the damage."

"Oh, that is on its way." My friend was observing my agony with the clinical indifference of a specialist considering a patient suffering from an uninteresting disease. "Ah, that is it being borne up the stairs now. Best leave your indignant protests concerning the damning of Mary Holder until after the deliverers have departed. They are a cut above your usual manual labourers."

As he spoke, there came the sound of much heaving and puffing, quickly followed by high pitched cries of protestation and distress from Mrs. Hudson mockingly echoed by the still higher shrieks of our little street Arabs. The door was flung open and a chaotic procession flooded in that might have served as the model for Richard Doyle's *Punch* cover, save that instead of the madman Mr. Punch coming along leading a bacchanal, there was Bacchus himself being borne in by two red-faced labourers. They carried it with a concern that was certainly quite uncharacteristic of the average English workmen, as if it had been an altarpiece been brought to a church for installation. It was the very reproduction of Titian's *Bacchus and Ariadne* I had observed Holmes admiring with his connoisseur's eye in Holder's dining-room. I deduced Holder had perceived my friend's excited admiration and hit upon the idea of presenting it as an expression of his deepest gratitude. As Holmes said, it would cover up the dented "*V.R.*" nicely.

"Magnificent," Holmes murmured appreciatively. "It is a genuine Yves Chaudron or I am very much mistaken. He is the king of the art forgers. Some carpers sneer that he is nothing more than the invention of the Argentinian fraudster Eduardo de Valfierno, but surely that is to split hairs. It is like those stories that Valierno is himself the creation of one Dr. James Moriarty – or vice versa. Think of those rumours that I am one of your less convincing fictional characters, which are not so wide of the mark after all. Some say the same of your occasional collaborator Arthur Conan Doyle. Or are you a character in one of his stories? I forget."

Such talk has always left me feeling uneasy and confused. I am told that if one thinks one exists, but this is little help since I am not entirely sure what thought is. It is probably best not to think about it. I realised Holmes was still speaking.

"Twenty-four hours ago, Holder would not have parted with this for the world. Now he could no more bear to look upon it than Georgiana Spencer's husband the Duke of Devonshire could endure the sight of Gainsborough's portrait of his wife once he understood the rosebud she proffers is not meant for him. He had nothing to hope from that plucked flower. Eh, Watson?"

I was not about to permit my friend to distract me again. "Holmes, I must speak out," said I with an unwonted firmness. "In matters of crime you are the undisputed master. In love you are a child. Now I have had numerous and varied experiences with women in no less than three continents. My dispatch box is crammed full of reminiscences and commendations. I may tell you, then, that am not one of those to be blinded by a pretty face. I know true spirituality when I see it. You were entirely mistaken about Miss Holder, who was, I assure you, a woman of quite outstanding moral stature and capable of heroic self-sacrifice. Her eyes alone told me as much. If she went with Sir George, it was doubtless to persuade him to write to the authorities confessing all so her cousin Arthur might be released. It is inconceivable to me she would in a moment have

342

turned traitor to her guardian and her country for the sake of a man she had repeatedly told her uncle she did not trust. And you were wrong, Holmes, when you supposed they had been meeting at that window almost every night to carry on a love affair. On the contrary, I can prove it was the first time he ever encountered at that window, and she had not anticipated the visit."

"Indeed?" Holmes seemed quite amused to see his modest lightning conductor flash forth so defiantly. Doubtless he had supposed he had bended me to his will as fully as he imagined Sir George had done Mary to his. "The worm has indeed turned, and a most remarkable worm it is to be sure. You think Holder should hasten to Sir George's domicile to enquire of his servants where he had gone. Proving the innocence of his son can wait till later. That is you opinion, is it not?"

"He is not on his way to his son," said I with certainty. "He may have said that out of embarrassment after you had casually consigned his poor niece to the bottomless pit. I trust he is even now hastening to save her. Besides, if he meant to urge the police to free Arthur, he would certainly have asked you to go with him, or at the very least he would have taken that boot." I nodded towards where Sir George's incriminating shoe now served as a doorstop. "How else could they match the footprints in the snow to it and prove Arthur pursued the thief to recover the coronet?"

"Oh, it is too late for that," said he disinterestedly. "It snowed last night. That evidence is gone forever."

I was horrified. "Holmes! Why did you not take the police with you yesterday once you had purchased the boots from Sir George's valet?"

"What makes you think I did not?"

"I know you did not. Holder saw you in the stable lane disguised as a tramp. He could hardly have failed to notice if you had brought the police with you."

"He did not see me. Mary Holder did. I timed our visit to end well before he returned from his bank that evening. He only saw a common vagabond. You may recall I had dressed as a loafer, which is a creature that hangs about rather than straying here and there as vagabonds tend by definition to do. It is their *raison d'etre*. Besides, my loafer could afford to pay almost twice a common labourer's weekly wages for a pair of boots too old for even one in Sir George's financial traits to consider resoling. And do you imagine I supposed Sir George's valet would instantly befriend a penniless tramp?"

"He might if he was feeling charitable."

"Then he would have bestowed upon said tramp such decrepit footwear *gratis*. But really, Watson, you are being quite extraordinarily unobservant. Do reconsider the boot. Can you see nothing singular about it?"

I studied it hard. "I am sorry, Holmes, I can see nothing special about it. It is just a very old, very battered boot. I have no doubt that with your remarkable powers, you are able to tell me how many hearts he has broken and which brothels he has frequented, to say nothing of what school he went to and what he had for dinner. All I can see is one old boot, much the worse for wear."

Holmes sighed. "I have just told you what is so very singular about it in asking that very question. Come, come, this is so simple. Oh, very well. Consider this: I purchased a pair of boots from the valet. How many boots are generally to be found in a pair?"

"But of course!" I cried. "There should be two! Holmes, what happened to the other one?"

"Hmm." said Holmes thoughtfully. "I had been planning to lend you *The Dynamics of an Asteroid*, but perhaps that should wait. You are perfectly correct though. There should be two. And your question is most pertinent. What did I do with the other one? As a concomitant query, one might also ask where it is now. But I will keep you in suspense no longer. Since there were signs that it might snow again, and the only hope of proving Arthur Holder's innocence was to match his bootprints and Sir George's shoeprints to his feet and Sir George's boots respectively, I went to the police and invited them to accompany me back to the stable lane to do so, bringing Arthur Holder with them. They matched. Arthur confessed to his actions, though without incriminating his cousin Mary Holder. I donated one boot to the Yard and kept the other for my little museum. Then I left with a promise I would return in two hours with the missing piece of the tiara as proof positive of Arthur's innocence. I did so shortly before seven o'clock.

"But then why did they not release Arthur?"

"You are on sparkling form. And the answer?"

"Holmes!"

"You have it."

"They did release him!"

"I might add I had already sent a telegram to my government insider, who communicated to the police the need for absolute discretion if a royal scandal was to be avoided. Neither the public nor the press will ever hear a word of this affair, save for a few vague rumours. I am of course excepting your account of it. I am relying on you to produce a ripping yard that will convince all who read it the whole affair was nothing more than a fairy tale. Just write in your usual style and nobody will believe a word of it. You can publish it once Mrs. Mary Holder has died of consumption. That should be in about five years."

I was annoyed but did not rise to the bait. Too much was at stake to distract myself with defending either my literary style or my diagnostic skills. "Holmes, you said you only got back to your bed at two this morning. What were you doing during those nine missing hours after you left 221b again?"

"That is self-evident. Did I not tell you I discussed the matter with Arthur after the recovery of the missing gems? Once he had been released, I took him in my cab back to Fairbank. We spoke on the journey and I managed to persuade him to lie in wait for my prey outside his old home. Perhaps I neglected to mention what the prey might be, for fear it would arouse his ire. I had so arranged things Mary would slip away with her uncle hard on her heels."

"You knew she would fly to Sir George? But how?"

Holmes rubbed his hands together in considerable satisfaction. "I did it brilliantly, Watson. You recall the look of fear in the then Miss Holder's eyes when I surmised the maid Lucy's lover was one-legged? Why do you suppose that terrified her so? It was because she was no fool. She must have bitterly regretted her blunder in failing to efface those footprints and shoeprints left in the stable lane snow. She understood I had spotted that some were left by a peg leg. She saw the game was up and so assumed I was but playing with her prior to an arrest."

I had indeed been surprised at my friend's carelessness, for he is usually well able to conceal his feelings and lull his victims into a false sense of security. It was best to be diplomatic. "Of course it is understandable that you were unable to hide your excitement at her signs of guilt, Holmes. Still, it is a pity that you did not manage to suppress your sense of triumph until after we had left. That look of eagerness in your eyes as they met hers must have convinced her you knew she was guilty."

"Five years I have known you, Watson, and still you manage to surprise me," said he with a sad smile. "Do you not recall how easily I soothed Holder after he had employed my 'V.R.' as a target for his head? And you seriously believe I could not have assumed a mask of indifference with her had I wished to? I met her fear with my evil eye to turn it into pure panic. A rabbit confronted by the gaze of a snake could not have been more petrified than she. Thus her flight was assured. Holder saw that exchange of looks. I knew I had them both in the hollow of my hand."

Holmes is a born predator and one ought not to disapprove of his nature, any more than one would of a tiger's failure to be a vegetarian. Nevertheless, I do sometimes find his pleasure in the pursuit a little unnerving. "You mean you deliberately sent her to her ruin and made sure Holder would witness it?"

"Say rather to the edge of a cliff with a Romantic view of the sea of troubles below. It was in a good cause, Watson. I was saving her soul. I have already explained how I cleverly arranged her saviour would be present."

"You cannot mean Sir George, Holmes," said I doubtfully. "You said he had previously cast aside a hundred women. Why should you have supposed he would take her with him at all when he fled the law? Would that not have increased the chances of an arrest and a conviction?"

"He did not. He was not."

"Did not what? And was not what?"

"He never did take her with him and he was not fleeing the law. Did I not say he knew he had nothing to fear from the authorities, since a royal scandal had to be avoided at all costs? On the contrary, he was in a position to blackmail the great and the good by threatening to reveal all should any legal action be attempted against him. No, Watson, if he was fleeing anyone, it was Mary Holder, who would have been a serious liability. Her sudden and very unwelcome appearance decided him it was time to make a fresh start with the handsome sum he had been paid for his part in this swindle."

I was shocked. Holmes did occasionally lie in a good cause, but why do so now? "You told Holder his niece was known to have flown with Sir George. Holmes, did you mislead him?"

"Not in the slightest. Do not look so upset, my friend. I assure you nobody was lied to, save for you. And you are my biographer. Holder already knew the truth since he witnessed it all. I have said he saw the panic in her eyes when I permitted her to deduce my activities in the stable lane. Those same expressive eyes had previously betrayed her feelings for Sir George at all those candle lit dinners he attended at Fairbank. Holder understood perfectly well what it meant when she spoke of him in Byronic terms as mad, bad, and dangerous to know."

I was confused. "But if she thought him disreputable, how could she have found him attractive?"

Holmes bestowed upon me an annoyingly piteous look. "Experiences with women in three separate continents and he still does not understand. Watson, believe me when I tell you the man who whispers insincere nothings into a woman's ear is the very one most likely to receive hard somethings in return. Ask my rascally friend Escott the plumber. I shall introduce you to him one day.

"But she was such a thoroughly good girl!"

346

"That was the problem. She had been a thoroughly good girl for far too long. Consider that she arrived at Fairbank after the death of her father, aged nineteen, the very time when even a thoroughly good girl would be desperate for romance, and instead for five years she was forced to fill the vacant peg left by Holder's deceased wife as the mistress of his household. Holder took care that during all that time she should never see a single eligible bachelor, save for Arthur. It was not so difficult to justify keeping her at home, given her pale and potentially sickly condition. Spreading the word she was suffering from incipient consumption would have further discouraged suitors."

"Well, even if he had done so, it would have been in a good cause. He hoped she would marry his son."

Holmes gave one of his cynical barks. "Ha! You think so? Not at all. He! Nothing could be further from his mind. You imagine she did not reciprocate Arthur's feelings? I tell you she did. She loved him as much as he loved her – else how explain why a woman you yourself have admitted was exceptionally self-disciplined should nevertheless have screamed and fainted when she realised Holder was intent upon blaming his son for the theft. One might account for her swooning by her condition, which you really ought to have perceived, but not her screams."

"Her condition, Holmes? Surely you do not mean she was with child?"

"Nothing of the sort. She was still a virgin – No thanks to her uncle for that. Do you not see that Holder's accusing his son of the theft on the flimsiest of circumstantial evidence was but the climax of a smear campaign he had been waging against him for five years? Why do you suppose he insisted so strenuously that Arthur was born with a criminal strain and bound to rise from crime to crime until he did something really bad and ended on the gallows? He worked to dissuade her from wedding his son by painting him in the blackest colours as bad to the bone. Feeling deeply indebted to her uncle for taking her in and showing her such trust, she could not go against his professed fears. It was partly out of compassion for the father that she stifled her passion for the son. Besides, she supposed it would be selfish of her wed Arthur, only to make a widower of him in a very few years."

This was a typical layman's error. Those with no medical training often mistake a pale skin for evidence of imminent sickness. It is why thin, attractive women are at once supposed prone to consumption. To have attempted to correct Holmes would have been futile and a needless distraction. "But then why did she throw herself at Sir George?"

"The more resolute the pressure cooker, the more powerful the explosion when all that pent-up pressure is ultimately released. Holder eagerly invited Sir George to dinner again and again as one of the inner circle of the Marlborough House Set. Such was the banker's desperate ambition to join its ranks that he turned a blind mind's eye to the glances that passed between Mary and the black knight, and by which he reeled her in. Holder was himself bent upon netting the Prince of Wales as a client so that he might boast his bank was by royal appointment – to say nothing of his dream that one day he, too, would be a knight, though heaven knows Sir George ought to have taught him that the title is less than worthless nowadays. True knights are never acknowledged as such."

This was perverse, and as such not atypical of Holmes. "You cannot mean Holder encouraged Sir George's visits?"

"Who do you suppose introduced Arthur into the Smart Set? It was Sir George, and wholly in accordance with Holder's most earnest entreaties. Moreover, Sir George easily convinced Holder he had the ear of the Prince and could pass on hints concerning the bank's readiness to supply unlimited funds. Arthur was to assist in the work. The poor lad was pathetically grateful that he should be granted any role in the service of the bank, even so questionable a one as that of playing the wastrel to please Prince Pagan. Little did he realise he was playing into his uncle's hands. It made it all the easier for Holder to pour still more poison into Mary's ear and insist here was proof positive his son was a bad 'un."

Holmes here displayed the professional satisfaction of an artist who has succeeded in portraying his subject in a bad light though working with him in broad daylight. I was willing to accept that in theory a woman might find a handsome scoundrel physically attractive despite his moral failings. I could not accept that she was his mistress, particularly since – if as he supposed she was still a virgin – their lovemaking at that window was best left to the imagination of a *Holywell Street Journal* subscriber.

"Holmes, you said that she and Sir George carried on their affair at that window at Fairbank almost every night. This is surely absurd. Her position was not that of the maid Lucy, who had no choice but to see her admirers secretly and at night since she was never permitted to go out. But Mary was more the jailor than the jailed. As the *de facto* housewife at Fairbank, she was required to visit the shops and perform other tasks away from the house. Why not pursue a love affair during the day? And if it was the case that the maid Lucy regularly met with her admirers in the garden at night, why risk being seen by them? I tell you, Holmes, I am convinced that was the only time Sir George ever came to that window and that his visit was quite unexpected."

"I entirely agree."

I was taken aback. "You do?"

"I do."

348

I was sceptical. "Really?"

"Absolutely."

Now I was convinced. "You are joking, Holmes!"

"Not at all. The only joke was a private one. I made that amusing claim she carried on a passionate affair at that window of questionable opportunity despite the dangers and discomforts involved partly to see if Holder would accept so hilarious an idea uncritically, which he did. That confirmed he was determined to write her off as a bad loss without hope of redemption. Besides, I was anxious he should not suspect there was a very special reason why Sir George had come to his home that night."

"And what reason did he have?" I asked eagerly.

"I shall not insult your intelligence by stating the obvious."

"Insult away."

"Why, it could not be coincidence he happened to appear on the very night Holder had the coronet stowed away in his disreputable bureau. Sir George knew it was there and he meant to take it."

"Impossible!" I cried. "How could he have known Holder possessed the coronet at all, and why on earth suppose the banker would have been so mad as to have taken it home with him?"

"Exactly!" Holmes's eagle eye glittered with a perverted delight. "It was an act of the purest insanity to remove that tiara from one of the safest houses in the City of London to store it away where anyone might take it. Can you not see that Holder had to have had some overwhelming need to do such a thing at the risk of destroying his life, his firm and perhaps even bringing down the monarchy itself? But let us proceed from step to step. To begin, then, with the most easily answered difficulty: How could Sir George have known the coronet had been offered to Holder as security? Answer me that, Watson."

I thought about it. I was certain Holder's illustrious client was the Prince of Wales, who loved to gamble and who enjoyed the company of men and women who were sometimes of dubious and questionable reputation. Whether Sir George really was of the inner circle at Marlborough House, he probably had connections with those who were. Holder might have supplied the knight with credit in return for his sowing the germ of an idea that the Prince might pawn some priceless artefact and receive a generous loan with no questions asked. I suggested as much.

Holmes listened with signs of faint approval. "Not bad. In support of your theory, Watson, I might mention that one of Sir George's gambling partners is a certain colonel who moves in both the best and worse circles. This colonel's ultimate chief is a master manipulator who is also something of a mind reader like myself. He knew Holder would be unable to resist the tiara. He meant the banker to take it home with him. The man who calculated the dynamics of the asteroid that destroyed the dinosaurs was easily able to predict the actions of one Alexander Holder."

There was an obvious flaw to my friend's diamond. He was ignoring the problem of free will. Even his favourite author confesses that you while in the aggregate man becomes a mathematical certainty, the dynamics of an individual cannot be calculated. I opened my mouth to say as much but caught the glint in my friend's eye and knew he had perhaps predictably anticipated my objection. I tried a different tack. "A bank is not a pawnbroker's, Holmes. Who could have imagined Holder would demand he take actual possession of the coronet? And who could have known that the Prince would have consented to so irregular a procedure?"

"Dr. Moriarty. I do beg your pardon and his. I believe it is now Professor Moriarty. But you must forgive me if I make one minor correction: Holder's client was not the Prince, though he was not to know that. "

It seemed to me that my friend, being denied the impossible as an option, was adopting the most improbable theory he could think of as a second best. "But that is inconceivable! Nobody could impersonate the Prince! Blue blood shows, Holmes."

Ever the cynic, Holmes was clearly amused. "Really? Have you ever heard of The Tichbourne Claimant? Oh, but you have. You must recall how the missing heir to a baronetcy was lost at sea. He was a fragile, effeminate fellow. His mother, Lady Tichbourne, refused absolutely to accept her loss. Now imagine if the monstrous Grimesby Roylott were to think to impersonate Oscar Wilde. Nevertheless, when a burly butcher appeared from Australia bearing no resemblance whatsoever to her son, her Ladyship at once accepted the serpent to her bosom. Rest assured, Doctor, when the willingness to suspend disbelief is strong enough, anything may be believed."

"But Holmes, Holder was no hysterical woman. He was a hard-headed English businessman!"

Holmes considered this pertinent objection. "It is true that City lore has it his massive, strongly marked face was the model for the door to Holder and Stevenson's burglar proof vault. Both were long thought to be equally impenetrable. But you know, Watson, every vault has its casket of orgiastic mysteries secreted deep down in its bowels. Any thief must take into account that their vault is time-locked, and the same is true of Holder's heart. The visit of that impostor was timed to exploit his darkest secrets to maximum effect. You recall the date?"

"The client called just two days ago. It was a Thursday. The date was February the nineteenth. What of that?"

"Only that it was the second anniversary of what you would doubtless have chronicled as 'The Adventure of the Philanthropic Prince'. I played a small part in it, supplying his Majesty with workman's clothes and accompanying him as a Virgil to his Dante as he descended down into the vilest alleys of the East End. To his credit he sincerely wished to see how his poorest subjects lived – and rather more to the point, died. It was with difficulty that we restrained him when he thought to pour sovereigns into the laps of a mother and her wretched children half-starved and freezing to death. Had he done so, I very much doubt that a single sovereign would ever have left that hellhole, including a possible future one."

"And did he not work to alleviate such conditions after his return?"

Holmes nodded approvingly. "He did. Four days later, he gave his only substantial speech in the House of Lords to date, urging the government to take action to improve the lives of poor naked wretches. As it happens, the day when that loan of £50,000 is to be repaid to the bank shall be the second anniversary of that speech. Of course Holder will never see his illustrious client again, so saving him the mortifying embarrassment of having to hand the tiara back bent out of shape and in pieces, to say nothing of stuttering out an explanation for his act of madness in taking it home with him. When he reads one day that Victoria has appeared in public crowned with it, he shall suppose it a replica made without her knowledge."

"But would not Holder ask himself why the money was not repaid?"

"Not for a second. The Prince sails for Monte Carlo tomorrow. I said this fraud was impeccably timed. Holder will deduce that the £50,000 was lost in the casino. But you see my point? When the Prince entered the East End, nobody recognised him. Might not the reverse illusion have been achieved with equal ease? It is evident that the clerk who handed Holder the visitor's calling-card never imagined it was that of the Prince of Wales. Had he glanced at it, he would have whispered excitedly to the banker that it was he. Holder would have had no choice but to send the clerk scurrying away to summon his partner and the possibility of removing the coronet to his home would have been lost. But the visitor did not greatly resemble the Prince. He was just enough like him so that he might seem to have been the Prince come in disguise, even as he had concealed his identity two years earlier to the day."

I could see no way that my readers would accept any of this. "Come now, Holmes. That is too far-fetched."

"Is it? Did you not see that a vagrant whom Holder had spotted was transformed by him into Sherlock Holmes as soon as the thought entered his mind? Holder saw what he expected to see. That is what humans do."

351

"But surely, Holmes, there is a '*je ne sais quoi*' about royalty that is not to be imitated."

Holmes chuckled in that superior way of his. "If the real Prince had visited Holder, then the banker would have demanded proof of identity. Sometimes an impostor can convince where the real item might not simply because he conforms more closely to the idealisations and the caricatures than the original could ever do. Here was a man who could speak of £50,000 as a mere trifle and who was ready to pawn a coronet or two that he had no right to without a qualm. Do you seriously imagine, Watson, that the real man would ever behave thus? But Dirty Bertie, a.k.a. Prince Pagan, a.k.a. Edward the Caresser would be perfectly capable of behaving every bit as disgracefully."

I shook my head. I was still far from convinced. "Nobody would mistake the Punch Prince for the true one, Holmes," I insisted.

Holmes paused to consider this. Then he snapped his fingers. "I have a convincing parallel, Watson. By heaven, I do believe that I am not the first to think of it. Moriarty did so too. You recall 'The Adventure of the Slave's Collar'?"

I did not. "I think it must have been before my time."

"A little, perhaps. This year marks the centenary of what once seemed like the trial of the century, though it was soon superseded by the trials of Marie Antoinette and her husband that it had helped make possible. I shall remind you of no more than the key facts as they relate to our present concerns."

"Proceed," said I.

"Know, then, that a clever impostor masqueraded as Marie Antoinette to persuade a very wealthy cardinal to purchase the fabulously costly Slave's Collar supposedly on Her Majesty's behalf. To play her part convincingly, the impostor took as her model not the real Marie Antoinette, but rather the Queen of an infamous portrait by Vigee Le Brun, a protégée of those excellent and underrated painters Jean Baptiste Greuze and Claude Joseph Vernet. Many supposed the Queen had posed for it in her undergarments and was provocatively offering some lover a suggestive rose, just as her friend the Duchess of Devonshire does in that stolen Gainsborough portrait presently located under Mr. Adam Worth's bed. When tried later at the insistence of the Queen the Cardinal was found not guilty on the grounds that he quite understandably mistook the impostor for Her Majesty, so convinced were many that the vicious caricatures of the Queen were accurate. That verdict ruined her reputation forever. A recollection of the scandal in this its centenary year cannot fail to concentrate royal minds wonderfully. If ever this present scandal were to be brought to court Holder would probably be found not guilty of any

352

wrongdoing on the grounds that he had been quite right to assume that Punch Prince he had done business with was a plausible enough imitation of the original."

"But even if one were to accept that Holder's client was an impostor and the coronet a replica, who could imagine Holder would not only accept it but take it home with him? And why try to steal it back again?"

"As for the theft, that was to break it so Holder would not wish to return it at all. Of course it had been broken before being passed to Holder and then glued back together again. The triangular piece of one corner was stuck on and then snapped off by Sir George just before Arthur caught up with him in that stable lane. Sir George mimed wrestling with Arthur for it and then suddenly let go."

"But surely, Holmes," I protested, "when Arthur failed to hear a loud crack as it broke, he would have realised that it had not snapped at all."

Holmes looked puzzled for a moment. "Ah, you are thinking of that nonsense I told Holder. You are picturing my feigned attempt at breaking the tiara and my farcical failure. You have seen me straighten out a poker, Watson. I could have crumpled up that tiara like wastepaper had I wished to. It was Holder's mettle and not the coronet's I was testing. The entire point of the exercise was to claim that when it broke, it must have been with the sound of a pistol shot. Now, if that had been true, then Arthur could not have broken it himself without awakening his father. Had Holder loved his son, he would have seized upon that straw as proof positive his son was innocent. Instead he dismissed it out of hand. That proved he had framed his son and was determined to keep him imprisoned."

I could not believe my ears. It saddened me my friend could be so cynical. What dark secrets in his past had resulted in such disillusionment with human nature? "Holmes, Holder loved his son!"

"Did he? Did he not say that before the theft he had not had a care in the world, and that in spite of his declared conviction his son was bound to turn to a life of crime? Or should I say *because* of it. That slander had achieved its purpose, which was to prevent the wedding of Arthur and Mary and so keep his niece with him. His great nightmare was that one day their eyes might be opened and they would see it was he who had worked to keep them apart. It was my task to open those eyes. Holder showed me how to do so. And ironically it was this very picture that supplied me with the vital clue to how to manage it. I might call it the clue of clues, for some would say it was first clue of all."

Holmes gestured towards the Titian copy. I could not for the life of me see what the depiction of an ancient myth could have to do with a Victorian banker in love with his niece. Holmes saw my bewilderment. He laughed.

353

"Oh, do not think me a freak, my dear Watson. Have I not said that I am not the only mind reader? Sir George reported back to his gambling partner, Colonel Moran, that Holder had this hung in his dining room and was evidently inordinately fond of it. Moran informed his chief in turn. I can picture the scene now. My mastermind has his back to the Colonel and is feasting his eyes upon the Greuze girl *Experience* as he thinks upon his own forbidden and lost love. None could have understood better what that Titian meant to Holder. Armed with such knowledge, our mastermind's plot practically wrote itself."

"Forgive me, Holmes," said I humbly, "but as I cannot read this picture with any certainty, so you cannot expect me to perceive what Holder would have made of it."

"But you know the story of Bacchus and Ariadne?"

"Of course. Ariadne was the princess who supplied a scarlet thread to the hero Theseus, whose mission was to enter the first labyrinth and kill the Minotaur. The clew of thread allowed him to exit safely and in return he promised to wed her. In assisting him, she had betrayed her father and so would have to fly from her land forever. Then Theseus abandoned her while she slept. I take it she is shown here caught at the very instant when she was waving towards his receding ship and crying out to him to return. No, that cannot be right. According to the legend, Theseus arrived back at Athens in a ship with black sails, which convinced his father the King of Athens he was dead. That caused him to die of grief."

"No, you are perfectly correct, Watson," said Holmes with a grim little smile. "Titian is implying that having betrayed Ariadne, the hero must next have betrayed his father to seize the throne. We are to imagine that as the journey proceeded it occurred to Theseus what a really splendid opportunity fate had put into his hands. So he changed the sails back to black again. But that is not the real point of this picture. What we have here is a moment akin to the one when Romeo, besotted with some girl or other, I forget her name, as no doubt did he, sees Juliet for the first time. Even as Ariadne is still waving towards Theseus" ship her eyes meet those of Bacchus as he begins his leap down from his chariot. You have heard of Empedocles?

"Never."

"He devised a theory that the eye sends forth a ray by which it sees. Between these eyes is a golden thread of light akin to that scarlet or gold thread Ariadne supplied Theseus with. The latter cut the painter when he first abandoned Ariadne, and then hoist black canvas to pursue the siren voices that called him on to a glorious future. By contrast, this thread cannot be cut asunder but reels Bacchus down to Ariadne, who might seem to some like a mermaid, but is actually more like a drowning woman he

354

would save by drawing her up out of the world maze and into the heavenly spheres.

"There he will make her a crown of stars so as to alter the fate written for her in the heavens. He will rewrite her fate to ensure her happiness in the hereafter. He does this as the god of tragedy as well as of honey and wine. This is truly a *deus ex machine*, where the machine is his juggernaut-like chariot, as also a sarcophagus. He falls to the world stage to change the course of the martyrdom of a woman, just as Christ lived and died to alter the martyrdom of man. In their own ways they both worked rather like you, Watson, when you strive to write accounts of our little detective adventures as tragedies with absurdly happy endings."

I was too impressed at this brilliant line of reasoning to be offended. "It is wonderful! Wonderful! And yet I still do not quite follow. What has that to do with Holder's cruel treatment of Arthur and Mary?"

"Watson, you stumbled upon the truth when you saw Holder running down Baker Street sawing the air with his hands thus and with a wild look of grief and despair in his eyes that caused you to declare him mad. A little simplistic, Doctor, but in general terms a perfectly valid diagnosis. But let us try to be more precise. If I wished for a medical precedent, I should take the case of Don Quixote, as he preferred to be called, who was actually an ordinary man like you or many another whose mind has been turned by reading far too much sensational literature of the kind you are so addicted to. When you are reading a Clark Russell sea tale, you sway your head from side to side as if you were aboard a rolling ship and especially when there is a tempestuous storm in progress in our own world. Fact and fantasy become so confused that you cannot tell which is which. What you would call madness is nothing more than a more exaggerated tendency to do the same. In his own mind, Holder had become a tragic figure. He modelled his look of intoxicated despair on that of Bacchus here."

"But why think of Bacchus if, as you say, his thoughts were forbidden as regards his niece? There are enough examples of incest in the ancient myths. Why not use one of those?"

"Because it would have been too obvious. He had to have an image that he could read aright but that others could not. Now observe Ariadne is dressed in blue and red, which are often the colours of the Virgin Mary. Consider next that the parallels between Christ and Dionysus, the Twice-Born, are too striking to be coincidental. Both die and are reborn, which is why Bacchus descends out of a chariot like a sarcophagus and is reminiscent of the risen Christ in the graveyard appearing to the Mary Magdalen, save that here it is a fallen woman who backs away and seems unlikely ever to touch the god. The blood of both heroes is drunk by their followers as the new wine and for renewal. Both enter the world stage to change the predestined martyrdom of man. Both make of mortal women their brides and queens of heaven to be crowned with the stars. Ariadne's stellar coronet is sometimes called the Crown of Thorns. But being a fallen woman, she is made a conflation of the Mary Magdalen with the Virgin Mary, where in my old faith the latter is both the Mother of God and the Bride of Christ. Do you see now what this image once meant to Holder? I daresay he fell in love with his Mary the moment their eyes met too. Her consumptive paleness only made her more beautiful and tragic in his mind, and justified his decision to ensure she never left him, for she was not long for this world anyway."

I was deeply disturbed. Could Holmes be right? Could I really have missed so obvious a diagnosis? I have written that I had never seen so pale a woman, but of course I had meant other than the consumptives I have treated. Had I not put her leprous complexion down to grief and horror, I would have arrived at the same conclusion in an instant. For some reason the incomparably spiritual face of Mrs. Conan Doyle came into my head. Holmes paused to give me time to recover from my confusion and then continued.

"By one of those cruel jest the gods so relish playing on us poor worms, he could never tell his love, as he would have had she not been his brother's daughter. She entered his household as a sunbeam might and it was a great deal to him just to see her dainty form about the house, and to hear the sound of her voice. By transforming her into a saint not long for this world he found the strength to keep her at arm's length. Yet he dreaded the day she would leave him, and he longed to crown her before then as his queen, just as Bacchus did Ariadne. You see that look in Bacchus' eyes? It is how Burbage's Hamlet must have looked when his were opened and he leaped into Ophelia's grave to embrace her corpse, having remembered at last how much they had loved each other. It is the look of a man who has fallen in love with a woman at the very moment he has learnt she must be dead of consumption in a very short time. You have heard of Zeno's Paradox? It denies the possibility of motion since every step can be subdivided into an infinite number of smaller ones without end. Bacchus shall never complete this leap. It shall always be eighteen seconds and nine minutes past the fifth hour on the feast of the Assumption of the Virgin in the eighteen-hundredth-and-ninety-fifth year before the birth of Christ.

"And what if he did complete this leap? All humans are consumptive in the eyes of the gods. Her life must be over in the blink of this god's eye and the golden thread connecting his eye to hers must be cut. He is not gaining but losing her. That was how Holder felt when he realised his Mary was consumptive. But if he could crown her with the tiara made for

Victoria by her deceased husband Albert, whom as a closet spiritualist, Her Majesty was certain she would be reunited with after death, it would be a kind of mystic marriage to be consummated in the hereafter. There flesh relations shall be meaningless. There Christ is himself married to his mother."

I could never publish any of this, not even in the *Holywell Street Journal*. "He might call it love," I muttered with some disgust, "but I would call it selfishness."

Holmes shrugged. "One might say the same of the selflessness of a god of love that makes men to know him, love him and serve him and would damn all those to hell who question that infinite goodness for an instant. In Holder's case, as in such a god's, love and selfishness are one and the same thing. We need not trouble ourselves with such matters. All that concerns us here is that our criminal mastermind pondering his own unattainable Greuze girl saw how he might exploit Holder's dream. He would offer Holder that tiara with its promise of a marriage and coronation in heaven. Just as Victoria dreams of being enthroned by her Albert's side in paradise as the mirror images of Christ and the Virgin Mary, so Holder could dream of being seated beside his virginal Mary after their deaths when the jewels in the coronet would turn into stars. As you know, a girl first wears a tiara at her wedding to signify the death of innocence and the crowning of love. Holder would crown Mary as still an innocent in death and so turn it into a martyr's crown. How, then, could he resist taking that tiara home with him to perform a coronation before this very image of a Christlike figure leaping down to his bride to assume her into heaven? He imagined it would be safe enough to do so. He supposed his son would be at his club. He could not know Sir George had called in Arthur's debts to ensure he would not dare show his face at Marlborough House."

"But how could Sir George had known the tiara would be so easy to steal?"

"Having been denied the supreme pleasure of crowning her, Holder hoped to at least tempt her to take a peek at it to crown herself Napoleon-style. Accordingly, he revealed its presence in his old bureau in the dressing-room adjacent to his bedroom. As he expected, Arthur warned him to remove the key to the cupboard of the lumber room since it could open the bureau. Once that thought had been planted in Mary's mind, Holder made sure the lumber room door was left ajar and the key to the cupboard was in its lock. She was bound to find it when she made her rounds to check the doors and windows. Of course recalling Arthur's warning, she would have removed it, meaning to hand it over to Holder, but his hope was that once she had it in her hand, she would be unable to resist the temptation to take a quick peek in Pandora's box. It was like Eve

357

finding herself holding the apple lest any serpent take it and thinking to steal a little bite. He also left both his bedroom and dressing-room unlocked and did not lock the case in which the tiara was stored. Thus instead of four locks to defeat her, there were none."

"But Holmes, if he eagerly anticipated her passing through his bedroom to his dressing-room, how could he have missed her? He said he was a light sleeper."

"I doubt he did miss her. He would have followed her after she had removed the tiara out of its box, perhaps hoping that she would crown herself before that Titian reproduction. Then he saw his rival and son Arthur following her too. He observed her at the window and witnessed Sir George snatch the prize out of her hand. He saw Arthur leave by the same window intent upon recovering the coronet. In an instant, he understood how he might frame his son and so eliminate the one reason why Mary might yet abandon him."

"By concealing the identity of the true thief, even if it resulted in a national scandal?"

"He had read of the Prince's imminent trip to Monte Carlo. He assumed that the £50,000 would be lost at the casino there. The disappearance of the tiara would be hushed up. To have Mary with him for the few years remaining to her would have been worth writing off a bad debt to a bank that dealt in millions."

"But how could Sir George had known Arthur would follow her down and then work to recover the coronet?"

"She had already collected that key and was still intent upon passing it on to Holder when she was startled to see an excited Sir George at that window anxious to pass on to her the latest gossip. He had learnt at the club that the Prince had pawned his mother's most prized tiara. She could not resist capping his news with the revelation that the coronet was even then in her home, an assertion he naturally laughed at, convinced as he was that Holder had been pulling her leg. A little offended, she determined to prove it. Before she went for the coronet, though, he impressed upon her the importance of removing it from its case lest Holder, awakening in the night and checking the bureau to be sure all was safe and sound, should find the box missing and so raise the alarm.

"That instruction would have reassured her, as it was intended to do. Obviously a thief would take the tiara in its box. A police constable might not think to stop and question a man encountered late at night bearing a little case in his hands. The dullest policeman in the world would by suspicious if he happened upon someone in the street late at night carrying Queen Victoria's famous emerald and diamond tiara.

"Sir George had two other reasons for insisting she remove it from its case. Firstly, he meant to rouse Arthur by the simple expedient of throwing some gravel at his window. I found a few pebbles beneath it lying atop the snow just as one would expect them to do if they had fallen from above. Hearing footsteps outside his bedroom door, the newly awakened Arthur thought to investigate. Had he seen Mary going downstairs with a box in her hands, he might have called out to ask her what she was doing and to offer his assistance. However, seeing that she bore the coronet he was rendered speechless and determined to pursue her silently.

"And the other reason?"

"The entire point of the theft was to have Arthur wrestle for it. That could hardly have been done if it was still in its case."

"What you say appals me, Holmes," I shuddered. "How could you have let her go to Sir George for that one slip? Surely we should work to find her even now."

"There is no need. I have already saved both her and Arthur. Holder will never see either of them again.

"But how?"

"By playing our mastermind at his own game. I used this picture just as he had done. Arthur and I lay in wait for Mary to slip out and hasten to Sir George's home. Her pleading with him to fly with her decided him. He would not have fled otherwise. He promised to do as she wished and then sent her indoors on some trifling errand. When she returned it was just in time to see his carriage disappearing into the distance. I knew Holder was concealed nearby clutching the coronet and preparing to leap out to play Bacchus to her Ariadne just as soon as her Theseus had shown his true colours as a pirate off to board and pillage other weaker vessels. Then at the instant Holder was about to do so, my iron grip on Arthur suddenly slackened as I was overcome by a crippling attack of incipient rheumatism. Arthur leaped out to Mary with a look very like that of Bacchus here. Their eyes met and hers were opened. Unlike Titian's Bacchus, he did achieve his Ariadne. I knew my work with them was done. After that, it was just a matter of adopting the voice of a constable catching sight of a very suspicious looking character concealed in the bushes. The banker hurried away in fright. We may leave him to a lonely and dishonoured old age. Whatever his sins have been, he shall receive a more than sufficient punishment."

Here I thought it best to interrupt Holmes with a warning that Conan Doyle was due to arrive with that perfect angel of a new wife of his to discuss our collaboration on what has since become *A Study in Scarlet*, its title inspired by all Holmes's talk of clews of thread through mazes. I knew how Holmes distrusted and despised my fellow doctor and would not wish to be present. At the reminder he started up.

"I really should post Holder's cheque to Mr. and Mrs. Holder, as they must now be, before their banker has time to stop it. They shall need it in their new life and to pay for her treatment when death approaches."

I was impressed and surprised. "That is extraordinarily generous of you, Holmes."

"Hardly. There was no fence, and I never did recover the real tiara since it was never missing. Besides, Holder only made out the cheque to silence me, and I do not wish to be entirely silenced. Once Mary Holder has expired of tuberculosis you must publish your account, which I trust will be even more misleading and inaccurate than usual. Besides, Holder will undoubtedly disinherit them both thanks to my actions, so I owe it to them."

I looked at my friend admiringly, for after five years he still amazed me. "I would never have pictured you as a matchmaker, Holmes. You have always expressed your disapproval of love." I gestured towards the painting. "Do you really think Bacchus is making the right choice at the crossroads and Theseus the wrong one? I seem to recall Dionysus had been returning from military triumphs in India when he forgot them all on seeing Ariadne. I would have thought your sympathies would be with Theseus for abandoning her to seek immortal glory as a hero."

"You forget, Watson, I have the example of an everyday hero returned invalided from India to remind me that the heroes of myth are but the pale shadows of those whom we pass every day in the street and who remain unrecognised."

"My blushes, Holmes." It was no mere expression.

"You see that boy satyr in the foreground of this painting? He does not heed the dog barking at him. He seems to catch some siren song his goat's legs take him towards without the use of his eyes. That is Theseus deaf to Ariadne's cries and heeding only his calling to a higher destiny. The boy drags a calf's head after him. That makes him a satirical portrait of Theseus emerging from the labyrinth dragging the head of the Minotaur after him. So much for such heroes."

I thought about how Holmes had saved me from a comfortless, meaningless existence. I had been his Sancho Panza to accompany him on one adventure after another. Yet an ungrateful part of me craved an average existence in which the only adventures would be ones I read about in the papers.

"The problem with making choices at crossroads," said he, eyeing me thoughtfully, "is sticking to them. Now, you would like to be like that old man in this painting bearing the casket of orgiastic mysteries. In your case, of course, it would be a battered tin dispatch box crammed full of accounts of our adventures. The alternative would be to leave it empty and instead become a happily married man reading the occasional yellow-backed novel. I daresay you shall sooner or later choose the latter option. But shall you stick to it? Eh? Well, we shall see."

Holmes was right, of course. In the relations with my friend and my Mary it had to be a matter of till death us do part. Had not Holmes died when he did I daresay I would have been buried at the crossroads as one of those who could not choose. I should then have lost them both. Was it really just coincidence he should then have happened to rise from the dead so hard on the heels of my dear Mary's passing? Was his concealment of his survival selfishness? Or should I call it love? Perhaps it was both.

Carlo Crivelli – *"The Annunciation with St. Emidius"*

The Adventure of the
Peachy Copper
Continuing "The Copper Beeches"

"You have it, sir, just as it happened."

"I am sure we owe you an apology, Mrs. Toller," said Holmes, "for you have certainly cleared up everything which puzzled us. And here comes the country surgeon and Mrs. Rucastle, so I think, Watson, that we had best escort Miss Hunter back to Winchester, as it seems to me that our *locus standi* now is rather a questionable one . . . ."

"Though not as questionable as the shape of that grasping woman," he added under his breath once we were out of earshot. "Let us just drop by the local telegraph office, which we shall find half-a-mile down the road on our left. I anticipate a reply."

Holmes had warned me that the Machiavellian smile of the countryside was that of a *belle dame sans merci* and concealed bloody fangs, so I maintained my hold on my smoking Webley No. 2, ready for any assault, be it human or otherwise. That mongrel mastiff hound I had just rid the world of might have spawned others. Since I, a doctor, was armed and Holmes was not, I was surprised – and perhaps just a trifle annoyed – that the seemingly distressed Miss Hunter chose Holmes's arm to hold onto. I observed that as she did so, she leaned her head towards his so that her cropped hair grazed his cheek. Despite the disgust my misogynistic friend invariably feels at any feminine approaches, he endured it manfully and overcame his desire to repel her. Had he failed to do so, I would then have felt obliged to offer her my own shoulder and best bedside manner, not because I found her in the least bit attractive myself, but out of a sense of professional duty.

When we rounded the corner, Holmes discovered doubtless to his utter amazement how wrong he had been about the isolation of the Copper Beeches, for there lay before us no howling desert – but on the contrary a sizeable town with respectable looking citizens walking the streets. There was even a policeman. The discovery seemed to have struck him dumb, for he said not a word, all the time concealing his astonishment with quite extraordinary skill. Only I, who know him ten times better than any man and a hundred times better than any woman could ever do, intuited the chagrin he must have felt at his uncharacteristic blunder. The very fact that he betrayed not the least surprise proved to me how taken aback he was.

We had to wait ten minutes to collect Holmes's telegram, for it was a busy office and there was a long queue. This was as I had expected. Miss Hunter had told us she had sent her telegram the previous night, and only an overworked office would have kept such exceptionally long hours. I was a little puzzled Holmes had not deduced from this that it must serve a large town. Yet this ignorance of the locality only went to prove he could not have been there before and that did relieve me. My secret suspicion he had made a trip without my knowledge was unfounded. He and Miss Hunter had not been working together as partners behind my back.

And yet here was another puzzle, for if the area was so densely populated and with the busy Southampton Road running straight past the Copper Beeches, how could that half-starved mongrel of the Rucastles have been let out at night? Surely the calf-sized brute would have leaped those low railings surrounding the property and been at the throat of the first passer-by it encountered. Moreover, it would surely have trespassed onto the grounds of the new Lord Southerton to tear the peer's prized Brazilian tigrina to tatters. The life of his Lordship, who had been crippled when he seized that adorable cub from its enraged mother, would have been at serious risk too.

Then I remembered Miss Hunter had only seen the hybrid hound at night from her bedroom window and so would not have perceived if it was on a long leash. Besides, she was one of those women prone to hysteria, even though my medical eye told me she did not wear a corset. Others would not have realised this.

Holmes read his telegram aloud for my benefit: "*Fowler flown.*"

"Cryptic but concise," he observed approvingly. "Terse but to the point. Why cannot you write like that, Watson? All has gone exactly according to plan. You will be glad to hear Alice Rucastle has just been released from her place of confinement."

Miss Hunter clapped her hands approvingly, but Holmes graciously waved away the compliment, though he smiled. Even the best of men are susceptible to flattery. I would have to look out for him, particularly since it seemed likely he had been experimenting with his hallucinatory drugs. What else could explain this latest blunder? That he was drugged would also explain his bizarre behaviour on being discovered by Rucastle in the room where the latter had been keeping his daughter Alice a prisoner. That Holmes should have accused the rotund brute of abducting her, and by means of the skylight! I had thought at the time my friend had gone truly mad, particularly when he leaped in front of Rucastle at the very instant he must have seen me drawing my Webley No. 2 to take aim at the villain. But no, it had to be the drugs. I had misheard him when he said he had been experimenting with cocaine. I had mistakenly thought he said

364

ketones. "You mean, of course, Holmes, from her locked room in the Copper Beeches. The one we have just left."

Holmes chuckled. Miss Hunter echoed him with an irritatingly ingratiating giggle in the manner of an infatuated schoolgirl working to curry favour with her teacher. "No, Watson, I do not. Perhaps it would help if you performed a trifling experiment. I mean a mental one. Do you picture that room in your mind. Now, can you see the skylight and a table some ten feet from it? Excellent. Just add our demonic Mr. Pickwick and picture him hopping up and down in a futile attempt to reach that skylight. You smile, my friend, as well you might. Ah, but what if he were to move that table to beneath the skylight? Then he could climb up onto it and begin to squeeze and squirm his way through. But what is this? Mr. Pickwick's wicked twin would appear to be stuck half way through! His legs are kicking helplessly in the air, as they would have done anyway in due course had not his recent maiming cut a blossoming criminal career so tragically short."

"You are forgetting, Holmes," I gently interjected, "that the door to Alice's prison was still heavily barricaded when we arrived. Rucastle must have made his way up to that room via the ladder placed by the side of the house. He never entered the room at all. He called down to his daughter and commanded her to climb up through the skylight."

"And do you suppose that she would not have thought to take that route long before had she been able to? Once on the roof, she would either have escaped by means of another skylight or ended her sufferings by casting herself from the roof. No, if she could have reached the skylight by standing on that table, then her tormentors would not have left it there."

"Well, then, she stood on the table and her father hauled her up."

"If that was what happened, then why was the table not still under the skylight? No, Watson, I would indeed have had to have needed to go mad on cocaine to imagine he had abducted his prisoner from her cell by so absurd a route. I never did. And I beg of you, do not do that cunning rogue Rucastle the injustice of supposing he imagined his daughter was ever taken that way either. The only thing more ridiculous would have been if he had thought it was *we* who had escaped with her when we were still in the room."

I was somewhat reassured. "I have to confess, Holmes, I had begun to doubt my own sanity, as well as yours and Rucastle's. I wondered whether some hallucinogenic drug had not been released into the air that was causing you both to talk balderdash. First you accused Rucastle of kidnapping his own daughter from his own home, and that via a rooftop flight and a precipitous descent when he might have used the front door. And then, as if not to be undone, there was Rucastle crying out he had us

365

in his power despite the fact he was unarmed, and I had my revolver aimed at his heart. His accusations were just as insane as yours. What game were you two playing?"

Holmes looked genuinely surprised. Not to miss an opportunity to ingratiate herself with him still further, Hunter copied him and even gasped in feigned amazement.

"Why, my dear Watson," said he, "is that not obvious? Well, it will be once you have thought about it. Obviously, everything turns on the fact that Miss Hunter here was instructed to cut her hair before going to the Copper Beeches."

"Why, that was to increase her resemblance to Alice Rucastle," I explained with a renewed concern, for certain drugs can cause temporary memory loss. To my considerable indignation, the woman had the audacity to wink conspiratorially at Holmes, who to my utter astonishment winked back! The world seemed to be going mad.

"Not at all, Watson. Quite the contrary, in fact. Miss Hunter, if you would?" Holmes had turned towards the woman as a schoolmaster might do towards a favourite student who has just raised her hand.

"It was to reduce it," said she, smirking in the most provocative manner. I was surprised at how very unattractive that superior smile now made her. Earlier on I had mistakenly thought her quite pretty, with that transitory extra bloom of the ripe peach that the wise Aristotle, master of them that know, observed youth possess. It just goes to show how misleading first impressions can be. Holmes, who knows nothing of women, nodded approvingly.

"Do keep in mind, my dear doctor," continued he, "that Alice's fiancé Fowler had last been permitted to see her before ever her incarceration had commenced. He still pictured her with long hair. He had no reason to suppose it cut short, nor would it have been until soon after Miss Hunter's arrival."

"But Mrs. Toller said – "

"Oh, we may safely disregard anything Mrs. Toller said. She was a double agent and loyal to whomever paid most. Let me ask you this. When as a doctor did you ever feel the need to play the barber? There was a time I grant you when all barbers were surgeons, but does it therefore necessarily follow that to this day all surgeons must be barbers? Clearly not, or you would certainly have moved your lamp from the left to the right of your bedroom mirror during the course of this morning."

I was about to ask how in the world Holmes had deduced this when I realised the woman was considering my chin in some amusement. I decided to press on. "But Miss Hunter discovered Alice's tresses in a drawer in her bedroom."

"As she was intended to do. They were placed there just before she did so. You stubbornly insist on missing the point, Watson. What matters is that Hunter was told to cut her hair 'quite short' and more importantly, she was to do so before ever she went to the Copper Beeches. Do you not see the immense significance of that?"

I had to confess I did not. What difference did it make whether she cut it before or after taking up her position? I waited patiently for Holmes to explain. To my annoyance, he looked towards the woman instead as a specialist might to a medical student accompanying him on his rounds.

"You see, Doctor," said she, speaking as if she were a detective herself, "if Rucastle really had meant me to impersonate his daughter, he would never have been so vague as to tell me to cut my hair 'quite short', for I might cut off too little or, which would have been worse, too much. Instead, he would have trimmed me himself once I was at the Copper Beeches." She gave a little shudder of revulsion at the thought of that sadist's touch, which briefly made her look almost attractive. "But of course, it is immaterial what length I cut my hair. Alice's would be cut later to the same length as mine. I was not there to impersonate Alice, you see. It was Alice who was to impersonate me."

I was confounded. "But Miss Holmes – I mean Mr. Hunter – I mean Holmes – whatever for?"

"Oh, Doctor Watson, sir," said she with a laugh that grated strangely on my nerves, "you are really too kind to your friend Mr. Holmes here. You must have noticed when he made his little trip while speaking to that beastly Mrs. Toller. His mistake says it all." She turned to Holmes for a second opinion.

To my surprise, Holmes did not stiffen at this brazenly forward criticism but took it in good part. "A well-deserved rebuke, Miss Hunter. Full marks for spotting my blunder."

Miss Hunter beamed. She was clearly teacher's new pet. He would be finding an apple on his mantelpiece next. She would hardly be the first temptress to behave thus.

"And the blunder, Holmes?"

"Oh, I could not resist making a childish joke that threatened our entire plot. You recall how I said that like a good seaman, Fowler had blockaded the Copper Beeches so Rucastle could not steal his daughter away?"

"Certainly."

"And you did not wonder how I knew that Fowler was a seaman?"

"I did at first. Then I understood. Only a seaman could have reached that skylight unaided."

Holmes nodded his approval and I flushed with pleasure, flashing a triumphant look at the woman as I did so. "Very good, Watson, though that was not how I knew. Of course, you have not forgotten that Miss Hunter said Fowler was a small man, and only one at least as tall as me could have managed such a feat. An ordinary man would have found it impossible – though by placing that table beneath the skylight even by an average-sized woman could have done it. But as we have already noted that table was not found there."

"Then how did you deduce his trade?"

"Oh, the same way as Miss Hunter did." Once again Holmes turned towards his new favourite.

"But I need not answer that Doctor," said she, in a transparent attempt at appeasement. "You know Mr. Holmes's methods. When he has no data, what does he do?"

I was growing increasingly galled at her cheek. "I have indeed known Holmes for rather longer than you have," I replied with great dignity, communicating by my tone she might do well to remember it. "Whenever he lacks data, he either detaches his mind from the problem until information is available, or he bustles about to collect it."

The woman had at last remembered her place. She could not answer but instead looked humbly towards Holmes. He chivalrously stepped in to rescue her.

"Of course, you are quite right, friend Watson. I congratulate you on deducing that I came down to Winchester in secret. Then I disguised myself as a vagabond and set to work observing the observer. I discovered the little man beyond the railings of the Copper Beeches standing with legs apart as if still on the deck of a ship in a tempest and with a mariner's telescope from Watson and Sons of 313 High Holborn to his eye. He was observing the arrival in an open dog cart of the neatly cropped Miss Hunter as one might a suspicious looking vessel. Later I saw him again through your excellent field glasses as he studied her more closely while she scurried this way and that in the grounds going about the charitable business of releasing finches and mice the young master had taken in his traps prior to performing what he called his 'crucifixions'. The furious dirty Bertie Rucastle was pelting her with pebbles."

Miss Hunter revealed a quite fetching violet-coloured bruise on one arm for my inspection. It made me think of De Quincey's observation in that very dangerous work "On Murder as One of the Fine Arts" that a perfect phagademic ulcer is in its own way no less beautiful than a faultless moss rose. As a doctor, I felt an almost irresistible professional urge to treat the bruised peach. She did confuse me.

"Another time I saw him observing Miss Hunter seated at a window and laughing uproariously at Rucastle's very risqué stories, some of which he was reading to her out of his copy of the *Holywell Street Journal*. She had a fragment of a broken mirror in one hand."

"To observe who was watching her."

"Not only that. She was flashing a Morse code message to Fowler: '*All in place.*' That was when I became knew for certain what Miss Hunter was, though I had intuited it the moment I met her. My mistake was to suppose she was a born but not yet a professional one."

"A copper!" I gasped.

"Actually I work for the Ladies Detective Agency, Doctor," said she with a touch of resentment, as though I had bestowed another bruise and this one to her pride in confounding her with the official detective force. "When Rucastle gave his previous governess her notice, Mr. Fowler saw his chance to introduce a trusted insider into the Copper Beeches, for he had begun to suspect Mrs. Toller was playing a double game. At Westaways, you know, they keep books in which prospective employers detail what they require in a governess. Studying Rucastle's entry, Fowler was amazed to find it amounted to a portrait of his fiancée, right down to the colour of her hair and her abundance of freckles, to say nothing of her precise statistics. He concluded the villain's plan was to have someone impersonate her. But what could he do? The police would not listen. They thought him mad. He would have to hire a detective. Under normal circumstances he would certainly have come to you, Mr. Holmes, but for all your skill at disguises it would have been hard for even you to have played the governess for several weeks undetected. So he went to Maurice Moser's agency instead."

"Moser had been a detective inspector, Watson," said Holmes with a critical frown. "I had always thought him a bit of a dullard and may inadvertently have told him so, though opening an investigative agency that only employs lady detectives was, I confess, a stroke of genius that puts him far ahead of the official force. Naturally he is jealous of me. That was part of the reason why he had Miss Hunter pay me a call."

Our female copper turned into a positive study in scarlet, and this time I was sure it was from genuine embarrassment. Either that or she was another Eleanora Duse in the making and, like that great actress, able to blush at will. "I confess my old boss's intention was to humiliate you by having me solve the case while making certain you failed. But I assure you, my dear Mr. Holmes, I would never have betrayed you. Every time I passed by your former rooms in Montague Street on my way to model for the very best Bloomsbury artists, I would look up and think of you." She blushed still more deeply, and Holmes had the good grace to look away.

"You modelled for artists?" I tried not to sound too obviously shocked. It helped to explain her brazen manner. Now I understood why she had boasted that her hair had been called "artistic". I remembered that the Pre-Raphaelites had a thing for what they called "stunners" who had just that Titian tint. I felt quite sorry for her, thinking how she had been forced to sell her body.

"She has nothing to be ashamed of, Doctor," said Holmes sternly. "I am told my own grandmother supplied her face to a painting on the execution of Lady Jane Grey. In fact, Miss Hunter, if by way of my fee you were to sketch yourself dressed in electric blue and seated at a window, I would certainly set your work on my mantelpiece next to Miss Adler's photographic portrait posed after Holbein's *Christina of Denmark*. If you are half the detective I take you to be, you can easily deduce what picture in the National Gallery you ought to use as the basis for yours. Ah, I see you have already done so. Of course, the parallel with the ventilator that did not ventilate in the case of the Speckled Band was fairly obvious and it is certainly an interesting example of a locked room mystery. Or should I say a locked womb?"

"But Holmes," said I, anxious to return to the matter at hand before things got entirely out of hand, "whenever I dropped by, I found you in a brown study and crying out 'Data! Data! Data!' in a state of the most desperate frustration. Are you telling me you had been slipping off to the Copper Beeches without my knowledge? Did you not trust me enough to confide your discoveries to me?" I was a little hurt, for I once more found myself suspecting Holmes had been partnering himself with the woman behind my back. It was bad enough that he had worked with my wife while we were all three lodging together at 221b following our marriage as I had struggled to find a practice I could afford to purchase. While I hunted about for one, my wife had taken my place. Using her was the only selfish action which I can recall Holmes ever committing in our association. But the partner is always the last to know and I certainly had no desire to see history repeating itself.

"Watson," said he with fervent gravity, "of all your admirable flaws please believe me when I say the one I envy most is your complete inability to dissemble. To have shared my findings with you would have been to broadcast them to the world. How many times have you commenced your reminiscences on experiences in three separate continents by loudly proclaiming to the readers of the *Holywell Street Journal* your utmost discretion and assuring all those involved in the adventure that your lips are sealed? Then you proceed to kiss and tell. What if I had told you Mrs. Toller was a double agent whose ultimate master was Rucastle? When I apologised to her for misjudging her, it would have initiated one of your provocatively vocal throat clearances. I could hardly take such a chance when doing business with so smart a mercenary as Mrs. Toller. But it may console you to know that those brown studies were not entirely feigned. I was genuinely concerned for Miss Hunter here."

This time the woman's freckles turned the colour of beetroot. I frowned. I was still a little confused. I had thought I detected signs of a mutual attraction between her and my friend, which I had told myself I ought to welcome, yet now that my intuition appeared to be confirmed I felt strangely disturbed. Could it be jealousy? She was not my type. Besides, I am happily married.

"No, no," said he with a knowing smile. "I am afraid you quite mistook my feelings towards the charming Miss Hunter. You will recall I said I would not wish to see one of my own sisters forced to cut her hair and sit like the Virgin of the Annunciation at the moment she realises she is a character in the story she is reading. Rucastle required you read *Jane Eyre* to him, did he not, Miss Hunter?"

She nodded. "And *The Woman in White*."

"Just so. He certainly took Count Fosco as one of his role models. But I meant what I said, Watson. When a girl takes the veil as a sister, she has her hair cut short. In my mind, I conflated the fates of a sister who became a governess with another who was made a bride of Christ." He grimaced.

I knew better than to seek an absolute confirmation that Holmes had had two or more sisters. He had yet to do so much as supply his French grandfather's name, so he would certainly have lapsed into silence had I pressed him and that would have been the end of it. But I made a mental note. Had he once been destined for the Church himself? Did that explain his celibacy and those hermit-like ways that caused some to call him the Diogenes of Baker Street? It was best to press on. "I think I understand you, Holmes. Rucastle planned to sneak his daughter out of his house under her fiancé Fowler's eyes. Dressed in blue and veiled with her hair cut short, he would think her Miss Hunter. Actually, it would be Alice disguised as Hunter disguised as Alice. I think that is it. It is. Isn't it?" I found my explanation confusing.

Holmes and Hunter were nodding in unison, so apparently they did not. I welcomed the approval of the one but not that of the other. Besides, I had been left thoroughly bewildered by my own solution, which I now began to doubt. "Wait a minute. That cannot be right. The real aim had to have been to deceive Fowler into believing the Rucastles had left with Alice, lest he suspect she was still in the house and unguarded. That has to be it. Rucastle left with Hunter disguised as Alice disguised as Hunter disguised as Alice. But Fowler must have seen through the deception, else why should he have entered the house and stolen Alice away?"

371

"My dear Watson, I had no idea you could be half so devilishly devious. Ah, but there is nothing sadder than when a brilliant theory has to be demolished by one inconvenient fact! Miss Hunter did not go with them. She was waiting for us when we arrived to rescue Alice, who was by then long gone. No? You still do not follow? Miss Hunter, kindly elucidate."

"You see, Doctor Watson," said she with a touch of the professional teachers determined to explain the past perfect continuous to the dullest dunce in the class, "Mr. Fowler had let the Rucastles know he knew they knew he knew I had been introduced to impersonate Alice. They did not only mean to smuggle Alice out under his nose. They meant to convince Fowler that she was still a prisoner and one left unguarded in that upper room. While Mrs. Rucastle proceeded to have the drugged and disoriented Alice committed under another name to a private asylum, Mr. Rucastle returned to the Copper Beeches to seize upon Fowler and myself and accuse us of helping his daughter escape via the skylight. That was why Rucastle had placed a ladder against a wall and left the skylight open. He moved the table away from under the skylight to make it seem I must have done so after lifting Alice up from it and into the arms of Fowler."

"That is surely far-fetched, Miss Hunter," said I reprovingly. I looked to Holmes for support. I sighed. He would not to give it. He would side with her against me.

"But surely, my dear Watson, you must have seen Rucastle was working to a script," said he with disappointment. "He burst into Alice's prison cell expecting to find none save for Fowler and Miss Hunter there. Instead he was confronted by no Fowler, but by two gentlemen he had never seen in his life. When I perceived you drawing your pistol, I had to leap between you and him so he would not see we had him in our power. I put myself in the line of fire, you see, and so concealed your weapon from his sight. Moreover, it prevented you from following him when he went for the police. I only accused him of abducting his own daughter by that absurd route to justify confronting him in that manner. Had I not done so his cry of 'I have you in my power!' would have been positively farcical. You must see that. But really, he was doing no more than speaking the lines he had rehearsed too well for his intended confrontation with Fowler. He was playing the prepared scene, despite the fact that unknown understudies had stepped into the parts he had allotted to Fowler and Miss Hunter."

"But Holmes, he was not going for the police. He was going for that Frankenstein's mongrel. Miss Hunter said so." I looked to her for confirmation of this obvious fact. She merely shook her head and smiled sadly in the most maddening manner.

"Oh, come, now, Watson, why would Miss Hunter have supposed such a thing? Rucastle had assured her only Toller would dare to handle that Ross and Mangles abomination. Rucastle had of course intended to rouse his servant Toller from his stupor when first he returned so he might stand guard with that titular dog at the door, but the drunkard was dead to the world. Or so his master thought. We had to make it look like an accident, you see."

I felt a sudden chill. "Look like an accident, Holmes? You are referring to the attack by the dog? You are saying it was not an accident?"

Holmes did something I had never witnessed before. He squirmed. "How could I have known the creature would be so savage? I had merely intended it would temporarily incapacitate Rucastle to give Fowler and Alice time to disappear before he was hot on their scent. That was why I insisted you bring your revolver. It enabled you to kill the thing before its attack proved fatal."

"But who released it?"

"Fowler's insider at the Copper Beeches. Toller."

"What, could Mrs. Toller have controlled it?"

"Not her. Her husband."

"But he was drunk!"

"And then suddenly as sober as a judge. No, Watson, he was never drunk. That deception was for his wife's benefit. As a double agent her ultimate loyalty was towards Rucastle as the man who paid her the most filthy lucre. It was Mr. Toller who was on the side of Alice."

I thought about that. "And that was why Toller left the door to Alice's place of incarceration unlocked on the occasion that Miss Hunter investigated the forbidden rooms."

"Ah. You still think Rucastle would have entrusted an alcoholic with the key to her place of incarceration. Hardly very likely, Watson. Of course, Toller never was that hopeless a drunkard, though the Rucastles spread exaggerated tales of his inebriation the better to lure Fowler into their trap. But it was Rucastle who left the key in the door. If it had not been him, then would he have waited patiently outside it for Miss Hunter to return from her little expedition? He would have dashed in to ensure Alice was not even then being rescued if not gone already. And do you suppose he believed Miss Hunter when she said she had discovered nothing? He meant her to communicate with Alice, as she did, and to assure her that help would soon be on its way."

"No, no. Miss Hunter, I remember you fled in terror on seeing a shadow under the inner door. You did, did you not?"

She arched her eyebrows. "What shadow, Doctor?" she enquired with feigned innocence. No, she was no Eleanore Duse.

"Why, the shadow cast by the light from the skylight."

"But it was evening. The sun would have been too low."

"From the moon, then."

"Did I not tell you I saw that mongrel hound of the Rucastles by the light of a full moon two weeks earlier? There was no moon that night."

"Miss Hunter," said I indignantly, "do you mean you deceived me and Holmes?"

"Calm yourself, my dear Watson, and rest assured she only deceived *you*. I have already explained why it was necessary. Of course, she spoke with Alice and promised to go to Fowler. It was just what Rucastle wanted her to do."

"Impossible!"

"It is impossible he did not. Do you really suppose that having caught Miss Hunter stealing into Alice's place of imprisonment, he would then have rewarded her by generously giving her half the next day off and far away from the Copper Beeches? Obviously, he assumed Fowler would approach her to ask for her help. She would then tell him Toller was dead drunk and the Rucastles would be going out leaving the dog locked up and the house wide open. It would seem like the perfect opportunity to rescue his fiancée. How could he resist? Fortunately, Miss Hunter and I saw through the plot. Fowler shadowed the trap that took Alice disguised as Miss Hunter disguised as Alice to the asylum. That telegram informed me Fowler has just rescued her from there and now they have escaped together."

"It was wonderfully done, my dear, dear Mr. Sherlock Holmes," said Miss Hunter a little too warmly. "But it is time for me to say *au revoir*. Goodbye, Dr. Watson." She shook my hand warmly and kissed Holmes on the cheek, which made him cringe inwardly. He concealed his chagrin superbly. Then she handed him a flat package and was hurrying off to catch her train. I heard her utter the most ridiculous schoolgirl giggle as she did so.

"A most interesting person," said Holmes thoughtfully. "I confess I can't quite make her out. She certainly showed potential. Later, perhaps. Now let us take a look at my fee. I am glad she did not offer to pay me with that coil of her hair. She might have been tempted to do so, you know, for she has a definite romantic streak. Miss Violet Hunt, whom I suspect was a Hunter role model, asserts that the painter Dante Gabriel Rossetti turned a coil of his deceased wife's hair into a bell-pull. What would Mrs. Hudson have said were I to do the same with Hunter's?

"I can well imagine," said I with a shudder. I felt quite ambivalent about the prospect of pulling on Hunter's hair to call for coffee. Of course, it would depend on one's mood. At that particular moment it might have been quite cathartic.

Now we were by ourselves in a compartment and flying back to London. Holmes began unwrapping the package. "A practical woman like that would not have sat idly by in her little room behind the British Museum and a stone's throw from Bloomsbury awaiting the next abortive trip to Westaway's employment agency. While she was a paid governess in the family of Major Spence Munro, impoverished artists taught her drawing and painting in return for modelling sessions. Once she had lost her old position, then assuming artistic new ones became her one source of income. Between modelling, she spent much of her time studying prints in the British Museum and sketching the paintings in the National Gallery a short walk away. Ah, here is her self-portrait. It shall hang as promised next to my photograph of Irene Adler as Christina of Denmark. I saw Hunter admiring it when she visited 221b. I suspect she read your account of that trifling Bohemian scandal in your little *Baker Street Journal*."

"She is not one of my subscribers, Holmes."

"No, but Inspector Moser's Ladies Detective Agency is. She would have read it there by way of research. You remember Moser was hoping she would collect dirt on his greatest competitor. Fortunately, she had her own agenda and merely wished to prove her worth to me. Have no fear, Watson. We shall not be standing in the dock to testify I did unspeakable things with the most cherubic of my Baker Street boys."

Holmes has a somewhat perverse sense of humour. I ignored his poor taste jest and considered the sketch. She had provocatively cast herself as the Virgin in the *Annunciation* by Crivelli that I recalled Holmes pointing out to me in the National Gallery. Now I understood Holmes's comment about its featuring a ventilator that did not ventilate. The Dove is shown descending through a tiny orifice in a wall like a bullet aimed plum at the Virgin's brows and smack into her brain. As a doctor, I thought that a very curious place to conceive.

"You see, Watson," said he with a smile, "Miss Hunter was always ambitious to cast herself as a character in her own story. Here she is playing at being Mary reading the prophecy of her fate and apprehending in a flash that an apparent fiction is turning into fact. In Miss Hunter's case, shutting herself away for six months to read nothing but sensational literature might not be such a good idea. And yet she was a woman after my own heart."

"She was after that all right," I muttered to myself. I had not forgotten how she had described lying awake half the night in her joy at the thought of being under his direction. Hers was hardly a very subtle hint.

375

Fortunately, my unsuspecting celibate friend had failed to pick up on it. "What are her plans?"

"I am posting her to a school for anarchists at Walsall."

"I beg your pardon?"

"You recall how she used her mirror to signal to Fowler? She adopted that trick from your description of my employment of a coffee-pot during that Baskerville affair. That was ingenious and proved I could use her. Now that you are married, I cannot use you to be my eyes and ears quite so much, Watson. Oh, please do not pout. I promise you she shall not be the other woman. Would you prefer your wife to think me the other man?"

"I see you have plans, Holmes," said I sadly. "You have no place for me in them."

"Not at all. Besides, all that is a long way off. The next world war in fact. Now, I cannot have your readers suspect what work I may put her to in the distant future, so I am relying on you to portray her as quite out of my life and reduced to the insignificant role of schoolmistress. You had better end your account with something along these lines. Let me see . . . .

> *As to Miss Violet Hunter, my friend Holmes, rather to my disappointment, manifested no further interest in her when once she had ceased to be the centre of one of his problems, and she is now the head of a private school at Walsall, where I believe that she has met with considerable success.*

About the Author

Nick Dunn-Meynell would rather have been born Reginald Kincaid. He has nothing in his life he need be personally ashamed of, but you will have to be content with his word for it. He once led a comfortless, meaningless existence teaching English and philosophy and had, to all appearances, a most brilliant career before him. He is now cared for by a resident patient with a suspiciously lumpy mattress. His doctor lectures him about never going out, but why should he go out when the proper treatment of but one of Watson's cases would take him three good months? His hobbies are demythologising Sherlock Holmes and crushing cockroaches with a Persian slipper.

 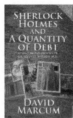 

The MX Book of New Sherlock Holmes Stories
Edited by David Marcum
(MX Publishing, 2015-   )

"This is the finest volume of Sherlockian fiction I have ever read, and I have read, literally, thousands." – Philip K. Jones

"Beyond Impressive . . . This is a splendid venture for a great cause!
– Roger Johnson, Editor, *The Sherlock Holmes Journal,*
The Sherlock Holmes Society of London

Part I: 1881-1889
Part II: 1890-1895
Part III: 1896-1929
Part IV: 2016 Annual
Part V: Christmas Adventures
Part VI: 2017 Annual
Part VII: Eliminate the Impossible (1880-1891)
Part VIII – Eliminate the Impossible (1892-1905)
Part IX – 2018 Annual (1879-1895)
Part X – 2018 Annual (1896-1916)
Part XI – Some Untold Cases (1880-1891)
Part XII – Some Untold Cases (1894-1902)
Part XIII – 2019 Annual (1881-1890)
Part XIV – 2019 Annual (1891-1897)
Part XV – 2019 Annual (1898-1917)
Part XVI – Whatever Remains . . . Must be the Truth (1881-1890)
Part XVII – Whatever Remains . . . Must be the Truth (1891-1898)
Part XVIII – Whatever Remains . . . Must be the Truth (1898-1925)
Part XIX – 2020 Annual (1882-1890)
Part XX – 2020 Annual (1891-1897)
Part XXI – 2020 Annual (1898-1923)
Part XXII – Some More Untold Cases (1877-1887)
Part XXIII – Some More Untold Cases (1888-1894)
Part XXIV – Some More Untold Cases (1895-1903)

In Preparation
Part XXV – 2021 Annual

. . . and more to come!

The MX Book of New Sherlock Holmes Stories
Edited by David Marcum
(MX Publishing, 2015-   )

Publishers Weekly says:

Part VI: *The traditional pastiche is alive and well . . . .*

Part VII: *Sherlockians eager for faithful-to-the-canon plots and characters will be delighted.*

Part VIII: *The imagination of the contributors in coming up with variations on the volume's theme is matched by their ingenious resolutions.*

Part IX: *The 18 stories . . . will satisfy fans of Conan Doyle's originals. Sherlockians will rejoice that more volumes are on the way.*

Part X: *. . . new Sherlock Holmes adventures of consistently high quality.*

Part XI: *. . . an essential volume for Sherlock Holmes fans.*

Part XII: *. . . continues to amaze with the number of high-quality pastiches.*

Part XIII: *. . . Amazingly, Marcum has found 22 superb pastiches . . . This is more catnip for fans of stories faithful to Conan Doyle's original*

Part XIV: *. . . this standout anthology of 21 short stories written in the spirit of Conan Doyle's originals.*

Part XV: *Stories pitting Sherlock Holmes against seemingly supernatural phenomena highlight Marcum's 15th anthology of superior short pastiches.*

Part XVI: *Marcum has once again done fans of Conan Doyle's originals a service.*

Part XVII: *This is yet another impressive array of new but traditional Holmes stories.*

Part XVIII: *Sherlockians will again be grateful to Marcum and MX for high-quality new Holmes tales.*

Part XIX: *Inventive plots and intriguing explorations of aspects of Dr. Watson's life and beliefs lift the 24 pastiches in Marcum's impressive 19th Sherlock Holmes anthology*

Part XX: *Marcum's reserve of high-quality new Holmes exploits seems endless.*

Part XXI: *This is another must-have for Sherlockians.*

Part XXII: *Marcum's superlative 22nd Sherlock Holmes pastiche anthology features 21 short stories that successfully emulate the spirit of Conan Doyle's originals while expanding on the canon's tantalizing references to mysteries Dr. Watson never got around to chronicling.*

The MX Book of New Sherlock Holmes Stories

Edited by David Marcum

(MX Publishing, 2015-   )

MX Publishing

MX Publishing is the world's largest specialist Sherlock Holmes publisher, with several hundred titles and over a hundred authors creating the latest in Sherlock Holmes fiction and non-fiction.

From traditional short stories and novels to travel guides and quiz books, MX Publishing caters to all Holmes fans.

The collection includes leading titles such as *Benedict Cumberbatch in Transition* and *The Norwood Author*, which won the 2011 *Tony Howlett Award* (Sherlock Holmes Book of the Year).

MX Publishing also has one of the largest communities of Holmes fans on *Facebook*, with regular contributions from dozens of authors.

www.mxpublishing.co.uk (UK)
and
www.mxpublishing.com (USA)

Lightning Source UK Ltd.
Milton Keynes UK
UKHW041541230321
380852UK00002B/12/J